THE ALIQUIAN

THE ALIQUIAN FOUR-PART SERIES
BOOK ONE

MARY COE

STREAMLINE
BOOKS

Contents

For Rebecca Vogelsang (1990-2008) and the Vogelsang family.

Becca,
Your pursuit of kindness, purity, beauty, and the arts is the very breath that fills Resi's lungs. The story of your life is still being told. Keep dancing and singing and ushering in even brighter sunshine through heaven's gates.

THE ALIQUIAN

Chapter 1

The River

Not even the moon's inconstant light through the trees could guide Taresia Flood's steps as she hurriedly stole away from her lean-to and made her way into the night. In the haze of having just woken up from deep sleep, she couldn't quite remember how many trips she'd made past curfew in the previous months. Four, maybe five runs. Somehow, she'd managed to make it back home before dawn each time, but tonight was to be her longest journey yet. How could she have overslept?

"Stupid...*stupid*!" she scolded herself as she threw her too-small cloak over her head.

The darkness of the wood loomed before her just as it always had on her nighttime jaunts. Many stories had woven their way through the tapestry of the Sept-Regions, and though the region of Ter, where the Offenheimer Farmhold lay, was far from the rumored terrors in the mysterious region of Sterch, Taresia couldn't help but look over her shoulder anytime an unknown sound echoed through the thicket. Even still, she moved more carelessly along the overgrown path than usual, nearly tripping over her untied laces, which she had left undone to make up for lost time. Only an hour remained before sunrise, and she had a mission to accomplish.

The first mark was to appear to the north, if it was still there. A slight bend in the path led her straight to it; a weathered ribbon tied to a branch further up a tree. She took a large breath of relief at the sight of it. Dumb trunk; it'd taken her nearly an hour to climb it on her first run.

Taresia continued to the second mark, ducking under one of the second tree's low branches to stray briefly from the path. She walked south for a time, listening for anything that wasn't the croon of the crickets or the crunch of leaves beneath her boots. Overseers, men put in place to watch over the Aliquian field hands, called 'Licks, were known to occasionally roam the woods in the night hours, and usually, they were accompanied by one of their slobbering, large dogs that had a particular appetite for those wandering the property out past curfew. With all the preparations for the upcoming Festival, Taresia was almost certain no one would be out yet—part of the reason she'd been so anxious to go tonight. But one could never be too careful.

The third mark was harder to find, in a small squirrel hole. It had withered since her last visit. She fluffed it, then moved on. After finding the fourth mark, she hesitated. She took a moment to peer through the wood and gather her determination before walking onward. It was the furthest on the property she'd ever walked alone.

She began to scout for a place to put her next mark. Where was a low-hanging branch, something that might throw off the trail? Her eyes scanned the ground. Ahead she spotted a small bush that brushed against molded leaves. She ran to it, lifting the sleeve on her right arm to reveal the fabric wrapped around her wrist.

Quickly, she pulled the ends of the fabric free and tied it tightly to the lowest hanging spot on the bush before turning back. But then as she turned, she heard a promising babble; water from a bit further east. She smiled, beaming at her own brilliance. As her pulse quickened, she reminded herself that it was not the time to act in haste. Run now, and she would surely be caught somewhere along the river in only a matter of hours. Her carefully crafted plan would work. It *had* to.

Taresia, or Resi as she was known to the others that worked beside her in the meadow, felt certain that a significant transformation had taken place within her that summer. Her time spent roaming alone in the darkness had been responsible for her transition from that of a quiet girl to a dangerously curious young woman. She'd become somewhat of a wayfarer these past few weeks, if such a thing were possible for someone like her. The woods gave good instruction, and unlike her parents, they were consistent. The pines surrounding the property had taught her wisdom, their ancient, formidable beauty remaining at peace even in the midst of seasonal swing; and the wind had taught her of loyalty, its constant lull through the forest enveloping her like two loving arms. The light mist of rainfall that settled onto her cloak never let up or waned for a moment. From what little Resi could remember of her mother and father before they'd abandoned her, it seemed they'd known nothing of what it meant to stick around through the worst of times.

In fact, Resi had come to realize that independence was much closer than she'd once been led to believe; as near to her as when she reached her hand out from the path to brush the pines with her fingertips. But her nightly outings to place her markings had proven to be not enough. She desired the kind of freedom that could live in broad daylight, and if her plan succeeded, it would be hers to grasp onto forever.

Enough dawdling. The rush of the river faded beyond the pines as she ventured back towards the path. She couldn't help but think of its cool waters streaming like silk down a smooth, wooden oar. Unbidden, the colorful memory of her first encounter with the River came to mind.

'Lick children were often recruited in the summer months to pick berries in the deep wood surrounding the farmhold. Resi had been just a girl then, her hair still in braids. That morning had been brisk, and wet, as most every morning during harvest season was. After pricking her finger on a thorn, she had tried to stop the bleeding by sucking on it, but the cut went deep. Without another thought, Resi had innocently crossed the patch to wash her finger in the nearby stream. After cleaning the wound in the cool water, her eye had been drawn to the other bank where a strange mound of pine needles waited. It covered something. Daringly, she'd darted across four thick boulders to investigate it. She'd wiped the covering away, and saw a handle of a wooden oar, one expertly crafted and coated with polish.

Then, a violent hand had grabbed her by the hair; an overseer.

"Sneak off again and I'll send the dogs after you, you understand?!" he'd seethed at her.

The overseer had kept a suspicious gaze on her for the rest of the afternoon, his dog at his feet asleep on his boots. Little did he realize that a growing seed of freedom had been planted deeply in a young girl's mind that morning.

Resi had been smart enough to count her steps on the return journey from the berry patch that afternoon. And when the dinner bell had rung later that night, she'd raced to her lean-to to etch the route onto the underside of a loose board with a rock. Sixty paces east along the main path, an hour's journey south, then down the rolling hills and over the berry fields. She wanted to remember that place, that beautiful, gleaming patch of sunshine where the rowboat waited.

With all that she had endured in the months after her discovery of the boat, Resi had waited and plotted. A long and painful eight years passed before she finally found the courage to plan her escape from the Offenheimer Farmhold. The upcoming day of the Fourth-Year Festival was the perfect day to run. Not a soul would wonder about an Aliquian girl bounding through the wood as the Governor's freshly painted carriage rolled through the town square. Every overseer, patroller, and 'Lick's attention would be delightfully consumed by the day's festivities in town.

The day of rest for the Aliquian people came once every four years in the space of the season between summer and autumn. If Resi was ever going to leave, it was now. If not, she'd have to wait another four years in the dirt for such an opportunity to present itself again.

She didn't fear being followed by overseers; she was certain she'd be followed by at least one. Much to her own consternation, it was the silly stories from the fields that threatened her peace; tales of bones crushed by the hands of hungry ogres, of fugitive 'Licks meeting their demise after being drowned in a lake by some murderous creature no one could quite name. She cowered in fear at the unknown of what awaited her outside the property lines.

But if *they* had done it, why couldn't she?

Resi often tried to remember her mother and father pleasantly; damp and spent after long days spent working in the fields. But all Resi could recall were the dark circles beneath her mother's hazel eyes, and the sorrow that had consumed her night after night in the weeks before she'd vanished from Resi's life altogether. And her father, his frail frame walking back to the lean-to every evening. He walked a few paces ahead of her mother, but never by her side.

Resi shook herself from her thoughts. She didn't dare think of her parents for longer than was necessary. Her anger at them often brought on the very thing she feared most in this world.

In the quiet of the woods, Resi's stomach suddenly flipped. She placed a wary hand on it, only to quickly pull it away. It was hot. *Too* hot.

For nearly a decade, Resi had swatted at the heat that lingered right below her ribs, trying to think of it as nothing more than an upset stomach. But in the last year, the heat had quickened, and Resi feared the possibility of whatever it was finding its way to the surface. As a girl, she'd regularly wakened with a fright and with a fresh red mark on her palm where her hand had rested on her stomach. Like the many creatures that lingered in the shadows of the neighboring region of Sterch, her fire within was a dangerous and mysterious force for which she had no name.

The whispers on the property amongst the other field hands were that Resi was a *witch-'Lick,* short for a witch-Aliquian. Or, so some believed. Resi couldn't be sure whether the others her age were deranged for believing in such nonsense, or if they were simply wise to keep their distance from her. Stories of magic dated back centuries to the fated King Aliquis, the namesake of Resi's people. The story of King Aliquis had been recited to Resi in the form of a lullaby as a child: the mighty king, the first of *any* soul to wield unfathomable power. As a child, nature had responded to him in an unnatural way, and that gift had ushered him into greatness.

According to legend, the first generation of Aliquian people were born through *belief*, and not through blood. The great King Aliquis bore no natural children, but had awakened many hearts to the idea that his power, pure and purposeful, was attainable for *anyone*. He delighted in passing on this power as a gift to the first generation of people who rallied around him and desired to be just like him. The first generation of Aliquians was entirely comprised of the original settlers of the regions, called Patrians. Their children and children's children would carry on Aliquis's namesake.

However, not all present-day Aliquians bore the same gifts as the Great King. The essence of Aliquian power was rumored to be built around the nature of the unique strengths of the human heart. *Power that wisely chooses its carrier*, as Resi's mother had told her so long ago. Though many believed in and feared Aliquian power, very few had ever successfully brandished it as a mighty sword. None, besides Aliquis, had ever experienced the fullness of this power without being tempted into darker practices. This fear of pure power turning sour and becoming something else altogether had tarnished the Aliquian namesake. The Aliquian people were brought to their knees many generations later when lawmakers and politicians eventually shackled them into chains of servitude.

The whisper of this kind of pure power was still alive and well, though no evidence of it had ever passed through the southern region of Ter. Only *Codians* were permitted to use a different source of magic: sorcery, but there were many parameters on its limits of use. Sorcery, and its potent allure, was widespread and popular amongst the Codians and was rumored to be on the rise in the larger cities in the West.

Suddenly paranoid, Resi pulled her cloak tighter around her. Stubborn, spiteful people the Codians could be. They had migrated into the Sept-Regions from the North more than two hundred years prior. Codians often sported red hair and boasted fiery tempers to match. The original settlers of the regions, the Patrian people, resided further to the West. Stories spoke of them sheltering behind great stone walls in the wealthy metropolis of Turbus; they desired no trouble or war. They'd seen plenty of unrest and violence in the previous ages after Aliquis's power had divided them, and now, they only desired peace.

Resi understood this desire too. Her need for peace outweighed her need for anything else. The slander surrounding her name had caused her to lose sleep for years since her parents had fled. According to the rumors, the sole reason why her parents had escaped the boundaries of the property was because Resi held a *darker* power within, a mutation of the past mistakes and failings of previous generations where Aliquian power had descended into darkness. Fearing Resi's forbidden power might one day bring them ruin, the story spoke that her mother and father had fled the farmhold without a word of warning to anyone. Most worrisome to Mags, Resi's only friend on the farmhold, was that Resi was beginning to believe this rumor. With every year that passed since her parents left her behind, Resi's shame deepened, and the flames inside of her spread wider and burned hotter.

Of course, the timing of their disappearance didn't line up with the discovery of Resi's internal heat; it was the winter *after* they'd fled the property that she first felt the stabbings of fire in her gut. But no one knew about that—the others only saw the girl with the unnatural green eyes and assumed the worst.

With a new determination, Resi turned back towards the path, allowing her legs to settle into a slow jog as she made her way uphill. When the path's dirt became visible to her through the trees, she looked up to see morning birds flying from branch to branch. She bounded expertly through the forest's terrain, finally arriving at the drive that led to the house.

She paused, momentarily transfixed by the mansion's haunting glow in the setting moonlight. 'Licks called the Offenheimer's home the Eye, and rightfully so. With its many windows, balconies, and porches, it made for the most elegant viewing place to watch all the comings and goings on the Farmhold, and, it was used as such by the

Offenheimers and their visitors, who spent their days undoubtedly taking their freedom for granted. The log fortress sat directly at the center of the property and overlooked the entirety of the land like a pestering brown speck in a sea of endless green. Dark smoke from the stone chimney on the east wing swelled high into the lightening sky. Resi sneered at the sight of it. The Eye's presence often reminded her of a hidden predator waiting for the right moment to ambush its prey, its surrounding trees creating a full canopy over the rutted, single-track drive that lead to it.

She quickly panned the meadows. No movement caught her sight. But just as she lifted her skirts to make a dash across the drive, she was alerted by the faint crunch of footsteps from behind her.

"Hello?" a thin voice breathed through the wood. Resi ducked and knelt behind the nearest tree, then cautiously peered around the trunk to see the path. A figure floated eerily towards her on the dirt, a lantern outstretched in front of the long cloak. A shaking, wrinkled hand clutched the wooden handle. Jowls peeked through the hood. Resi's inners immediately curled.

Gilda was known through the fields as the "*Snitch 'Lick*" and prided herself in being the most loyal confidante to the Mistress of the Farmhold. She often roamed the property in the early hours to keep tabs on the 'Lick quarters. In recent years, however, Gilda's body had grown old and fragile. The woman's memory had slipped so terribly that she'd been ordered to stop laboring in the fields the previous summer. Many had rejoiced in suspecting that the Snitch's trouble-making days were over, but clearly, they weren't.

Resi rose to her feet. If it were any earlier in the night, she would have waited it out, spent the early hours mulling over the final details of her escape amongst the shadows. But she didn't have the time to remain hidden before the overseers returned to their morning posts. She had a plan, albeit a ridiculous one, but still, it was something.

"Hello?" Gilda called again, her voice rattling like a snake. "I know the sound of sneaking when I hear it!"

Resi's weight shifted on the leaves. It was now or never. She took a deep breath, then walked decidedly towards the road.

"Halt!" Gilda squawked. "I see you there, walking through the trees!"

Despite every impulse to make a run for it, Resi slowly made her way forward. She'd nearly made it to the path behind the lean-tos when a bony hand quickly yanked on her shoulder.

"Just what do you think you're doing?!" Gilda yelped. The woman's eyes bulged so far out of her head it looked as if they might fall from her skull onto the gravel. "Taresia Flood…" she said slowly as she pulled the hood of the cloak to unveil Resi's face. "Roaming the woods alone like a vagrant on the run. How do you choose to explain yourself?!"

Resi didn't respond. She didn't even blink.

"Girl, do you hear me?!" Gilda screeched.

Still, Resi said nothing. Her feet shuffled forward again on the path, her eyes fixed on the horizon.

"You will answer me!" Gilda piped. She brought her frail arms forward and placed them firmly on Resi's shoulders. The woman did her best to shake her, but the attempt was weak. Wildly, Resi fell to the ground in a spastic heap and Gilda stepped back in fright. After a few moments of strained silence, Resi spoke.

"Where am I?"

Gilda huffed. "Clear out to the wood."

"What time is it?" Resi asked as she rubbed her eyes.

"Nearly dawn."

Resi huffed in a far-off, sleepy way. "I was dreaming."

Gilda's legs shifted underneath her and the lantern in her paw swung like a delayed pendulum. "Dreaming? Or *scheming*?"

Resi tried to remain calm and unbothered, but she couldn't help but snicker at the way Gilda's voice quivered from behind her toothless mouth. "Like I said, I was dreaming," she answered as she bent to wipe the dirt from her knees.

Gilda's yellowed eyes stayed fixed on her. She pointed her shaking fingers towards the log home on the hilltop. "And, and, what should I tell the Mistress about all this?"

Resi's stomach churned. "I think you needn't tell her a thing," she

9

replied. "And shouldn't I be just as curious to see your shriveled self, walking the dirt this early in the morning?"

"Mistress always has someone walking the property in the weeks leading up to the Festival. Surely, out of all people, you should know that."

Resi knew this to be true. It was why she usually left her lean-to when the sky was darkest. But the heavy rains this week had fatigued her so, made her body heavy as bricks at the end of harvest season. She should've known better than to leave after waking so late.

"If an overseer had caught you," Gilda threatened, "you would've been marked already."

Resi felt a snarl curl her lips. Marked; or branded with a circle. It was the overseers' cruel way of flagging a 'Lick as dangerous.

Without missing a beat, Resi continued walking. "Sleepwalking isn't a crime."

"You make me to be a fool, Taresia!" Gilda said as she trailed behind.

Resi stomped towards the 'Lick quarters, trying her best to ignore the anger inside her that began to warm her stomach. The monster always showed itself when her temper flared.

Gilda wasn't finished with her. "What should I tell the Mistress when I tell her that it was *you* that I found wandering your way around?"

Resi turned back menacingly. This was getting out of hand. Any minute and an overseer would be able to spot either of them through the trees. "Tell her this," she began. "I fell asleep, I had a dream, and then I woke to you screaming in my face like I was guilty of dragging a dead body to the woods for burial! Now...unlike *some* folks, I have actual work to do today. I'd be gladdened by you leaving me be so I can return to my lean-to."

Gilda staggered again, her weak knees swaying underneath her weight. But then, a realization crossed her eyes, along with a gleam of triumph. "Strange thing..." she said as she reached one of her hands to brush Resi's cloak. "You managed to have time to put your cloak around that skinny little neck of yours before *dreaming* your way into the woods."

Frustrated and with not a minute to spare before sunrise, Resi yanked herself from the woman's grip. The cloak, once thought to be a source of shelter and safety, a blanket to hide behind, had given her up. She turned back for the path, leaving Gilda alone in the early daylight. Unless the hag's faulty eyesight had miraculously improved overnight, she wouldn't be able to spot the markings in the woods. Even so, Resi couldn't shake the look of suspicion in Gilda's eyes. The last thing she needed was to be watched in the coming days.

The western-rising sun began to peek through the forest trees as Resi rounded the path back to the huts. She raised a watchful look to the Eye, noticing that a candle on the second floor had been blown out. Finally, she came to her lean-to and stepped over two sleeping bodies before finding her own place beside them. Only a few minutes passed before the morning horn rang out from The Eye. Another day of work awaited Resi, and no differently than if she'd slept the entire night, she sat up and answered its call.

CHAPTER 2

THE MARK

It wasn't even midday when Resi looked down at her hands and noticed they were already stained blood red.

"Another damp one," she spoke to Mags, who worked quietly beside her in the fields. As the rain began to pick up, Resi adjusted the hood of her cloak to better cover her face. She then placed the freshly picked crimson root responsible for the stain into the basket that hung over her arm.

"Yep," Mags responded. She was never much for talking in the chill. But Resi knew that even a single word from Mags often mean so much more.

"Going to be a harsh winter," Resi sighed.

Winters in the peninsula of Ter came in ruthlessly and devoured the land in feet of snow. The bitter chill from the ocean seemed to work its way inside every nook and cranny. But, of course, there was always work to be done on the farmhold, including logging and fur-trapping. While 'Licks continued to toil and trudge through the snowfall, the Offenheimer family remained either locked inside the Eye enjoying drawn warm baths, or they traveled on long holidays to the temperate regions of the west.

What Resi wouldn't have given for a bath after a week of hard work. She watched Mags's portly frame bend down to pick another root, noticing how her hair fanned out on either side of her hood. She'd cut it short that summer, which often caused it to fluff in all directions, especially in the rain. Resi couldn't help but let out a snort at the sight of it.

"What?" Mags asked her.

"Your hair is doing that thing again."

Mags rolled her eyes at her. "Can't help what it does in this humidity."

Resi resumed her work, but took a moment to survey the fields; four dozen or so 'Licks worked beside them that morning. She briefly relished in the quiet, only hearing the sound of light rain hitting against the large leaves of the Folly plants.

Soon enough, however, Mags turned to her with a commanding eye. She playfully snapped her fingers at Resi to stay on task.

The hours spent by Mags's side were the only aspect of Resi's life that had ever held her back from the idea of escaping. After all, Mags had looked after Resi as if she were her own child ever since Resi's parents had left. In the months prior, Mags had lost her husband of thirty years and needed someone new to tend to. Resi supposed that they'd helped ease each other's loneliness when they'd both needed it the most. After eight years together in the fields, Resi had found a sort of rhythm working beside Mags that she feared she'd never find with anyone else.

"This is a harvest to remember, Resi," Mags breathed, looking about the fields. "In all my life I haven't seen such an abundance."

"To *remember*?" Resi huffed. "I'm already trying to forget it. There's never been this much work to be done."

Mags nodded, then shrugged. "Work is better than no work."

"And why's that, exactly?"

"Overseers. Gets them on edge when the crop count is low." Mags said the words under her breath, her eyes scanning the meadow. She then passed a collection of roots to Resi, and Resi placed all but one in her basket. She rolled the single root in her hand, contemplated crushing it, then thought better of it. The root grew in darkness, and had also brought darkness into the world. Resi had grown to loathe

the very sight of it. When ingested, Folly Root caused a silly sort of euphoria; hence the absurdity of its name. The wealthiest socialites from far and wide knew all too well the delicacy of Folly Root, but the effects were highly addictive. There was only one place in the regions from which to get it, and that was on the Offenheimer Farmhold.

Resi blew air through her lips, trying her best not to let the panic from earlier that morning close in on her. She'd been keeping an eye out for Gilda but had yet to see her. She turned her focus back to Mags. "Next few days should be busy, huh?"

"We can count on it," Mags responded.

Resi glanced to the monstrous log columns of the Eye. Friends, relatives, and socialites from out of town had arrived earlier in the week to stay with Offenheimers for the Fourth-Year Festival. That morning, a colorful group sat bundled up on the porch drinking warmed mugs of Fet, a wine from the western region of Rowan. It was often mulled to piping hot temperatures to warm the bellies of the social elite in the rainier months.

"Any news of the feast?" Resi asked, hopeful Mags had inquired to one of the other 'Licks about it. She needed to learn as much as possible about the plans for the night of the Festival, and if there was anyone she could count on to spill information, it was Mags.

"I hope something good; a great meal and the best selection of ale and Fet," Mags said jovially. "Pickled Folly Root too."

Resi groaned. The scent of pickled Folly Root was intolerable; like dirt and overripe fruit. "Just don't come looking for me while you eat that nasty stuff. I'll be somewhere in the next region plugging my nose."

The words came out in jest, but Resi couldn't help but feel the weight of their truth. She planned to be long gone from the farmhold by the start of the feast. How far would she make it that day? And where might she be when Mags turned for her during the Festival and found she was missing?

Mags laughed. "It's too bad I can't eat it more often. Could use a little time away from you laughing at my hair."

"Ha-ha," Resi sang sarcastically.

Mags wiggled her eyebrows, then continued. "Who's to say what they'll be serving us for the feast; different every year. There'll be stories told, the usual ones. No doubt, the overseers will be quick to belittle the power of our people. They'll claim that the gifts of our ancestors turned great power into evil. Still, I'm just waiting for that first sip of Rowgar. Ooh, I can taste it now." Mags had always delighted in the delicacy of Rowgar, another sparkling wine from the region of Rowan. Her cheeks raised to show a crooked grin Resi had grown so fond of ever since she was a young girl.

"You'll never stop believing those tales, will you? No matter how ridiculous they get," Resi said.

Mags smirked and her eyes brightened beneath her hood. "Mark my words, Resi. One of these days you're going to come across an Aliquian with the ability to pick you up off the ground with just their thoughts! And when you do, don't come running back to me unless you're looking to hear the words, '*I told you so.*'"

Resi snickered uncomfortably, wondering if the heat in her stomach would decide to reveal itself today. It was always so sporadic, so testy. Resi had never wanted this kind of burden on her life, and telling Mags her secret would only add to the anxiety she fought off day after day when the heat came alive inside of her. And besides, the woman worried about her enough as it was.

Resi fought against her thoughts, asking more questions to distract herself from something that she didn't fully understand. "What time is the parade?" she asked.

Mags looked at her, confused. "Aren't you full of questions today."

"What?" Resi asked, trying to sound innocent.

Mags sighed. "I'm just not used to you getting so curious...well, about anything. Least of all the Fourth-Year Festival."

Resi attempted a casual shrug. She needed to ease off the questions, be more subtle. But who else could she ask but Mags about such things? The woman was her only connection to what was discussed on the property. She still didn't know when the overseers would leave the Festival to get to their posts in the forest. She racked her brain to formulate an excuse.

"It's my first Festival as a woman," she finally said. "Not so unnatural to wish to partake alongside others my age."

"No," said Mags with a huff under the weight of the roots in the large baskets they carried. "But it's unnatural for *you*. You recall last Festival?"

Resi tried to push away the thought of last Festival; how she'd barely slept in the days leading up to it, how she'd been unable to breathe at even the thought of it. It had been her first Festival without her parents, and as much as Mags had tried to cheer Resi up on that day, Resi had remained quiet and distant during the Feast. While everyone around her had danced and celebrated, Resi had sat numbly and watched, seething with envy at the happy expressions on the faces of her people. Her mind had drifted to simpler times when her mother had hand-stitched her a dress for previous Festivals. Her father had thrown her atop his shoulders to see over the crowds of people along the cliffs. They'd been happy then. If she'd known that her time with them would be cut so short, she would've clung onto them more tightly.

"Forget I brought it up, dear," Mags said, her face worried.

The two walked on, searching for the nearest cart of Folly Root that would be collected by the overseers, but all of them were stationed beyond the furthest barn.

Just then, Mags tripped over a rogue tree root and landed forward on her hands. Her basket fell to the ground, and red Folly scattered across the dampened grass.

"Dumb tree root, gets me every time," she said as Resi reached to help her collect the Folly and bring her to her feet.

"You alright?"

"Fine," Mags groaned, her eyes squinting in pain. "Just get so stiff in this chill."

Resi wondered when Mags would be pulled from her duties; part of her was grateful she wouldn't be around to witness it.

Mags squeezed her arm. "Pray that when you're my age you won't get put to work the way I have. Moving about in these conditions is just about the worst thing for an old woman."

Resi playfully turned in all directions, holding her hand as a shield over her eyes. "Old woman?" Where? I don't see one."

Mags smacked her on the shoulder. "Stop your nonsense!" she teased. "Believe me, I'm as old as a woman wants to be out in these fields. If I know one thing for certain, it's that this Festival will be a welcomed relief, most especially by me."

Guilt rumbled inside Resi. In three days, she'd be leaving without a goodbye or even so much as a warning. She knew it was for Mags's own safety that she didn't tell her about her plan, but the thought of not spending the days in Mags's company sent a wave of sadness coursing through her. Who would be there to care for Mags as she aged? Who would keep her mind fresh and sharp with conversation?

As they walked, they looked behind the house to the main field, a green-rowed expanse that dipped beyond the furthest hill on the property. *Jee!* an overseer cried at his horse as his cart filled with hundreds of folly roots took a left turn. More 'Licks twisted the bases of the folly plants through the rows. As they neared the barn, a group of 'Licks led by a stocky overseer came down the row. The group carried burlap bags filled with horse feed on their slumped shoulders. The foggy conditions of the day made it difficult to see the forest past the field, but Resi was certain every 'Lick had been called from their lean-tos to work on gathering roots for the Festival.

"Buncha 'Licks!" bawled the overseer as the group trudged along. "Slowing down won't get the job done! Get to it!"

Resi looked to see a scowl cross Mags's mouth. The woman didn't blink until the group passed. The slang term was familiar, but that didn't make it any more enjoyable to hear from the mouth of a Codian. "*You're not worth a lick,*" was another popular phrase used by overseers, and was often followed by a spit to the dirt.

When Resi and Mags came to the barn, they went to the rear and threw the contents of their baskets into a large bin to be cleaned.

As they returned to their post in the fields, she and Mags walking arm and arm, Resi swept the front strands of her hair behind her ears inside of her cloak. "Should've thought to put this mess up today," she said. She'd let it grow to her waist the previous year. It was all one length except for two gold strands that stuck up at the top of her head; they'd been that way since she was a kid.

"Don't cut it. Come winter, you'll be grateful for its warmth. " A reminiscent grin spread Mags's plump cheeks wide. "When I was your age, mine was as thick as syrup. Of course, it was much darker. But now? I don't have as many as three strands to collect on the top of my head."

Resi felt a sudden pain in her heart. "Don't make me feel worse about laughing at your hair earlier."

Mags looked at her with a quick wink. "I wouldn't dream of rubbing your cruelty right back in your face."

As a girl, Resi had longed for raven hair, having heard the many lyrics in songs of old of foreign princesses with cascading, raven locks. But as she'd grown older, she'd become increasingly fond of the uniqueness of her coloring. Her bright green eyes and golden-brown hair had been passed onto her by her mother, but the brushstroke of freckles across her nose were all her own.

The rest of the day passed slowly. Resi glanced every so often through the mist towards the Eye, her mind shifting to her unwelcome meeting with Gilda from the night before. She hadn't seen Gilda amongst the fields all day, and as the hours ticked by, she couldn't decipher if that was a good thing or not. Finally, when the bell rang out to signal the end of work, the Aliquian field-hands belonging to the farmhold tromped back drearily to their lean-tos.

Nightfall was soon to cast its shadow on the day as Resi savagely finished her dinner of onions and peas in chicken stock. After sipping up every last drop of it, she sat on the steps of the lean-to, listening to the sounds of rain. It was a pleasant night, rare for this time of year, when windy storms usually came rolling through the meadows. It was the kind of night Resi would've normally enjoyed, if she weren't so on edge. The desire of her heart, her escape, wrestled with her mind. Perhaps, it wasn't the right time for her to run. Maybe it was better to wait.

Feeling desperate for relief, she darted under the sheltering of the lean-to and stealthily grabbed a stubby piece of charcoal and a faded piece of parchment that she kept hidden beneath her cot. Adrenaline coursed through her, and her stomach's heat raised from its slumber. Sketching had a funny way of rousing the monster from its sleep, but not violently, as when her anger drew it out quickly and without warning. Her artistic inclination was still new to her, and unpracticed, but she knew above all else that her hidden sketches had sparked color and light in all the places that the farmhold had once darkened. Since the Ban of Aliquian Education, artistic materials were forbidden for 'Licks to carry, but items so small could easily fit into the breast of her dress if an overseer drew near. Resi smiled to herself as she recalled finding the parchment many years earlier in the wildflower meadow, probably left behind by a drunken overseer before he turned in for the night.

She looked down the lane. Mags wouldn't be back for a little while, which gave her some time to sketch. She looked upon the parchment, her hand caressing the lines of her precious sketches. It was loaded with drawings, all minimal, and all constrained to a sliver of space. She chuckled quietly as she looked upon the familiar renderings—a sketch of her hand, a bird guarding her eggs in the nest, and her favorite, a small portrait of Mags.

She crossed back to the stoop of the lean-to and rested her boots on the second step, laying the parchment on her right knee. She looked up just in time to see a slight break in the clouds. The warmth of the sun kissed her cheeks for the first time in what felt like weeks, and Resi exhaled with joy. She heard gasps from somewhere nearby; 'Licks in their lean-tos reacting to the emerging shadows from the nearby trees stretching long in the grass.

Resi closed her eyes and thanked the clouds for parting. Her hand scribbled a rounded line along the paper and gradually, her paranoia concerning Gilda and her escape waned. It was what she adored most about sketching; every fear was drowned out by the sound of the charcoal against the parchment.

Her focus narrowed in on the scene before her; light—golden and pure, piercing through cloud cover.

Black and white sketches wouldn't do this kind of beauty justice. She'd been hungry for color for months now. For *paint*. She'd yet to experiment with blending and the progression of a new medium, and she ached for the chance to try her hand at it.

The monster seemingly agreed; it begged warmly inside of her at the idea.

She'd only just started sketching the clouds when Mags returned from the gardens with more ingredients for dinner that week. Picking vegetables from the patch was Mags's favorite way to end a day, especially on a pleasant night like this. With her was Uza, the other woman who shared their lean-to. Uza's figure looked more skeletal than ever, Resi noted, as she and Mags closed the gap between the vegetable patch and the lean-tos. The two strolled in silence up the road with baskets very full of onions and carrots. When they neared the stoop, Resi stuffed the parchment and charcoal into her dress and took their baskets to help.

"Beautiful night we have here," Mags said as she wiped her brow.

Resi set the baskets down on the dilapidated chair at the edge of the stoop. Uza didn't say a word. In silence, she brushed past both of them without so much of a glance and made her way inside the lean-to. A heavy sadness filled the air in the wake of her departure.

"Anything from her today?" Resi asked Mags quietly.

"Not a word."

Resi's eyes lingered on Uza for a time. "She'll come around. She just needs time."

Mags wiped her hands on her day-dress, something she did anytime she felt annoyed. "Yeah, well...how much time does one person need?"

"We can't begin to know what she went through," Resi sighed, then folded her hands in her lap and turned towards the sunset. Uza, her husband, and their children had each been dispersed to different properties in separate regions. Since her arrival to the Offenheimer Farmhold only two years ago, Uza had remained close to silent.

Mags's tone went rough and icy. "What right does she have to be more entitled to grief than the rest of us?"

Resi shuddered, but didn't say anything more as she watched the sun sink lower before it disappeared once more behind dark and foreboding clouds. She feared it would be the last she'd see of it before winter would snatch away its warmth until spring.

As day gave way to night and a fresh spit of rain descended once more upon the meadows, Resi and Mags sat together in silence and watched the others returning to their lean-to's for the night. Mags greeted those she knew, asking them about their day and their children. As usual, Resi kept her distance from anybody that drew near. The cautious looks from the others ensured that she remain quiet and withdrawn.

When the traffic of the lane through the lean-tos finally slowed, Mags turned to Resi with a firmness in her eyes. "You know, you might try speaking up one of these days. Saying hello won't kill you."

Resi avoided her eyes as she pulled the hood of her cloak over her head once more.

"Like you said, you're a woman now!" Mags continued. "You certainly can handle a few conversations with some new people."

Resi's lips curled. "It's not a question of whether I can handle it or not. It's whether they can handle having a conversation with *me*."

"Don't let their gossip get the better of you," Mags ordered. "Sooner or later, they'll see that you're as harmless as a field mouse."

Resi had no response. She watched Mags rock in her chair to fill the silence between them.

"I almost forgot!" Mags then blurted out suddenly. "I heard that the girl down the way, the one about your age? She went and got herself engaged! The Gillis's son asked for her hand not a few days ago! Isn't it wonderful? What a celebration this Fourth-Year Festival should be for them! And for their families!"

Resi turned to Mags with a huff. "*That's* what your griping is all about?"

"Oh, come on, don't shrug me off," Mags groaned. "I was only telling you news from the fields."

"Right."

"Calm down, will you? Most girls your age enjoy hearing about upcoming nuptials!"

Resi turned again towards the lane. Strikes of lightning stabbed at the horizon, followed by low rumbles of thunder. She wanted to go back to the escape of her sketches, but she knew better than to let Mags ever see her practicing a forbidden craft. She sighed. "You know more than anybody that I don't care for that kind of thing."

There was more silence, but Mag couldn't take it for very long. "Can you blame me for wanting such a thing for you too?" she said with a burst.

"I've told you a thousand times—I'm never getting married."

Mags huffed, then shook her head. "Don't be so sure of that."

"If I'm sure of one thing, it's *that*."

"How can a young woman be so sure of anything..."

Embarrassed, Resi felt an uncomfortable laugh leave her. "Why does it matter so much to you?"

Defeated, Mags sat back in her chair. "When I heard you talking about going to the Festival today, I got excited. It might be nice for you to start meeting some of the others around here, especially the ones your age. You can't spend the whole of your days and nights clinging to me. I won't be around for much longer." The woman's face softened as she looked Resi deeply in the eyes. "You're such a beautiful girl —and educated, too. Any man would be lucky to take you as his wife."

Resi recalled the summer after her parents' disappearance when Mags had taught her to read and write. It had been a temporary distraction for Resi, until that autumn when Governor Sequis had declared the Ban of Aliquian Education. Aliquian children Resi's age and younger had not been taught. Overseers had ransacked the lean-tos, removing books and parchment. Any Aliquian caught with such materials was liable for a heavy punishment, and an even worse punishment came to those who were ever discovered teaching.

Resi knew Mags was right, though, and she hated it. She'd feared approaching the others her age—and why would she, after all they'd done to distance themselves and tarnish her reputation? They were few in number, but close all the same. "Like I said, I don't want it," she said, shrugging off her thoughts. "And that's that."

Mags's tone lowered as her head dropped. "I'd hoped you'd someday find someone who could make you feel at home."

Resi tried to ignore the growing heat in her stomach, her monster. "And a husband is the very thing to make me feel safe?"

"Well!" Mags said, astonished. "It certainly helps!"

"I shouldn't be pressured to find a husband on the off chance that he might get snatched up by another girl in the meantime."

Mags shook her head towards the road that led to the Eye. "You're not going to have many options around here if you don't start thinking about it."

"So be it, then!"

Mags's face went as red as Folly Root. "Resi, if I weren't wise, I'd swear you were Codian, judging only by your stubbornness! What are you going to do with your life, huh? Work your way into spinsterhood?!"

"Maybe! I mean, look at you! You're doing fine!"

Mags relaxed as many years worth of wisdom sparkled behind her dark eyes. "I may look fine, dear, but I had my chance at love. And when it was taken from me, I was stupid enough to think the same things you're thinking now. *Why was he taken from me? Why me?*" Her voice went soft as she recalled the memory of her lost husband, the love of her life who had gotten sick with a field cough in the months before Resi's parents had fled. "But I couldn't ask myself those questions for very long. When you lose someone you love, you know you'd rather go through the pain of losing them five hundred times over than never having them in your life."

"I guess that's where we differ," Resi said stiffly, her gaze forward. Her mother's face suddenly flashed to mind before the heat in her stomach sparked and she batted the image away. "They *chose* to leave me behind. Asking questions is the only way that I can make sense of it."

Mags looked at her sadly before she started rocking her chair again. "I know you miss them around the time of the Festival."

"I don't want to talk about it anymore," Resi spoke sternly.

"Alright then," Mags said with a frown; but in the next moment, a new light came to her eyes. "Just don't pretend you haven't noticed the handsome boy looking at you every night from up the way."

"You're lying," Resi mumbled.

Mags's lips pursed. "You turn that pretty little head of yours around and you just might catch him making big eyes in your direction right now."

Resi skeptically narrowed her eyes on Mags, then faced north. A few lean-tos up the road sat a boy her age on the steps. She recognized him. He was relatively new to the Farmhold; he came in a few years prior with a large group from the West. He often worked in the barns. And Mags was right—he was looking right at her. He stared a little too long after her eyes met his before his gaze shifted to the road.

"He isn't looking at me like *that*," Resi sulked.

Mags laughed. "Trust me. He's looking at you *like that*. And he likes what he sees. I know that kind of far-off look."

Resi kicked the dirt. "Doesn't matter. I'm not so sure I agree with thinking him to be handsome."

"Hmm...I guess my eyes deceive me," Mags said teasingly.

Resi fought the urge to turn back for a second glance, but her curiosity won. The boy still watched her, only this time he didn't remove his eyes from her when she reciprocated the glance. There was something goofy about his face; he hadn't quite filled out like the others his age. His thick, copper-brown hair went in all directions, and caterpillar eyebrows rested above big, deep eyes that reminded Resi of the color of soil after rain. A slight smile came to his upper lip before she turned away.

"Not handsome, huh?" Mags probed.

"Would you shush?!" Resi said as she reached to swat Mags's leg.

They laughed, forgetting their earlier spat, but soon enough, the sadness that Resi had fought off moments earlier came back to her as the chilly night air silenced around them. She'd miss this—these talks before bed, the long hours spent with her only friend in the world. Mags had requested that Resi stop clinging to her. If Resi went through with her plan, she supposed she was only days away from doing just that.

After the sun had set, and fires were lit up and down the lane, a sudden commotion erupted to the south. Deep voices called out over the twilight, then came loud shrieks. Those in the nearby lean-tos craned their necks to see what was causing the ruckus.

"What is it?" Resi asked with a concerned look to Mags.

The woman leapt from her chair and came to where Resi stood. "Get behind me."

Three overseers emerged on the path wearing crisp, gray uniforms. Max and Christoph, the lesser in rank of the three, dragged a woman no older than Resi in their arms. Her feet scraped the mud beneath her as tears streamed down her face. The third member of the crew, Horris, was the Foreman of all the Overseers on the property.

"This isn't good," Mags said. "It's Horris."

"Who's the woman?"

Mags shrugged her shoulders. "Not sure."

Max and Christoph threw the woman down at the center of the road. The shoulder of her dress had been torn, and three deep gashes swiped sharply down her left cheek.

The sight of Horris never brought cheer. Most Aliquians knew to stay quiet whenever he drew near. In many areas of the regions, some would consider Horris to be an attractive man. But to those who knew his antics, he was anything but. Resi watched his long, thin frame stride up the lane. A large mustache broke up the lines of his narrow face. The ends of it curled up his cheeks like two rounded billows of smoke.

"Good evening, folks!" Horris called to the small crowd that had gathered. His voice was gruff and power-hungry. "Sorry to shake up your night, but we couldn't resist a little show after cleaning up the mess up the road!"

The woman whimpered, her frame shaking from head to toe.

"I can't watch," Resi whispered to Mags.

"Don't turn away," Mags said with her eyes glued to the scene. "You know what he does to those of us who do."

"Well," Horris said, taking a quick sniff as he surveyed the bystanders. He then rolled his sleeves from his arms. His circles widened as he walked around the woman. "I'm sure you all would like some clarification on why we've interrupted your peaceful evening..."

The woman's whimpering rose in pitch, keening into the night sky.

"I believe an explanation from the cause of the trouble would be the most reliable source. What do you think, boys?" Horris asked.

"An intelligent idea, boss," joked Christoph. He looked to Max for reinforcement; Max only nodded with a vacant expression.

"Oh, pardon me," Horris apologized sarcastically to the crowd before turning back to the woman. "I do believe many of these folks have yet to make your acquaintance. A mistake on my part. Tell us your name, 'Lick." Horris said the command with a cruel kind of joy, but the woman could only say her name in a whisper. "Oh...you can do better than that!" Horris beckoned to her as if speaking to a frightened child. "One more time! For everyone to hear!"

The woman's voice quivered. "Shina."

"Lovely...and what, Shina, made us drag you all the way out here on a pleasant night? I'm sure these kind people would be interested to know what forced them away from the warmth of their suppers."

Shina mumbled again and Horris laughed maniacally. "Oh, Shina, this business of speaking under your breath just won't do! Again, please! And much, *much* louder," he commanded.

"I—" Shina paused as she heaved long breaths that bobbed her chest. "I stole from the Mistress."

A gasp came from the gathered crowd.

"Ahh, yes, indeed," Horris called out. "You stole from the Mistress, Shina. And what exactly did you steal?"

"A—a hairpin, sir."

"A hairpin! And a nice one, too—probably worth much more than one might even pay you in a lifetime if you worked for a wage!"

"Yes...yes, sir."

"You know..." Horris changed his pacing, his speech growing faster. "I do believe that getting caught stealing from the Offenheimer's home requires a severe punishment, does it not?"

Shina didn't respond. Horris leaned in close to her, his arms still resting smugly behind his back. "It does, Shina," he said, his tone reverting back to pointed accusation. "A severe punishment indeed." He then turned to reengage the crowd. "Shina is a favored attendant of the household! Slept with a pillow under her head and woke to hot food prepared for her in the morning. She was the tutor for the Offenheimer's only son!"

Horris crossed back to Shina. "Unfortunately, our little explanation has come to an end. The punishment must be served. Pity. What will it be, Christoph?"

Christoph unveiled a scroll from his pocket and cleared his throat. "Any house attendant caught in possession of a stolen article shall be removed from their position and must bear the Mark for the remainder of their days."

A collective gasp came from those gathered. Resi put a hand over her mouth. She'd yet to ever see the Mark given in person. Only, the Mark would not be given by any old branding iron; not if Horris would be executing the punishment. Certain authority figures and politicians within the regions were given the rare permission to use sorcery in moderation, if only to keep Aliquians in line. The practice of basic sorcery required a permit, which could only be obtained through specific training. Horris was the only Codian on the property with such permission.

Resi felt a white-hot flash rumble in her stomach. She hadn't seen Horris use his magic in years.

"Mercy..." Mags whispered beside her, her lips quivering.

Shina's face went blank as she processed her punishment. Her head fell back and she looked to the sky.

"The Governor's orders are the Governor's orders," Horris spoke low to Shina as he knelt beside her. "I'm sure you understand."

As if the news of the punishment had some malicious ability to transform him, his eyes suddenly went dark. A chill ran down Resi's spine as she watched a surge of maleficence overtake him.

In preparation, Christoph and Max raced to the woman's sides and they lifted her from the mud. Christoph yanked at the woman's sleeve, revealing the untouched skin of her forearm, and Horris stepped forward. He outstretched his hand, and using only the pad of his index finger, he drew a circle on Shina's arm. Tears streamed down her face as she looked at the initially unbothered skin. But after a few seconds, her eyes met Horris's dark gaze as a painful cry left her. The Mark gradually appeared branded on her skin, and all the while, Horris kept his eyes locked on hers.

Horror came over Resi as her heat fanned and sparked within her. It was as if it desired to be freed from the prison of her body. Her eyes scanned the faces of those nearby before they landed on the boy she'd seen from the stoop. He stood tall on the dirt, his fist clenched, the veins in his arms strained. He didn't look away from Shina for a moment.

As Shina's cries subsided, Resi's earlier doubts concerning her escape suddenly fled her. With or without placing the final marking, she knew she wouldn't deviate from her plan, not as long as her people were subjected to such cruelty. She made a vow to herself in that moment, one that marked her soul as permanently as Horris's sorcery had marked Shina's skin. If, in time, she found herself in the safety of the western regions, she'd see to it that every last person standing beside her on the dirt lane would come to know freedom too.

CHAPTER 3

THE EYE

The day before the Festival sprung up on Resi as quickly as a weed in the field. That morning, she had been ordered to carry water to and from the stables on what was shaping up to be the muggiest day of the season. As she went about her tasks, she tried to hold back a yawn, but couldn't; she'd barely slept the last two nights. She couldn't decide if it was because of Shina's punishment, or because of the impending day of the Festival. More than likely, it was both.

The usual hum of thinly-veiled excitement that could be heard about the meadows in the days leading up to the Festival was eerily absent, as was the buzz of chatter in the evenings. Instead, it appeared as if every field-hand was focusing their efforts on the work that needed to be done, each trying their best to forget Horris and his dark eyes; to forget Shina and the screams that had ripped through the forest that night.

Strange as it was to see the spirits of her people so low, Resi preferred working this way; with fewer distractions and less chatter. It often meant quitting earlier in the evenings. But even with the extra time in her lean-to, Resi feared sleep wouldn't find her again tonight.

Tomorrow, the Aliquians, overseers, and members of the household would stroll into town following Governor Sequis's carriage in the afternoon. When the feast was complete after sunset, everyone's stomachs would be filled with plenty of food and ale. Mags had gossiped to Resi the previous night that the assigned Overseers for the Festival planned to drink heartily while on the job. They would more than likely leave their posts after sunset to continue drinking in town. If Resi waited to dash to the boat until the evening, she had reason to hope the overseers would be too drunk to worry about anything other than where their next drink might come from. Still, she had her doubts. She hadn't placed the final marking that would lead her to the river, not after her run-in with Gilda.

After another long walk to the water pump, Resi turned back towards the stables with a full bucket. Her hands were beginning to callus from the rough wood of the handle, but she moved quickly, averting her eyes from an overseer that strode past. She was certain her plans were written all over her face.

She came to the wildflower meadow, spotting Mags in the middle of the field with a basket of colorful blooms resting on her hip. Her stance was low to the ground to keep her wide frame balanced, and the unparalleled humidity of the day had caused her hair to practically stand on end. Resi couldn't help but smile as she continued moving. It wasn't unnatural for them to see each other on one of the rare afternoons they weren't paired together in the fields, but today, Resi could sense something was amiss. Mags looked up at her from the meadow, and her face tensed.

"Taresia!" she called out suddenly.

Resi felt her heart quicken. Aliquians were forbidden to shout in the fields, and were ordered to keep their heads down. Panicked, she pretended not to hear her friend's cry.

"Resi, wait!" Mags called again. Urgently, she set her basket down on the grass, grabbed for her skirts, and awkwardly began to jog to the road. Resi watched in shock as the same overseer that she'd walked past only moments prior had turned back on the road. He matched his pace to Mags's disjointed run. "Resi, please! Hold up a moment, will you?!" Mags heaved when she drew closer.

Suddenly aware of the many gawking faces that had looked up

from their work, Resi set her buckets down on the gravel. "Mags, what're you doing?" she asked in a whisper, eyes darting towards the overseer who was only seconds behind.

"Someone came to look for you today. A man from the Eye," Mags said with heavy breath. She bent at the waist and clutched her knees.

"Who?" Resi asked.

"An older gentleman. Seemed pressed to find you," Mags answered, her eyes wide.

Resi kept her composure, but a sour feeling began to work its way through her.

"What is the holdup?" the overseer barked. Resi attempted to dodge the spit that came flying at her from the corners of his mouth, but failed.

"Sir, I apologize," Mags spoke as she stood protectively between the overseer and Resi. "I was merely informing Miss Flood that a fellow from the house was looking for her today. Told me it was a matter of importance. Asked me to send her up the road if I saw her."

"What sort of fellow?" the man asked.

"An older man. Wearing a tattered suit."

The overseer rolled his eyes and placed his hands on his hips. He huffed and his gaze went to the road behind them. "You, boy!" he suddenly yelled to someone approaching. Mags and Resi turned to see the same brown-eyed boy from up the lane on the night of Shina's punishment. Resi's stomach flipped as she watched his eyes widen on her. She glanced down at the sleeves that were rolled up to reveal his strained forearms. He too was on water duty, as made evident by the full bucket swinging near his hips.

"Yes, sir?" he responded. His voice matched his stature—youthful, a tad unsure.

"You have a name, 'Lick?"

"Corey, sir."

"You have enough strength to carry two buckets?"

Corey looked to Resi with confusion. Tensing, he rolled his shoulders. "Yes," he said haltingly.

"You'll take on her duties," the overseer commanded as he pointed to Resi. Corey looked at her again with questions in his eyes. He readjusted the full bucket in his arms.

"That'll be all," the overseer ordered.

Resi picked up her bucket, embarrassed, and passed it to Corey. Their eyes met briefly during the exchange, and she found herself wishing she'd encountered him for the first time under different circumstances. He then turned back for the barns, his arms shaking with the extra effort.

The overseer glared menacingly at Mags. "If I ever see you drop your work again, I'll see to it that you never speak another word in your life. No such thing as a talkative 'Lick without a tongue. Got it?"

Mags withered before nodding. Briefly, she looked upon Resi with concern, then lifted her skirts and returned down the hill to the meadow.

"Let's get a move on," the overseer said to Resi as he turned towards the house. Fearfully, she trailed after him. Her heart feared the worst, but she wouldn't let her thoughts linger in dark places for too long. Her gaze lifted to the Eye through the fog where she noticed a gathering of women on the northern extension of the porch. They drank Rowgar from crystal glassware between bites of pickled folly root. All at once, they cackled in unison, their heads tilted back, their mouths wide. Then, they just as quickly returned to their gossiping when one of the women leaned in conspiratorially with more information. Together, they resembled something much like a squawking flock of birds, their feather-tips of their wide-brimmed hats wiggling as they laughed and cooed.

One of them, however, stood apart from all the rest. The woman's back was turned towards the fields, and her gold dress caught what little light filtered through the cloud cover. A fur shrug draped around her shoulders and the tilted hat atop her head was decorated with feathers of every color. Finally, she turned out towards the expanse of the property with watchful eyes.

Resi gulped. It was just as she feared. It was rare to ever see Marion Offenheimer, Mistress of the Farmhold. She often kept herself as far away from the mud and stench of the fields as possible. But all that changed on the week before the Festival. Marion couldn't help but boast and gloat over her property to her friends during their stay. She'd held complete control over the property all week as her husband, Theodore Offenheimer, owner of the farmhold, had been engaged with business outside the home. Marion and her guests had celebrated frivolously during the day hours on the back porch, and their debauchery often overflowed well into the night.

Resi craned her neck to better see Marion. The Mistress appeared to be engaged with another woman, someone seated beyond Resi's view from the road.

"Keep up, 'Lick," the overseer called back to her.

But Resi had stopped, paralyzed on the gravel with her eyes fixed on the familiar wrinkled fingers that extended themselves to Marion. Much as she wished to bolt for the woods, to take off in a run for her markings, she pushed on towards the house, knowing she was headed for trouble.

A middle-aged man matching Mags's description noticed Resi and the overseer approach and crossed the porch to welcome her. "Miss Flood?"

Resi nodded as she attempted to push her dampened hair back from her face.

"I thought I'd never find you in the fields," he sighed with relief as he wiped a bead of sweat from his forehead. "My name is James. Come. I'd like you to meet Mistress Marion," he said proudly as he gestured Resi up the porch stairs. He was dressed in a moth-eaten burgundy suit. Marion heard his introduction, and like a slow-moving portrait, she turned to face her newest arrival. She had a youthful glow for a middle-aged woman, but the expression of permanent discontent across her face couldn't hide her true age. Eyes the color of the most ominous green sea shone brightly over her rosy cheeks and two strawberry-blonde curls hung loosely at her collarbone.

Resi had the sinking feeling she should bow. Or was she expected to curtsy? Clumsily, she settled for something between the two, a sort of bend at the waist and knees that left an uncomfortable informality in the space between her own ragged skirts and Marion's expensive gown.

"Thank you, James," Marion spoke as her eyes instructed the man to leave their presence. She then turned with a smile to Resi. "A pleasure, Taresia. I take it you know Miss Gilda?" Marion gestured to the haggish woman, and Gilda smiled hollowly. "That will be all for now, Gilda. Thank you for your time."

As Gilda hobbled towards the steps, she winked at Resi, her eyes proud and victorious. Did she think this was some kind of sick joke? Resi nearly yanked her by the hair, but Marion's questions halted her.

"Alright if I call you by your first name? Miss Flood has sort of a depressing ring to it," the Mistress said as she removed her gloves. Resi couldn't respond. She was too transfixed by the details of Marion's hair, her dress, her emerald stare. "Have you lost your hearing, 'Lick?" Marion asked, her head tilting to the side.

"I'm sorry ma'am. I've just, well, I've never seen such a beautiful dress in my life, is all."

"Well, aren't we well-mannered!" said Marion as she turned to witness her own reflection in a nearby window. "Compliments will do you well in this house. Mind coming inside from the mist? I like to retreat to my private drawing room with guests at this time of day. But tonight, I'm going to say farewell to my friends and you and I are going to have a little chat. Just us girls."

Marion threw Resi a counterfeit smile before turning back to her friends and bidding them farewell. As soon as the group noticed Resi lingering by the stairs, they scowled. Their critical eyes scanned her from head to toe, taking in the whole of her worn attire as if she were dressed in nothing but her own filth.

James and Marion crossed the threshold into the house, and Resi, stuck somewhere between reality and hallucination, lagged behind. As she moved forward and into the hallway, her breath caught in her chest. The interior of the log mansion was certainly a feast for the eyes, and not at all what she had expected. A giant, crystal chandelier hung high above their heads and dark oil paintings dotted the walls, looking like windows into different worlds.

What was most alarming to her was the display of wide-ranging taxidermy that decorated the foyer. A stuffed whimsical bird, hung high over the stairs and poised in flight, particularly caught her attention. She withheld an insatiable urge to laugh. In all the years she'd daydreamed about the grandeur of the Eye, she couldn't have imagined it to be so opulent, and somehow equally as tawdry and tacky.

"Do try to keep up, Taresia. We have only a short while before dinner is served," Marion ordered over her shoulder as she removed her hat and furs, hung them on a coat rack, and strode into her drawing room.

Resi tripped over herself as she came into the room. A fire was already roaring in the grand stone hearth. The space was decorated in warm colors with a green-bolted chaise that sat before a large window overlooking the fields. Lazily, Marion plopped herself down on it and motioned for Resi to sit in the wide-backed chair opposite her. Awkwardly, Resi sat, but she dared not get too comfortable. Her sweaty rags needn't brush against the smooth fabric of the back of the chair if they didn't have to.

"Would you like anything? Tea?" Marion asked her kindly.

"Uh, no, ma'am. I'm fine."

"There's no need to refrain out of politeness, dear. Please, indulge me! You look as if you just got caught in a monsoon!" Just then, a young 'Lick woman entered the room and placed a tea tray on the small side table next to Marion. The Mistress glared at the woman until she saw herself out of the room and she and Resi were alone once again. Marion then poured her a cup of tea and crossed the space of the room to hand it to her. Her eyes momentarily lingered on Resi as she took her first sip.

"Warm," Resi remarked, but then she noticed the bitter aftertaste of folly root. She hadn't been expecting that. Her face pinched at the center as her mind began to spin. The effects came on quickly.

Marion nodded once, then returned to her chaise. "I enjoy the root best when it's brewed."

Resi gulped. The last she'd tried folly root was at the previous

Fourth-Year Festival; the only time Aliquians were allowed to partake in the pleasures afforded to Codian people every day.

"Now," Marion continued, her smile wide. "I don't want you to find any reason to be uncomfortable. I'm sure you're curious about what this is all about. Getting brought into the home, and all! And now, a private meeting with the Mistress of the property in her private quarters! Quite a day for someone like you, I imagine. I know it sounds ridiculous coming from me, but please, do try to relax."

Resi didn't move. She couldn't even breathe, or think. The root's vicious toxins were working her over even worse than Marion.

"Miss Gilda's told me quite a lot about you," Marion said with an arching of her brow.

The insides of Resi's stomach clenched. Her eyes closed in panic. Just maybe when she opened them, all of it—Marion, the house, the warm glass in her hand—would go away.

Marion settled into her chair. "She's informed me that you're one of the few remaining 'Licks your age that can read. Of course, I recall the ban of reading and writing amongst your kind in this region when you would've just been a girl. After all, it really isn't necessary for 'Licks to have an education. But even so, I find yours to be of value to me today." The words trickled out of Marion's lips like sweet syrup.

Resi's head tilted. "I don't quite understand, ma'am."

"The reason I called a meeting with you today, Taresia, is because I have need for you," Marion smiled. "Here. In the household. I'm sure you're aware that I've recently dismissed my son's tutor. My boy needs to resume his studies, and preferably as soon as possible. And I have a feeling you're the exact person for the job."

Resi blinked rapidly. Relief washed over her as she realized that maybe she wasn't in trouble after all. "With all due respect, ma'am, I'm not certain I have the experience. I have no understanding of children, and I'm not one to teach."

"Oh, don't be so modest!"

"I don't aim to belittle myself out of need for flattery. I only speak the truth."

Marion's gaze furrowed. "Scottis is twelve years old. He's hardly a child. All I ask is that you look after him and see to it that he commits time to his studies. And," she said wistfully, "I'm sure you know of his condition."

Resi cleared her throat. "Condition?"

Agitated, Marion fixed a loose piece of hair at her neck. "He's... slow. Well, at least, socially speaking."

"Oh. I didn't know that."

"Well, now you do," Marion said sternly. She uncrossed, then quickly crossed her legs again. "I think it's imperative for him to be around a young lady only a few years his senior. It'll help him to engage in conversation. The boy can barely say a word without losing focus, even to the likes of his father and myself!" Marion flung the curls from her shoulders and her décolletage flushed a bright red. She caught her breath, and then the color subsided. "Mind if I ask you a few questions?" she asked, her voice suddenly pitching higher.

Resi nodded, taking notice of the creeping fear that sat at the top of her spine at Marion's slight outburst.

"You're not obligated to anyone on the property? No family? Children?"

Her mind went to Mags. "I suppose not."

Marion looked upon her suddenly with pity. "My husband's informed me of your parents. I remember them, of course. Stupid, really, to leave such a...beautiful property. We treat our 'Licks as family here, and it always strikes me odd to think anyone would *choose* to leave such a wonderful establishment."

Resi said nothing. She only kept her focus on taming the lit fire in her stomach.

"Horrible thing, abandoning a child," Marion continued, her lower lip pouting. "But, it's for the best they left you behind. I'm sure their fate was decided not soon after their leave. Few 'Licks, if any, make it out of this region alive. Governor Sequis's militia is highly skilled. They don't rest a minute until they've found the 'Licks they're looking for. And when they do, well...let's just say they certainly get a kick out of torching their catches until there's nothing left of them!" The Mistress let out a bird-like laugh. Resi felt sick at its sound.

"Oh!" Marion piped when her fitful cackling subsided. "How insensitive of me—I don't mean to be so crass, Taresia. Surely, you must have your own suspicions of what's become of your parents."

Resi's breath slowed. Her eyes found her lap. In all the years that had passed since they'd departed, Resi had no comprehension of what had become of them. No hunch. It was why she was leaving, after all. She needed her most desperate questions answered, no matter their outcome.

A knock then came at the door. It was thunderous, abrupt. "This isn't a good time, James!" Marion barked. "Tell the kitchen to hold dinner for another twenty minutes!"

"I hardly think your kitchen 'Licks would rejoice upon seeing the likes of *me*, Mistress," said the voice through the door.

Marion flounced her way to the door almost giddily. She opened it, and in the doorway stood none other than the Foreman, Horris, dressed in his gray uniform. He slipped into the room like a serpent through grass.

"Didn't think you had company," he said when he noticed they weren't alone. His twisted mustache was uneven on his face, and Marion, gracious to adjust it, brushed her finger carefully along his cheek. Horris gave her a strange look, then turned to find Resi watching their encounter. His face suddenly went stern, anxious.

"I need only a few more minutes," said Marion softly to him. "Will you be available after dinner?"

Horris nodded, then shot a cool glance towards Resi before making his way out of the room. The door clicked quietly behind him.

"Apologies." Marion turned back with her brows drawn together at the center of her face. She returned to her chaise, her skirts swinging beneath her hips like a feather duster. "Many things still left to discuss before tomorrow. Which brings us to our next order of business. Tomorrow. I'd like you to start then."

Tomorrow. Marion wanted her to start tomorrow. But, tomorrow was the Festival. Tomorrow was the escape.

"Tomorrow?" Resi repeated.

"Oh, I know it's the Festival! But do try to understand. Scottis is not suitable to attend. I need someone to look after him here while Theodore and myself do the usual business of attending and mixing with the other socialites of town. You know how it is."

Resi readjusted in her chair. She certainly *didn't* know how it was, but she felt certain that she should simply nod and agree to Marion's terms without a fight. Seeing Horris, though, and the way he had brushed against Marion—it had further provoked the fire within her, and she was powerless to extinguish it.

"Ma'am," she burst. "I know the boy's welfare is your main concern. Forgive me for being forward, but is it possible to have one last day of celebration with my people before I commit a new life to him?"

Marion's fingers played with a curl, but she dropped it to her shoulder as Resi spoke. Her smile followed suit. "I hope you realize the gift I'm giving you, Taresia. I am inviting you into the greatest home south of Esur. You will take up in your own chambers. You'll be delivered a new day-dress, because we can't have you walking about the house wearing—well, *that*." Her hand brushed the air in the direction of Resi's muddy linen skirts. Her tone went sharp. "You've been promoted, 'Lick. You've exceeded the standing of many of your peers. It's an honor. And I expect you to receive that honor, one that demands you to begin your duties tomorrow. No ifs, ands, or buts."

Resi looked to the ceiling. The room had become smaller since she'd first entered it. The folly root had either taken deeper hold, or she was losing her sanity. She'd be living in the house? And further, she'd be taking care of the Offenheimer's son? And there was no getting around it—no way to fight for one last day, one that could lead her to freedom. She felt the fire inside her stomach tame, then simmer into nothing.

"Yes, ma'am," she answered.

"I also ask you to be available in the mornings to help me dress for the day. It'll be a good opportunity for us to discuss Scottis's progress."

Resi's hand went to her head, which was beginning to throb.

"Everything alright, dear?"

"I'm sorry, ma'am. I'm just—"

"Processing? That's fine. A lot of change, and good change at that, is headed your way! Now...you will be expected to keep Scottis focused on his studies, ones that will force him to keep his sights set on becoming Master of the single greatest Farmhold in the region. So, no distractions. He has this *fascination* with paper animals. Ridiculous, really. Keep him focused on numbers, socializing, and interaction."

Marion's voice was drowned out by the pulse in Resi's ears. Maybe, just maybe if she could get back to the lean-to tonight, she could up her escape by a day and hope to find the boat before dawn. Gilda wouldn't be patrolling the woods on the morning of the Festival. Every Aliquian, by law, was required to rest, save for the at-home help. She needed to leave the mansion, and fast, if only for one last night with Mags before she'd be shunned away in the Eye for the foreseeable future. She needed to leave, and she needed to leave now.

"Very well, Mistress," she said suddenly. "I thank you so much for this honor. I will do my very best to give all that I can to the development of your son. I look forward to seeing you first thing tomorrow." She stood quickly and curtsied. She'd paced to the door and reached for the handle—

"Taresia?" Marion called to her. "It would behoove you to wait to be released by your Mistress. Don't you agree?"

Resi froze, then turned to find Marion draping soft and sensual on the chaise. "Yes, ma'am," she answered.

"And may I ask *where*, exactly, you're heading off to in such a rush?"

"Oh..." she answered with a nervous chortle. "I was only trying to be polite, ma'am. I know that dinner is to be served soon. I was returning to my lean-to to free you so you may attend to more important matters."

"Your lean-to?" she giggled. "Oh, Taresia! You wouldn't expect me to send you back to the woods? Not after what I've offered! You will stay here tonight! And besides, much has to be done to fix your appearance before you meet Scottis tomorrow. You will march straight upstairs, take a bath, and sleep in the comfort of your own bed. Doesn't that sound nice?"

Resi's pulse pounded like two drums in her ears. "Oh, really, it's no trouble for me to—"

"I insist," Marion said sharply. Her chipper smile quickly snapped into a stern frown. A nod was the only thing Resi could think to do. There was no more fighting it, no more ideas to get her out of it.

"Thank you, ma'am. You're too kind."

The Mistress stood slowly from where she sat, her gown filling the space. "I expect you to be washed, dressed, and fed when you enter my chambers at dawn. I release you," she nodded, without breaking eye contact.

Resi curtsied again, her nerves shifting her balance on the carpet. "Good night, ma'am."

She exited the room with her mind in a whirl before James, the same man who had initially greeted her, approached her. Another woman, older, with long, braided hair stood beside him.

"Welcome, Miss Flood," James said to her kindly. "We hope your introduction to the house is warm. This here is Lucille," he said, pointing to the older woman. Lucille smiled. "She will show you to your chambers and explain all the ins and outs of the home and what's to be expected of you come tomorrow."

He pointed to the back of the home, presumably where the servant stairs were located and Lucille walked on, her eyes looking to Resi to follow.

Resi turned over her shoulder to find Marion facing the window in the drawing room. She was out of earshot. Quickly, Resi turned back to James, her voice low. "Could you send a message for me? To the woman I share a lean-to with? You met her today in the meadow, I believe."

"It's not advised," James said under his breath, then he noticed Resi's heavy breathing. "But I'll do what I can, Miss. What would you like it to say?"

Resi's heart rattled against her ribs. Her knees almost buckled.

"Just...that I'm safe at the house. That I won't see her tomorrow for the Festival. And," she paused, choking on her breath, "that I'll try to see her soon."

James's smile dropped. "Yes, Miss."

Lucille led her to the back of the home and up the narrow stairs before showing her to her room, a plain and small space with a bed, a side table, and a chair. After a short bath, Resi sat vacantly at the edge of the feather-down bed, feeling as if she'd tripped and fallen into someone else's nightmare when she should've felt as if she'd landed in a dream.

RESI WOKE before sunrise in front of the fireplace in her chambers; she had tried the bed, but its softness was alien and impossible to get used to. Her eyes adjusted to the room. Momentarily, she forgot where she was, but upon remembering, she stood quickly to her feet. Much of her had hoped she'd awaken on the floor of the lean-to, next to Mags, back in the familiarity and comfort of everything she'd known for so many years.

Quickly, she dressed in the simple day-dress that Lucille had laid out for her, all the while trying to escape the thought of what had occurred last evening. An offer into the house was considered an honor for many Aliquians, but those on the Offenheimer Farmhold believed otherwise. The master, though rumored to be fair and just, was distant and too busy with matters of business to have any sort of interaction with his in-home help. And in his absence, the Mistress Marion was said to be cruel, ever-present, and always watching; the darkened pupil inside the Eye.

Resi went to the small mirror at the edge of the side table. Much as she wanted to continue where she'd left off the night before by crying into the bed pillows, she managed to pull herself together long enough to put her hair into a braid. Even after all the times she'd seen her sweaty face reflected in the pools of water in the puddles of the fields, she didn't recognize her own face. This face, unlike the one she knew, was etched with worry, anger, even madness.

Minutes later, Lucille knocked on the door, and it wasn't long until the two took the back stairs into the kitchen for a small helping of porridge. After much instruction from Lucille on what to do, and what *not* to do in the presence of the Mistress, Resi found herself at Marion's door.

"You may enter," Marion called.

As expected, the following hour proved to be tense. Marion was quiet and, based on the stale stench of her breath, hungover. Resi had heard voices raising from the porch until the late hours, as was usual in the days before the Festival. Resi styled Marion's hair and aided her into her elaborate gown. The gown's fabric was plush, shiny, and fanned out extravagantly behind her. Its hue was the exact color of her eyes, a dark emerald. At Marion's request, the bust was corseted ludicrously tight. Once fully dressed, she appeared to Resi like some sort of oddly proportioned flower, a top-heavy sort of thing with a stem that might snap under even the slightest of pressure.

Though exhausted from minimal sleep and reeling with nerves, Resi was pleased with the job she did on Marion's hair. She'd pinned it into a full up-do at the back of the head with bouncy curls framing the Mistress's round face. Though Marion hadn't expressed even the smallest bit of gratitude, Resi could tell she was impressed; the Mistress had turned her head to the left and right in admiration of her own reflection in the mirror with a coy smile on her face.

There was little to talk about, considering Resi had yet to even meet Scottis. Marion did, however, ask her about her first night in the mansion, which seemed to Resi a kind, albeit, expected gesture. But she couldn't be sure of the Mistress's intentions; if she was hiding the knowledge of Resi's planned escape, she certainly didn't show it.

"Where is Scottis?" Marion finally asked Resi as they came into the upstairs hall.

"I'm not sure, ma'am. I was awaiting instruction about when I would meet with him."

Marion rolled her eyes, then she stomped off. "It's like I have to do everything around here."

Suddenly alone, Resi paced in the quiet hallway. She'd seen Scottis only a handful of times as a young child. He used to run about the fields as a very young boy, but now spent the majority of his time indoors.

As the clock chimed behind her, Resi suddenly felt the beginnings of panic. She knew nothing about tutoring. She tried to settle her breathing by pacing to the nearest window at the front of the home and looking out on the circular drive. It was washed with bright light, as it was most every morning. The only noticeable difference between that day and every other was the absence of her people. Everyone was sleeping in, merrily dreaming of their pints of ale and the feast that awaited them that afternoon.

A weird lump settled in Resi's throat. What she wouldn't give now just to be able to attend. Her mind went to Mags and momentarily, she calmed. At least Mags would be able to enjoy it. The thought alone was enough to warm her.

Still feeling helpless, she turned away from the window, but then noticed a labyrinth of lines and words blurring together on the adjoining wall: a map of old Caplia, now called the Sept-Regions, spanning three feet across the damask wallpaper, encased in glass. The paper of the map was old, its edges worn and curled. Resi had never seen something so intricate, and yet, so delicate. A map of this nature would've taken a cartographer months to plan and create.

Her monster poked at her stomach warmly as she felt an unexpected and feverish urge to bring color to its negative spaces. What might it look like then?

"It's something, isn't it?"

With a fright, Resi jumped. She turned to find Theodore Offenheimer, owner of the Farmhold, looking at the map alongside her. He was dressed in a crisp, white suit the same color as his well-trimmed beard. There was a mysterious calm about him, as if the world moved at full speed around him and he was careless to adjust his own pace to match it. As his mouth curved into a contented smile, Resi noticed how the soft lines around his light blue eyes crinkled pleasantly at his amusement.

"My apologies, sir," Resi said with a curtsy. "I'm awaiting the introduction of your son. Silly of me to get distracted."

"Oh, it's quite alright, Miss...?" he asked.

"Miss Flood, sir. Taresia Flood."

His smile widened as he turned to her, and Resi found herself thrown by its sincere warmth. "I've had this map for many years," Theo stated proudly, his hands pinned behind his back. "Given to me by an old friend. They don't make maps like this anymore—not for nearly three hundred years. Worth quite a lot back then, I imagine." He turned to her, then winked. "Worth even more now."

"A souvenir from the past," Resi heard herself say, but then regretted it. Lucille had warned her about speaking out of turn. But Theo didn't seem to mind. He nodded, his gaze still on the map.

"Precisely," he nodded, then chuckled. "The Misses, however, hates the sight of it. Thinks it doesn't match the modern decor of the home," he said with a shrug as he looked to the crystal chandelier hanging over the main stairs. "Even so, I can't find the courage to dispose of it. Some things are worth more than money can buy."

Resi eased. For years, she'd only ever heard stories of Theodore's quiet presence, his lack of backbone in matters dealing with his wife. No one—at least, no Aliquian—had ever spoken of his humor, his wit, his kindness.

"You seem nervous," he spoke lightly. "May I offer some advice?"

Eagerly, she nodded.

"At first, Scottis may display shy behavior," he started. "But he is bright. I can assure you that he will keep you on your toes. Towards the end of Shina's time with him, she was struggling to keep up with him in his studies."

The mention of Shina made Resi's heart jump. She wondered what she would be doing on the day of the Festival, if it were possible to find reasons to celebrate after such cruelty.

"He's quite gifted when it comes to numbers," Theo continued. "And he's very perceptive. But I must warn you," he said with a knowing laugh, "he puts things bluntly, but he doesn't mean to offend. In recent years, I've learned to become quite fond of his odd sense of humor."

Resi curtsied once again. "Thank you," she murmured.

"The gratitude is all mine," he said with a nod. "I have a feeling you'll settle into your new duties well."

A flurry of noise erupted from down the hall as Marion abruptly appeared with Scottis by her side. The boy was taller than Resi remembered, lanky and lean, but his fair coloring was exactly the same as when he was a child. He looked immensely like Theo, with a sweet face and a messy mop of nearly white hair.

"What are you two doing?!" Marion snarled when she saw Theo standing beside Resi.

"I was just giving some parting words of wisdom to Scottis's new tutor," Theo said assuredly. "We only just met, but I gather they will do just fine together."

Resi earnestly looked to Scottis, but his eyes remained on the hardwood floor.

"Scottis!" Marion barked. "For goodness' sake! Bend down and tie your shoes! A proper man can't be seen undone like that!"

Scottis didn't respond. He stood beside his mother, motionless. The air went still as the Mistress's hand raised to slap him clean across the face. Without hesitation, and without much thought, Resi quickly moved to fill the gap between them.

"Here!" she offered, gathering Scottis's laces in her fingers. "Allow me."

She began to tie his shoes, all the while feeling the heat of Marion's breath coming down on her like a fiery warning. She looked up, and Scottis's eyes met hers briefly. They were almond-shaped, innocent as a baby's, but wise with the years of having to live under the same roof with Marion as his mother.

"Delightful," the Mistress smiled smugly. "We will see you both in the morning. And Taresia—" she snapped as she and Theo headed to take the stairs to the first floor. "You're to have Scottis to bed by sundown, and no later. I expect to not be bothered until tomorrow morning." She looked at Theo with a smile. "Understood?"

Resi nodded.

"Might I also remind you, 'Lick," Marion continued as she delicately placed her fingers into her lace gloves. "Today is a special day, but not one to be taken advantage of. The house is guarded from the outside by overseers. But, of course," she paused, smiling sinisterly. "You probably already knew that."

Resi's heart quickened. It was the first indication that Marion had learned of her plan from Gilda, and though the realization was startling, it wasn't altogether surprising. But why not scold her for planning her escape? Punish her?

Resi snapped out of her thoughts only to find that Marion and Theo were already off and headed down the stairs. Sinisterly, Marion snickered something callous under her breath at Theo before Resi turned to find Scottis sitting on the floor. Despite the growing ache to rush out the front door, despite every impulse she had to find Gilda and demand answers, she couldn't help but pause and smile as she watched Scottis defiantly untie his shoelaces.

CHAPTER 4

THE PORTRAIT

Scottis and Resi sat in the sunlight of the upstairs hall for some time, watching her people through the front windows depart from the fields and down the long drive to head to town. Both were silent. Resi was still reeling in the wake of Marion's warning, but Scottis, it appeared, was transfixed by the floor, his eyes never leaving his untied shoes.

"Your father tells me you're smart," Resi finally spoke. "Maybe you can show me what you're working on?"

Scottis didn't even so much as blink in response.

Eventually, Resi blew the air from her lungs through her lips. Her hands found her hips. This was not how she wanted to spend a day, especially *this* day. "Look...you know as well as I do that we need to make this work. Either you show me to your room, or I'll have to tell your mother that we stayed here in the hall like two idiots with nothing to do all day."

"Mother wouldn't like that," he finally spoke. His voice was high, boyish.

"No," she said matter-of-factly, recalling the nasty smile on Marion's face as she turned for the stairs. "I don't think she would."

Scottis flicked at his shoelaces again, then he suddenly stood and turned back from where'd come from with Marion only a few minutes prior. "Follow me."

Resi did, noticing as they went the peculiar way in which he trudged down the darkened hall. His posture was stiff, too erect for someone so young. Quickly, he lead her to the last room on the right and opened the door to reveal a bright, youthful study. At the sight of the room's adornments, Resi's jaw dropped.

"Did...did *you* make these?" she asked.

The four walls were covered in darkly stained wooden shelving, and on each shelf rested dozens of paper animals and shapes in every color imaginable. Her hand reached for the one on the nearest shelf, a blue paper elephant.

"No!" Scottis yelled.

Gradually, Resi lowered her outstretched hand. "Alright," she said calmly. "*No touching.*"

She watched Scottis pace swiftly to a table at the center of the room. Resting atop it was a clean stack of paper. His hands found a chair, and in silence, he sat. He reached for a green sheet and began folding it.

"What are you making?" she asked him as she hesitantly approached him. As expected, he didn't answer. He folded with intensity, his eyes never leaving his hands. She settled on watching, realizing that the best way to get Scottis's attention wasn't by showing interest. His fingers moved feverishly, folding the paper to precision. When he'd concluded his project, he laid the shape in front of her. It was the same as the one she'd tried to pick up earlier; an elephant.

"You can keep this one," he said quickly, flatly.

Resi smiled slowly as he handed her the gift. "That's very nice of you."

He didn't look at her or even acknowledge her appreciation. "Folding is easy for me," he said simply, his gaze forward and distant.

"So I see."

His eyes shifted vacantly to the wall in front of him. "Shina taught me."

Resi took a deep breath. She wondered if hearing Shina's name would ever get easier—if she'd ever block out the memory of her freshly marked arm, of her screams rising over the whistling wind.

"Seems I have some big shoes to fill," she said quickly to change the subject. She flipped the elephant in her hands.

"Seems so."

Scottis went quiet again as he stood and crossed to the other side of the room. He rustled around in a drawer. Finally, he returned to the table with a quill, some ink, and a lined piece of paper. He looked quickly to Resi, then sat back down.

"Mother wouldn't let me say goodbye. She said what Shina did was unforgivable."

Resi took a breath. "I'm sorry to hear about that."

"Two numbers," Scottis then said to her suddenly.

"Excuse me?"

"Give me two numbers."

"Uh," she thought, feeling put on the spot. "Two and seven."

"Too easy," he said sharply, looking only at the paper in front of him. "Bigger."

"Alright," she said. "How about twenty-nine and—and four hundred thirty-three?"

Scottis stared ahead, his eyes switching back and forth in his head. It was only a few seconds before he wrote something down on the piece of paper. He turned it to face her.

$$12,557$$

For a moment Resi was confused, but after a time, she understood. She looked at him with wide eyes. "Did you just multiply in your head?"

Scottis nodded.

"How?" she said, looking back at the number.

"It's easy for me."

She laughed. "I'm beginning to think a lot of things are easy for you."

Scottis tried to hide his pride, but couldn't. A smile curled the outer edges of his mouth.

"Is this how it works?" she asked. "I just give you numbers and you multiply them? Or, do we need to attend to some sort of scheduled lesson?"

"For the next hour, I read," Scottis said with a sigh, as if nothing could be more boring.

"Do I read with you?"

Offended, he glared at her. "I can read *by myself*, thank you."

Try as she might, Resi couldn't hide the laugh that broke free from her lips. "No, I—I know you can read. I'm just not quite sure what to do with myself in the meantime."

"Do whatever you wish," he answered.

"What did Shina usually do?"

Scottis sighed, clearly perturbed by the length of their conversation. "Fold. Play cards."

Neither sounded appealing to her. She turned about the room, looking at the animals that lined the shelves, then stopped when an idea presented itself to her like the sudden burst of sunlight through the window.

"Could I sketch?" But then, a better idea. "*Paint?*"

Scottis stood from the table again and made his way back to the desk. He pulled open a different drawer and removed a large piece of parchment paper, a painting palette of bright colors, and a paintbrush whose handle bore the remnants of previous painting endeavors. He paced to where she stood and passed on the items. He then went to a table that held a pitcher of water and poured some into a glass. He promptly brought it to Resi. "You dip the brush in the water. That spreads the paint."

"Really?" she asked. "I'm allowed to do this?"

"No," Scottis said with a flat face. "I'm kidding."

She let out a small laugh. "Look who has a sense of humor."

Scottis gave her a cool look, one learned from his mother, Resi presumed.

"One whole hour?" she asked him, and again, he nodded without a word. She'd only ever had that kind of time to herself during her nightly strolls to plant her markings. But a whole hour just to *paint*? She smiled at Scottis as she watched him make his way back to the table. She followed him and sat across from him.

"Are you any good?" he asked as he flipped open a thick book.

"I'd like to think so," she answered, although, she really had no idea. Her fingers brushed the paper in anticipation.

"Shina wasn't," he said disdainfully.

Resi laughed, then cleared her throat. Another idea came to her. "How about I paint your portrait?" she asked him.

The book slid a few inches in Scottis's hands as he turned to look at her. His expression went hard.

"It's okay if you'd rather I not," she said. She watched him look to his book.

"Fine," he sighed.

"You have to promise to be still."

Scottis kept his gaze on the words of the book. "Because so many people move about when reading..."

Resi took in the space of the paper, overwhelmed with the prospect of using its entirety. But then, Marion's request from the night prior echoed loudly in her mind. She'd been specific in asking Resi not to distract Scottis from his studies, to keep him focused. Painting wasn't the escape she'd initially planned on for the day of the Fourth-Year Festival, but it would certainly be a welcomed distraction.

She waited with her hand and the brush hovering over the blank parchment, suspended in a moment of disbelief. Finally, she dropped her wrist and let the paint gently touch the paper. She felt the heat inside her gut flame, and for a minute or so, she felt unsure of its presence. But soon enough, she easily fell into what came most naturally to her, and time no longer existed in the space of Scottis's study. Her eyes switched from Scottis to the parchment, and the brush moved rhythmically in her hand as color, light, and shape introduced themselves to her paper for the very first time. In the portrait, Scottis balanced the book on the table between his two hands, his face focused, lips pursed into a pout. She made some final adjustments to his eyes, then flinched as Scottis quickly stood from his seat and paced back to the desk.

"What do you think?" Resi mused as she passed the completed portrait to Scottis. Impressed, he took in his own image as if he were finding his reflection in a pond. He stared at it, seeming to pore over every detail of her work. The wonder she saw in his eyes was the first indication that he was still, in fact, a boy of only twelve. Everything else about him spoke of maturity at too young an age, a boredom with life when it was supposed to be at its most fascinating.

"I get to keep it?" he asked.

Resi didn't know how to answer. Marion had warned her not to encourage Scottis's practice of nothing that went against his studies. But as she looked upon Scottis's pleading eyes drooping like two drops of water off of a flower petal, she couldn't imagine denying him the portrait.

"That's only fair," she answered. "You made me something too. But what do you say we keep it a secret? You know, just between you and me."

He looked at her with reassurance. "Mother won't know."

And somehow, only relying on his promise, she believed him. Scottis then stood again from the table with the painting in hand. He crossed to the desk, opened a drawer, and gently placed it inside. He found his desk once more, a knowing smile playing across his face.

After finishing his studying in the late afternoon, Scottis was willing to show Resi his paper animals, but not without her pleading. He gave her permission to touch only one of her choosing. "Mother broke one of the shelves last year," he said solemnly. "My favorites were ruined."

Resi nodded. She understood. She couldn't imagine her one simple piece of parchment in the lean-to being blown away by the wind, or worse, being found by an overseer. She looked on with excitement as he removed her choice from the highest shelf, an intricately folded pink rose. Afraid she might crush it just by looking at it, she held it outstretched in her open palm.

"How long did this take you to make?" she asked.

"Not long. I picked one from the garden and used it as a guide."

Resi looked over the rose with fascination, knowing Marion could not have been more wrong about her own son. Scottis wasn't behind —he definitely didn't have a condition. He was the most impressive person, young or old, that she had ever met.

Later, they ate dinner together in the main dining room, an extravagant space with golden wallpaper and an intricate tapestry that skimmed the floor. Scottis watched in disgust as Resi scarfed down the meal made by the kitchen help. She couldn't name half of the food on her plate, but she was certain it was the best meal she'd had since the last Fourth-Year Festival. It was the next best thing to the feast that awaited Mags in town.

It was nearing sundown when Scottis decided he wanted to sit on the porch before going to bed. Resi obliged. Their walk through the house from the dining room was quiet, as much of their time together had been that day, and for the first time since that morning, Resi was reminded of her foiled escape. The empty fields were a peculiar sight, eerie and lonely.

When they found a set of rocking chairs, she let her eyes wander down the lane towards the Aliquian quarters. She imagined Mags drinking a pint of ale, merrily conversing with those around her about the beautiful day she'd had in town; the rain had miraculously held off. She wondered if the woman might be relieved to not have Resi tagging along for once, which made her ache inside.

"You're quiet," Scottis said, breaking into her thought.

Resi looked at him quickly before bringing her attention back to the dim light of the fields. "I thought you liked silence."

"I do. But *you* don't."

She laughed, and Scottis let out a snicker of his own, hard as he tried not to. It was confined, restrained.

"Believe it or not, I'm more like you than you might think," she paused, noticing Scottis's attention turn to her. "I avoid talking as often as I can."

A glint of disbelief sparkled in Scottis's almond-shaped eyes. His gaze went back to the fields and the two of them sat together, enjoying the quiet of evening as the sun fell beyond the furthest trees on the property.

"Are you disappointed? That you had to spend the day with me instead of going to the Festival?" she asked him after a time.

Scottis shook his head, and she was surprised that he'd finally answered one of her questions. "Are you?" he asked back.

She sighed. It was her turn not to answer.

"You wouldn't have been able to paint," he said softly, his eyes watching the sun fall beyond a cotton-like cloud.

She smiled. He was right. Even though her escape had been ruined, even though she'd been denied the privilege to go to town with her people, perhaps there was something precious hiding in this bad stroke of luck after all.

THE WEEK CAME and went as if it were a sluggish season all its own. News of the Festival had spread rapidly from the Aliquian quarters, and the few house 'Licks, including Resi, that had not been excused for that day were not spared from the others' glee about just how perfect the day had been. The weather had held up the entire afternoon into dusk. The fireworks display went off without a hitch. It seemed the only disappointing news from the day had been when rainfall had settled on the long walk home from town as if it were a grisly omen of another four years without a celebration.

Resi had been confined to the inside of the lodge that week and had adjusted to her new routine as best as she could. She woke with the sun most mornings, and after a quick meal from the kitchen, she reported directly to Marion's suite. She often dressed her in absolute quiet, but on the off-chance that Marion had a question about Scottis and his progress, Resi would answer as concisely and articulately as she could.

Even with all the other guests that had kept her occupied that week, Marion had kept a watchful gaze on Resi. After her sly word of warning on the day of the Festival, it was apparent she had been briefed by Gilda, and her paranoia surrounding Resi's escape was all but evident in the way she lurked around every corner and glared her down in her mirror's reflection as Resi delicately pinned her hair every morning. But Resi had kept her wits about her. She had half a mind to be just as wary of Marion, and often felt her presence before she even drear near. She steered clear of Horris too; he appeared to find his way into the warmth of the lodge every time Theodore Offenheimer was called into town for work. She avoided anywhere that wasn't her chambers when she heard the sound of heavy boots coming down the hall in the evening hours.

The only thing keeping her sane was her time with Scottis; she'd grown increasingly fond of his odd manner, his intelligence, and everything about him that made him especially unique. But the thing she most often looked forward to was painting in the afternoons whenever he settled in to read. As promised, he'd kept her renderings hidden in the same drawer, and Marion was none the wiser.

In the evenings after she put him to sleep, she often found herself seated in the windowsill of her chambers watching the rain trickle down the glass like tears. Her view of the fields was limited, but gave her a direct line of sight to the lean-tos, which were barely visible through the trees and fog. She thought of Mags every night as she fell asleep, and often dreamt at night of running barefoot through the trees, her hair caught in the breeze and a smile spread wide on her face.

She'd awoken from one of those dreams late one night when a loud thud came at her door. Initially, she'd thought she was still lost somewhere between sleep and reality, until Marion's shrill voice rose over the incessant knocking.

"Wake up, Miss Flood."

Quickly, Resi raised from her bed and brought herself to the door. "Ma'am?"

"Open the door, 'Lick!"

The door flung open and there waited the Mistress, her hair pinned atop her head, her nightgown slightly disheveled and off one shoulder.

"Explain to me—" she said cruelly, removing an item from her breast. She unfolded it and handed a crumpled paper to Resi. It was the portrait of Scottis, now ruined. Resi shuddered.

"Don't be so surprised that I found it," Marion said, picking something from underneath a fingernail.

"Ma'am, I—"

"Scottis used to steal cutlery from the kitchen. He doesn't know that I do a thorough sweep of his study every week to ensure he hasn't slipped into old habits."

Resi's heart sped rapidly beneath her nightgown. "I had the time to paint it on the day of the Festival, ma'am. It was a gift."

"A gift?!" Marion remarked with a smile of disbelief. Her hands slapped her thighs. "It's quite a rendering. Especially by 'Lick standards." She snatched the portrait out of Resi's hands. "Tell me. When did you have the opportunity to learn such a craft? Certainly not in the fields."

Resi froze as she listened to the sound of her own heartbeat over Scottis's yelping.

"Answer me, 'Lick!" Marion barked.

"It's the first I've ever painted, ma'am," Resi replied. It was the truth, she reasoned, even if she was hiding the simple fact of the one small piece of parchment in the lean-to that made the rest of the world fall away anytime she held it in her hand. Her stomach churned.

"A natural!" Marion said sarcastically. She slowly folded her arms beneath her exposed décolletage.

"It won't happen again. I did it only as a gesture of kindness."

"Scottis doesn't need kindness! He needs someone to keep him on track! Keep him focused on what his future responsibilities as owner of the farmhold will entail! We don't need you to further instigate distractions. He's slow enough on his own!" Marion seethed the words out in one breath, careful to check the staircase with her eyes in case someone approached.

The entire house was no doubt awakened by Marion's wrath in the middle of the night, and Resi's embarrassment at what whispers she'd hear the following morning in the kitchen pawed at her insecurities. The familiar heat within her sparked. Words bubbled in her throat, and desperate as she was to keep them to herself, she simply couldn't. She'd been holding her tongue all week.

"He's not slow," she heard herself say.

The Mistress glared at her. "What did you just say?"

"*He's not slow*. You'd know that if you spent any time with him."

Marion's chest flushed red before her face followed suit. "You will not speak to me as if I do not know my own son!"

"I will!" Resi said defiantly. "Because you don't! He's brilliant! And artistic, and funny, and beneath the surface, he's kind."

Marion writhed beneath her corset. "Spend one week with my son and you're an expert, are you?" she hissed. "I'd watch your tongue, 'Lick. There are Codians that would slit it right out of your mouth if you spoke so frankly to them."

Resi's fire coursed through her veins with rage. But she'd said too much already. She watched Marion adjust her skirts.

"After your careless behavior, you should be grateful I'm not throwing you back to the fields with the rest of the rats," the Mistress spat. "And if you so much as sketch a single line in this household again, I will see to it that your life on this farm is shrouded in misery. But for now, I have something else better in mind as punishment," she said with a small chortle. "There will be a burning tomorrow. You can tell Scottis that he can count his precious foldings and your paintings as firewood because of your foolish remarks."

Resi's heart sank. "You can't do that to him."

"Ah, ah, ah!" Marion warned her with a wag of her finger. "It's already done."

Without another word, Marion disappeared down the hallway, leaving Resi and her heat to simmer in the darkness of her chambers all night.

CHAPTER 5

THE ADVISOR

Marion delighted in Resi's discomfort the following morning as she prepared her for the day. A twisted smile lingered on her tulip-fresh lips as Resi silently adjusted her hair and did her best not to yank on every tendril she pinned.

As expected, Scottis took the news poorly when Resi sat with him over breakfast that morning. Resi blamed only herself for thinking Marion wasn't shrewd enough to find her paintings, but Scottis wouldn't let her feel sorrowful for even a second.

"She broke the shelf on purpose, you know," he confided in her. "Threw her boot at it and then crushed my foldings with the other boot on her foot."

Resi couldn't find the right words to say to comfort him. But she supposed she didn't have to. Scottis had spent twelve years comforting himself. The only person who was adjusting to Marion's cruelty was her.

A door from the porch squeaked, then closed, and moments later, Horris entered the dining room from the darkened hall. Resi's back straightened in her chair.

"Morning," Horris said to the pair of them before his eyes landed on Scottis. "Son, why don't you take the rest of your breakfast upstairs and give me a moment to speak to Miss Flood."

"Mother doesn't usually let me—"

"Run along," his tone quickened, and Scottis didn't object. He scooped up his plate and cutlery and beelined it for the stairs.

Resi shuddered as the house quieted around them. Marion had run into town early that morning for a dress fitting. The other 'Licks were already busy pinning clothes on the line outside. They were truly and utterly alone.

"Nice day, today, isn't it?" he spoke softly as he found a chair on the other side of the table. He kicked his feet up on the table as if he owned the place. His tone hardened. "Look at me, 'Lick."

Resi didn't respond, and resisted the urge to run. She squeezed her eyes shut before turning to him.

"No need to be afraid of me, Miss. I won't hurt you—at least, not if I don't have to."

Resi waited with her hands on her lap, frozen with fear despite his words.

"Lots of things happen on this property," he drawled, slimily rolling his tongue over his teeth. "It's my job to pay attention to it all, every tiny detail. And, as I'm sure you've noticed," he continued, "lots of things, big and small, happen within this very house."

Resi's breath quickened.

"Now, Miss Flood." His voice deepened as he casually folded his arms behind his head and leaned back in his chair. "I don't imagine you're a stupid girl. Although," he said, his eyebrows gathering, "I guess I wouldn't hold your kind to any type of standard. But I have a feeling you and I could get along quite well within these four walls. That is," he paused, his smile fading, "if you and I come to some sort of understanding. I'm sure you know what I mean."

She cleared her throat, then nodded her head without a word.

"Good," he replied, and his manner eased. "We shouldn't have any problems so long as you keep whatever your eyes see in this house a nice, quiet secret. Are we clear?"

Another nod.

Horris groped at his pants, shook one leg, and nodded in return. "By the way," he chuckled as he pulled a toothpick from his trouser pocket, "quite the painting you did of the boy..." He let the air settle for a brief moment. "Can't say I've ever seen a 'Lick with such a—" he paused, smiling slyly, "—gift."

The front door squeaked open and Horris stood as Resi flinched at the pinching sound. He threw her a quick wink before mockingly curtsying before her. "Pleasure talking to you, Miss Flood."

Marion appeared then in the hallway, her cheeks flushed. She removed her wide-brimmed hat and the fur draped around her shoulders and flopped both items on top of the table. "What in the Sept-Regions could you two be talking about?" she snarled.

"Nothin' you need to worry about," Horris said charmingly as he stood to his feet and strode his way towards her. The Mistress kept her eyes locked on Resi as if she were suspicious of her drawing Horris's attention in an inappropriate way.

"Mistress," Horris nodded to Marion. Resi watched Marion's eyes brighten at Horris's fleeting attention, and then wilt as she watched his lean frame disappear from her line of vision. The back door to the porch squeaked and then slammed before both of them saw Horris skip down the back steps of the lodge.

"Is Scottis awake?" the Mistress asked abruptly.

"He's upstairs, ma'am."

Marion sneered. "I assume you informed him of the discussion we had last night?"

Resi nodded.

"The burning will take place this afternoon, before dinner. You'll gather what's needed for it. *All* of it," Marion reiterated. "Until then, you know of your responsibilities. No need for me to repeat them." She gave the command casually.

There was something distant, something bitter, Resi thought, about Marion's relationship with her son—something so far removed from motherhood. Resi couldn't help but be reminded of her own mother; her sad eyes looking down on Resi as she bent to kiss the top of her forehead before they both gently fell asleep in each other's arms. She'd been a good mother to Resi, hadn't she? That is, until she'd left, anyway.

Suddenly, Marion's attention went towards the windows that overlooked the front drive. "What—what in the Sept-Regions?"

A carriage, black and ornate, was rolling its way up the front drive.

"Who is it, ma'am?"

"*That*, Taresia, is a carriage from the governor's estate," said Marion, with equal parts excitement and dread. She raced down the main hallway to a mirror and attempted to cool her flushed cheeks with the back of her hands. "Oh, it's no use!" she wailed.

Resi stood in the shadows of the back of the house nearest the porch, bemusedly enjoying the mayhem. She watched the Mistress anxiously fiddle with the fabric of her dress as she waited for the new arrival in the foyer. It was entertaining to see Marion this way, Resi noted—frazzled, nervous.

The front door opened and Theodore Offenheimer entered the foyer looking refreshed. With him was a man about the same age— fair, with thinning copper hair. The newcomer sported a yellow and discontented smile as his eyes darted about the foyer. He was dressed in a navy uniform, similar in style to those of the overseers.

"Well, goodness me!" cried Marion, all signs of her nervousness suddenly vanishing. "Luther! To what do we owe the pleasure?"

The newest arrival smiled at her. "Mistress Marion...ever the beauty. All these years have passed and you have remained the same." His voice was shrill, high-pitched, quite the opposite of what Resi had been expecting. As he stepped into the light, Resi noticed the pale and paper-thin skin of his face.

"Hello, there, Miss Flood," Theo addressed her from where she lingered at the back of the home. He tilted his bowler hat politely.

"Good morning, sir," she said with a curtsy, her eyes finding the floor. She'd quite hoped she'd go unnoticed.

"I'm sure Marion's informed you of our visitor," Theo went on after a quick look to Luther. Luther's eyes continued to roam the foyer; he looked displeased.

Resi stalled with a look to Marion, who met her glance with panic.

"She's informed me our visitor is from the Tristeland, yes?" Resi inquired.

"Taresia, this here is Luther Cane, Advisor to the Governor," Theo announced.

The room blurred in Resi's vision. The governor's advisor? "Sir," Resi curtsied to him. All Luther could muster was a silent nod in her direction.

"Whatever brings you here this morning, Luther?" Marion asked. "And might we offer you some breakfast? Lucille has just brought folly tea to our southern porch." Marion's arm swept grandly, albeit awkwardly, to the back of the lodge.

Luther smiled politely at her, then clasped his arms behind his back. "Could be quite pleasant to be seated for breakfast," he started, then popped onto his toes. "But it's no trouble if there hasn't been a third place set."

Marion snapped her head in Resi's direction, then smiled thinly. "'*Lick.*" She said the word with venom in a clear attempt to impress the newcomer. "We demand a third setting. Quickly."

Resi nodded. She'd never been asked to prepare a place setting before, but she didn't dare defy Marion. She curtsied again before leaving them, then headed into the kitchen to find Lucille, who was working over a boiling pot of porridge that puffed steam in thick white clouds over her face.

"We have a visitor," Resi told her.

Lucille didn't look up from her work. "Well, who?"

"It's—" Resi paused. "The Advisor of the Governor."

"Well, I'll be..." Lucille replied, staring into a dark corner of the kitchen.

"We need a third place setting for breakfast," Resi urged anxiously. "Mistress has asked me to prepare it. I have no idea what I'm—"

"Alright, alright, Miss Flood. Let's not panic," Lucille said swiftly. Her experience in the house was abundantly clear as Resi watched her walk gracefully across the kitchen, her hands cleaning themselves on her apron. Lucille found the utensil drawer and pulled out what was needed, then quickly laid out the place setting for Resi to learn.

"They'll be expecting you to wait on them too," Lucille instructed as she went back to the porridge and poured it into three bowls. "Mistress doesn't like more than one house 'Lick presented to guests on their visits, especially to one from the Tristeland." She paused, looking Resi straight in the eyes. "Don't say a word during the meal. Wait on them only if they ask. And don't be hovering over them either. Stay closer to the door if you can."

Terrified, Resi nodded. Lucille kindly placed her hands on Resi's shoulders. "I'll tell James and the others that you've been called upon. We'll stay out of your hair. Don't want to put the Mistress on edge any more than she is. *Although*—" she mused playfully, and Resi laughed.

The next hour passed arduously. Resi waited on the far end of the porch as she listened to the crunch of crumpets and the slurp of folly tea. Much of what Marion, Theo, and Luther discussed was out of earshot, but from what Resi could tell, the conversation was pleasant and of no pressing matter. Theo remarked every so often on the beautiful feast from the week prior. Luther returned his compliments with a nod and a flash of his mossy, yellow smile. What was most audible, however, was Marion's outlandish attempts at laughter; with each word that came from Luther's mouth came a horrid, ear-splitting cackle that even caught the attention of many in the fields.

Resi let her eyes wander over the property from her position on the porch. She felt as if she were watching the other 'Licks through a glass window or from beyond some great, sound-proof shield. If she screamed to catch their attention, she was certain no one would turn in her direction. No one, not even Mags, would be there to help her.

After a time, Marion snapped at Resi again, a command to clear their plates. "Do tell me of the governor's travels, Luther," she continued as Resi approached. "I've heard so little of his work these days."

"I wish there was more news to tell of what brings him out of town so often. Boring affairs, really," Luther confided. "He's been in meetings with all of the Sept-Regions officials for the last few months. Spent some time in Dirig with the Patrian King, but that's a trip he makes once a year. Usual business," he said with another disturbing smile.

Resi began to clear the plates promptly, but lingered momentarily upon their conversation.

"Luther has informed me that he's in need of our product for an upcoming event," Theo happily informed his wife. "Something rather grand, I'm to presume. How much again did he ask for?" he turned back to Luther.

Luther sat back in his chair and raised his eyebrows proudly. "Quadruple our last order. Then, double that."

The three went quiet for a time before Marion leaned forward ever so slightly in her chair with a stunned expression. "To what event do we owe our gratitude?" she smiled as she fanned her face with a delicate hand.

"I'm afraid that's private," said Luther with a knowing smile. "Just as of now."

"Well, of course!" said Marion excitedly. "Discretion is *vital* in preparation for an event, especially for one of such scale. I tell you, with all the guests we had arrive before the Fest—"

"It's an honor, Luther," interrupted Theo. "We're pleased you thought to come to us."

As she cleared the last plate from the tablecloth, Resi tried not to laugh at the scowl on the Mistress' face.

Then, all at once, Luther stood from his seat. "Much as I'd like to stay for the day, there's much to be done. So much clean-up after every Fourth-Year Festival! Must be going. But I can't thank you enough for—" Luther's voice muffled beyond the porch door as he went inside. Marion and Theo scurried after him, Resi noticing Marion's occasional side glances to her husband. The Mistress was riding a high. Such an order would be a cause for celebration, especially after the Fourth-Year Festival, which was the greatest provider of income for the farmhold every fourth year.

"Taresia!" Marion hissed after Theo ducked inside before her. "See to the door!"

"Ma'am?" Resi looked up at her with confusion, her arms filled with dirty dishes and glassware.

Marion's eyes bulged. "*The door,* 'Lick! Open the front door for our guest!"

Unsure of what else to do, Resi placed the mess back on the table before jogging back inside. Once in the foyer, she paused just in time to see Scottis at the top of the steps. His expression startled her, though she recognized its pain. His face was ghostly white.

"Ah! There's our boy!" called Theo from the hall. "Scottis, you remember Mr. Cane? He's the governor's friend!"

Scottis didn't change his position at the top of the steps. His gaze was inaccessible, as if he were looking down on the three of them like some great king.

"Sure have grown, young man!" called Luther up the stairs, his voice shrill and insincere.

"What's that you got there, son?" said Theo, whose face went hard with concern as he took in his child's misery.

Marion quickly entered the foyer from the drawing room, where it appeared she'd quickly escaped to powder her nose. "What's going on?" she asked cautiously. She followed their gaze to see Scottis. Her back went stiff when she saw the small folded portrait in his hand.

"Scottis..." she said with dangerous calm. "Scottis, where did you find that?"

Scottis remained still on the landing. His lips quivered as if they would part to unleash a sickening scream at any moment.

"Marion?" Theo inquired, his hooded eyes swimming in worry. "What's that he's holding?"

Marion's face heated to a dark crimson, and without a word or even so much as a reassuring glance to her husband, she marched up the stairs after Scottis. Her boots cracked like a warning on the wood.

"Marion, what in the Sept-Regions—?" Theo called after her.

But Marion didn't reply. She was on a mission. No sooner had her skirts hit the second floor than she was clamoring to rip the painting from Scottis's hand.

"You. Will. Give. Me. THAT!" she cried as she clawed and

scratched at Scottis. Scottis's arms thrashed violently in protest. Then suddenly, the paper flew out of Scottis's hand and the foyer went still.

Everyone's eyes went to the portrait as it hung over their heads like a thunderous cloud. Slowly, and much to Marion's chagrin, the delicate parchment descended towards the foyer floor. It sank lower and lower, every so often getting caught in the breeze from the fields and altering its direction, as if it had a mind of its own to change. It fluttered gracefully, like a bird, then came to land perfectly on the toe of Luther's boot.

Resi's heart pounded against her ribs. She was certain it would have been heard by everyone in the room if their focus wasn't drawn to the parchment.

Curiously, Luther bent to retrieve the paper. He unfolded it, gazing upon the painting. He then looked to Marion.

"Who..." he paused, then looked back to the painting. He soaked in the picture, then turned to Scottis. "Who did this rendering of the boy?"

Marion's eyes went to Resi. The glare she threw might as well have been a dagger.

"It was her, sir!" Scottis said as he pointed a finger to the shaded corner where Resi had retreated.

Luther's eyes widened as he took in the sight of the shrinking girl in the darkness. Then, he nearly doubled over with the kind of cackle that could be heard clear out to the woods. "My boy!" he finally managed to bellow. "Such a thing is unheard of! Surely this painting was not done by a 'Lick woman!"

Resi's breath held tight in her chest as she turned to Marion. The Mistress's eyes nearly bulged out of her head. Then, an idea came to her. "But, yes!" she burst out dramatically, clutching her hand to her chest, almost pleading. "I too, am surprised by such a discovery. But it is true! Scottis's new tutor is quite the artist, as made evident by that rendering in your hand."

Another few moments of dumbstruck silence fell, but the room's energy changed from that of chaos to confusion. Luther and Theo both looked at Marion as if she were deranged.

"How long, may I ask, did it take you to paint this?" Luther asked Resi directly, but a great lump had already settled in Resi's throat. She couldn't muster a single word to reply.

"An hour," Scottis proudly stated. "It was her first time, too."

"*First* time?" Luther inquired further as his head tilted to inspect the portrait more deeply.

"You must understand," Marion suddenly blurted with a sense of control and command. "Such practices are not permitted on this farmhold. Taresia has assured me that it is the first of her efforts to try her hand at painting, but between you and me, I suspect otherwise. We plan to have her lean-to excavated this afternoon for further information. If my predictions are correct, she could be liable for a very severe punishment."

Resi's heart leapt to her throat. She had no reason or need to contradict the Mistress's statements, and even if she did, she wouldn't have had the courage to do so. Not in front of Theo, and most especially, not in front of Luther.

"Is this true, Resi? Did you paint this?" Theo turned to her, his eyes displaying a surprising show of concern.

Resi's mouth went as dry as sand. Hesitantly, she nodded.

"Well, Miss Flood," Luther said, his tone low. "Creative practices of any kind amongst the 'Lick population are strictly prohibited. Evidence of any sort of pursuit of this kind of artistry would be a severe crime."

Marion's face lightened. She took a step towards Luther, hesitant, but curious. "I'm glad you agree, Advisor."

Luther's stance widened before he crossed his arms before his chest. "Your Mistress is right," he said, acknowledging Marion. He quickly looked down to the rendering, his eyes searching the portrait for any flaw, before looking back up to Resi in fascination. "But today might just be your lucky day. Turns out, the region of Ter may be in need of your help."

Resi thought she'd misheard the Advisor, but it was Marion's outburst that indicated the contrary.

"Ex—excuse me?!" the Mistress stuttered, almost laughing in shock at the Advisor's change of tone.

Luther was still searching the terrified expression on Resi's face as he began to roll the parchment in his hands. He stuffed it into the pocket of his uniform. "I'm afraid it's rather simple, Mistress Marion," he said, his voice wispy. "In preparation for this upcoming event, the Tristeland Estate is in desperate need of a portrait artist."

"A *portrait* artist?" Marion chortled, her hands finding her hips. She was coming undone at the seams.

"Why, yes," Luther said simply.

Theo and Resi watched in fascination as the scene between Luther and Marion unfolded.

"Surely, you're not requesting the use of a 'Lick in this matter!" Marion burst, her weight shifting beneath her to keep her balance.

"On the contrary, ma'am." Luther's simplicity played at Marion's sanity. Her eyelids fluttered in protest.

"An explanation seems fair in this sort of situation," she retorted. "If the 'Lick is needed by the region, then *our* son will be short of a tutor." Marion looked to Theo for any sort of aid, but Theo didn't speak a word. Instead, he looked up to Scottis, who had made his way to the middle landing of the stairs. The boy's face was as ecstatic as Resi had ever seen it.

"Certainly," Luther answered Marion pleasantly, although Resi could see that his patience was beginning to wane. "Sequis has moved up the date of this event by three months. As you can imagine, this is not a matter of rank or stature, but a matter of very," he paused, indicating his efforts had been exhausted, "*very* little time."

"I see," said Marion, whose awkward smile had gone cold and hard. "But there must be someone—*anyone* else that is suitable for such a high honor! And a Codian, at that!"

"Afraid not." Luther shook his head, wiping a new bead of sweat that had appeared on his temple.

"It is Sequis that desires this artist?" Theo finally piped up. "Whatever for?"

Luther sighed, apparently realizing that he'd revealed more information than he'd intended. "The Governor wishes to have a portrait painted of himself," the Advisor said resignedly. "To be revealed at the upcoming Ball."

A crash then rang out from the kitchen, a mishmash of breaking plates and dishes landing on the floor. Theo, Luther, and Resi turned towards the interruption only to find Marion unfazed by the alarm. "There is..." she gulped loudly, "to be a Ball?"

Perturbed and running out of tolerance, Luther pursed his lips. "I've said too much."

"Well, how marvelous!" said Theo in an effort to ease the tension. "We will speak nothing of it, of course. Keep it entirely private."

At that, Marion's eyes flew open wide. Her face ignited with absolute delight, as if none of her earlier qualms had mattered in the least. "We promise to do everything to maintain absolute secrecy!" she assured Luther enthusiastically. "That is, until invitations are to be delivered. I can only imagine the guest list you've acquired for such an event!"

Resi's lip quivered to hide her amusement. If there was one thing for certain, it was that Marion wanted nothing more than to be at the center of every social event. And if Luther was true to his word, the Governor's Ball would be the social event of the decade.

In an effort to gain any sort of ally, Resi turned to Theo, who was already looking at her with heavy eyes. "So," Theo said, his gaze snapping to Luther as he adopted a businesslike tone, "when will the girl be needed?"

Luther huffed, exasperated. "You mean *if* she'll be needed. I'll arrive at the Tristeland by dusk to gauge the Governor's opinion." He turned to Scottis, his voice tone changing slightly. "If you don't mind, son, I'd like to take your portrait to the Governor."

Scottis's eyes widened to the size of saucers before he sternly cleared his throat and adjusted his collar. "I suppose that would be alright."

At the boy's reaction, Luther and Theo smiled, but Marion was too absorbed by the prospect of an invitation to turn from Luther for a second.

Luther cleared his throat. "If Sequis is impressed with the painting, we will send word by nightfall."

A chill rushed up Resi's spine. An invitation—to the Tristeland. It was the most exclusive estate in the region.

Marion let out a jealous whimper. "How *lucky* for her."

"And what of our boy?" Theo asked Luther. "How long will he be without his tutor if Sequis chooses Taresia for the job?"

"If the Governor is pleased with her work, then we will need her for the duration of the month."

At that, Marion's jaw dropped. "But surely that's an absurd amount of time to spend on one painting?!"

"Let's not jump to conclusions," Luther hissed. "Only if Sequis approves of Miss Flood's work can we discuss the details of her time away from her regular duties. Now," he paused, readjusting the neck of his jacket. "Have I made myself clear?"

Marion slowly slid her arms behind her back, and her eyes darted about the foyer before landing on her own feet. Her voice went small. "Crystal."

"Excellent," Luther piped, again bobbing onto the balls of his feet. "Must be off."

He turned for the door, and Resi scurried to open it for him. "It's been a pleasure, Miss Flood," Luther said to her with an air of formality. His eyes proudly glanced back down to the portrait in his hand. "Mighty fine work, too."

The door came to close behind him, and when Resi turned back to the foyer, she was met with a cruel face from the Mistress.

"Neither of you," she glowered at Resi and Theo. "Not one word." In a huff, she whirled towards the stairs, as her eyes sought out Scottis on the landing.

"Mother?" the boy said as the Mistress began her ascent after him. Then, realizing she was on her way to punish him, Scottis scampered up the remaining stairs, his face breaking into a bright and proud smile.

CHAPTER 6

THE LETTERS

The house was quiet for the remainder of the afternoon. Many of the house 'Licks kept to themselves in the kitchen, whispering in a tight huddle about the morning's events as Scottis and Resi quietly giggled in his study. Like two spies, they shushed each other as they rested their ears on the wall. Marion and Theo were having heavy words in their adjoining suite.

"You can't be serious, Marion!" Theo roared. "Threatening our son in front of a government official? Burning his creations? It's ludicrous! Have you lost your mind?!"

"Oh, don't you talk to me about *losing my mind!*" Marion hissed. "I might as well have been standing next to a vegetable for the duration of the discussion! Were you even listening to a word Luther said?!"

It became abundantly clear that there would absolutely *not* be a burning, at least according to Theo. His firm decision had eased Resi's heart so much that she'd grabbed Scottis and lifted him up in the air. She'd half expected the boy to scream and punch in protest, but much to her surprise, he'd obliged her with a smile.

After a rather unproductive day as a tutor, Resi ushered Scottis downstairs for dinner. As they took their chairs, a strange mix of emotions warred within her. There she was, moments away from enjoying a full meal in the comfort of the Offenheimer mansion, when only days ago she was on the stoop of the lean-to, chewing out Mags over a lukewarm bowl of broth. What was even more strange was the prospect that she might be delivered to the Governor's estate in the coming days. How was it possible that she could go from absolute obscurity to a possible meeting with the region's leader in just a matter of a few days? Alongside her shock and guilty pleasure, these questions just made her miss Mags more than anything. Desperately, she needed someone, anyone to talk to.

For a brief moment she looked to Scottis, wondering if there was any infinite wisdom locked away in that brilliant mind of his. Scottis, however, seemed oblivious to Resi's nerves. He spoke a mile a minute as he chewed his dinner, recounting the way in which Luther had addressed him personally. He was delighted that at this very moment, the Governor of Ter might be holding the same portrait that he'd held in his hands only hours prior. Resi cleared her throat and readjusted herself in her chair, trying to settle herself by stuffing her face with as much roasted vegetables as she could manage.

After she'd seen Scottis to his chambers, Resi finally went to her room, grateful for the time alone. Exhausted, she leaned her back against the door, allowing every emotion within her to come rushing to the surface. She clutched her chest, then heaved forward and covered her mouth so her sobs wouldn't be heard.

She let her mind run rampant. The mansion. Scottis. Marion. Being so far removed from Mags and the others. And now, recruited as a potential portrait artist for the Governor? It was all too much.

Numbly, she went to the window and pulled the ribbon from her hair. She combed through the tangles with her hands as she viewed the fields. As far as she knew, her markers still remained intact in the darkness of the woods, waiting for a girl that would never come to retrieve them.

Soon, slow footsteps came down the hall. Resi froze when they stopped before her chambers. She waited for a knock, but instead was surprised by a small envelope slipping underneath the door. Without hesitation, she rushed to it. It wasn't addressed.

Fiercely, she opened it, smiling when she saw for the first time Mags's own scribbled handwriting.

Dearest,

Can't recall the last time I sat down to write a letter. All the same, I only know how easy it will be for you to make fun of me if you find any mistakes.

James was kind to give me the supplies necessary to write to you, for which I could not be more grateful. I've been worried sick. The day you were taken in was one that I felt, in part, responsible for. I never should've told you to go to that wretched lodge. It should be me cooped up inside that prison, not you.

Can't risk trying to meet, although it's all my heart wishes for. I'll settle for knowing you received this letter, but please, I beg you, do not respond. It's not worth the risk. And at my age, I've stopped worrying about myself. Either way, I've got enough worry in my little finger for you, which is more than I care to have at all.

There's much talk going around, Resi. Folks are saying you were snatched up by the Mistress before you'd do something stupid. I know it can't be true. At least, I pray that it isn't.

Be good. Be respectful. Try to think of me every now and again. Maybe, if we're lucky, I'll spot you on the porch with a smile on your face. Only then will I rest easy at night.

Love, M
PS Burn after reading.

Resi couldn't help but gasp as she read Mags's final words. She clutched the letter tightly to her chest in hopes that the gesture would somehow reach Mags as she lay in the lean-to. She was so close to her, only a short walk to the south. And yet, she was worlds away.

She returned to the letter to reread a worrisome sentence.

...you were snatched up by the Mistress before you'd do something stupid.

News must've spread about Resi's plan to escape. The realization made Resi angry enough to crumple the note in her hand. Then, immediately regretting it, she unfurled the wrinkled parchment and gently placed it again at her heart. Delirious, she wandered back towards the window, hoping to get a small glimpse of the 'Lick quarters through the mist.

She fought her memories, but couldn't win. She smiled as she remembered the summer before her parents' disappearance. It had been a happy and remarkably beautiful season, one filled with laughter over dinner and fireflies dancing about the fields as Aliquians turned in for the evening. Rebecca, Resi's mother, had allowed Resi to stay up into the late hours of the night on many occasions. Cozily, they'd snuggled together on the floor of their lean-to, whispering secrets and stories to each other until Resi's eyes became heavy. Sometimes Rebecca would take a holed quilt and drape it over their heads, then they'd play pretend—once they decided they were at sea on a rolling ship, and another time, they'd imagined visiting the northern regions to tromp through the many feet of snow.

"There's a city, Resi," Rebecca had told her then, "one so beautiful that only few have ventured to see it. The way is dangerous and very risky. But once the city's gates are opened to whoever dares to find it, that person is home."

Though she'd been small, Resi often recalled how young her mother had looked every time she'd told the story of the Hidden City, a realm where fugitive 'Licks were rumored to flee. Her face would light up, and her voice would slow and grow warm. Resi enjoyed remembering her mother that way—blissful and utterly absent of worry.

It had been Resi's father, Tristan, who'd finally put an end to these stories when he'd returned to their lean-to one evening in a rampage. The memory of it was violent. Resi only recalled the furious look on Tristan's face, how he'd struck Rebecca on the cheek, and how Rebecca had cried herself to sleep that night as she held onto Resi tightly. It wasn't even a month later that Resi had awoken in the early hours of the morning to find their lean-to empty, her parents gone. Her twelfth birthday had come the following week.

It was true, Resi supposed, that every Aliquian parent told stories to their children in the months leading up to the Festival. But now that Resi was approaching twenty, she often wondered if Rebecca had believed the myths of the Hidden City to be true—and worse, if they were in part responsible for her slow progression into madness before leaving the farmhold behind.

The legend of the Hidden City was now somewhat of a laugh in the fields. Some were even convinced that the realm was nothing more than a hole in the mountains where fugitive 'Licks hid from their adversaries to wait out their inevitable death. Even if such a place were to exist, Resi couldn't understand what person in their right mind would leave the comfort of Ter to retreat to the mountains, where all kinds of formidable creatures loomed in the hillside shadows of Sterch.

Thinking of the many mysteries of Sterch brought Resi's thoughts in a roundabout way to the Governor; Sequis was what some referred to as an Araf, or in other regions, a giant. But he wasn't like the usual giants found in the region of Sterch—broad, savage beings that could stand up to forty feet tall, and often boasted only a small level of intelligence.

Stories held that as a boy, Sequis was considered as normal as any. It wasn't until he'd hit adolescence that his body began to shoot in all different directions and he'd sprouted taller and more muscular than any other man rumored to have roamed the Sept-Regions. It had appeared that Sequis was the first and only of his kind: not quite man, not quite giant.

During his teenage years, he'd developed a passion for combat, earning himself a reputation as a notorious fighter in the region of Malig. It was also around that time that his name began to resound throughout the regions, most significantly amongst the women. His physical appearance was striking to behold. Sought-after socialites and wealthy daughters of kings from overseas were rumored to fall at his feet with just a single glance from him.

Eventually, Sequis was sought out by the great Patrian King, King Romilius, who still resided over the region of Dirig. The Patrians were the original settlers of the Sept-Regions, and as such wielded great power in the Western regions. Much to the Patrian peoples' dismay, Romilius had recruited Sequis as head of his army.

Although Sequis had been born in a completely different region, many suspected that King Romilius' attempt at friendship was to ensure that Sequis would find no need in the future to overthrow him. After all, Sequis had been born of a Codian woman, and the history of Codian and Patrian alliances and simultaneous betrayals extended back hundreds of years. Sequis had fearlessly served the Patrian army as leading Commander, fighting battles overseas to protect the thriving coastal metropolis of Turbus, Dirig's capital city.

The years had passed, giving way to a new era. Much of the Codian population had migrated to Ter and began seeking a new leader, one resilient enough to overthrow the Governor who'd been in long-standing position for many years. This Governor, a Codian man named Humphries, had been in favor of the abolishment of Aliquian servitude from within the region of Ter. Humphries had pitched what would be his final campaign as one that would see the peoples of the Sept-Regions—Codian, Patrian, and Aliquian—united as one.

Naturally, there were many in favor of seeing this Governor set on fire, particularly amongst the Codian population. So, after much hullabaloo and gossip, Sequis had left his rank as Commander of the Patrian army behind and raised an army of his own. He then eventually raided Ter, supported by an army of Codian men willing to give their lives to see that the bondage of the Aliquian people would remain intact. Those men would one day become the illustrious Eastern Guard, the most formidable militia in the Sept-Regions.

Resi had been but a girl when this all took place, only remembering the cry of her people on the day the news of Sequis's and the militia's attack had spread through the fields. Rumors swirled that Sequis's unyielding strength and violence had ripped Humphries' head right off of his body as he refused to leave his throne. Many Aliquians had rejoiced earlier that summer, hoping that freedom was on the horizon, but no such thing was to be.

It had been just four years ago that Resi had seen Sequis for the very first time, at the last Fourth-Year Festival. Despite his reputation as a sword-thrusting, power-hungry monster, the Aliquian crowd had been all but busting at the seams to catch a glimpse of him as he exited the giant tent that had sheltered himself and his officials.

As the Governor had taken to his podium, grown Aliquian women had swooned. Men had stood on tip-toe over the crowd to get as best a look as they could at Sequis's face.

"I'll tell you this much," Mags had whispered to Resi. "He may be an Araf, and a murderer too...but even a blind woman wouldn't turn away that bone structure."

Resi had sneered at Mags, even loathed her for such a statement as she'd tried to get a better view of Sequis. He was large; very large, Resi recalled. He'd sported a three-piece suit and had worn it like a true politician. Still, the attire had looked bizarrely unfit on his massive stature. In Resi's mind, she'd always pictured him in full battle dress, his face dirtied by the blood of his enemies, his mouth wide in a war cry as he stampeded across fields in search of anyone who might dare to stand against him.

Resi couldn't remember Sequis's speech that day. She only recalled that the rain had cleared along the bluffs just in time for the Festival to start and that all had been good and right in the world in the moments after the applause died and he'd sauntered his way back to his tent.

Only, it wasn't good and right. Not for Resi. She was still minus a mother and father. Her people were still under Codian rule. And they would be forever, so long as Sequis was in power.

Resi came back to herself as loud voices called out to one another, interrupting the silence of the night. She tried to peer out the open window to view the front drive but saw nothing in the darkness. Overseers yelled out for an incoming arrival, a messenger of sorts, one on horseback from the Tristeland Estate.

Quickly, Resi threw herself across the dark room and landed on the bed. Noticing Mags's note was still in hand, she dove to stuff it beneath the mattress. She managed to throw the covers over herself, hoping to hide from whatever awaited.

Minutes passed before a knock came to her door. Fearful, Resi peeked above the covers to see Lucille waiting in the blackened space of the open doorway. A lantern ignited her face, which was so pale Resi nearly didn't recognize her.

"Mr. Offenheimer wishes a word with you in his office," Lucille whispered.

Rigidly, Resi rose from the bed. She grabbed her cloak to cover her nightgown, then brushed by Lucille without a word. Taking a breath, Resi threw her long hair defiantly over her shoulder and marched down the steps.

For a while, she paced in the hallway, noticing that Theo's door was open a crack. Light poured into the hallway in a thin line near her feet.

"Come in, Miss Flood," Theo finally called to her.

Resi entered the office, noticing at first the aroma of folly. The space was dimly lit by only the glow of a large, thin candle. The office walls were entirely covered in rich, wooden shelving—similar to Scottis's room, just more grown up. Resi had never seen so many books together in one place. It wasn't until she faced towards the desk at the center of the room that she noticed Theo tucked away in a tufted chair in a corner of the room, his face hidden in shadow.

"Take a seat," he ordered.

Resi found the chair in front of the desk and sat, discreetly wiping the sweat from her hands on the hem of her cloak.

"I'm sure you know why you're here," Theo said, as Resi suddenly noticed that his hands were clasped tensely before his face.

"The Governor already sent word?" she asked, trying to hide the shaking in the base of her throat.

"Just now." He stood abruptly from his chair, crossing into the light. He sat down rigidly at the desk, his eyes fixed on a small package lying on the surface before him.

"Oh?" Resi piped, then cleared her throat as she took in the package's wrapping. Brown paper covered a dimpled cylindrical shape. A note was attached with a gathering of dried flowers, and the package was laced at the middle with a black ribbon.

"I was strictly informed not to open it," Theo murmured, finally managing to look up through his white eyelashes. His eyes were bloodshot, strained. "It is addressed to you." He picked up the package and passed it over the desk.

Tentatively, Resi took it in her hands, cradling it carefully. She had never received a wrapped gift. She released the note from the ribbon, noticing that, unlike Mags's letter, the envelope had her name written on it in large, scrolling letters. How bizarre that in the span of one night she'd received not only one letter, but two, when in her whole life up till now she'd never received any.

Unsure if she should read the note aloud, she opened the envelope and began to skim the letter. The penmanship was large, commanding, and as beautiful as if it had been crafted by a calligrapher.

To Whom It May Concern:

I was rather impressed by the painting of the boy and wish to seek an audience with you at the Tristeland Estate. Please accept this gift as a sign of my appreciation for your talent. I admire your work tremendously. A carriage will be sent tomorrow morning. The choice to take it is yours.

Sincerely,
Sequis, Governor of Ter

Resi sat in her chair, stunned.

"Well?" Theo asked, his torso leaning in towards her. Speechless, she passed the letter to him, but he pushed it back to her. "Please. You read."

Resi murmured the contents of Sequis's letter aloud. Once finished, she gently folded it, then placed it down on the desk beside the package, clasping her shaking hands together tightly in her lap.

Sensing her fear, Theo took the liberty of opening the package himself. Slowly, as if he were cutting into a living organism, he unwrapped the ribbon and flowers from the paper, then removed the covering. Once opened, it proved to be a brush organizer with many small pockets, containing an entire paintbrush set.

Resi couldn't help herself. She reached out in fascination, grabbing the smallest brush of the set and removing it from its pocket. The bristles were made of fine, white hair, and the handle, long and thin, was painted the deepest black. At its base was the gold Governor's crest, the same as the one on the door of Luther's carriage from the Tristeland.

"You must be delirious with excitement," Theo said weakly.

"More like delirious with fear, you mean?"

A chuckle came from beneath Theo's thick, white mustache. "To be honest," he replied, "I'd be lying if I said even I wasn't nervous."

"*You?* Whatever for?"

"Many things, really. The upcoming shipment of folly root for the Ball is merely one small task on a long 'to-do' list. There's the matter of Scottis's well-being, and of clean-up after the Festival. Least of the items is my wife's sanity amongst all this." He smiled uncomfortably. "I'm an old man with many responsibilities, and with that comes the anxiety of overseeing it all. But I must admit, in regards to you, I find this whole ordeal rather strange."

Resi went still in her seat.

"You see," Theo continued. "A leader such as Sequis would normally find every reason *not* to hire an Aliquian artist, and yet he finds your work very appealing—so much so, he's willing to hire you over a Codian. Very strange."

Equally as confused, Resi shrugged her shoulders. "Could be he's particular. At least, that's what Luther conveyed."

"Oh, yes. Very. Either way, it's quite the honor to you that he would ask you to paint his portrait. However, it's important that a young girl like yourself be cautious of such a..." his eye twitched, "*man*, especially one in great power."

Resi waited, feeling her pulse begin to climb. She watched Theo readjust himself in his seat.

"I never had—" Theo paused, "*If* I'd ever had a daughter, maybe it would be easier to explain. I'm not quite sure how to convey the nature of my concern."

"Sir. It's quite alright," Resi said as she stood from her chair. She wanted to save Theo the embarrassment, although, she didn't have the slightest idea about what he was going to say.

"Sit down!" Theo finally exclaimed, his voice bellowing into the hall.

Startled, Resi dropped back into her chair. It was the first time she'd ever heard Theo raise his voice, and the feeling of being on the other side of his temper sent her head swimming.

Surprised by his own reaction, Theo put a hand to his temple. His tone was remorseful, weighted. "You'll excuse me. I didn't mean to frighten you."

Resi cleared her throat. "It's me who should be apologizing, sir. I cut you off."

Theo looked at her, his eyes heavy. "You must heed this advice upon entering the Tristeland. Do you understand?"

Urgently, Resi nodded.

"The Governor is widely known to favor the company of Aliquian women. There isn't a man, woman, or child from here to Dirig that would argue otherwise. Which is why I feel somewhat bothered about you going to the Estate on your own."

Bewildered, Resi let her eyes fall from Theo's face.

"You see, Sequis prides himself on his reputation, especially when it comes to wooing and—" unsure, Theo chose his words carefully, "*seducing* Aliquian women."

Resi's eyelids fluttered rapidly. She looked down to her lap, noticing the brushes laying in a disorganized collection. "I don't believe a man such as Sequis would find anything even remotely appealing about me.'"

"Oh, quite the contrary, Miss Flood," Theo replied. "I think you should have every reason to be wary. What I'm trying to say is that Sequis's decision to make advances has nothing to do with whether he finds you fetching. For some men, it's nothing more than a game of power."

Shocked, and almost humored, Resi looked up at Theo with her eyebrows raised. "I can safely say that no amount of wining and dining would ever convince me to go against my virtue."

At her reply, Theo snickered mildly. "I've heard stronger women say the same thing and fail." He then gave her a limp smile, and swept his hand towards the door for her to leave. Resi obeyed, wishing that Theo had waited to deliver her the paintbrushes until the following morning. There was little chance she'd sleep after all this fuss. But it didn't matter; sleep had been hard for her to come by for many weeks now.

"Miss Flood?" Theo called after her.

She paused in the doorway, sensing the presence of the house 'Licks eavesdropping from the hallway. She turned back to see the many books about the shelves and the flickering flame of the lantern lighting Theo's tired face.

"The Governor is as lucky as any to call upon you as his artist."

All Resi could think to do was nod. A thank you felt out of place, too intimate. She turned towards the hall.

"Get to bed! The lot of you!" Theo called out to those gathered in the hall. Startled, the group clumsily bumped into each other on the stairwell before making their way back to their own quarters.

Finally, Resi made it back to her room, falling into a messy heap on her bed and clutching the paintbrushes against her chest. She could barely comprehend receiving a gift from someone like Sequis, a leader who had kept her people in bondage, withheld her own education, and bedded Aliquian women who didn't have the will or power to say no.

Suddenly, Resi's stomach went white hot. Violently, she flung the brushes across the room. They landed in the corner, making somewhat of a racket as they bumped against one another in their linen carrier. Numbly, she huffed in the dark for a few minutes before she went to retrieve them. One by one, she extracted them from their pouches, reveling in their beauty as she wished away the angry tears that had begun to fall down her cheeks.

CHAPTER 7

THE TRISTELAND

The following morning, the crunch of carriage wheels could be heard approaching the small town of Esur from the north. A decorated white horse led it forward, its neighs causing a group of young children playing with sticks and a ball along the street to jump and scatter in all directions. After blocks of being admired by the townsfolk, it crossed paths with another modest carriage on its way out of town. Two wide-eyed women with ample cleavage craned their necks out of the second carriage's windows, ogling the first carriage and pointing with excitement at the governor's crest on the right door—a simple, golden circle.

A few more blocks of cobblestone led the elegant carriage to a dirt road that continued out of town. It was only another small descent down a steep hill overlooking miles of green fields and forest before it wheeled onto Offenheimer Lane. Every Aliquian in the front field paused to glance at the elongated shadow as the carriage rounded the front loop and came to an abrupt halt. From their vantage point, they could just see a pair of booted feet present themselves out of the side door before they dropped firmly to the ground.

Anxiously, Resi waited on the back porch of the Eye. She was dressed in one of Marion's hand-me-down gowns, a sapphire-colored nightmare of a dress with velvet and lace anywhere it could be added.

Theo waited calmly beside her, his gentle hands resting at the top of his cane. Every so often, he glanced at her. It was his own subtle way of showing he cared. Though she sensed his worry, Resi was just doing her best to avoid the glares from the other Aliquians in the meadows by looking down at her knuckles, which were clenched tightly around the brush set that Governor Sequis had gifted to her.

Much to Resi's relief, the Mistress had not left her suite since the news of Resi's invitation to the Tristeland. She'd feigned an early autumn cold, but everyone, 'Lick and free, knew that Marion Offenheimer had come down with something else entirely—a bout of green envy.

When a light knock finally came at the front door, Resi flinched in her chair.

"Quite a jumpy girl, you are," Theo remarked as he stood and aided her to her feet.

"The nerves...and this *thing.*" She prodded at the corset at her waist. "It certainly doesn't make breathing any easier."

Theo chuckled softly. "I'll never begin to understand why women subject themselves to such discomfort," he said with a shake of his head. Tenderly, he placed Resi's hand on his arm and guided her towards the front of the house. "Just remember," he said calmingly, "it is the highest honor to be invited to the Tristeland. It's not every year that even *I'm* called upon by Governor Sequis." He halted to fix her bonnet, which had slid a few inches forward to shield her eyes. "Don't forget to enjoy it." He gave her a wink.

Immediately, Resi felt some of her panic settle. "Thank you, sir."

"Come now," he said as he led her further down the hall. "It's time."

After an unsteady breath, Resi nodded to him before he opened the door with a swell of pride evident in his eyes.

Waiting beyond it in the early morning sun was none other than Luther. He flashed them a wide, unholy smile. "Good morning!" he piped, with a light bob onto his toes.

Resi gulped. She'd hoped for a solo trip to the Tristeland, one where she might gather her nerves before meeting with Sequis. She held her breath as she watched the two men exchange pleasantries, something about the length of the drive, before Luther's gaze came back to her. His hand, a long and thin collection of bones, extended to hers. Resi was thankful she'd chosen to wear gloves as he bent to kiss her hand. The thought of Luther's dry lips against her bare skin made her momentarily queasy.

"My, my, Theo," Luther spoke softly. "Who could guess that the same 'Lick I met two days ago was standing before me now? Do tell whoever is responsible for this transformation that Sequis will be most pleased to look upon such beauty after months of travel."

Theo cleared his throat, a clear signal for Resi to respond to Luther's strange albeit back-handed compliment. Resi felt her grip tighten on Theo's arm. "Good morning, Advisor," she said with a curtsy.

Surprised, Luther turned to Theo in disbelief. "An articulate 'Lick, too! Where in the Sept-Regions did you find such a thing?"

Uncomfortable, Theo cleared his throat again. "What brings you to our door this morning, Luther?" he asked. "I was told to expect a carriage, but certainly not you!"

Luther bobbed on his feet once again, and briefly, Resi wondered if it was some sort of nervous tic. It was a silly notion to imagine: Luther Cane, Advisor to the Governor, second in command, nervous to speak with Theodore Offenheimer. "Delighted as I'd be to accompany Miss, uh...Miss?" Luther stalled.

"Flood," Resi finished for him.

"*Flood*," Luther repeated slowly. "As much as I'd like to accompany the 'Lick, I unfortunately have some business to tend to in town. Thought I'd save the hassle of preparing two carriages and hopped a ride. I'll be dropped off in Esur. But you, you blossoming thing—" he reached his hand to brush Resi's cheek, and she flinched for the second time that morning. "You will continue on to the Tristeland. The Governor is anxiously awaiting your arrival."

"Well, best be on your way," said Theo gently to Resi. "Wouldn't want to keep Governor Sequis waiting." A few uncomfortable seconds passed before Theo extended his hand to the Advisor. Luther then turned for the carriage.

"We'll have her delivered back to you as soon as possible," Luther called over his shoulder. He snapped two fingers for the coachman, and moments later, a petite man with a monocle and a strawberry beard flew across the gravel from the rear of the carriage. He aided Luther inside before returning for Resi's small suitcase. The carriage driver sat idly at the front of the cart.

"Remember what I said, dear," Theo spoke quietly to Resi. She nodded, then turned to grab the hand of the coachman before climbing inside the carriage. The door closed sharply behind her petticoats, and not a moment later, she and Luther jolted forward in their seats as the horse pulled away from the drive.

Resi dared not be the first to speak. Terrified, she looked down at her gloved hands twisted together in her lap.

"Quite a season, I must say. Damp as ever in those fields," said Luther, who appeared to have no idea how to make small talk. Resi looked up and nodded slightly, but her attention was soon drawn out the window. Theo waited by the front door, and as her eye caught his, he gave her one last wink of encouragement.

Her eyes then went to the top window of the lodge. Waiting before it were Marion and, by her side, Scottis. The boy's face was forcibly celebratory, as if he were hiding his true disappointment for Resi's departure. Limply, he waved before Marion, whose mouth was rigid as she yanked his hand down and pulled him out of view.

"I take it you're happy with your new position inside the home?" Luther continued.

Resi took a deep breath. "I am very grateful to the Offenheimers for granting me the position of tutor. Grateful even more to rest my head on a comfortable bed every evening."

"They're good people, the Offenheimers," said Luther. "Wealthy, hospitable...Known them for years. You should be grateful you ended up at this fine estate. There's not a better place for a 'Lick in the whole region. Other than the Tristeland, of course!"

Resi gave a weak smile, then looked back down to her lap. She found herself wishing that at any moment the whole interior of the carriage might swallow her whole. She drew her attention to the fields passing slowly out the window, trying as best she could to ignore the persistent pain against her ribs from the ill-fitting second-hand corset.

Then, from the front garden, a pair of deep brown eyes met hers, the same pair she'd seen watching her from her stoop. Corey slowed his picking as he watched her pass. He simply smiled a sad, pitying grin at her, gave a slight nod, then resumed his work.

A blurred hand dangled in front of Resi's face, shaking her from her thoughts. Luther's dirtied nails were inches from her nose. "Hello?!" he called to her.

"Apologies, sir," she said.

Luther brought his hands together around the underside of his knees, a childish sort of pose for someone of his rank. "I was beginning to wonder if you'd left your manners at the farmhold!" he said, looking at her from beneath a raised brow. "Now, I'm to assume you heard at least *one* word of my instructions, yes?"

Resi tensed. It wasn't the first time she'd tuned out in the last few days. "Forgive me, sir."

Luther readjusted himself in his seat. "Attention must be paid today, Miss Flood!" he said with a nervous sort of laugh. "I'll start from the beginning." He cleared his throat. "I will be dropped off in town. From there, the carriage will see you to the Tristeland, where you will be greeted by Commander Lee. Lee will then escort you to the Governor's wing, where you will be granted a private audience with Governor Sequis."

Resi's stomach dropped. "*Private...audience?*"

Luther gave her a look of absolute certainty. "Governor Sequis has asked for no distractions during his portrait sessions. There must be no others present for you to do your best work. After all, the portrait is to be presented at the Ball for all his attendants to see! Oh, it will be a historic occasion, indeed. Now..."

Luther continued on with more crucial information, but Resi was too focused on continuing to breathe to hear a single word of it. A private audience. With Sequis. And further, a reminder that her very first professional piece of work was to be presented at the Ball.

"It's important, Miss Flood, that you understand, er, one particularly important aspect of your stay at the Estate," continued Luther. "The Governor, although highly impressed with your talent, has no awareness of your, eh, standing...well, rather, your low ranking in... well..." He stopped himself and readjusted his collar. "I haven't informed him of your position at the Offenheimers."

Resi adjusted herself in her seat. "I don't quite understand."

Luther laughed nervously again and crossed his legs. "He doesn't know that you're a 'Lick."

"...Oh."

Luther smiled weakly, clearing his throat. "He saw your sketch last night and immediately made up his mind that you were the right artist to capture his likeness! Had I told him of your ranking, he would've required a further search for an artist of your talent, and one that wasn't a 'Lick. As I mentioned earlier, there just isn't the time, not before the Ball in a few weeks. But not to worry! I've drawn up a description that I think will suit you."

Luther reached into his breast pocket and presented a piece of parchment to her.

"Feel free to read it aloud," he told her before his face went white with worry. "You do know how to *read*, yes?"

Resi's eyes squinted at the words on the page. "Miss Kensington. Of Portfish?"

"Small fishing town in the northernmost part of Ter," Luther proudly stated as the color returned to his cheeks. His yellow teeth gleamed in a rare spot of sunshine that crossed on his side of the carriage. "Sequis has yet to travel there. He won't suspect a thing."

Resi's eyes fluttered before she continued reading the remaining contents. "Patrian. The daughter of a fisherman. Minimally educated."

Luther nodded, seemingly proud of his plot. Resi, however, felt her vision spin. The Patrian people were the original settlers of the Sept-Regions, and the same people from which the Aliquian people had descended. Resi had yet to ever meet a Patrian, but she knew they were rumored to usually have darker hair and light eyes—Resi could certainly pass for one.

"Patrian?" she asked.

Another yellow smile graced his face. He then reached across the carriage and swiped the parchment out of Resi's hand before he stuffed it back into his coat pocket. "As long as you keep your head down and don't say a word, the Governor won't suspect a thing."

The carriage fell quiet again for a time, and soon enough, the wheels rolled onto the cobblestone road to lead them through the charming town of Esur, which was just south of the roadway that would lead to the ascending drive to the Tristeland.

"Sir," Resi finally spoke boldly. "Surely it's not in my best interest to be dishonest with the Governor."

An explosive outburst of laughter came from Luther's slight frame. "Miss Flood," he said. "As you're soon to discover, the Governor is a man of very few words. I'd be surprised if he even remembers you're coming, with all the preparations for the upcoming event. Let one thing be made very clear...he's invited you to the Tristeland for your talents, not for your acquaintance. Understood?"

She nodded.

"And besides," he went on, "if you *were* a Patrian, you would stay within the Tristeland as a free woman. Surely, that can't be all bad! You can enjoy the grounds in whatever way you see fit. If anything, darling, you should be thanking me. I just gave you a few weeks of freedom. Not too many of your kind would think to complain after such an offer."

Resi eased. A few weeks of freedom within the Tristeland Estate was a chance that she had to take; if not for herself, then for every other Aliquian man, woman, and child at the farmhold. She would keep to herself. Speak to few. She'd play the part of a Patrian woman. In any event, she'd keep her mouth shut.

The majority of the carriage ride was uneventful, but as they pulled through Esur, Resi felt a familiar dread come over her. It was the first she'd seen of the town since the last Fourth-Year Festival.

The carriage soon passed the water well that stood at the middle of the Center Square before coming upon a series of small storefronts. They rolled past window after window filled with cakes, meats, spices, and scarves. Banners still hung from the awnings, evidence of a Fourth-Year Festival that had come and gone too soon.

As they made their way north, the streets began to fill with red-haired Codian folks, each pausing to point at the carriage as it creaked past. The carriage finally came to a stop in front of a darkened alley.

"This is where I leave you," Luther said quickly, buttoning his coat jacket. "I trust you'll do our Governor justice in your rendering. Good day, Miss Flood."

The carriage door swung open with a thud, and the monocled coachman aided Luther out of the carriage. Luther gave instructions to the driver to pick him up promptly in the afternoon, and Resi watched as the Advisor strolled down the shadowy alley before walking through to a door and disappearing out of view.

Resi jumped in fright when she lurched forward in her seat as the carriage pulled away. Finally, she was on her own. She opened the bundle of brushes in her lap, examining each wooden brush as if it were its own rightful treasure. She pulled the largest from its pocket, one with a thick wooden handle and squared bristles. Her eyes found the Governor's crest, the same as the one positioned right outside her window.

The plush hills surrounding the town of Esur had already turned into rock along the journey. Clouds often rolled in over the lower peninsula of the region, where the farmhold was located, but north of Esur seemed nearly a world away in contrast; mild and pleasant. Resi's eyes squinted in the harsh sunlight as she searched the hillsides until she spotted it; a fortress raised high above like a jewel box in the sky. The Tristeland.

As the carriage climbed higher, the Tristeland's many corridors, towers, and courtyards consistently gave way to more and more property. Black dots lined the Estate's large, grid-iron entrance gate. They appeared stationary from a distance, but as the carriage approached, they proved to be men dressed in charcoal armor; Sequis's militia, his notorious Eastern Guard. Hundreds of them ranked along the perimeter of the gate, some standing completely still with their stances wide and assured, while others paced slowly along the wall.

Shouts suddenly sounded from the east, and Resi strained to see a dozen men stationed along the battlements atop a tall tower. Minutes passed as the gate's shadow slowly engulfed the horse and the carriage. Then came the blare of a horn before the gate opened and the carriage pulled forward once more.

It took every ounce of Resi's course to tear her eyes away from the view outside the window. She didn't trust this place. How could she? It had been built on the blood of her people, spilled in battle.

An impressive and sprawling courtyard awaited. It bustled with guards, all dressed in the same dark charcoal armor. Some led horses to water at a trough; others seemed to be taking a much-needed break in the shade, talking quietly to one another as they took sips from their hip flasks.

Up close, the Tristeland Estate appeared as if it could swallow the Offenheimer Eye in one bite. It bore an intimidating, and intricate facade, with wide stone steps along the inside of the courtyard that led to two tall darkened doors with gold circular door knobs.

Resi could barely catch her breath as the coachman flew to her door, and her skirts bunched in the opening before she toppled out of the carriage. Her eyes landed on a man, waiting alone at the top of the stairs. One by one, she slowly ascended them, recounting the details of her new identity to herself, and feeling as powerless as an insect trapped beneath a very great stone.

Resi curtsied to the man, whose face bore harsh lines. "Commander Lee," she said, her eyes squinting as the sun exposed itself in the courtyard.

"You received the governor's gift?" he said as he turned towards the stairs.

"Yes, sir. And may I express my gratitude? The brushes are absolutely exqui—"

"There's no need for pleasantries, Miss Kensington," Commander Lee interrupted her brusquely. "Consider the gift a necessity for you to do your job, and for you to do it well." He turned abruptly, indicating for Resi to follow him.

Two guards greeted them before the set of gargantuan black doors. Resi thought the men's armor to be in better condition than Commander Lee's. This was unsurprising as the two men looked to be no older than she, both still fresh and eager to be on the job. Their eyes widened upon Resi's approach, and awkwardly, they scrambled to open the heavy doors for the new visitor. Resi's lip curled into a smile; it appeared Marion's dress was doing all the work for her.

She watched the darkness swallow Commander Lee as he crossed the threshold. Resi followed after into the cool of the Estate, her eyes quickly adjusting to the dimness of the room before her, and as they did, her mouth fell open.

They were warmly welcomed by an ornate and cavernous foyer. An arched ceiling displayed a richly painted mural over their heads. Gold molding swirled and churned into unique shapes on every wall, and a crystal chandelier the size of her lean-to floated above a curved marble stairwell, which led deeper into the castle.

Resi paused to behold the mural, but then recoiled when she realized what the artwork conveyed; the battle of Sequis and the Eastern Guard's attack on Ter. Sequis's back was turned as he looked over the nearby cliffs and his face was completely out of view. His massive frame was armored in gold and towered over his onlooking militia, who were resting in the aftermath of battle. Everyone appeared exhausted after hours of fighting, their muskets at their sides. Resi had been so transfixed by the intricate detail of the mural that she nearly glanced over the one defining horror of the entire piece. In one hand, Sequis grasped at the hair of a decapitated head.

At once, Resi's stomach flipped with heat, and her cheeks burned.

"Welcome to the Governor's home, Miss Kensington. We hope it will suit you for the duration of your stay," Commander Lee called to her as he began to ascend another stairwell. His tone was casual, normal.

Once upstairs, they came upon a large room filled with plush, velvet sofas. Fresh bouquets in shimmering vases lined the tables, and further along, a polished fortepiano gleamed in the sunlight. The view from the windows overlooked the entirety of the Tristeland's gardens. A large circular fountain silently pulsed beyond the glass windows. The whole scene brought Resi's attention to the sea, which glinted gold and navy on the horizon past the Eastern cliffs.

Resi gulped. From the dirt of her lean-to to the lap of mind-boggling luxury.

"Only a little further, Miss," Commander Lee said.

He led her through a hallway, beyond which the rooms grew smaller to become elegant guest chambers. One door was open, and Resi glanced inside to see a plush bed with a gold velvet canopy. Three women with dark hair and dressed in matching grey livery worked quickly to stretch the sheets on the sprawling mattress. Resi lingered as she watched them work before one woman's attention came to her. Embarrassed, Resi made a small curtsy, took one last glance at them, then continued on.

She quickened her pace to match Commander Lee's, and after he took her up a darkened stairwell that led them towards the cliffs, he paused before a tall door in the hallway. He turned to her, his face shrouded in shadow while he drew a quick breath.

"There are a few matters to attend to before you are to meet with the Governor," he announced.

Resi gulped.

"First, there is the issue of your reaction upon meeting His Lordship, Sequis." Commander Lee cleared his throat, and he repositioned his feet beneath him. He was courteous, much more so than Luther. Still, he was strict, concise. His voice became a quiet murmur. "As you can imagine, many act rather strangely the first time they find themselves in the company of a giant. The best advice I can give is to remain as calm as possible, to keep quiet, and to refrain from any questions. Second, you are to address him exactly as I have just now: His Lordship. Are we understood?"

Resi flinched slightly, then nodded.

"Now," the Commander said even more quietly and glanced at

the door behind him. "You should be made aware that the Governor is—well, he's not in the best of spirits this afternoon."

The pulse beneath Resi's corset stopped. "Is everything alright?"

"Well," Commander Lee paused again, looking back a second time towards the stairwell to be sure they were not heard. "What with heavy travel and fatigue, his mood has been rather shifty the past few weeks." Lee sighed. "He's refused any other visitors this morning. The only person he wishes to speak to is Luther, but the Advisor has been out all morning attending to the preparations for the Ball. Naturally, I offered to have the portrait session rescheduled for the end of the week, but he refused. There is so little time ahead of the celebration, and with you being in Esur for only a few short weeks..." Commander Lee rolled his shoulders, then shook his head disapprovingly. "I must also warn you..." he continued, "he's been drinking."

Resi's weight shifted on the rug beneath her feet. "I—I see..." she said softly. She tried to hide her fear, but couldn't. At that very moment, a crash came from beyond the door that sounded much like glass shattering on the floor.

Commander Lee winced, then gathered himself. "I can't make any guarantees for an even temperament. But, I can speak on behalf of the Governor when I say that your talent is unmatched by any other artist in the region. His words. It was on his authority to have you retrieved today. And it was you, and *only* you he desired for the job."

The pressure in Resi's chest mounted to the point of feeling as if she might burst from the inside out. "Very well," she said coolly.

Lee nodded before lifting his fist to the door. "Now. Shall we meet the Governor?"

CHAPTER 8

THE GOVERNOR

The door gave way to an expansive parlor with high ceilings. The chamber's adornments were lavish but comfortable. White pillar candles twinkled softly on the mantle, and sheer window curtains rested over a bearskin rug on the floor. A giant stone hearth roared with light and heat, and at the center of the room sat two gold velvet couches built with Sequis in mind. They were monstrous. In the midst of the chaos, however, there was one glimmer of hope: a large easel with a blank canvas resting atop it placed in the corner. Resi's eyes clung to it as if it might have the ability to steady her at such a time.

As Lee had warned her, the room was in disarray, its floor littered with battered books and papers. The rug was flipped over at the corner nearest the chair and the minimal light that poured in from the windows displayed a mess of glass, presumably once a vase, that had been shattered and left on the floor.

Lee took in the disastrous sight with wide, searching eyes. "Sir," his voice croaked over the cracking logs in the hearth. "Sir, the artist has arrived for your portrait session." He moved deeper into the room, and Resi followed close behind. It was then that she noticed a white wing-backed chair hidden in one of the darker corners of the room by the fireplace.

"Your Lordship?" Lee inquired again.

As Resi neared the hearth, her fear intensified. She continued to scan the room; every piece of furniture was gargantuan.

A low grunt suddenly startled them from beyond the chair. "Leave us."

Resi had heard Sequis's voice boom in front of a crowd of thousands. But hearing its deep timbre now—here, in the dimness of a contained room—made her tremble.

Lee turned to Resi with an uneasy smile. *Good luck,* he mouthed to her before heading to the door. He gave her one last gaze of reassurance before exiting the room.

Resi stood frozen, unsure of whether she should be so bold as to speak before she was addressed. As the silence became thicker, she sank deeper into her dress.

"You're from the North, I'm told." Sequis's voice rumbled over the fire. A sniff and a deep breath followed. "From a small fishing town I've never heard of." The words were harsh and arrogant, as if he'd felt snubbed by the fact that his portrait artist wasn't from his place of rule. "Don't tell me you're a mute," he chuckled after a time.

Resi shifted her weight nervously on the bearskin rug. She gathered her nerves, which were bundled into a tight knot at the center of her chest, and spoke. "F-forgive me, Your Lordship."

A harsh, slurping noise followed; Fet being sipped from a goblet. "Ah...she speaks."

The chair gave a scoot before a shadow grew on the adjoining wall. It eclipsed the light of the space as Sequis stood mighty before the hearth. He stretched his back from many stiff hours in the chair, then his frame slowly turned. His size made the once cathedral-like space seem infinitely smaller, but his features remained hidden in the dancing shadows cast by the fireplace.

Resi did her best to remain calm, to not ask questions. She tried to refrain from staring at the massiveness of Sequis's girth, so much so that she hadn't noticed until that very moment that his thin, loose shirt was unbuttoned to show a smooth patch of exposed skin on his chest.

The corset grew tighter against Resi's middle. "I—I suppose we should get to work, Your Lordship?" she inquired thinly.

Sequis waited stiffly before the hearth, his mass still concealed in silhouette as he took in the sight of her. "You're practically a child," he seethed. "Luther mentioned to me that you were young. How old are you?"

Resi gulped. "Nineteen, Your Lordship."

More hissing and cracking from the fireplace. Candlelight flicked and played along the dark walls.

"Just a girl," he said quietly.

The floor groaned as Sequis moved his way around the chair. She watched as his angular jaw, sharp enough to cut through stone, tensed, then relaxed. A tendril of golden hair fell over steady blue-green eyes as they met hers.

Resi gulped. The rumors didn't do him justice. He wasn't just handsome—his beauty was astonishing to witness, almost other-worldly.

Recollections of sleepless nights spent beneath milky starlight and vast darkness pooled her memory as they both studied each other. She'd spent an entire summer after her parents' disappearance tossing and turning in her lean-to. The stars had become a fascination of hers, the shapes and names of the constellations a comfort to her despite their eternal distance and mystery. Sequis's beauty and size had this kind of effect on her, and she felt fragile and powerless by comparison.

"Your talent far exceeds your reputation," his voice thundered. His arms, the size of an average man's torso, found his waist. "I'd not heard of you before yesterday. Someone as gifted as you should have a name amongst the great artists of Ter. But no...You prefer to live quietly, modestly. I can't understand why."

Stupefied, Resi watched Sequis take another sip of his wine from a sizable goblet. Colorful ideas for his portrait swirled within her. Her eyes darted about the space. The sinking sun over the sea, and the candlelight and fire that warmed the room...mere minutes had passed since their introduction, but the study had already transformed into a mirage of oranges and gold. The window of use for this kind of light was fleeting, but the tones and shadows of this time and place suited him. After the glass was finished, he plunked it down on a hefty table nearest the hearth.

"Tell me your name, Miss."

Resi blushed. "Miss Kensington."

"Yes, yes, *Miss Kensington of Portfish*, I know..." He glazed over the title with a pitying wave of his hand. "What I wish is to address you as my equal."

She nodded sheepishly. Didn't Luther say the Governor was a man of few words? He may have asked her to withhold certain information, but she couldn't justify any more unnecessary fibbing.

"Taresia," she said without so much as a blink. "It's Taresia, Your Lordship."

Sequis slurped his wine again, then crossed to a table decorated with many substantial goblets and a glass decanter of Fet. With each one of his steps came a vibration that rippled across the floor. He poured, then returned with two sizable goblets in hand. When he reached to extend her a glass, half the room fell into shadow.

"Drink," he commanded her. "It'll help with the nerves."

Resi didn't ask any questions. She struggled to lift the heavy goblet to her face, then took the contents of it down in consecutive large gulps. The bitterness of its flavor sent a rush of adrenaline coursing through her. She emerged from her drink with a loud and exasperated gasp to find Sequis smiling at her from across the room. His gaze was unsteadying.

She cleared her throat. "Sorry, Your Lordship. I'm not one to drink during the day. Or, or really much at all, for that matter." Hesitantly, she wiped a leftover drop from her lower lip.

"I know a woman's first drink when I see it." Sequis reached again for her glass, swiping it aggressively from her grasp with a strange smile, then returned to the table to pour her another.

"Oh, that's plenty for me, really—"

But it was too late to object. The wine gurgled its way into the goblet, and when Sequis returned with the freshly poured glass, Resi took it.

"Very, er, very kind of you, thank you..." She took cautious sips, then held the heavy goblet with two limp hands.

Sequis laughed, and the room shook. "This business of 'Your Lordship' is very formal. I meant what I said earlier about addressing you as my equal. My name is Sequis. You will address me as such. That is a command."

She took the hint. "Very well then...Governor Sequis."

At the sound of his own name, Sequis's eyes widened, then focused again on her. "For being so young and so talented, one would assume you were well-traveled, well-read—you must receive compliments on your achievements daily."

"Quite the opposite, I'm afraid."

"I find that difficult to believe. Tell me, how was it that you discovered your gift?"

Resi waited for a plausible response to come to mind, but none came. Diversion seemed like the best tactic. "I'm as common as any commoner you'd find roaming the streets. Might I spare you the boring details?"

Sequis moved the space of the room and found the couch opposite her. Again, the room responded to his size with a groan. Resi stepped back slightly as he sat wide on the plush fabric.

"I'm afraid I must insist, Taresia. You see, you've been asked here on my command to paint my portrait. And if you are to execute your job well, you need to be comfortable. I think it best we get to know one another before we take on such a task together. Don't you agree?"

His reasoning was sound, but not what she had anticipated. Resi nodded.

"Good," he said, relieved. "Now, please, sit...I'd like to know how you became an artist."

As close to the truth as possible, Resi reminded herself, perching hesitantly on the other couch. "I came upon sketching, first, Your Lord—"

Sequis interrupted her with a wag of his finger.

"Sorry...*Sequis*..." she corrected herself. "I came upon sketching a few years ago. I've grown up very poor. I found a pencil and parchment in a field near my home. Sketching became somewhat of an escape."

"But why not use pencil and paper to *write?* For *mathematics?*"

"I guess sketching just came naturally," she replied. "I find that all great joys do. I'm still quite new in my understanding of art, but I'd like to think I'm learning quickly. I could only assume ruling came just as easily to you."

Sequis's head tilted at her response. "I'd once hoped it would," he mused, "but it took many years to master the ins and outs of legislature. Quite boring, if I must say. Sometimes, responsibilities get thrust upon you before you even know what to make of them. My work certainly has its perks," Sequis said with a wave to the room. "But you—your talent is beyond your experience, which is impressive. What's more, your heart soars when you speak of your art."

Resi fought the smile that desperately wanted to break free on her mouth.

Sequis took another sip. "And your family?"

Her hands tightened around the goblet. She would've been comfortable with any other question; any question but this. "Wh-what of my family, sir?"

"I understand your Father is a fisherman. What does he make of your talents? He must be proud."

Resi's breath intensified, and one of her hands found her waist. "Excuse me. It's just, I haven't had much to eat today, and with all the Fet..."

Immediately and with great conviction, Sequis stood, his great mass taking four barreling steps to the door. Resi couldn't help but flinch at his sudden movement.

"Lee," he commanded through the door. "Call for some refreshments."

"Yes, sir," Lee called from somewhere down the hall.

Resi felt she was at the edge of a very steep, very mysterious ledge.

She'd narrowly avoided a question about a topic she wasn't sure she had the power to keep secret. At least, not with Fet in hand.

Sequis found his way back to the couch. "I should've thought of this hours before your arrival," he said apologetically. Still, a ripe anger lingered in his eyes. It hovered there briefly, then flitted away like a bird taking flight from the sea. "Stupid, really—no refreshments prepared for a guest."

"Oh, not to worry," Resi assured him. "My welcome here has been more than warm."

"Of course, you are called to Court for the duration of your stay. I insist. We have all the finest foods served daily from every region. I cannot guarantee that our fish will be as well prepared as it is in the North, however."

Resi waited before taking another long sip of her Fet. She'd never been one for socializing, and now she was expected to mingle with Patrian and Codian dignitaries and socialites at Court. Another quick sip of Fet, an afterthought, made its way down her throat, and she nearly choked on it.

"Besides your art, how else do you spend your time?" Sequis inquired curiously. He sat back on the couch more comfortably, allowing his legs to fall open again.

The adjoining room, a bed chamber, was just barely visible to Resi from where she sat. The door was halfway opened, and she couldn't help but let her eyes hover over the ruffled sheets of the bed. Its fabrics by candlelight appeared soft, inviting. She found herself momentarily repulsed at the thought of how many women the Governor had entertained within the same four walls. She imagined them all lit by the same glow, sitting on the same couch, probably wearing equally as atrocious of gowns. Or perhaps some had worn 'Lick garments— Theo had warned her of Sequis's taste for Aliquian women, after all. It suddenly occurred to her that free or otherwise, perhaps the women who were invited here didn't feel like they had much choice in the matter, either.

"Humor me, Taresia. There must be other delights for an artist besides painting and sketching," she heard Sequis finish.

Picking folly root, planning secret escapes. She laughed nervously, took another sip, then looked to the fire. "I'm a woman of few hobbies, sir."

Sequis continued to gaze at her in disbelief. "You don't like talking much, do you?"

"Pardon?" she asked as another sip of Fet met her mouth. Its earlier bitterness had weakened. It was becoming flavorful, pleasant even.

He shifted forward in his seat, his eyes searching her. "I find it ironic that an artist who captures her subjects to perfection somehow manages to also shield herself from anyone who dares try to see *her.* Who taught you to do that?"

Resi was vaguely reminded of a time long ago when she'd stumbled upon a dead bird in the fields on a chilly autumn day. She'd poked at it for a few minutes with a long, sharp stick before Mags had called her back to work. That winter, she'd often wondered how it would've felt to be dissected, to be pulled apart and investigated. Sitting here with Sequis gave her all the answers she needed.

"I mean no harm by what I said," Sequis stated calmly. "I simply wish to draw you out from hiding."

"I wasn't aware," she cleared her throat, "that I was holding back, sir."

His intense eyes sparkled with a dash of playfulness. "Do you have any idea what made me choose you for the task of painting my portrait for the Ball?"

Resi shifted on the couch, and the goblet, now much lighter than before, fell slowly to her lap. "I'm told you like my work. Your desire to call upon me is beyond flattery. It's—well, it's—" she drew a breath. "It's the largest honor someone like me could accept."

Sequis smiled a boyish grin. It drew Resi in like a breath, and then all at once faded into calm austerity.

"A few things to know; I've had the finest oil paints delivered all the way from Turbus," he told her as his arm motioned towards a table near the door. Metal tubes presumably filled with paint rested atop it. "Newly developed paints, I'm told. They dry within minutes, which will allow us to work quickly and with minimal breaks. There are also pastels, pencils, plenty of brushes, and any essentials you might need to do your best work. And this room is at your disposal at any time of the day, any day. Consider it your study as much as mine, although I might only be present during our scheduled sessions. With all the preparations for the Ball, I will presumably be busy with other matters."

Curiously, Resi peered towards the decorated table. An eagerness, impulsive and primal, came over her.

"Please," Sequis nodded at her. "Take a look."

Without hesitation, Resi leapt from the couch and crossed to the table. Her eyes danced across the array of paints, and her hand opened the many drawers that displayed a vibrant array of unused pastels. As if she'd called the monster by name, her heat warmed in her stomach and spread into her chest.

"Are you pleased?" he asked her.

Resi turned back to face him with a wide grin. "Beyond," she admitted.

"And of course, there's the matter of payment for your time. I presume you work by the hour?"

Payment; Resi had yet to even contemplate being compensated for her work, although the idea of it enticed her tremendously. The Offenheimers wouldn't allow such a thing, and she couldn't return to the farmhold with money in her possession, not without it being confiscated. Mistress Marion was much too clever not to rummage through her belongings once Resi was settled back into her duties within the Eye. She had to deny it, but how? When a quick and humble answer came to her, she smiled. Her glance shifted back towards the table of supplies.

"The honor of painting your portrait is payment enough. But if you don't mind parting with the paints and pastels, I'd—"

"Done and done," he agreed to her terms.

Delighted, Resi nearly skipped her way back to the couch. Marion would have a harder time chastizing Resi for accepting a *gift* from Sequis. After all, it would've been rude to deny the Governor such a thing. If Marion threatened to destroy the materials, then Theo would presumably stand up for Resi, maybe even keep them locked away in his study for her use, so long as no one else knew.

The sound of the crackle of the logs in the fireplace filled the space as Resi nestled back into her seat. After a few more sips of Fet from his goblet, Sequis reached into his trouser pocket, then extended a hand to her with a piece of parchment. Accepting the parchment, Resi opened it slowly—the painting of Scottis.

She sweetly doted on it as if Scottis himself had just entered the room. Her hands traced the lines she'd brushed so joyously on the afternoon of the Festival. She couldn't help but giggle at the memory of Scottis's pinched-up face; so focused, so adult-like.

"You *see* people, Taresia," Sequis said quietly. "This boy, a complete stranger, is now a sort of friend to me. I see his life. I see his desires."

"You can see all that? From this?" she chortled hesitantly as she held up the parchment.

Sequis reached his hand for Resi to pass the parchment back. She did so, and as Sequis took in the image, his eyes squinted. "I see a boy. But, one who wants nothing more than to be a man. He's curious. Restrained. Different from others his age."

Resi tried to conceal the blush of her cheeks with a raised hand. If only Sequis knew she'd painted it in secrecy. She cleared her throat. "I think you doubt your own perception, sir. Could it be that you have the remarkable ability to see what most cannot? Not many would say the same of such a—" she stalled, "—dismal, rushed painting."

"But I'm correct, aren't I?" Sequis asked. His eyebrows, thick and darker than the hair on his head, raised in two beautiful arches. "And that has to count for something."

"I guess you'll never know," she joked. "A secret I'll now have to take to the grave."

Sequis laughed, and the boom of it shook the room yet again. "You take a compliment like a sword to the rib," he mumbled, then drank.

"Maybe so. But I think I prefer it that way. Better to be humble than an egotistical prat."

Sequis choked on his Fet, then chuckled again. "I dare say, Taresia! Quite a blow!"

"Oh! Oh, no, sir, I don't mean you!" Her face was on fire. Stupid Fet. Mags had told her that Fet made women say foolish things. "I only meant that I don't wish for your compliments to go to my head. I can see how it might be easy to accept them. One remark too many from you and I'd be marching around the Tristeland with orders of my own."

Curious, Sequis leaned forward on the couch. "And what might be your first command?"

Resi shuddered. Sequis's striking features were dizzying to observe up close, and she was particularly aware of them anytime he changed his position. The sharp, symmetrical jaw. The muscular shoulders and wide chest. As gorgeous as he appeared by candlelight, he was equally as menacing, as if at any time the facade might snap.

"Probably something silly," she giggled to lighten her fears. "I'd command that every window be opened so the fresh air could pour in from the sea."

Sequis's hands rolled together. He chuckled. "Not silly."

A thump came at the door, and Sequis stood again. He crossed to answer, talked with someone at the door, then brought in a large, silver tray that appeared no bigger than a tea plate in his hand. It was decorated with a plethora of cheeses, colorful fruits, and nuts.

Resi refrained from gasping. She hadn't seen a plate so filled since the last Fourth-Year Festival. She told herself to wait to reach out and grab as much as she could to devour, but her appetite was ravenous. She blamed her nerves. And the Fet.

"Go on, now," Sequis said, noticing her widened eyes. "I can imagine you're hungry after your journey."

Tentatively, she reached for a piece of cheese, brought it to her lips, then plunked it into her mouth. Its salty, creamy goodness slid down her throat with immense satisfaction. Her hand reached out again for more, and before she could contain herself, she was stuffing food into her mouth from the left and the right.

"Quite the appetite for a woman. If I didn't know any better, I'd suspect you were a 'Lick," Sequis spoke with a laugh.

Resi's pace slowed, but her heart sped rapidly. *Don't blow it. Just don't blow it.* "Sahry. So hungwy," she said with a full mouth. She took a deep gulp, then settled back onto the couch. She couldn't imagine why Sequis wasn't digging in; a giant's appetite was rumored to be insatiable.

"Might I ask you another question?" he asked after a time.

She nodded.

"What do you have in mind exactly? For my portrait, that is."

"I think that is entirely up to you. Although…" she paused in trepidation as her mind went back to an hour or so prior when she'd first seen the horrific mural in the foyer. It was difficult to imagine the same charming person seated before her unleashing such violence. "I could never match up to the grandeur and scale of the war mural in the foyer. Who…who painted it?"

The room fell quiet once more as Sequis's light mood suddenly darkened. The corner of his eyes winced before his gaze shifted towards the cliffs out the window. "*Grandeur*…" he echoed her with a slight roll of his eyes. "The piece was made by many artists. Took almost a year to complete, and they still couldn't manage to put my face in it."

Resi's shoulders pulled forward in her dress. "A *year*?"

His eyes came back to hers with clarity. "I didn't ask you here so that I could be immortalized in another lousy war painting. I demand your talents because I desire a more…intimate take on my rulership."

His answer surprised Resi, and in some small way, it delighted her. "My wish is to please you."

Sequis's mouth curled into a smile, and the smell of Fet wafted to Resi's side of the room. She noted the bloodshot tinge of his eyes. "I suppose it's all a question of how I'd like to be remembered…how my name will go down in history along with the rest of Ter's rulers."

His voice trailed off before he stood abruptly. He landed before the hearth, his stance wide. He was lost in thought, somewhere between where he was standing presently in the room and someplace else—perhaps beyond the sea, over the cliffs. Resi couldn't help but stare again at the mass of his arms.

"How do *you* wish to be remembered, sir?" she asked. She was startled she'd had the courage to ask him such a thing. But Sequis was unfazed. He turned to her, his expression calm, as if he were still watching the sun's reflection on the water.

"You are a civilian of this region. You must have an opinion on the matter."

"I couldn't be prevailed upon to give you my opinion, sir. It is of little value."

Sequis's eyes went hard and severe. "I demand it."

Resi shuddered, this time out of fear. Sequis' growing temper was palpable, as if at any moment the pendulum might swing the other way. One wrong question, one statement too far, and she could find herself in the wake of an angry giant.

"I see..." she began nervously, noticing the tremble of her voice, "a man of integrity. A man that's seen every corner of the Sept-Regions. A man who would die for the people of Ter."

Sensing that she was running out of steam, his nostrils flared. "Don't tell me what I wish to hear. I wish for the truth."

"Sir, I—"

"What I wish for is honesty. Go ahead. Look upon me!" his tone sharpened to a deadly point. He turned in a circle with his arms outstretched. "What is it you see?"

Resi waited fearfully in the light from the window that was making its way onto the couch. She was momentarily frozen in Sequis' emerald stare. "I see..." she began, "someone who has worked far too hard, for far too long. With a heavy weight on his shoulders. Weight from the world—from himself. I see..." she paused, "someone who carries much sadness in his heart." She suddenly remembered Scottis. "A man that desperately wishes to be a boy. And to be seen for who he *really* is. To be known."

Sequis simply looked at her, his face blank. He rubbed his forehead with two massive hands, and Resi watched him closely, taking in the stubble on his chin, the sorrow that hid behind his eyes. She watched him make his way back to the window, as if something awaited him on the other side of the paned glass.

"It was my mother who told me I would be the greatest leader in the East," he said proudly, gesturing with his goblet in one hand. "Always had high expectations for me. But then again, who wouldn't have high expectations when they birthed not only a bastard, but a giant?" A sad laugh left him. "She didn't love, me of course. Even in the end, she didn't," he barked, his hand barreling the wine canister off the side table with vigorous force. Red Fet flung violently on the bear-skin rug like splattered blood.

Frightened, Resi pulled back on the couch. She didn't want to move or breathe, but she had something in mind; something crazy, something beyond her control. It came on like a fever—fast, powerful, able to knock out every inhibition. The vibrant light from the gardens boasted a marvelous display of lavender and magenta over Sequis's shoulders out the window. His golden hair was pulled back, but the front strands softly framed the striking angles of his anguished face. A picture in her mind, one powerful enough to shut off every warning voice in her head, told her to obey her instincts. And the fire within— it lit like a torch against her ribs, as if it were agreeing with her crazy idea. Was it inspiration? Or just the Fet?

It didn't matter. She didn't care.

Without a word, she hauled herself from the massive couch, her legs reaching awkwardly down from its height to find the floor. Sequis was now too drunk to do anything but wait as he watched her dart about the room.

She crossed to the easel, taking in the sight of the enormous blank canvas as if it were already consumed by color. "Don't move," she heard herself command him. "Don't move an inch."

CHAPTER 9

THE COURT

S ketching out the lines of Sequis's face, a quiet focus enveloped the chambers; it was all a hazy, magnificent dream. Resi could've stayed lost in her mind and hands for the rest of the day. And her monster—this had been its first appearance in days without the accompanied anger, as if her passion for painting was somehow beginning to form a bond with it. For all she knew, her time within the Tristeland walls would be the only chance she would get to practice her painting publicly; the thought in and of itself was both exciting and somehow equally as devastating, so she surrendered herself both to the task and her inner fire, following its lead as her hand flew across the canvas.

Resi had just finished outlining the painting with a pencil when Sequis suddenly began to button his shirt. Judging by the absence of light, she'd been working for close to two hours.

"I can keep going," she assured him.

"No," he commanded, his eyes red and weary. "You will rest for tonight. We will resume tomorrow."

He paused to rub his temples. Too much Fet, too much exchanged in such a new introduction. Resi couldn't help but wonder if he felt embarrassed, maybe even ashamed of his earlier behavior.

The air went suddenly tense between them, as if somehow the previous two hours had never happened, as if they'd meant nothing.

In a whirl, Sequis withdrew to his bed chambers, pausing slightly with his back to her when he came to the door. "I will see you at dinner," he sighed. He then shut himself in his room, leaving Resi alone and confused.

Would every session be so tense, so unnerving?

Feeling trapped in the silence, she threw a sheet over the canvas. The paints had dried in an instant. Unsure, she waited for a time before exiting the room. She came out to find Lee standing patiently in the shadows of the hall.

"Seems your time went well," he said to her, his tone pleasant.

All Resi could manage was a nod. Her mind was still lost in the parlor, looking upon Sequis and then the canvas and then Sequis again, memorizing the way in which he leaned on the window as the last light of day graced his tortured face.

Lee seemed to be in a better mood than before. Cheerfully, he led Resi back through the Estate, pausing every so often to point to something for Resi to take in its splendor. They marched by corridor after corridor filled with lavish, empty bed chambers, through giant entertaining spaces glittering with crystal chandeliers and colorful tapestries. They passed the main dining hall, a cavernous space decorated with deep burgundy wallpaper and elegantly dressed tables. Many members of Sequis's Court were already making their way around the candlelit tables.

Resi's favorite place of the entire Estate was the marble foyer, save for the mural overhead. She was captivated by its impressive stonework, which was more than one might ever hope to come across in the span of a lifetime. The sight of it took her breath away for the second time that day as Lee waltzed onward, leading her to another long hall. It took a brief moment for Resi to catch up, noticing along the way the intricate carvings adorning each of the large wooden doors. Eventually, Lee stopped before one, opened it, and gestured for Resi to go inside.

"Your chambers, Miss Kensington."

The room was spacious, giving way to a beautiful terrace that overlooked the gardens, and further on, the sea. A circular canopy bed lay directly in the center of the room, covered in crisp white linens and fur blankets.

Stunned, Resi turned back to him. "This should do," she said, hoping her eyes weren't giving away her true amazement.

He chuckled, then composed himself. "Dinner is served promptly at sundown. Which was..." he glanced around Resi to where the sun had disappeared beneath the sea beyond the terrace, "nearly half an hour ago."

"I hope I didn't delay His Lordship," Resi spoke with a nervous rattle in her throat.

Lee said nothing to calm her, and she took it as a sign of his own anxiety at Sequis's schedule having been interrupted.

"I haven't the proper attire," she continued before looking down at Marion's outdated gown with a grimace. And besides, she planned on using any excuse during her time at the Estate to stay away from matters of Court. "I may turn in for the night, if that's alright. It's been quite a long day."

Lee gestured to a small set of doors at the other end of the room. "I'm afraid the Governor won't stand for your absence. Giants consider it an abysmal discourtesy if dinner is skipped by an invited guest. And no need to fret over what to wear. You'll find some options in your closet. The Governor sent for a few dresses. But please, dress quickly. His Lordship is usually very punctual when it comes to mealtime." And with that, Lee nodded to her politely and shut the door behind him.

Quickly, Resi ran to the closet. She shook her head. "Oh, just a *few* dresses, then," she said to herself, eyeing the expansive collection of colorful gowns. She came to a chartreuse one, immediately remembering the lovely getup Marion had worn on the day Resi had been brought to the Eye. With tremendous satisfaction, she plucked it from the rack.

Moments later, a knock came at the door.

"Who is it?" Resi asked timidly.

The voice was soft, unassuming. "Chamber 'Lick, ma'am. Come to help with your dress."

"Oh, uhh," Resi hesitated. "Come in, please."

A petite woman with dark hair entered. Her face remained youthful, but held the kind of experience that came with years of working within an estate like the Tristeland. Without even a look at Resi, the woman approached her and began to lace up the back of the dress.

"Thank you," Resi said with a smile over her shoulder. "I'm Resi." But the woman didn't reply. Instead, she focused all of her attention on the gown, lacing it as if she were being timed. She finished, then just as quickly made her way out of the room.

Resi hadn't planned for it to be difficult to make friends with the Tristeland 'Licks, but then again, she'd never been one for making friends. Plus, now that she was "Miss Kensington of Portfish," it would be next to impossible to have any confidantes of her own kind during her stay. The thought left a giant pit in her stomach, but she supposed she was used to being on her own.

Once she exited her chambers, she made her way back towards the West Wing of the Estate. Candles had been lit outside the entrance of the dining hall since she'd last seen it. She walked through the doors into a beautiful entryway filled with aromatic flowers and candles. The whole hall was dimly lit, giving a romantic glow to the many smiling faces that mingled about the room.

Awkwardly, Resi stood just inside the entrance. As she looked about the room, she smirked contemptuously. It was as if every one of Marion Offenheimer's relatives had been invited to dine with the Governor. The Codian men wore their finest suit coats and hats. And the women frolicked about the hall in gowns that would've made the Mistress's attempts at fashion seem weak at best.

Resi's face twitched as a rancid and all too familiar scent hit her nose: Folly. She watched on as the members of Court huddled together in groups of threes and fours, arms interlaced, heads tilted back in glorious merriment. Insecurity rushed over her. She didn't belong here, and never would. To ease her nerves, she fiddled with her dress. For a fleeting moment, she wanted to be angry with Luther for putting her in the middle of a terrible lie. But the longer she looked out over the dazzling crowd, the more she realized she had only herself to blame. She'd had every opportunity to tell Sequis the truth in his parlor. But now that she'd lied to the Governor, now that he seemingly trusted her, there was no turning back.

Resi had many questions of her own in regard to why Luther had thought it acceptable to betray the Governor's trust. He was his advisor, after all. If Sequis couldn't trust his closest companion, then who could he trust at all?

She huffed out a breath, suddenly feeling anxious and very, very exposed. It was well known throughout the Sept-Regions that Luther had been Sequis's closest friend, aiding him in building the Eastern Guard. They'd risen in power together, leaning only on each other along the way to achieve Sequis's dream of one day ruling. Was it possible, Resi wondered, that Luther knew Sequis better than Sequis even knew himself? And if so, was true friendship the only exception to breaching someone's trust?

A set of double doors suddenly flung open on the other side of the hall. The Codian Court all gasped and applauded as Sequis entered the room. He was dressed in a navy military coat adorned with silver and gold medals on his left breast. Resi felt her stomach drop. Sequis appeared just as out of his element amongst the crowd as she was. In the dim hall, his shoulders hunched forward slightly, almost as if he was trying to hide his enormity.

Resi's mind drifted back to the parlor, to his unbuttoned shirt and his endearingly messy hair. Then, out of sorts as he had been, he'd at least looked comfortable, more himself. But here, he appeared as distant and removed from his Court as if he were a far-off dying star beyond the glass windows of the hall.

It wasn't until the crowd settled and fell back into conversation that Resi saw Luther at Sequis's side, his eyes dark and roaming. He was in a state of dishevelment, his hair slicked back with sweat after a day away from the comfort of the Tristeland.

The crowd continued to guzzle Rowgar from their flutes as Sequis made his way to a lavish throne. It sat opposite the many tables, a perfect perch from which to look out upon the Court. Luther followed after him, his steps tiny in comparison to Sequis's long strides. Every so often, he appealed to Sequis, apparently pestering him with questions. Did he ever stop talking?

Resi was relieved when a young 'Lick man with a tray of sparkling Rowgar finally approached her. She didn't even so much as thank him before swiping a flute and taking a large sip. The effects of the Fet from her session with Sequis had long worn off, but heady as the experience had been, she now understood its appeal—it seemed to ease her nerves. If there was one thing she knew for certain, it was that endless amounts of Rowgar and Fet would have to be in ample supply so long as she was staying at the Tristeland.

Somewhere, a string quartet began to play a rousing melody. The tune stirred up a group of drunken Codian women, who began to wave their delicate fans in Sequis's direction. Sequis, however, was unamused, even embarrassed by the attention. Passively, he waved back to the group, then turned back to Luther.

"Good evening," came a voice over Resi's shoulder. It was Commander Lee, dressed in his finest; a black uniform suitable for a formal event. Resi sighed in relief at the sight of a warm, familiar face. "Are you finding your first Court experience pleasant?" he asked.

"A bit overwhelming, I must say," Resi admitted.

"Ah, you'll get used to it. And I apologize, I would've escorted you into the hall, but I'm in charge of the Eastern Guard's responsibilities concerning the upcoming Ball. Had to see to some things before dinner was to start."

"It's no bother," Resi said pleasantly. "I escorted myself."

Lee surveyed the room, then turned to her with an impressed expression. "A young Patrian woman should never arrive to dinner alone." He gave her a wink and a smile that made Resi feel uneasy. *Patrian woman.* In an effort to hide her discomfort, she turned away and took another sip of Rowgar. Her eyes landed on Sequis; he was watching her. He looked on her briefly, then turned back to Luther.

"Everything is breathtaking," Resi remarked, her cheeks flushed.

"Yes, quite," said Lee. He brushed his hands over his buzzed head.

"Although, nothing in comparison to what you should expect at the Ball in the next few weeks."

Resi froze with her glass suspended in front of her mouth. "Forgive me, Commander, but you make it seem as if I will be invited. I can't imagine Sequis being in favor of such an idea."

"On the contrary," Lee piped as he surveyed the room. "I'm sure he will be delighted to share your artistry with the world. He'll want to show you off there. Hopefully, the news of the portrait will be spread across the regions, and you'll be gifted with many new opportunities."

The remaining contents of Resi's glass went down her throat. *Many new opportunities?* Just how far could this charade go? To Dirig? To Rowan? Sooner or later, the truth would have to come out, and when it did, the consequences had the potential to be massive.

It was settled. She needed to clear the air with Luther. If not tonight, then as soon as possible.

A hush then came over the crowd, turning Resi and Lee's attention towards the throne. Sequis stood with a raised glass. His face was strained, tired.

"If it pleases the Court," he started, his voice strong and sure, "my desire is that we shall come together in celebration tonight. It is a special evening because we have a special guest in our midst. She is an artist, and a rather great one at that."

Resi's knees swayed. Ever the gentleman, Lee bent to grab her arm. "Quite the honor," he murmured, misinterpreting her nerves as a sign of humility.

"She comes from a town I've yet to know in the North," Sequis called out. "She has no name for herself, and yet, her unparalleled talent has utterly bewitched me. If you would all give your attention to the center of the room, I would like to introduce the newest guest of the Court, Miss Taresia Kensington."

Sequis's long arm extended to her and the crowd turned in one choreographed movement. But all Resi could do was look at Luther, his already pale face growing whiter. An instant wave of applause flooded the room, some enthusiastic Codians even going so far as to yell, "Hear, hear!"

"Give a curtsy, Miss Kensington!" Lee said to her as he took a few steps away to join the applause.

Meanwhile, the world had fallen into utter disarray in Resi's mind. A strange feeling came over her, one similar to the heated fire in her stomach, the hidden monster that reared its ugly head whenever it so pleased. Only, it wasn't her monster. This was humiliation.

Her eyes fell to her chartreuse gown, reminding her of Marion. How might she handle the attention? Surely, the Mistress would have relished the opportunity to be honored before the members of Sequis's Court. If Resi was to be believed as a free woman, she'd have to go to great lengths to pretend.

She bent for a curtsy, then smiled demurely, reminding herself again and again of Marion's delicate mannerisms among her friends. She hunched her shoulders forward, clutching her heart in a gesture of gratitude and hoping she looked as if she'd always belonged amongst the free. Some members of Court smiled at the new arrival's humble display. Others were unbothered and continued sipping from their flutes. Many looked intrigued by this mysterious newcomer. What wasn't surprising, however, was the reaction of the many Codian women in the room; most tried to conceal their jealousy for Sequis's admiration by curtsying with a devious look behind their eyes.

"A splendid evening for you, Miss Kensington. I can only imagine your excitement," said an enthusiastic Lee as he offered his arm.

Frantic, Resi took it. "There are no words," she said, and for the first time in hours, she knew she was speaking the truth.

Lee began to lead her to a large rectangular table placed in the center of the room, one decorated with white pillar candles and cream-colored flowers. Lee took her to a chair near the middle of the table. Momentarily, Resi was grateful she wasn't seated in some position of honor. There was a chance she might be able to spend the remainder of the evening unnoticed, or at least, unmentioned.

Moments later, every member of Court was seated. With breath held, the crowd watched the Governor stride from his throne to the table. Following him were three members of the Eastern Guard. Together, the three counted before pulling out the massive chair at the head of the table to seat him. Their breath staggered as they placed it back down on the floor. Sequis took his place, then pulled his chair in on his own, forgetting to thank the three guards as they sulked off.

"Begin," Sequis said simply. At his request, a parade of 'Lick men dressed in red uniforms came out the double doors, each with their own pewter tray. One by one, they settled behind the chair of each guest, then served them over the left shoulder in perfect unison.

Resi ate her meal quietly, remembering the way in which Marion had dined with Luther on the morning of his arrival. She kept her serviette in her lap and tried her best to never let an elbow hit the table, all the while admiring the many people to her right and left. An older couple across the table was kind enough to congratulate her on her high honor amongst the Court. Many others, however, kept their distance, only eyeing her from behind their raised glasses.

After dinner there was to be dancing, which pleased many of the guests. Resi, however, asked Lee if it would be appropriate for her to see herself to her chambers now that dinner was over. The day had been tasking, and Lee indicated that he'd inform the Governor of her retirement.

She gave another curtsy, then turned for the exit, but not before glancing to where Sequis lingered at the other end of the room. He was surrounded by Codian women, their fans flapping, their cheeks red from the Rowgar. She was surprised to find him already looking at her, his face sullen, maybe even disappointed. She smiled at him, and he smiled back, his eyes never wavering from her face. She then turned the corner into the hall and ran as fast as she could to her room. Once inside, she satisfactorily locked the door behind her and collapsed onto the bed in an exhausted heap.

———

MUCH OF THE next week was a blur: Each morning, Resi was wakened and readied herself in her quarters. She ate breakfast in privacy, then was brought to Sequis's parlor for a morning session. Once two hours had passed, Resi was dismissed for lunch, which she could take at her leisure in her room, near the kitchen, or her favorite, amongst the gardens. After lunch came a shorter session with Sequis, usually only an hour before he was whisked away by Luther or Lee for matters concerning the Ball. Then, Resi had free time to roam the grounds until dinner. She usually spent this part of the day on the balcony of her chambers, touching up elements of the portrait at her leisure and admiring the sea. It was imperative for her to take the brief time of solitude to collect her thoughts.

One evening, Lee had knocked at the door to check in on her progress. "Remarkable work, Miss Kensington," he'd said as he observed the beginning stages of color on canvas. Then after more observation, "If you'd rather use Sequis's study so you can work with the light at this time of day, I could hire a stand-in model when he's not available. Of course, no one will stand at Sequis's *height*," he laughed, "but we could arrange something to help you."

"It's quite alright," she assured him as she returned to her work. "Thank you for offering, but I enjoy working from the balcony."

Lee hovered over her as he further inspected the portrait. "You can paint from memory?" he asked.

She turned to him, bemused. "That's not normal?"

Lee's eyebrows raised as he laughed under his breath. He then turned for the door.

It hadn't occurred to Resi that a reputable artist painted any other way. From the very moment she'd first witnessed Sequis with his back leaned against the window and the vibrant swirl of color in the sky behind him, she'd locked the memory away into a bright and easily accessible place within her mind.

Contrary to his behavior during their first session, Sequis had grown quiet, almost anxious during their sessions. Every now and again, he'd offer some commentary concerning the nature of the weather as he looked out the window. Resi, more focused on her work than on conversation, would indicate for him to remain still and focused, and Sequis, amused by her bossiness, would settle into a contented laugh.

"Nice not to be in charge for a change," he'd said one morning. With much satisfaction, Resi had returned to her work, knowing he'd meant it.

Much of their time was spent in silence, for which Resi was grateful. It allowed her to focus on her skills and on the work in front of her. Marion had been right; she was a natural.

What was most evident was Sequis's desire to engage with her. Often, he'd wait until the fleeting moments when she was gathering her brushes to leave before he'd attempt to strike up a conversation. "You look awfully fetching today," he'd remark, or, "Wonderful afternoon to walk the cliffs," or, "You were in some other world there, weren't you?"

Their exchanges were always brief and pleasant, but there was a new nature of awkwardness to the way he addressed her. Maybe, she'd thought, he was too used to the company of men. Or possibly, their first meeting had left him feeling as if he'd shown too much of the softness of his underbelly. He was a ruler with a fierce reputation, but in the space of the parlor, he'd somehow become vulnerable, strangely likable in a way that made Resi question her own sanity. Sequis had been responsible for so much catastrophe, so much carnage and devastation in Ter. But whenever he engaged with her during their sessions, Resi found herself swelling with the kind of pride that usually came after receiving recognition from someone of a higher social importance; much like Marion's interaction with Luther upon his visit to the farmhold. Whether she wanted to admit it to herself or not, Resi had become dependent on daily attention from him, and found herself disappointed anytime Luther whisked him away from their portrait sessions. The notion of it all made it difficult not to smack herself anytime she faced her reflection in the mirror of her chambers at the end of a long day.

After their fifth session was completed, Resi noticed Sequis's face wilt when she went for the door. "Have a pleasant afternoon," he'd offered to her.

She looked back to him confidently, then smiled at the thought of taking her afternoon to stroll in the gardens. "Same to you, sir."

There had seemed to be something more he'd wished to say, but he'd avoided it. He had given her a placid smile before he'd brushed past her and joined Lee in the hall.

The most laborious time of day came at dinner, when Resi was forced to chat up foreign dignitaries from overseas or spend time with Codian women who only approached her to ask her about Sequis. Though strained by these conversations, Resi was always on the lookout for Luther, who it seemed was consistently on the move in preparation for the Ball.

She was lucky enough to come across him as he left the dining hall late one evening. She practically had to chase him down as he went for the exit.

"Sir, I wish to speak with you," she called to him.

He sneered. "Get in line."

"It will only be a moment," she begged as she ran after him. "I—" she faltered, then whispered, "I can't lie to Sequis. Not anymore. He needs to know the truth about me."

Luther scoffed. "Don't be ridiculous," he said over his shoulder. "What Sequis doesn't know won't kill him. Trust me. I've known him a long time. And besides, you should be relishing your time here. Mingle with the other guests of Court. Play the part," he winked, then stalked off, leaving Resi all the more anxious in his wake.

Depleted, she tried to hide herself in the shade of a tall tropical plant. But, as it always went when she was alone at dinner, two Codian women, one plump and the other thin, spotted her and trapped her in their conversation.

"I heard Sequis is throwing the Ball in an attempt to further win over the people," whispered the plump one, her breasts bulging out of her dress.

"I've heard he plans on making some sort of announcement at the Ball," said the other, a skinny debutante who seemed particularly obsessed by the topic of their conversation. "It could be that he plans on taking a wife."

The other sighed. "Don't taunt a poor woman."

The thin woman smirked, then shrugged her shoulders. "For all we know, he could be scouting the Court for a wife right this very minute." Both women leaned to look past Resi to where Sequis sat on the other side of the room. The Governor was detached from any form of amusement, lounging on his throne. The skinny woman smirked. "Lucky chair."

Both women giggled behind their fans before turning to Resi. Desperate as she was to make a bolt for it, she couldn't.

"You're with him every day, yes?" the plump one asked.

Resi nodded silently, then took a fizzy sip of her Rowgar.

"Surely, you must have some knowledge of what he's looking for in a woman...tall, fair...maybe a little fuller around the waist?"

"You wish!" the thin one snickered.

Again, the ladies fell into a tangle of laughter and snorts. Like two hyenas, they playfully pawed at each other as they continued to giggle at their own ridiculous jest. Resi took their distraction as a cue; they didn't even notice her turning for the door.

The gardens were a welcome relief to Resi anytime she felt the need to get away, and tonight was no exception. She couldn't help but be amused by the fascination surrounding Sequis. The women of Court were always feigning some sort of injury or dropping handkerchiefs to get his attention. Sequis, however, seemed consistently bothered by their efforts, always resisting their advances with an excuse of needing to be elsewhere or by simply nodding and walking away.

On more than one occasion, Resi had noticed Sequis staring at her from across the hall, but never for very long. It was as if he was making sure she was pleasantly entertained without ever having to do any of the entertaining himself. He kept his distance at Court, only mingling amongst his guards or stealing away to meetings with Luther. He often lingered in the shadows, as if there were some wall that existed in the space between himself and his subjects. There was much on his mind, of that Resi was certain.

As the days came and went, Resi was pleased to see the portrait coming to life. It was taking longer to come together than she had expected, but she wasn't bothered to stay longer at the Tristeland than was originally allotted. She wanted this portrait to be unlike anything the public would expect, and she would go to whatever lengths she could to make sure Sequis didn't see the rendering until it was completed. Further, she felt herself beginning to slowly engage with the heat inside of herself. Day after day, it proved itself loyal, and not in the kind of way that was threatening. For years, she'd questioned it, fearing that whatever lingered under the surface had poor intentions for her well-being. But as the portrait progressed, the heat had become as dizzying and intoxicating to Resi as her nightly pour of Rowgar. Maybe she was always meant to discover painting. Maybe, just maybe, it was the cure for her little monster.

Ever curious, Sequis attempted multiple times to glimpse a peek of Resi's work, but in true artistic preservation, she would shield the canvas with a sheet before he ever had a chance to see.

"Forgive me, but wouldn't you wish to see the finished portrait alongside your guests at the Ball?" Resi asked playfully one afternoon as she packed up her brushes to be washed.

"The suspense is killing me, Taresia," he said, feigning agony by stabbing himself in the heart with an invisible dagger. "Any idea of how much longer?"

"Patience, sir. It'll be any day now."

Out of the corner of her eye, Resi saw a nervous smile dance across his mouth.

That evening, Resi snuck out of the dining hall and stole away to the gardens, desperate to escape from the small talk of the Court. She hated the boasts of wealth, the name-dropping, the frivolity of it all. Glad of at least a temporary reprieve, she walked the paths, enjoying the newly cool air of autumn on her face before coming to the cliffs. She let her eyes roam the face of the rock; it was a jagged descent down to the shore far below.

"You make escaping look so easy."

Resi nearly jumped as she turned to find Sequis, his hair tied back, standing beside her. How had he managed to follow her out?

"I might have to say the same about you," she replied, relaxing a bit. "And you're a *giant*."

A chortle escaped him, and Resi found herself taken aback by its friendly sound.

"Didn't you know? One of the perks of owning a sizeable estate is knowing all the secret corridors and trapdoors on the property and never telling anyone else about them," he mused quietly. "I get the sense you're not one for Court."

Feeling caught, and suddenly aware of how alone they really were, she took a hesitant step away from him. This spot along the cliffs. This *place*. Blood had been shed here. "Is it that obvious?"

His mouth quirked wryly. "I find it equally as heinous."

She tried to fight the words that wanted to come out, but the Fet from dinner made her bolder than usual. "If you think you're doing a good job of hiding it, you might want to reevaluate," she said, smirking slightly.

He grinned devilishly, then his face grew thoughtful. For a time, he was quiet. "Perhaps I'm too used to a lonely existence, being as I am," he finally said.

Surprised, Resi finally turned from the cliffs to look at him. Pensive, he faced the rock face, his eyes glued to the black horizon, his shoulders wide and broad, towering above her own. The mural in the front foyer came to her mind, and her heat flickered from the inside out.

"*Being as you are*?" she asked as she instigated walking back towards the gardens.

Amused, he raised an eyebrow, then followed her. "I'm one of a kind—*not quite man, not quite giant,* as they say."

In as many times as Resi had heard the phrase repeated in the stories surrounding Sequis's wartime escapades, she'd yet to hear it spoken with such dismay. For the first time since meeting him, she felt a wave of pity the size of Ter wash over her for Sequis.

"I grew up alone," she offered. "It's why I like the quiet."

He took a steadying breath, his eyes alight with interest. "You're an orphan?"

Orphan—a term that had long echoed in Resi's mind, but one she couldn't accept no matter how angry she'd grown at her parents. "Abandoned."

The breeze whipped around them, somehow fusing the air with more tension than was already there. Resi couldn't look at him confidently, but out of her peripheral vision, she could make out lines of Sequis's face twisting in disgust.

"No child should ever be made to feel alone," he declared.

She felt a slight irritation at his efforts to console her. The number of Aliquian families that had been separated and displaced across the regions during his time of rule seemed to nullify his sentiment completely. "I suppose that's the one and only thing that someone like you and someone like me could possibly share in common," she sighed. "Loneliness."

"It's universal," he said with a dark laugh, clearly missing the subtle anger under her words. He turned to her. "But I would argue that there's much more that we share in common. At least, one can hope."

At that, he reached past her and swiped a small white flower from a nearby tree in the gardens. Gently, he placed it behind her ear with a smile.

Resi felt her breath catch. This was not how she wanted things to go. She needed to leave, *now*. Frantic, she took another small step back as his eyes searched her face. "Goodnight, sir," she stammered.

"May I walk you?" he offered earnestly, his hand extended to her.

Like sudden rainfall, a new bravery came over her, one that felt rooted in the heat inside of her. "Sir, I think it best we maintain a professional relationship until I finish my work."

"Professional?" he repeated.

"Yes...I take my work very seriously."

His eyes dazzled over her face as the wind settled. "But do you take *me* seriously, Taresia?"

She watched Sequis's face drop in disappointment before she curtsied. "Goodnight, sir." She then turned her back on him, and fought with her thoughts as she raced back to her chambers. Once inside, she locked the door. Theo had warned her that Sequis might make a pass, but she didn't dare believe that she would struggle so much to push him away, and not because of temptation. That feeling waged war within her every time he drew near to her. Her will to push him away stemmed from the fear she felt of his unyielding need to possess what he didn't already own.

The days passed uncomfortably in her following sessions with him. It was obvious to Resi that Sequis was tense with embarrassment at being turned down by her, but Resi appeared unbothered. She relished in those two days of focus and discipline, and she felt proud of herself for holding her ground against the more carnal part of herself, a side of her personality she'd only recently become acquainted with.

Much as she held resentment for the Governor, for the man who had wielded his power so selfishly over the region, she felt forcibly drawn in by the way he kept meeting her gaze during their final sessions, and she loathed herself deeply for it. There was a difference between lust and love; even she knew that. But she couldn't fight off the hunger in Sequis's eyes as she finalized the portrait.

She wakened one night with a jolt after dreaming of her first memory of seeing his face dimly lit in his parlor. A feverish spell kept her snuggly tucked between sleep and consciousness all night, in a place where her obsession with shape, light, and color danced freely. Eventually, she escaped to her balcony to feel the cool air on her face with only the thought of Sequis, so raw and unguarded during their first session, and how it had inspired her. His belief in her talent had awakened her artistry with a vengeance. She ached and groaned with these new feelings alongside the heat in her stomach. All the while, she fought off Theo's words of warning to her as they repeated over and over again with the sound of the sea clashing against the cliffs until darkness became light.

She was relieved when the portrait was finally completed just a few days out from the Ball. Astonished at her own work, she looked upon the rendering while Sequis posed unaware by the window. For that brief moment, she tried her best to appreciate what had taken place in the space of this parlor. All of the work, the stress of Court, the *lying*: it had all brought her here, to this simple moment of pride. She looked upon Sequis's gleaming blond hair and enormous stature one final time before standing and covering the completed portrait. With a newfound sense of purpose, she packed her brushes one by one, wondering when, if ever, she'd have the chance to paint again.

"Done," she told him.

Sequis nodded only once, his face shifting between distress and elation. Hiding himself, he began to button his shirt. "Miss Kensington," he said suddenly. "I can't begin to express the depth of my gratitude for your service."

Resi turned to her brushes. "The pleasure was mine, sir."

"If there were some way I could convey—"

"Oh, really, it's not—"

"No!" he bellowed. The parlor quaked. "These past few weeks have—" he nervously shifted his weight. "It would very much please me if you would accompany me to dinner. Tonight. As a show of my gratitude."

She turned back to him only to see his face shriveled at the brows. Was he actually worried she might say no?

"That's very kind of you, sir," she replied, noticing the relief that washed across his face. "I look forward to sitting with you at Court."

He stopped her, taking a step closer. The room grew darker in his shadow. "You don't understand. I mean to ask you to dinner, with me. Tonight, in the gardens." Then, a clear of his throat. "Alone."

Resi suddenly felt every impulse to disappear from the Tristeland, from existence, all together. "Oh," she replied.

"I thought we might talk more," he said charmingly.

"Sir, this isn't appropriate—"

He grabbed her hand, and she froze. " You asked that we keep our relationship professional until you were through with your work, Taresia. As far as I can tell..." his hand motioned to her packed paintbrushes. He smiled a dashing, boyish grin. Resi hated to see that it suited him perfectly.

"I'll have Lee arrange everything," he assured her. "Say yes."

Resi shuddered, wishing it were easier to draw away from him, to remember the war stories, the tales from the fields surrounding the handsome giant's mysterious escapades with women from far and wide. But, Aliquian or free, Resi knew that any woman before and after her would have the same reply. There was no alternative. "It would bring me great honor, sir."

"Please," he said, a smile lifting the side of his winsome face, "I like it when you call me Sequis."

CHAPTER 10

THE PLAN

Returning to her suite, Resi was greeted by the cold bursts of autumn air through the open doors of her balcony. In a panicked rush, she ran to close them, then found herself in a daze on the edge of the bed. Too many questions bounced around in her head.

"He's making some sort of announcement at the ball."

"I hear he's taking a bride."

Quickly, she stood, then found herself yanking at the back of her dress. She couldn't breathe. She needed it off. She needed the air on her skin to remind her that she wasn't living in some parallel reality where it seemed everything was upside down.

"Ma'am?" a voice suddenly alerted her from outside the door. Her chamber 'Lick. When she let herself in, Resi turned to hide the brimming tears in her eyes.

"Oh," the woman said, "I'm sorry, Miss. I can come back."

She went to leave, but Resi ran after her to hold the door. "Help me with my dress?"

The woman nodded, her eyes wide and unsure. Resi led her to the closet, wiping her face of the tears that couldn't help but spill onto her cheeks.

"I'll need something elegant for tonight," Resi managed to say.

She cringed, hearing a tinge of Marion Offenheimer's condescension in her own request. The realization of it made her want to crawl out of her skin.

The woman didn't speak. She simply reached inside the closet and pulled out a lavender gown. It was adorned with small white flowers along the neckline, and a beautiful cream sash rested at the waist.

"I noticed this one when I brought them in," the woman spoke softly.

"You picked these?" Resi asked.

The woman shook her head. "The Governor put the order out for a month's worth of gowns. I just picked the ones I thought were best."

"Well," Resi said with a faint smile. "This one is perfect."

Delicately, the woman aided Resi out of her day dress. Resi noticed that her touch was lighter than normal.

"Would you mind telling me your name?" Resi asked.

"Ana, Miss."

Resi remembered a woman who'd been brought to the Offenheimers with the same name. She'd been from Pangus, the northernmost region in the Sept-Regions. "You're from the North?" she asked.

"Yes," the woman said after some hesitation. "From a small village I presume you've not heard of."

Resi smiled to Ana over her shoulder. "Do you ever miss it? Your home?"

Ana held the expansive fabric of the lavender gown as if it were breakable. "Every day, Miss," she answered.

All was quiet as Ana helped Resi into the dress and quickly pinned her hair into a loose style. Soon enough, she was at the door, but this time, she paused to smile at Resi before leaving. It was a step in the right direction, but Resi still felt an ache in her heart for a true confidante in the midst of all this mess. She'd always shied away from making friends. But without Mags by her side, she'd realized just how lonely her life had been without pursuing friendships with those her own age.

As she looked upon her reflection and admired it, Resi felt her pride snap like a twig. She looked too much like Marion in her fussy gowns, too much like every other woman vying for Sequis's attention at Court. She needed to find Luther and demand the truth be told to Sequis, no matter what the cost. If rumors of Sequis's desire for a bride were true, then her time at the Tristeland was leading her down a road she could no further walk.

Determined, she gave herself one last look in the mirror before pulling out the two short golden strands at the top of her head. *That's better.* It was decided; after her evening sessions with Sequis, Luther usually greeted him at his chambers. With any luck, she'd intersect him.

She exited her chambers and turned towards the hall. Desperately, she clipped towards the other end of the Estate, passing a group of curious Codian women headed to the dining hall along the way. She came to the foyer, then the opposite wing, then stopped dead in her tracks when she spotted Luther ahead in the darkening hall. She'd been lucky. Briskly, he stalked towards Sequis's wing. He was flipping through a giant stack of papers.

"Sir!" she called out, then spanned the distance between them.

Startled, he turned back to her. His mossy yellow teeth showed themselves in the form of a weak, unpleasant smile. "Miss *Kensington*," he said as he folded his arms. "Shouldn't you be in the dining hall with all the others?"

"Did Sequis not tell you?"

"Tell me what?" he said, his gaze narrowing on her.

Resi couldn't help it; she looked at the top page in his hand. It appeared to be an account of who would be in attendance at the Ball, a list of surnames ranging from N to P. She scanned for Offenheimer, but was taken aback when she didn't see it listed. Marion and Theo? Not invited?

"Someone's nosey," said Luther, yanking the papers back and shuffling them in his grip.

"Advisor," Resi begged. "I can't lie to Sequis. Not anymore."

Luther turned his back on her. He continued down the hall. "How much does it take for me to make myself clear?" he snarled.

Quickly, he looked behind her, making sure no one approached. "I've asked you to keep this matter private, 'Lick."

"Sir, this is a matter of Sequis's happiness, not mine."

Luther stopped in his tracks. "Since when do you care about the Governor's *happiness*?" he inquired, his gaze skeptical. Then, just as quickly, a realization crossed his eyes. A high-pitched laugh settled in the back of his throat. "You wouldn't be the first 'Lick girl to fall in love with him."

Resi could feel her fire rising within her, the strange feeling of tension that could explode at any second. "You underestimate the allegiance I have to my people?" she burst. "After all that you've put me through?"

"Oh, I'm *sorry*," Luther started. "Please do forgive me for gifting you two weeks' time to gallivant as a free woman."

She steadied herself. "How free could I possibly be if I'm being forced to lie?"

Luther's mouth twisted. "Let's remember that it was *I* who gave you this opportunity. And I who could just as easily take it away," he seethed.

"Funny," she said, her hands finding her hips. "I recall that it was Sequis who requested me. You were only the person to have passed on my portrait to him."

She watched as Luther's blood boiled beneath his skin. He fought to find words, but couldn't.

"He has asked me to dine with him," she continued. "*Alone.*"

Fancifully, he sighed. "So, the widely respected Governor fell for the homely farm laborer...How sweet."

"You think I'm making this up?"

He laughed. "You expect me to believe that after two weeks, the most sought-after man in Ter is besotted by the likes of *you*? After all the women he's bedded?"

Resi shuddered, her mind going to the rumpled sheets in Sequis's chambers. "I wouldn't have said anything if there was even the slightest chance it was untrue."

Now angry, Luther leered over her. A dark shadow crossed over his pale eyes. "You 'Licks are all the same. Always making up silly stories and fantasies from the past to play out in your weak little minds."

Resi took a step forward at him, feeling the heat swell in her belly. "Wasn't it you who conjured up a fake identity for me?"

All at once, Luther snapped. With giant force, he grabbed Resi by the collar, then threw her against the adjoining wall. His voice went icy cold.

"Who do you think Sequis will believe when the time comes, hm?! The man who risked his life for him in battle? Or the mousy 'Lick girl parading around in Patrian woman's clothes?"

Resi gasped on her own breath as Luther's hand slowly wrapped around her throat. It somehow made sense now—the lying, the secrecy. He was hiding something. But what, she didn't know.

"What are you not telling him?" she managed to choke out.

Luther's eyes widened. "You would be wise, 'Lick filth, to keep those pouty lips tightly shut," he ordered. "If not, I'll see to it that you're thrown from the cliffs, even if I have to do it myself."

Resi's vision was closing in. She was drowning in her own head, falling asleep with the fear of never waking up. But inside, the heat was boiling to the surface.

Then suddenly, Luther reared back in pain. He looked down to where his palms had pressed against her throat; they were burned red. Without a trace of surprise, his eyes met hers, and a sinister smile crept over his face.

Her heat...it had finally revealed itself to another.

Just then, Commander Lee came around the corner. Resi took the moment to catch her breath.

Luther looked up at the Commander as if he'd just committed a serious crime, then stood to his feet. He smoothed his hands over his suit coat. "Please tell the Governor to cancel his dinner plans with Miss Kensington," he to ordered the Commander. "He has pressing matters to attend to concerning the Ball." Then Luther pushed back his brassy hair and stalked off down the hallway.

Lee, however, couldn't seem to tear himself away, his eyes lingering over Resi. They brimmed with questions.

"Now, Lee!" Luther called.

Confused, Lee turned after him with his head low, his shoulders drooping.

Resi sat against the wall for a time, lifeless, transfixed by the one simple truth she'd now confirmed since Marion had brought her in from the fields.

Her plans, big or small, never seemed to work.

HOURS LATER, Resi gently placed a hand at her bruised throat, feeling the ache of its swelling. The same hand then fell to her stomach. Searing pain forced her to yank it away. *White-hot.*

After her run-in with Luther, she'd locked herself into her chambers. It was now the middle of the night, and try as she might to find sleep, she couldn't. She was too terrified of him reappearing to drag her to the cliffs.

As she lay wide-eyed in her bed, she let her hand run along the heat of her belly. For so long, she had pictured the monster as a rage-filled enemy and a constant annoyance, a reminder of how her parents had abandoned her. In the last few weeks, as she had begun to relate to it differently, she had wondered if it could possibly be what fueled her artistic passion. But perhaps, she reasoned, it was even more than that. Maybe it always had been.

Her mind suddenly floated back to the Offenheimers, to the moment she'd first noticed Corey looking at her. His eyes had been so soft. So warm. Hadn't Sequis looked at her the same way in the dim light of the parlor? What on earth could she do about him—or about Luther, for that matter?

In a whirl, she ripped off the covers and opened the balcony doors to the breezy evening. Her bare legs grew bumps as she tentatively peeked over the rail. It was possible, she thought, to end it all. Right here. Right now. She could have the escape she'd wanted for so long.

She could let the darkness of night consume her fully. All it would take was one jump.

Shakily, she climbed over the rail and stood at the brink. Her will was the only thing holding her back from falling to the darkened stone below, and though she desired the chance to reach for a free life, she didn't see a future of it, not since she'd been yanked from the fields by Marion, not after everything that had happened since she'd arrived at the Tristeland. Now that Luther was wise to whatever dark mutation brimmed within her, it was only a matter of time before she was punished, or worse, publicly executed, for such a crime. Mags, she hoped, would understand if she chose her own way out of this mess. In time, her wound of grief would scab over.

Resi clutched her breath and lifted one foot from the balcony. Curiously, she let it hover over the air for a brief second, wondering if death would take her in like a friend.

But then, past the garden wall came voices, muffled and deep. Two darkened silhouettes turned the corner of a hedge and continued walking the path. Immediately, Resi gripped the rail and threw herself back to safety, clutching her chest and gasping for air as she hid herself against the cold stone of the balcony. The voices grew louder over the growl of the distant ocean.

"You can't continue with this. You're acting crazy," said a man.

"If he doesn't show the people now, then when?" said the other with a shriveled tone that Resi could place out of a thousand. Luther.

"You can't be so sure of that. The people worship him," replied the other.

"But they don't *fear* him. He's become soft, too approachable. If they don't see him for what he really is, we lose everything!" snapped Luther. "All these years together, all the plans and the hard work will have been for nothing! He needs to be provoked. It's far past time."

"You realize you're exposing the public? People could die!"

"That's the point, you idiot! They need to see it with their own eyes."

There was a short silence, followed by the strike of a match. Cautiously, Resi looked over the ledge. Nearest the cliffs, two men lingered in the darkness. Their voices bounced off the stone of the gardens. She watched the flame of the match light a pipe. In the glow, she saw Luther puffing at it with forceful repetition. With him was Lee; his tall frame paced back and forth along the gravel.

"Is this about his last trip to see Romilius?" Lee asked.

Romilius, Resi repeated in her head. The Patrian King that resided in Turbus, the same king that had recruited Sequis to lead his army all those years ago before he'd seized Ter.

Luther sighed, bringing his long fingers through his thin mane of hair. "It didn't go as anticipated. Sequis needs to move now or else the public will lose interest in him."

"And what of the girl? How does she fit into all of this?" Lee demanded.

Resi put a hand over her mouth to cover the gasp that inevitably slipped its way out.

"She's asking questions," Luther snarled as he released a chimney's worth of smoke from his mouth. "It's thanks to good timing the Ball is only days away."

"Yes, well, she's smarter than she looks."

Luther's face twisted as if he were trying to hold something back, but couldn't. "She's *Aliquian*, you oaf."

Lee took a step back, shocked. "And you brought her *here*? For what?"

Luther simply shrugged, then doubled over in laughter. The reaction sent a chill up Resi's spine, as if her demise were as simple to him as the winning trick at the end of a card game. Once he'd calmed himself, he looked at Lee with a peculiar glint in his eye. "She's gifted, Lee. She shows signs."

Resi felt the flush of her heat work its way from her stomach to her cheeks; the monster's rage was growing. As she waited expectantly for Lee to reply, she was suddenly startled by the presence of a third member of the party, someone shadowed beyond the nearest hedge. He was completely hidden, just a tall silhouette in the darkness wearing an oddly-shaped hat.

"There's no doubt that she's a contender," the stranger's voice called out. It was quiet, husky.

"A contender?!" Lee barked. "What in the Sept-Regions, Luther? Are you planning some sort of a duel?"

Luther snickered. "If we're lucky, it won't have to go that far."

The shadowed man joined in Luther's merriment by laughing deeply. "She may show signs, Luther, but she's weak. She'll be no match against him."

Luther sighed, then folded his thin arms across his body. "This all has to remain quiet. She has to be revealed at the right time. I've planned everything down to the second."

Lee pointed a finger out and poked it into Luther's chest. "You'll be liable for her death," his voice quaked.

Resi's pulse ripened. She couldn't believe what she was hearing.

In an effort to keep his cool, Luther looked down at Lee's hand and lifted it away as if it were a breadcrumb. "Nothing a weighty check and a replacement 'Lick for the Offenheimers can't fix."

Resi had to remind herself to breathe. She wanted to blink them all away, to wake up from this horrible nightmare. But it was all real, *too* real. Luther was up to something, and she only blamed herself for having fallen prey to his schemes. All the while, she kept hearing his words:

She shows signs.

"And Sequis?" asked the shadowed man.

"All is falling into place," Luther giggled. "According to our artist, he's positively smitten."

There it was. It had all been prearranged. Resi shivered. Luther had wanted this to happen, had wanted Sequis to meet her. But why?

Lee shifted his weight on the gravel, his face bothered. "He'll be crushed when he learns who she really is. He cares for her, Luther. He's spoken of—"

"Ah, see, that's the fun part," Luther interjected as he released another trail of smoke. "Once I break the news to him that his dear Miss Kensington has *lied to us all* about the true nature of her identity, he'll never be able to wed her. It'll anger him enough to see to it himself that she is..." he turned his head to the side, trying to choose the best word, "*disposed* of. Then, we'll get our show."

"She's been nothing more than a pawn," Lee said blankly.

"But a very talented little pawn," piped Luther. "Couldn't have picked a better 'Lick for the part if I tried."

The shadowed man widened his stance. "If we're correct, she could put up a good fight," he said.

"And if she does?" Lee asked.

Resi felt a pang in her heart. She was certain she heard a drop of hope in him.

"All the better," Luther replied. "The second the people witness his strength against hers, his name will be all the more respected. Let's not forget—there's nothing Codians love more than a good show."

"Sequis needs to be kept away from her, even if he objects," said the shadowed voice.

"And she," Luther paused as he dumped the pipe and squished his foot over the ashes, "needs to be watched."

All Lee could do was stare vacantly at Luther, his gaze unsure.

"Are we clear?" Luther confirmed.

Lee hesitated, then nodded. The three then trotted off down the gravel in silence.

Fiercely, Resi's hands gripped her nightgown. *She shows signs.*

All of the secrets, all of the preconceived plans—they were all in an attempt to put together some sort of display. A show. And Sequis was none the wiser.

The fire leapt in her stomach, its embers and flames sparking a new sort of determination within her. She wouldn't jump. She wouldn't run. No.

The heat within—it was evidence of something greater within, something she could possibly learn or control. Something *ancient*. Somehow, she'd always known this, always feared this. Like her grief, she'd buried it deep beneath the earth. But even now, it couldn't be ignored. Perhaps the others in the fields had been right to alienate her. Perhaps her parents were right to have left her behind. Even Luther had known she was different from the moment he'd picked up Scottis's portrait from the tip of his boot. This monster, this fire, was her curse and her destiny, and somehow, it connected to her greatest joy of painting. Her artistry was responsible for capturing Luther's attention that day on the farmhold. It was what had brought her to the Tristeland, what had brought her to Sequis.

The fire bit at the hand resting on her stomach. Quickly, she pulled it away, noticing the redness of a fresh burn on her palm. There wasn't much time before the heat might leave her, might destroy something more than just the inside of her hand.

Then a crazy plan, one diabolical enough to actually work, suddenly came to mind. Quickly, she closed the balcony doors behind her. If she was expected to play the role of a Patrian, then she would. Without a beat, she raced to her bedside table, removed a piece of parchment from the top drawer, and began to address a letter to the Offenheimer Farmhold.

CHAPTER 11

THE DRESS

There was talk that an impending storm was to arrive the evening of the Governor's Ball, and as Resi trudged to her balcony the following morning, she feared the rumors to be true. Dark, gloomy clouds hung over the sea like a bad omen.

Resi had remained awake for most of the night, running the proceeding days in her mind in a torturous loop. She was still lost in thought when Ana let herself in. In her small hands was a silver breakfast tray and draping over her arm was a large garment bag. As she went to place them both on the bed, her eyes went wide.

"There's a note for you, Miss Kensington," the woman paused to gulp. "From the Governor."

Resi's eyes darted to the tray. A cream envelope rested amongst a beautiful array of jelly-filled pastries and fruits.

"I have this to send out too," Resi said as she handed her an addressed envelope. She nodded to the door. "Please, make it discreet."

Disappointed, Ana meekly made her way back to the hall. Once the door latched tightly shut, Resi snatched the envelope from Sequis and ripped it open.

Dearest Taresia,

I cannot begin to convey my regret for canceling our dinner last evening. If I'm being honest, it was Luther that demanded it. The man is insistent that every detail, even down to the exact placement of the dessert spoons, be perfect for tomorrow.

"Yeah, *I'll bet*," Resi said aloud.

I can only hope you will forgive me and allow me to make it up to you in one way or another. I must say, I find myself exhibiting the strangest behavior in your presence. The truth is, I feel rather clumsy around you, Taresia. The hours spent with you this month have unhinged me, and equally as such, have healed me. Your humility and forthrightness are qualities I've come to admire. To have known you, and to send you away after the Ball displeases me terribly. The Tristeland can be your home if you wish it to be. You can paint with a view of the cliffs, and I can make you happy here.

Please do me the great honor of accompanying me to the Ball tomorrow. With you on my arm, I'll be sure to be the envy of every man in the room.

Yours, Sequis
PS Stay. Please stay.

In a daze, Resi's hand fell to the bed, the letter in tow. Her eyes hesitantly drifted to the garment bag. She opened it; the dress inside was the purest white and was embroidered with diamonds and lace. The skirt was narrow and fluid, flowing from top to bottom like a wave. It was simple, elegant; different than the gowns she'd worn to Court.

Resi felt her stomach drop. It looked too much like a wedding gown.

Half an hour later, Ana knocked at the door again, then let herself in. It was a welcome distraction for Resi. The two worked in silence to dress her in a pale-pink day dress.

"Miss Kensington," Ana said as she sat Resi down at the vanity. "I hope you don't mind, but, the Advisor has asked that I show you around the grounds this morning. I thought you might be up for a small tour before the rains come in."

Resi agreed, knowing Luther would have had every guard on the lookout for the two of them. Still, she was grateful to stretch her legs. Some fresh air and new scenery would do her well.

After Ana finished the final touches to her hair, the two set off for the gardens. The Estate was buzzing with preparations for the grand event. Members of the Eastern Guard yelled orders to each other over the arrival of flowers, linens, and Fet from the region of Rowan. 'Lick women could be spotted changing over the bed sheets in many of the guest chambers for those staying the night.

As they neared the gardens, Resi noticed a guard on their tail. He lingered back, feigning disinterest in their conversation. Still, Resi couldn't help but be paranoid. It appeared Luther already had eyes and ears on her.

Ana, however, was ecstatic to be asked from her usual tasks. Her quiet demeanor was replaced by a youthful lightness, as made evident by the occasional skip that worked its way into her legs. In the heart of the gardens, she went into a deep explanation of the history behind the redesign of the space each year. Resi couldn't help but be impressed, pausing every so often to inquire how Ana had come to know so much about the Estate.

"I'm no historian, Miss," Ana spoke as they walked the perimeter of the garden nearest the sea. "But I try to know as much as I can about my place of residence. So few 'Licks do."

Resi knew the feeling. So many times that summer, she'd prided herself on her growing knowledge of the boundaries of the Offenheimer Farmhold. Ana, too, was smart enough to have learned every aspect of the Tristeland's grounds, and she used that information to her advantage.

"You must know of a few hiding places," Resi whispered with a glint in her eye.

Ana looked at her skeptically. "A few. There's the passageways beneath the Estate, hidden paths the 'Licks take to remain unseen during events."

Regretfully, Resi looked to her feet as they continued walking. She'd gone too far, inquired too much. She knew she couldn't have adversaries here, not while Luther had a guard on their heels.

Then, an idea came.

"Want to have some fun?" Resi asked Ana, peeking quickly over her shoulder to where the guard waited near the center fountain.

"Miss?" Ana said, her eyes following Resi's. Once she caught on, she smiled.

Quickly, they rounded a tall hedge, then hid behind a stone bench along the cliffs. They both covered their mouths, trying to hide their laughter as they waited. Moments later, the guard appeared from around the hedge to come after them. Confused and out of breath, he turned to his right and left, his eyes panning the cliffs for any sign of them. When he didn't spot them, he ran off from where he came.

"Did you see his face?!" Ana cackled as Resi pulled her from their hiding spot.

Perhaps it was the crisp fresh air. Perhaps it was being in the company of another Aliquian. Either way, Resi allowed herself to feel the weight of the last few days leave her, even if just for a moment.

"Miss Kensington."

She and Ana snapped to attention as a monstrous shadow grew on the garden path. Sequis. In the shade of the afternoon, the angles of his bone structure appeared as perfectly carved from stone. He was dressed in a loose white shirt and trousers, much like what he'd worn for his portrait sessions. The skin under his eyes was blue; fatigued from lack of sleep.

"I'm sorry," he apologized. "Didn't mean to frighten you."

Immediately, Resi curtsied. Her eyes danced about the cliffs for any guards on the prowl. But none revealed themselves. She could hardly believe it. They were alone.

Surprised, Sequis's eyes went to Ana. Within seconds, the woman curtsied and rounded the hedge back to the gardens. Desperate for a way out, Resi looked after her as she disappeared from view.

"Forgive me for sneaking up on you," Sequis said, his smile widening.

"It's quite alright," she replied. "We were just, uh, playing around."

Awkwardly, he shuffled his massive boots on the stone path. His eyes couldn't meet hers. "Must be nice to have that kind of freedom."

They stood there for a few seconds, Resi toying with the fabric of her dress near her warming stomach. The irony of such a statement coming from him certainly didn't miss her.

"I don't have much time," he went on, his emerald eyes darting over the hedge. "Seems I can't get away from Luther for two seconds without being chased down."

"I understand," she answered. *All too well.*

"You received the letter?"

Resi nodded, feeling a thumping in her chest. "I did."

"And?"

"Sir, I—"

"Sequis, please," he reiterated, taking a step towards her. "Sorry, I'm..." he laughed again, this one leaning towards maniacal. "I don't usually act so strangely in the presence of women."

Resi waited in his shadow, feeling every voice inside of her scream.

"I'm sorry for the other night," he said. He rolled his eyes, then swept a hand through two loose strands of his golden hair. "Luther."

"So much to be done," she sighed.

"I wanted more time with you," he spoke candidly. "Before the Ball. Seems we have to settle for secret rendezvous just to bump into each other."

Resi cringed. "So it seems."

"I dared to think you were avoiding me," he said, his eyes darkening.

Resi's stomach dropped. Sequis knew so little of his Advisor, what he was capable of. All this time, he'd assumed Resi was being distant, keeping her space. When really, it was Luther who was pulling the strings in his own favor, keeping them both busy. Or, in Resi's case, *watched.*

"Oh, no," she said, her head shaking wildly. "Not at all, sir—"

He caught her eye. "Please...I like hearing you say my name."

She sighed, letting her nerves come out with the air in her lungs. "It's hard for me to get used to saying."

He took another hesitant step forward. "Taresia, I know this is sudden. It's sudden for me too."

His large hand, rough and warm, touched hers. Goosebumps went up her arm. She looked up at him, seeing the urgency in his face. The *need.* It frightened her more than the war stories, more than when Luther's hands gripped tightly around her neck.

"I have to tell you something," she gulped.

Sequis's face lit up expectantly. "I'd hoped you might."

"No, no, it's not that," she started. "When I leave in the next few days—"

He moved closer, put his large arm around the small of her back, nearly lifting her off her feet. "I don't want you to leave..." He looked at her mouth, his need intensifying. Slowly, he bent to her, brought his hand to her chin, and lifted it. Resi couldn't breathe, couldn't speak.

Then, pounding footsteps came up the path, interrupting the moment. Relieved, Resi caught her breath. Sequis turned around in a whirl before bringing his hand to his mouth. He peered out over the cliffs, waiting for the intruder to show himself.

"Sir, some guests have arrived for this evening," a guard informed him. If he had any indication of what he was walking into, he didn't show it. "They wish for a private meet and greet with you ahead of the Ball."

Not a moment later, it was Luther that came flying around the hedge. He narrowed his eyes on Resi before approaching Sequis.

"I'm afraid, Sequis, this is urgent," he demanded. "And Miss Kensington should be taking measures of her own to see to it that she's the most beautiful woman in the room upon her painting's presentation tomorrow. Isn't that right?"

Resi looked him square in the eye, the fire never waning. "I suppose," she said. She curtsied, noticing the desperation in Sequis's eyes as she turned the hedge.

Quickly, she made her way back to her room, trying her best to ignore the guard that followed after her. Once in her chamber, she collapsed with a thud onto the bed. She lay there vacantly, wishing she could blink away the last two weeks. She wanted to go back to the night that Gilda had found her hiding in the trees, wanted to change the past so that she would never have been brought in from the fields, so that she never would've met Luther or Sequis.

Then, a faint click came from beyond the door. Frantic, she ran to it and tried to turn the handle. She waited in shock before trying a second, and then a third time. But the door wouldn't budge. She was locked in.

For hours, it seemed, she did nothing but go mad in her confinement. She ripped the sheets from her bed, threw her pitcher of water to the floor, smashed the trays of food along the lavish rugs of her quarters. The fire waged war inside of her, felt as if it were controlling her. She was nauseous with the feeling, anxious it might find its way out into the world and destroy whatever was in its path.

As the night wore on, however, she felt nothing—no fire, no peace, just a dull numbness that dried her tears against her cheeks and left her blankly staring out over the sea. Her legs went stiff with the chill of autumn as she watched the storm begin to drift its way across the water, the winds becoming evermore violent as the sinking sun went dark behind a black cloud. Until tomorrow evening, she was trapped under Luther's slimy thumb, and nothing, no matter how hard she thought about it, could change the destiny that awaited her.

THERE WAS much chatter in the halls in regard to the effect the formidable weather might have on the Ball. The fear of many guards was how the arriving carriages would make it up the steep ascent that would bring them to the Tristeland. The potential of a wheel getting stuck in the mud became more and more of a possibility the longer the rain beat against the cliffs.

The following morning, Resi waited in her clothes from the day before. She'd been unable to undress herself without Ana's help. Somehow, she'd found herself on the floor leaning against the bed with the comforter wrapped around her head like a shawl. She'd watched the storm roll over the cliffs, leaving the balcony doors open so she could feel the rain on her toes, so she could hear the thunderclaps bounce off the seawall.

She looked about the room. The once vibrant cloth of the walls now seemed gray and foreboding, like the walls of a dungeon. After all, she was no longer a guest. Luther had made sure of that.

For a brief period of time, she'd pressed her ear to the door, listening for any word she could. Much of the time, the halls remained vacant, but every so often, a grouping of 'Licks would pass, their mumbling low beneath the thunder. As far as Resi could tell, many of them were unhappy about the amount of work that had been placed on them in preparation for the Ball. She could relate. The days leading up to the Fourth- Year Festival had nearly killed her and Mags. Resi had contemplated yelling out for one of them to help her, then thought better of it. Luther was smart enough to punish anyone that might aid her.

As the morning approached, the hall began to fill. Resi tried to peek under the door to get a better glimpse. The only thing she saw was the muddied bottoms of skirts.

"The obscenity!" a woman said as she was ushered into a room down the hall. "You'd think the Governor would know not to throw a Ball during the rainy season!"

"My bonnet blew clear off of my head and was thrown over the cliffs," cried another an hour later. "It was my favorite, don't you know!"

"Surely, the Tristeland will provide a replacement for the return journey, darling," her husband quickly replied. The door then closed behind them and the conversation became private once more.

The rain continued to pour outside well into the late morning. Finally, somewhere around noon, the door to Resi's chambers clicked open, and there, standing wide in silhouette, was Luther. He was dressed impeccably in a burgundy coat and linen shirt.

"Get up," he seethed when he saw Resi lying on the floor. Resi flinched against the bed, then stood to her feet without a word.

Suddenly, a flurry of 'Lick women in black dress-gowns and bonnets came around Luther and into the room. Some carried towels, others sponges. One held a pitcher of water and a bucket. Frantic, Resi searched for Ana, but she wasn't among them.

"Undress her," Luther ordered them sinisterly as the door closed quietly behind him. Horrified, Resi reared against the nearest wall, but the women encircled her and soon began to poke and prod at the back of her dress.

"No!" she cried out as she looked on to where Luther stood in the corner of the room. But the women wouldn't pull from their task. They pushed Resi into the center of the room and soon enough, Resi stood stark naked, shivering in the wind and rain that pulsated through the open doors of the balcony.

"Bathe her," Luther called out numbly, his face shadowed.

A woman poured the pitcher of water into a bucket before the group forced Resi to step into it. Resi kept her arms over her chest as she suffered attack after attack of bone-chilling water. Her knees buckled together as she gasped for breath. Silently, the 'Licks scratched at her skin with harsh sponges, lifting her limbs in all directions as if they were preparing a prized stallion for show.

"Dry her," Luther called, and all at once, the women blotted at her with towels. Resi tried to snatch one away to cover herself, but the women quickly gathered the belongings in hand and forced her out of the bucket.

"Leave us." Luther said the words and within seconds, the women quickly fled the room. Humiliated, Resi swiped a fur blanket from the bed and draped it around her. With each passing second, she felt herself slipping further and further away from where Luther waited in the darkness.

"I can see I've done my job very well," he said calmly. "It's as if everything about you was made for him."

Resi's stomach dropped. Still, the fire raged on within her. "I would think someone in your position would be more cautious about where they chose to have their private conversations."

She motioned with a glance to the gardens. When she looked back at him, Luther's face went pale.

"I know what you're up to," she said finally. "And I suppose I should thank you. At least now my death won't come as a shock."

Luther brought a hand to his chin. "I wouldn't be so sure of that." He bobbed on his toes with the same nervous energy he had on the day he arrived at the Farmhold. "You don't know when it's coming. Not how. Not where."

"Don't pretend that you have this all figured out," she said blankly. "You're scared. I see it. Even now."

Luther laughed deeply. "What exactly do *I* have to be afraid of?"

With a smile, Resi waited, then bobbed on her toes to mimic his nervous habit out of spite. *Checkmate.* "Me."

Luther's eyelids flitted about, his face growing tense. He then stepped forward, coming within feet of her. But Resi didn't waver.

"There's nothing you can do to reset the future. *Nothing*!" He said the words with a finality that cooled all the heat in Resi's stomach.

"That may be so," she said. "Still, you suspect something about me. Something that frightens you, something that you can't control.

It's the only stone left unturned in your plan. And you can't quite put your finger on it, can you?"

Luther scowled, then drew closer still. "Then why don't you tell me what that is, 'Lick?" he spat.

The air settled around them as Resi waited for the right answer to come. But it didn't. He was testing her, but the strange heat in her stomach couldn't reveal itself just yet. Timidly, she recoiled from Luther, then watched in horror as his face sizzled with satisfaction.

"Your determination is commendable, but useless," he mused. "Years of work have led to this day. And you, sweet 'Lick, are the tiny cog that makes the whole machine run with seamless precision."

With much satisfaction, he reached out a slimy hand to brush her face, but Resi withdrew before it could land on her.

"I won't have the chance to say it later," he said quickly as he readjusted one of his sleeves. "Thank you for playing your part. You can die honorably knowing you served your region with bravery."

A horrible dread filled Resi as she watched him turn for the door. He opened it, and standing in the light of the hall was a young 'Lick girl with large, round eyes that she didn't recognize. It wasn't until Luther grabbed her forcefully by the arm that the girl even realized the door had been opened. Startled, she resigned to Luther's grip and came stumbling into the room.

"This here is Alby. She'll be prepping you for the ball," he said. Cruelly, he waved his hand in front of Alby's face and she jumped in fright at the sudden movement. "We keep her around for special circumstances such as this. You see," Luther cooed, his tone mellowing, "Alby is deaf and mute. Hasn't heard a word since the last time she withheld important information from a member of the Eastern Guard. Isn't that right, Alby?" his voice raised.

All at once, Resi's breath caught in her lungs. Where Alby's ears should've been were two long and crooked scars.

"You—you mutilated her," Resi stammered.

"That's the price 'Licks pay for listening in on the wrong conversation. Would've done the same to you if it weren't for what awaited you tonight," Luther said with a knowing grin. "Besides, I thought she might be better suited for you than your last little helper."

Resi's heart jumped into her throat. "Where is Ana?" she demanded. "What have you done with her?!"

Luther laughed again, this time allowing his amusement to take over him completely. With a sinister wink, he closed the door behind him. The lock clicked again.

"You snake!" Resi threw her fists against the closed door. "Don't harm her! Don't you dare harm her!"

"I'll expect you to be dressed by sundown. You have a big night ahead of you!" he called.

Resi kicked and pounded at the door until her fists were throbbing. It was no use. Exhausted, she finally gave up and rested her head against the wall.

When she finally turned towards the room, she met Alby's fearful gaze. The girl's whole body shook like a leaf as she crossed to the closet and hesitantly removed the garment bag Sequis had delivered the day prior. Her young, unassuming face went hard as she outstretched the bag in her weak arms.

Knowing what she had to do, Resi threw off the blanket from her shoulders. She let her hand float over her stomach, feeling the fire as it danced inside. The air beneath her hand was simmering, shifting the space between them. *That was new.* She then crossed to Alby. The girl's mouth was agape at the sight of the heat. She registered everything, knew everything immediately.

Decidedly, Resi snatched the garment bag from her hands. "Didn't anyone tell you it was rude to stare, Alby?" she raised even though she knew Alby couldn't hear or respond. In a rage, she flew to her vanity and looked at her reflection. Before her was a new Resi, one unafraid of the Advisor's schemes. She was done with hiding and running in the dark, cowering with her internal inferno and hoping it would never see the light of day. It needed to break loose and find its own place in this tortured Estate. And besides, she had tricks of her own waiting up her sleeves. It was only a matter of time before Luther would discover what she was capable of.

With the fire controlled in her belly, she turned to Alby with a fierce look. She didn't care if the 'Lick girl couldn't hear her. It didn't matter. "Make me the most beautiful woman the Governor has ever seen."

CHAPTER 12

THE BALL

After the rain had settled, the sky became a vision of pale pink and periwinkle clouds along the horizon. Resi ached to paint the sea and sky, to mold it into something tangible, but she knew such a time would never come. It was a sad, complicated thought, one overshadowed by the looming question of whether all sunsets were this captivating, or if this one might just be the last one she would ever see.

Below her, the gardens were a radiant sight. Large, ornate floral arrangements had been placed about the paths, and further, nearest the center fountain, a long, decorated table awaited the arrival of all the best preparations from the Tristeland kitchens.

Resi managed to tear herself away from the view when she felt the sting of tears in her eyes. She came into the dim room. Waiting in the corner was Alby. It'd taken the girl some time to realize she'd been locked in with Resi. In the time since her discovery, she'd been pacing the room, biting at her already chewed nails. They were down to the quick.

Much as she'd wished to ease Alby, Resi simply didn't have the stamina. For the majority of the afternoon, she'd tried to keep her mind on Mags. She wanted to remember every detail of their time together; the many nights spent bickering on the porch of the lean-to as the sun sank lower over the trees, the days in the fields spent tossing jokes back and forth. Every few minutes, she thought of Scottis with a smile, of his folded creatures, of the funny way he walked about the Eye.

And, every now and again she'd find her mind drifting to Corey. His warm eyes and soft temperament. He was a stranger to her, just another face in the fields, and yet, he'd felt so familiar to her as she'd passed him her bucket that afternoon. Would he cry alongside Mags and Scottis upon the news of her death? Or, would he simply clench his fist like he had on the night of Shina's punishment?

She noticed Alby watching her from the corner. The girl's eyes scanned the white dress with sincere admiration. Paranoid and anxious, Resi turned to the elongated mirror that delicately balanced on the wall. The dress fit her impeccably. Gone were the childish lines of her figure. With all the food she'd been served at the Tristeland over the previous month, there were curves in places where straight lines once had been.

She placed her hands cautiously on her waist, feeling the cool texture of the silk on her palms. The dress was fit to be displayed, a true work of art. The sleeves were long and tight along her arms with small white buttons along the cuff. She'd been shocked when Alby hadn't put a corset around her waist; the dress already had one built in.

It was odd, she thought; awaiting her death in a wedding gown. At least she wouldn't be burned at the stake, as she'd so often imagined if news of what she'd carried inside of her became public knowledge. She'd take her last breath in a gown fit for a queen. She'd be radiant. Somehow, the thought was comforting.

The door suddenly clicked. Without a thought, Resi took Alby by the hand and brought her a few steps deeper into the room.

Commander Lee. He waited in the doorway in a royal blue waistcoat. His hair had been groomed since last Resi had seen him, and for a brief moment, she saw the vision of him twenty years younger waiting outside on a cold night to retrieve a pretty Codian girl. He'd been less tense then, his posture taller, his hair less peppered with gray.

His eyebrows raised. "Miss Taresia. You look astonishing."

She managed to curtsy, ignoring the faint look of pity in his eyes when she met his gaze.

Lee then turned to Alby as he signed a command to her with his hands. Alby's eyes flickered to Resi, then landed on the floor. She then curtsied and left the room.

"I suppose the Advisor sent you," Resi turned to Lee. "Let me guess: too busy to retrieve his prisoner?"

Lee's face tensed as he pressed his hand against the other side of the door frame. No words came to mind.

"Let's get on with it, then," she finally said with a huff.

In a whirl, she brushed past him into the dim light of the hall. Lee closed the door and stood at her side. When he attempted to take her arm, she declined it.

Slowly, they drifted down the corridor. Resi recognized their route to the foyer. The hall was empty, but further on, the foyer awaited, and the busying sounds of arriving guests soon met her ears as they came to the interior balcony above the bustling crowd.

Resi looked down into the chaos with surmounting fear. Men and women were dressed in their finest; printed gowns, colorful gowns, gowns with sleeves, and gowns without. Hundreds of dazzling hair pieces extended into long feathers. A soft breeze trickled in from the open doors that lead out to the front entrance where more guests stepped out of decorated carriages. A queue had formed on the grand walkway, and there, standing near the entry with his back to her, was Sequis.

Resi stopped in her tracks. Proudly, he stood with his chest out, his shoulders and head hovering over the crowd like some sort of protective gargoyle. Unlike all the other nights at Court, he was beaming. He was dressed in a dark emerald coat and matching cape embellished with swirling gold designs. His hair was pulled back by a black ribbon. Sequis took time with each arriving guest, smiling and shaking each hand with enthusiasm.

And then, her eyes went far up to the space of wall above Sequis's head. The portrait had been hung there, but was covered with linen. The crowd surrounded it closely in anticipation of its grand reveal. It seemed everyone was waiting for one final arrival, and that was Resi.

"He's waiting," Lee ordered to her over his shoulder as he began to descend the grand stairs that led into the madness. It appeared he too was no longer in the mood for games.

She took a breath as she descended after him, feeling as if she were voluntarily choosing to enter a viper's pit. With each conquered stair, she became more aware of the number of eyes that had shifted towards her. Before she could blink, the whole room had turned to watch her. Still, she knew no one would miss her. No one would remember the girl who wore white. She was irrelevant, invisible inside this crowd. Eventually, all memories of her would disappear.

But then, a hush fell over the foyer, causing a bizarre sort of impulse for everyone to simultaneously burst into applause.

No. Not this. Anything but this.

Resi turned her attention to where Sequis waited in the doorway. Breathless, he watched her, taking in the sight of her in the white dress as if he were watching the sunset over the cliffs for the very first time. His beaming expression softened before he joined in the applause.

Resi descended the remaining stairs and when her foot hit the floor, a pathway magically appeared through the crowd: a direct route to Sequis. Try as she might to avoid it, she was drawn to his beauty like a moth to a flame. The noise of the hall quickly fell into static as she drew closer, closer.

Mesmerized, she watched as Sequis extended his hand to her. She took it, feeling the warmth of it send heat through her entire body. He bent at the waist before bringing his lips to her hand.

"You're a vision..." he spoke.

The walls were caving in. Luther's plan was in motion. She could feel herself wanting to say the words to Sequis. They were on the tip of her tongue. *Luther's lying to you. He's deceived you.*

Just then, Sequis motioned over her head to a nearby group of guards.

"I wanted to be with you," Sequis then whispered to Resi. "I wanted to be with you when I saw it for the first time."

The guards quickly took position beneath the portrait, each grabbing a rope attached to the linen covering. Once all was set, Sequis hushed the gathering of people closest to him.

"Now that our artist is here, I think it's high time we unveil what she's been working on these past few weeks. Is everyone in agreement?"

The crowd cheered in reply. Still, Sequis wasn't pleased. He cupped a hand behind his ear, leaning forward.

"I said, *is everyone in agreement?*"

Again, the crowd replied, but this time with gusto. Sequis smiled broadly, looking to Resi with great anticipation before the guard yanked on the ropes and the linen fell to the floor.

The crowd gasped. In the portrait, Sequis stood with his back pressed against the window frame, his gaze fixed over his shoulder on the sea. His bare chest gleamed in the sun as he wistfully held his filled goblet. There was the faint look of tears in his eyes. Even after all the time she'd spent on it, the portrait was foreign to Resi, as if someone else entirely had spent those days studying Sequis's face in the parlor. The effect was dizzying, like being awakened to her own talent after years of questioning it.

Quickly, Resi tore her eyes away from it, suddenly realizing that the accolade of being the Governor's portrait artist came with a hefty price: her life.

Sequis turned to her, his eyes filled with a new sort of dedication for his once timid and shy portrait artist. He felt seen, known.

"To my talented artist, Miss Kensington," he said raising a glass. "I suspect I will have to compete for your talents moving forward. But you will always have a home here at the Tristeland."

"Hear, hear!" a voice in the crowd cried. The guests followed suit, raising their glasses before sipping their Rowgar. As Resi had expected, the crowd surrounded her, each asking their own set of loaded questions about the portrait. Many congratulated her, some even asked her if she was available for freelance work. It would've been a dream on any other day, but not today.

Within seconds Lee was at her side. His face was rigid. Without a word, he grabbed Resi by the arm and ushered her away from the crowd.

"If you'd excuse us," he nodded to the surrounding guests.

Resi didn't dare believe Lee was aiding her out of the situation, didn't dare think he had the kind of heart to look after her at a time like this.

"You look miserable," she threw at him.

"I should say the same to you," he responded without a glance in her direction. Together, they walked into the crowd, allowing Sequis to further mingle with his guests.

She scowled. "At least I have an excuse."

Beyond the doors, the sky grew darker. Carriages were arriving fewer and fewer, and soon, the doors leading into the gardens would be opened for the guests to continue their evening.

Resi's mind went to Luther. The *leech*. Where in the Sept-Regions was he? Somehow, she knew he was near. She could feel him. The room was too damp, too stuffy. Her eyes darted about the foyer before finally finding a figure at the top of the stairs; Luther. His rat-like eyes twitched about the many faces below. At the sight of him, Resi felt her monster roar inside of her.

"Finally, the coward arrives," she huffed.

A few minutes passed before she watched Luther descend the stairs. His lips were curled in a soft smile. When he reached the middle landing, he looked proudly once more over the crowd.

"Ladies and Gentlemen!" he suddenly called. "The Governor and myself are honored to welcome you to the Tristeland Estate for a night of merriment and music," he smiled. "It brings me great joy to see these halls filled with your smiling faces. It brings me even more joy to know how eager we all are to celebrate the life and accomplishments of the greatest ruler south of Sterch!"

Necks snapped again to Sequis. Resi couldn't help but do the same. Sequis's mouth widened into a large grin as he looked upon his most trusted and loyal friend. The sight of it made Resi nauseous.

"Please," Luther continued, "if you could raise your glasses."

The fire inside Resi all at once flickered, then waned as she watched the crowd obey his command. It was to be a historic evening for those in attendance; an execution masked as a celebration.

"To His Lordship!" Luther called.

"To His Lordship!" the crowd repeated before guzzling down the Rowgar from their glasses. The room went joyously silent as the guests ruminated over Luther's words when suddenly, the front doors swung wide and in tripped none other than Marion and Theodore Offenheimer.

Resi shrank into the wall at her back, silently congratulating herself. On the night she'd first learned of Luther's plan, she'd carefully written to Marion in her best handwriting, apologizing for missing the Offenheimers on the long list of invites. She'd felt a great sense of satisfaction when she'd signed it from Luther. Still, there was no guarantee that they'd show up with such a last-minute invitation. But it had worked. Marion's vanity would certainly not permit her to miss such a prestigious event, and the temporary relief at having played Marion's own game in her favor had her giggling with satisfaction.

Exhilarated by all the attention, Marion took the moment to bask in her own glory. She was dressed fashionably in a magenta gown with ample amounts of white lace decorating the bust. On her head rested a giant plume of three bright green feathers and in hand she played with a matching fan. Theo, on the other hand, was appalled by their late arrival. Horrified, he swiped the hat off of his bald head. Resi turned just in time to see Luther's reaction. Upon the sight of the newest arrivals, his back stiffened.

After hearing all the stories surrounding the Mistress, Resi couldn't help but be curious to see how she fared within the Tristeland's walls. It was commonly known about the fields that Marion once sought to be a member of Sequis's Court, but was denied the opportunity.

Seductively, the Mistress batted her eyes as she approached Sequis, took a deep curtsy that almost sent her sideways, then met his gaze with practiced assurance. Clutched in one of her hands was the hand-written invitation. Proudly, she waved it around for those nearest to get a glimpse of it.

"Mistress Offenheimer," Sequis said to her humbly before taking her hand and kissing her glove. "It's been quite some number of years."

"Has it?" she cooed as she brought her fan to her face. She turned her closed eyes to the mural ceiling as if she were basking in the warmth of the sun. "Of course, you remember my husband, Theodore?"

Sequis turned to Theo, his face warm.

"Honored to see you again," Theo said boldly, his arm wobbling like rubber in Sequis's firm grip.

"The honor is mine," Sequis obliged. "Really, it is I that should be thanking you for your generous shipment of folly for tonight."

Playfully, Marion swatted at Sequis's arm; a poor attempt at flirting. "I was beginning to think you'd forgotten about us. I must admit, when the invitation arrived, I was certain there was too much to be done to prepare for such a quick turnaround. But lo and behold, Theo was emphatic we make an appearance. So, here we are!"

Resi snorted. It was just like Marion to play it cool, to feign disinterest.

Marion and Theo squinted at the portrait directly above Sequis's head. Theo smiled, taking in the colors of the rendering with pure delight. Marion, however, did her best to pretend she was unimpressed. She took one fleeting look at it before adverting her eyes back down to the fabrics of her dress.

"It appears our artist has truly outdone herself," Theo said proudly. "We were beginning to think she might not ever return to our lowly mansion after staying in such a fine estate," he said with a laugh.

Here it is. Here it finally is, Resi thought.

Sequis shifted his feet. "You know of Miss Kensington?" he

inquired, his head turning to the side as he looked down on the couple. "I was under the impression that the people of 'Ter had very little knowledge of the girl."

He began to peer over the crowd, looking for her, but Resi tucked herself further beyond the shadows of the plant. She was still within earshot, but out of sight.

Confused, Theo took a disoriented step forward. "Perhaps I'm mistaken. Miss Taresia was delivered here a few weeks ago, was she not?"

All of sudden, Marion's interest returned to the conversation. She'd been measuring her own gown against all the other women in attendance. "Yes, where is the girl?" she asked passively. "Wouldn't blame you for locking her up on a night like this."

Sequis looked at them with a polite, but strained sort of smile. "You speak of Miss Taresia Kensington? The artist from Portsfish?"

Resi leaned so far into the plant she thought she might tip it over. She peered through its leaves to see Luther struggling to make his way through the dense crowd. His face was strained; eyes bulging, veins popping at the neck.

For a matter of seconds, Marion gazed awkwardly at Sequis before letting out a forced laugh. "From *Portsfish*? No, no! Our farmhold is located south of Esur!" she answered, almost insulted. "Did Luther not explain?"

Resi watched with great satisfaction as Sequis processed the information. He was lost somewhere between confusion and absolute rage. It was the exact reaction she'd aimed for, and then some. Luther's name had been involved, and now, a new plan was in motion; her plan.

"I'm s—sorry," Sequis stuttered. "How do you know Miss Kensington?"

"Who in the Sept-Regions is *Miss Kensington*?" Marion squawked. Her fan fluttered in her hand so quickly that it almost disappeared in front of her face. "We're speaking of the 'Lick girl that you stole from us because you just *had* to have her as your portrait artiste! Never mind what it's cost us to replace her as our son's tutor.

And just when he was growing so fond of her...It set us back a few days, but nevertheless, we eventually found a suitable replacement."

It was clear that Marion's words were spoken to provoke empathy. Sequis, however, had lost complete interest in anything she had to say. Resi could see the wheels in his brain grinding against each other as he began to unravel all of Luther's plotting. Then, like a flick of a switch, he knew everything.

"Would you," he paused, bringing a fist to his mouth as if he was going to be ill, "would you excuse me?"

Resi scooted to the other side of the plant as Sequis bounded away from the conversation. Marion curtsied and Theo bowed, their gaze following after the Governor as he turned towards the gardens. Frantically, the crowd parted in an effort not to be knocked over by his speeding pace, and without so much as a glance to find Luther, Sequis exited the room.

It was only seconds later that Luther emerged from the crowd, and desperate for answers, Marion approached him, her face and décolletage red from embarrassment.

"There better be a good explanation for all of this," she bristled at him. "We just made absolute fools out of ourselves. And in front of the Governor, no less!"

"Mistress Marion," he replied as he slicked his greasy hair beyond an ear. "You have to forgive me, I—"

His eyes narrowed on the invitation in her outstretched hand. Furious, he snatched it from her, then devoured its contents. Once finished, he crumpled the note in his fist.

"Well, excuse me!" Marion called out, drawing attention. "That is *mine*, thank you very much!" Theo did his best to restrain her, but his attempt only caused more commotion. Luther, however, didn't move a muscle. He looked to where Lee stood in the crowd, his eyes brimming with the realization of Resi's idea to send the note. Sensing trouble, Lee crossed the space to him.

"The 'Lick," Luther breathed. "Where is she?"

Suddenly realizing he'd misplaced Resi in the crowd, Lee turned around himself.

"You had one job, you idiot!" Luther snapped at him. "Find her!"

Suddenly realizing the planned events of the evening had just taken a serious turn, Lee nodded sheepishly. He ran off towards the gardens and Luther, left with a bewildered Marion, angrily turned to the nearest tray of Rowgar, snatched a flute, and chugged until it was gone. Limply, the glass hung in his hand as he barreled his way towards a guard stationed at the perimeter of the room.

"Have the Offenheimers escorted from the premises," he demanded. Politely, the guard nodded.

"Luther, what is happening?" Marion barked out as the guard ushered them back towards the doors. "I demand to know what is going on at once!"

Resi watched Theo look about the room, certain he was searching for her, before he eventually disappeared out the front doors. Marion, however, was all but devastated as her cries went quiet outside. Ready to get back to the party, the guests returned to their earlier conversations without so much as a second thought or inquiry as to what the fuss was all about.

Resi let the victory of her plan swell in her chest. She didn't know what was more satisfying to watch: Marion's humiliation or Luther's plan coming undone before her very eyes. At least, now, the score was even.

Hidden, but only feet from where Luther shook with anger, Resi watched him roll his shoulders and his nostrils flare wide. He then took off to find Sequis, his hands twitching at his sides.

CHAPTER 13

THE GALLOWS

Thoroughly pleased, Resi moved her way through the crowd. She wanted to be there when Luther confronted Sequis. She wanted to see the terror fill his eyes upon his reckoning.

She'd nearly made it to the entrance to the gardens before a gentle pull came at her shoulder. Angered, she turned to see Lee, his face bothered.

"That's not a good idea," he warned.

She was done being controlled, done with the lies, the secrets. "Who was the other man with you in the gardens?" she snapped at him. "The man that told Luther about me, and these so-called *signs*?!"

Lee took a calming breath before attempting to place his hands on her shoulders.

"Don't touch me!" she snarled, pulling away. "Who are you protecting?!"

Lee's eyes scanned the crowd, anxious at the thought of someone overhearing their words. "Calm down," he said through bared teeth. "We wouldn't want you doing anything that could put yourself in any more danger than you already are."

The fire ignited in her stomach in one quick switch. It had been building all day, ever since Luther had busted into her suite without warning. She was swimming in the heat, could feel it in the space under her eyelids. She was feverish with rage.

Just then, Lee tried to grab her by the arm. "Ah!" he let out a scream. Startled, he looked at his hand. It was burned red.

A nearby woman looked on in horror as Resi and Lee watched the heat, like steam rising off the ground, rise from Resi's fingertips. Something like a shockwave rippled from her chest into her hands, tickling her like a feather being stroked down her arm. Stunned, she took a step back.

It was true, and there was no turning back. An ancient power existed within her, and though the knowledge of such a fact answered many questions, she still felt as if she were roaming in the dark.

"Sorceress..." the woman whispered, her plump cheeks jiggling as she shook her head in disbelief. The air was buzzing in the space between the three of them, Resi's fate hanging in the balance. And then, it all came crashing down. The woman lifted her shaking arm to point at Resi, her shriek splitting through the room like a whistle. "*Sorceress!*"

All at once, the room descended into madness. The guests yelped and cried as they frantically tore themselves through the open doors to the gardens, scrambling past each other as if they were avoiding the aftershock of an earthquake. The foyer roared with the stampede. Distressed faces sped past in a blur, desperate to get away from the scene and into the cool air of night.

"Seize her!" a baritone voice suddenly boomed through the foyer.

Resi turned to find Sequis at the top of the stairs, his hands gripped tight on the banister. Had he seen it? Did he know what she really was?

Hesitantly, a group of guards surrounded Resi as she managed to get to her feet. One by one, they inched closer, until finally, one was brave enough to put their hands on her shoulders. The others followed suit and soon, she was overpowered. Ravenously, they spat on her, ripping the sleeves of her grown and grasping onto her hair.

Despairingly, she screamed. She begged the fire within her to come forth once more. But it wouldn't. It had a mind of its own, a power to decide when and where it would be revealed.

"Enough!" Resi could hear someone cry out. "That's *ENOUGH*!"

Lee ripped his way through the young guards, his eyes wide. Forcefully, he grabbed her by the waist, pulling her away from them and into his arms. She shook as he carried her from the crowd.

"Not a word out of you," he said to her.

Resi didn't object; she let the fever take her deeper into herself until it was the only feeling left. It was enough to make her pass out. Still, she clung to her consciousness, reaching for it like it was her final breath.

The angry mob of guards followed after them into the darkened hallway leading out of the foyer. Together, they chanted, "Kill her!" as they threw white-knuckled fists into the air. They rounded a corner into the heart of Tristeland, the back of the Estate nearest the cliffs.

"Where are you taking me?" she asked Lee as she weakly lifted her head.

But Lee didn't reply. Together they marched on, leaving the angry mob behind. Even beyond the many layers of stone, Resi could hear the terrified screams of the guests as they reached the gardens.

They passed a roaring hearth that soon lead them to a set of descending stone stairs. One by one, Lee took them slowly, bringing them ever closer to the darkness. The stairwell was ripe with the smell of rat feces and mold.

Resi heard a door creak open at the base of the stairs. Beyond, waited a dark room only lit by two small torches mounted to the stone wall. Briskly, Lee brought her inside and set her down on a cold, wet floor. Resi looked up in time to watch him exit. She could swear there were tears in his eyes.

"Bind her," a voice called from the corner. Sequis stepped into the light, followed by two other guards with rope. Eagerly, the guards tied Resi's hand behind her back, then brought her to her feet. But Resi was too weak. She lost her balance and the guards hoisted her up.

"It appears we've had some sort of misunderstanding," Sequis breathed. "As one might expect, I don't tolerate liars."

"You should talk to Luther, then," Resi chimed. Her voice belonged to someone else, someone brave.

Sequis smirked. "You expect me to believe a Witch-'Lick over my most trusted colleague?"

It was as she had feared; it was Luther's word against hers.

"I tried to tell you in the gardens," she sighed. "But Luther gave me no choice! He threatened to throw me from the cliffs if I told you the truth."

The muscles in Sequis's jaw hardened. "And what of your little display upstairs, hmm?"

Resi put a hand to her stomach. The fire had cooled, slowed. But her head was still drunk with the sensation. "I—I don't know."

A deep grumble came from Sequis's throat before he let out a laugh so violent that Resi's hair blew back from her face. "Tell me..." he spat. "Is it fun feigning innocence?"

Resi coughed on the heat in her mouth. "You have to believe me. I —I don't know what that was."

Sequis bent at the waist again, his massive hand stretching to her hair. Tenderly, he stroked the strand, his eyes widening at the softness of its touch. "After all that I told you," he whispered, "you *weakened* me."

Resi waited, feeling the weight of his words land on her like a tidal wave. Then, he pulled her in closely, forcefully grabbing her face in his large hand. "You fooled me into thinking I could take you as my own! And I wanted you..." he groaned. "From the first moment I saw you, I wanted to take your innocence, to make it mine."

Horrified, she reared her head back. But Sequis's grip tightened again around her face. She could feel her teeth piercing her cheeks, could taste her own blood on her tongue. His words were biting, harsh.

"This is what you Aliquian women do...flaunt your fragile beauty until the exact moment you choose to blindside your enemies. What was it that you had in mind exactly? A massacre? A siege?!"

Resi let out a groan of pain before, finally, he released her.

He laughed. "And to think, everyone in attendance showed up

tonight because I'd pondered the idea of taking Miss Kensington as my bride."

Resi shuddered. "I think it's safe to say we don't make a great match."

Sequis's upper lip snarled. "Offending me won't keep you alive." He took a deep breath, one longing and pained. "This Ball was organized for one purpose, and one purpose only. According to Luther, the people of Ter find me too approachable. Too human. Too *weak*." He paused, ruminating the word in his mouth as if it were a rotten grape. "This event serves purely as a means to change my reputation. The people thought it a good idea for me to take a bride, but it seems Luther disagrees. Since marriage is no longer on the table, I say we leave your fate entirely in the hands of the people."

Resi gulped. "And, what of Luther's planned display?"

His brow quaked above his eye. "*What* did you say?"

"Oh, you don't know?" she asked smartly.

"What kind of display?"

"A duel of some sort," she breathed. "Something he's been planning for quite some time, so it seems."

"Between who?" he asked.

Resi brought her face up to the light. "Better question: what is it that Luther wants the people to see?" She watched a shiver of fear cross his eyes. "What aren't you telling them?"

Sequis went into a frenzy. Crazed, he pushed his hair back, then smacked himself hard in the face in an attempt to wake himself up from the nightmare that was crashing down around him. He paced the room before nodding to the guards to take her away.

Without warning, the two men began dragging Resi towards the door. They forced her into the wet hallway, gripping her arms with bruising force. Sequis stomped his way after them, leading them further into the dungeons before he disappeared down an adjoining hall. Resi shivered. The guards were going to lock her up, let her go mad in the dark until she begged for death.

Deeper, they marched until a set of double doors opened before them. Resi could hear the pulse of the center fountain. They'd marched her under the gardens and had appeared near the cliffs.

To the south, a winding cue of manic guests tried to wrangle their carriages to go home. Others huddled together by the center fountain, hoping the party might continue as they nursed their glasses of Rowgar. Guards lined the perimeter nearest the cliffs with their hands placed fiercely on the butt of their swords, keeping their eyes on the guests as if they were herding a group of paranoid sheep.

Resi marched forward, the guards leading her towards a structure posted beyond the gardens. In all the times Resi had taken her lunch near the cliffs, she'd yet to see it. The construction was of steel and wood, resembling a stage of sorts. Resi noticed a peculiar network of connecting wood that bridged over the top of the entire structure. But as they drew closer, she felt her stomach flip. Two nooses dangled beneath the wooden rafters.

Gallows.

Murmurs came from the crowd when a group noticed the guards and Resi working their way through the gardens. Soon, voices began to ring out closer to the Estate. Resi turned to see Sequis not far behind. Sharply, he stalked down the gravel path after them.

Resi tried to push her feet into the earth, but it was no use. This wasn't the way she was going to die; not like this.

"That's right! Hang her!" called a man from the crowd as the guests drew closer. Men and women cheered in reply.

Soon enough, Sequis tromped up the stairs with his head low. After him, came a large group of guards with lit torches. Together, they ignited large bowls of fire around the perimeter of the gallows. All at once, Sequis's perfect face lit up the night, his expression tense and certain.

For many minutes, he stalled as the people grew restless; women cried out, their voices shrill and demanding justice. Codian men began chanting to burn Resi at the stake. Soon, a rowdy group began to throw their shoes at Resi. Most flew right past her or landed at her feet until, WHAM!; one hit her square in the face, sending her to her knees. The guards lifted her back up to her feet, and she looked up just in time to see Sequis staring back at her with concern. The skin under his eyes tightened.

"*No more!*" he roared. The crowd went silent as the command ripped out of him. It was the sound of a warrior, the sound of a giant.

Resi panned over the crowd. Luther had been right; the people had become too comfortable with Sequis. Even members of the Guard were shocked by his sudden outburst.

Suddenly, the large doors of the Estate that overlooked the gardens opened with a jolt. A group of four guards led out a prisoner, a weak man dressed in a torn blue suit. Resi's fists tightened beneath the twine when she realized it was Luther.

"Unhand me!" he cried out over the silence of the crowd. "Do you realize what crime you are committing?!"

Puzzled, the guests began to whisper amongst themselves. Resi tried to fight the swelling in her chest as Luther's threats intensified. The sound of his panic was music to her ears.

Finally, the guards hoisted him onto the stage. The once perfect suit had been torn near the chest. He was shackled at the feet and his hands were bound behind him.

"Your grace," Luther squirmed. "This is unnecessary torment! Have these men release me! We can talk about this!"

Sequis remained silent, his head low.

"You know how much you mean to me!" Luther cried. "You're my brother! The only family I have!"

Resi's throat tightened. She looked up to the two dangling nooses. Two ropes for two necks.

"I know you don't want to hurt me...you *need* me, Sequis," Luther bellowed. He wriggled in the grip of the strong guards. "After everything we've been through, this is how you choose to repay me?!"

More silence followed, driving Luther into madness. All at once, he lunged forward at Resi with hate-filled eyes. A woman in the crowd shrieked, but the guards kept him restrained.

"It's her, isn't it?!" Luther cried wildly. "The Witch-'Lick! She's poisoned your head! She doesn't love you. She wanted access to you!"

Sequis's weight shifted on his feet. The whole crowd waited for his response, but still nothing.

"Don't you see?!" Luther continued as if he'd just gained complete clarity. "She's fooled us all! Sure, I knew she was a 'Lick, but it is *she* that kept her forbidden powers a secret!"

Luther's eyes darted from Sequis to the crowd, to his guards. He was desperate for validation, but he wasn't getting it. Blank faces stared at him from the gardens as Sequis's hand rubbed at one of his temples. Finally, the Governor spoke. His tone was thoughtful, reminiscent.

"I remember when I realized I was different," he started. "As a boy, I was frightened of what I might become. I was growing so fast that I could feel the ache of it in my bones."

Suddenly, he turned to Luther and crouched down on his haunches. His eyes went someplace deep in the past.

"I was only fifteen when I made the journey to Dirig. I had the weight of the world on my shoulders. I was to lead the largest army in the Sept-Regions, and I had no one to turn to. And then, I met you," he said, finally looking into Luther's eyes. "Initially, I thought little of you. You were small, feeble—scared shitless of war. But I came to learn that you saw more of me than I even saw of myself. I suppose you always have."

Luther eased, his chest bobbing with new, hopeful breath.

"What I didn't realize," Sequis continued, his tone sharpening, "was to what lengths you would go to ensure my reputation as a politician."

Slowly, he began rolling up the sleeves of his shirt, revealing bulging blue veins in his forearms. The crowd reared back in reaction, Resi included. She'd yet to see them all this time. They were unnatural, powerful in a dark sort of nature.

"You think that I'm not privy enough to know why you brought *her* here?" he asked Luther with a nod to Resi.

Luther's eyes widened into panic. "No, Sequis, no—"

"You planned this Ball to humiliate me!" Sequis said, leaning in to

Luther. "You lured a young 'Lick girl as bait in front of my face, just waiting for me to bite!"

"Sequis, *brother*!—"

"Do not address me so informally!" Sequis shouted as he turned again towards a shivering crowd. "Really, I couldn't have thought of a better plan, myself!"

"I intended nothing of the sort!" Luther defended himself. "I only wish for your subjects to see you as I do! They deserve to *know* their ruler. The real you, the true leader that you are! They need to see what you're capable of!"

Decisively, Sequis looked over his shoulder to the guards handling Resi. " Bring her to me."

Together, the guards reared her forward, but this time, Resi didn't struggle in protest. She didn't want her fear to be the last memory that Luther would have of her; of her shaking, scared, conquered.

"After all these years by my side, after everything you've taught me, you aim to make a fool of me!" Sequis spit back at Luther. "You knew all along about what she carries...you lied to me."

In the shadows, Luther waited. He didn't answer.

"And yet, you still brought her to me?" Sequis raged on. "Knowing full well that I'd fall prey to her, knowing that the news of what she is would be the ticket to my undoing?"

"I know I lied!" Luther sneered, his face shaking violently. "But don't punish me, not like this—"

"But isn't that what you wanted?!" Sequis posed with his arms outstretched.

"I only wish that you would free yourself! That you would rise up to be the politician I know you to be!"

"And publicly destroying a Witch-'Lick proves it?" Sequis sneered. Out of nowhere, he reached out his arm and grabbed Resi by the collar of her dress. In one quick move, he lifted her from her feet by the throat. Desperate for breath, she swatted uselessly at his mighty paw.

"My size and strength was never enough for you, was it?" he threw at Luther. "Just like it wasn't enough for my mother. No, I have to be *ruthless*; more than a man, or a giant. More than a ruler. I have to be an almighty *sorcerer*!"

Blue light, pure as the waters below the cliffs, began to grow from Sequis's free palm. It appeared as a small, fragile glass sphere, but soon began to swirl and move like liquid fire. The crowd sent a wave of awe and fear through the night air.

In all of Resi's nightmares, she'd yet to envision such a disaster as this. Sequis; practicing sorcery. It was what Luther had wanted all along, to raise Sequis up as a great and almighty ruler, one that could wield again the powers of sorcery into a new age.

But what she couldn't comprehend was that she potentially carried the same dark power inside of her.

Sequis roared at the crowd. "Is this what will finally prove my dedication as your ruler?!"

Resi watched the blue light grow in Luther's eyes. She didn't know what would take her life first: the strange blue orb or Sequis's hand wrapped around her neck. She spasmed in the air, her feet twitching and kicking as a groan ripped through Sequis. He brought the sphere inches from her chest, but faltered. She could see the fight in his eyes. He didn't want to do it.

But then, the flash of light ripped across the gallows. The blue sphere launched in the opposite direction, and immediately Resi fell to the floor.

She caught her breath, noticing Sequis beside her on his knees, his face hollow and scared. She was convinced the moaning was coming from him, but soon enough, she realized it wasn't. Her eyes rose to the guards gathered around Luther. The Advisor lay paralyzed on the wood. In shock, he clutched at his chest. Blue light shone out of a gaping, bleeding wound.

"I didn't want to do it, Luther," Sequis said through thick sobs.

Luther continued to yelp out, the blue haze continuing to grow from his chest and into his limbs.

"Why did you make me do this, Luther?!" Sequis ranted on. He pushed his hands against his knees to aid him to his feet. He crossed the gallows, his massive legs dragging behind him. Terrified, the guards scattered in all directions, launching themselves from the gallows as if it were a sinking ship. Luther's eyes widened with panic when Sequis set a hand on the wound. Immediately, the blue light began to recede.

Resi gasped. Could it be? Was Sequis healing him?

Then, out of nowhere, she felt her stomach lurch in protest. She brought a hand to it, only to be greeted with searing pain.

Fearful, she stood to her feet. She gagged on the heat from her own breath. The burning was spreading like fire ants inside of her. The itch of it was unbearable. She wanted to claw out of her own skin, to yell to the crowd to run as far away as possible, to help themselves while they still could. But it was too late. The heat had spread to her brain, to her extremities. She was rendered helpless, dizzy with the might of the power that had stayed dormant within her for years. The fever spread, and soon, the soft candlelight of the gardens turned completely black.

BLURRED SHADOWS. Muffled cries. Resi held out her hand in front of her face, certain it had been blown off. A ringing painfully pierced her ears.

There had been an explosion, an attack.

Weakly, she rubbed the soot from her eyes. Dust consumed the darkness above her in thick, tan clouds. She looked up to the gallows only to find them destroyed. The rafters had split at the center and fallen into a broken heap all around her. One of the nooses lay still by her legs, coiled around itself like a sleeping serpent.

Shadows raced and raged through the night, screaming and shrieking terrible pleas at the top of their might. But the dust was so thick that Resi couldn't see past the gallows.

It was pandemonium.

Shakily, she scrambled to her feet. With cautious steps, she navigated herself across the wooden planks, noticing as she did that one of her shoes was missing.

More screams. Or was it just the same as before, but closer? She shifted forward along the garden gravel until she nearly knocked herself over a stiff pile near her feet.

"Help me," a gruff voice came from the ground. But there was nothing Resi could do. The man was too violently burned.

She moved onward, noticing the dust was beginning to settle and clear. Soon, the silhouette of the Tristeland revealed itself atop the dusty aftermath. It had been badly hit. The grandiose facade had been mauled, leaving giant piles of rough brick along the perimeter of the gardens. The interior was exposed as if it'd been sliced into like a cake. Mangled books, chairs, and harpsichords leaked out of the bleeding wound.

Resi knew she should run, but her feet could only go so quickly as she passed face after face left burned and alone along the gravel path. The gardens were a war zone.

She brought her hand to her stomach. Nothing, as if all of the heat inside had been put to significant use.

An elderly woman reached out a wrinkled hand and clung to the bottom of Resi's dress. She was shaking, confused. Both of her eyes were blackened with blood and soot. The explosion had blinded her. Resi reached to her through the dust, bringing her to her feet.

"I'm sorry," she said, her own voice distant and unfamiliar. "I'm so sorry."

She pressed on with the woman, leading her out of the dust and to a safe patch of wilted grass. She looked toward the center fountain. It had been blown over like a birdbath in a wind storm. Three men were pinned beneath it like mice, yelping and screaming in gut-wrenching pain. Through the haze, a woman clutched at her burned husband, her tears marking clean lines down her sooted face.

Resi stood paralyzed over the blind woman. She couldn't have done this; not this. She wiped more soot from her own eyes, hoping the whole scene would disappear. Instead, her gaze drifted to the other side of the decimated gallows.

Sequis—his hunched, broad shoulders; his golden, soot-stained hair. For a brief moment, she watched him, mesmerized. She couldn't understand why he was crying. But there, smeared across the stone in front of him, was Luther. His legs lay broken on the stone, twisted and tangled together like woven branches. Gray, nightmarish eyes were opened to the sky.

The unthinkable had happened. Resi's inferno had destroyed the Tristeland gardens in one dizzying blow, and with it, the second most powerful man in the region.

Sequis stood to his feet, then turned towards the madness. His once-perfect face was badly gashed on one of the cheeks. Like a hawk, his eyes searched for Resi until they found her clear across the gardens. For a brief moment, they stood paralyzed amongst the chaos, both caught in the aftermath of the wreckage they'd caused.

But then, a single tear fell across the gash at Sequis's cheek. Resi stood to her feet, taking fearful steps forward. He'd only meant to hurt Luther, to inject fear into his heart. But this? He'd never wished for this.

Knowing what would come next, she watched the agony in his eyes suddenly switch. Terror and rage merged within him. The blue sphere lit on his palm, the flames spitting and cracking, igniting his face with cool, bright light. It wasn't a second later that Resi turned for the cliffs and ran for her life.

CHAPTER 14

THE STRANGER

last after blast followed, smashing into the dirt, the sky.
Sequis's roars echoed over the dust, over the screams of the
civilians.

A sting of blue light ignited the stone at Resi's feet, then burst
into flames. She bolted further down the path to the cliffs, trying to
avoid the inevitable gaze into the chasm below. Finally, she looked.
The sea stirred a foamy yellow against the rocky shore.

She turned to her right and left; she was stuck. The rock only
went straight down to the sharp stones that dotted the water. But
suddenly, as if by fate, a moonbeam struck a jagged shelf leading down
the cliffs. A path. Shaking, Resi ripped the train of her gown, freeing
her legs, then raced for it.

WHAM! Another blow from Sequis came blasting into the rock
above her. The remnants of what remained showered on Resi like
falling bullets, stinging the skin of her arms, biting at her legs. Still, she
kept moving, jumping over thick boulders and ducking beneath large
overhangs.

BAM!; another shot to the path near her feet. Horrified, she
watched as the blue light pierced the ground, then rolled the stone
over the edge to fall the many feet to the shore. Cautiously, she

scooted along the newly narrowed path with her back to the cold stone.

She glanced up the cliffs. Nothing was visible, not even the sky through the dust. But soon enough, the cloud lit up a bright blue before descending again on the path.

Resi's ears screeched in protest. The blast had hit just above her head. She landed on her side, inches from escaping over the thin ledge.

Where was Sequis? The path was dark behind her. It wasn't wide enough for a giant. He must've been blindly shooting from above.

Muffled shouts, droned out by the ringing in Resi's ears, sounded from somewhere over the cliffs; she'd thought too soon. Any moment and the path would be flooded by members of the Eastern Guard. She kept scaling the wall, looking for dips in the path ahead.

Again, the cliffs lit a bright blue. The blast collided with the rock in front of Resi. She fell back on the path, coughing into her arm as the dust parted. The route ahead was obliterated. Jump, and she was dead in the water. Wait, and she was trapped.

The guards' voices began to rise over the roar of the sea. "There!" one cried, his rough face appearing out of the sky.

Hoping for a miracle, Resi peered over the stone of the cliffs, but nothing revealed itself to her, not like before—just gray stone flickering blue and black as far as the eye could see.

Voices clashed against the rock wall. Resi anxiously ran her hands through her hair, then turned to the right; a patch of wood in the stone. It was unmistakable. Unconvinced, she took a double-take. There was no time to waste. To get to the trap door, she'd have to jump over the missing path.

Determined, she took a few steps back before throwing herself into the air. But she'd undershot it. Her upper body slammed into the stone, taking the breath from her lungs. She wheezed as she struggled to bring her legs to the path. She looked up just in time to see the trap door fly open. A hand waved out of it.

"Come! Now!" a voice called. Resi darted to it, then allowed the arms of the stranger to lift her feet from the rock and into safety.

The door shut behind her with a gratifying thud and a latch bolted shut, indicating the door was locked from the inside. Finally, she was safe, at least, for the time being. All was silent in the black until WHAM!; another blast echoed beyond the many layers of stone.

A match lit before a small, youthful face. It ignited a torch to reveal Alby, the Aliquian girl without ears, her sweet eyes wide with terror.

All at once, Resi clamored to hug her. "I'm sorry," she apologized, out of breath. "Just good to see a friendly face."

Quickly, Alby stepped aside, and waiting behind her was Ana. Resi was beside herself. She swept Ana into her arms and held on tightly.

"Did Luther hurt you?" Resi asked.

Ana simply shrugged. "He can lock me up, but that weasel of a man couldn't hurt me if he tried."

Resi shuddered. Luther would never hurt anyone again. "How did you find me?"

Ana looked at Alby with a grin. "Commander Lee. He sent us here to search for you. Said if you were smart, you'd find the path to the tunnels."

Resi hadn't had the time to wonder where Lee had run off to in the hour since he'd delivered her to Sequis. And here, she'd found the tunnels that Ana had told her about on their tour of the gardens. She'd nearly forgotten about this fact, and she'd forever be in their gratitude.

"You don't have much time," Ana said, panic setting in her eyes. She tossed a change of clothes at Resi; a pair of trousers along with a men's shirt and boots. Alby held out a brown wool cloak, and with it, a small satchel. Resi looked inside. Bread packed just for her.

Undressing, Resi went to remove the diamond necklace at her throat.

"Keep that. You can sell it," Ana instructed as she fussed with the cloak at Resi's shoulders.

"But, where will I go?" Resi asked, all the while hating the tremor of fear in her voice.

Ana sighed. "Follow this passage north. Don't make any turns or you'll end up back where you started. A few days and the tunnels will lead you to a path into Derton. There's an inn on the outskirts of town. Hide out for a few days, then move on."

A shiver of cold fear ran down Resi's spine. For months, she'd dreamed about fleeing the boundaries of the Offenheimer Farmhold and making it to Derton. She'd wanted this journey, hadn't she? But now that it was here, all she desired was to duck out until the world forgot about her.

"You both risked your lives coming here," Resi sighed. "I'll never be able to repay you."

Ana stepped forward and placed two sturdy hands on her shoulders. "You staying alive is payment enough."

Resi felt guilty for accepting her kindness. She wouldn't, not after what she'd done to the guests in the garden, not after what she'd done to Luther without having meant it. But her plan to escape Ter had to take action. All summer had been leading up to this very moment. She was born to run. She just hadn't known then that she'd be fleeing the region on the basis of being wanted for murder.

Ana and Alby both chuckled at her silence. "I had a feeling you were one of us," Ana started. "Did from the moment you asked me if I was from the North. Not many Patrian women would know the history behind an Aliquian name." Her eyes gleamed with fresh tears. "You're gifted, Resi. It's about time someone stood up to Sequis. And now that we know what he truly is..."

The three of them came together to embrace in the darkness, Resi hating the feeling of guilt that wanted to latch on to her for dear life.

"I won't say goodbye," Resi said.

"Well then," Ana shrugged. "—Until next time."

She passed the torch to Resi before she and Alby linked arms and turned back for the pass that would lead to the Estate. Resi waited until they disappeared into the darkness before she turned North. With a new mission, she threw the hood of her cloak over her head, then marched onward.

RESI ONLY KNEW two things about the town of Derton. The first was that it was a fishing town. The second was that it existed for those simply on their way to bigger and more accommodating destinations.

After three days trapped inside a silent, damp tunnel, all she desired was a warm, dry place to rest her head. And, seeing as the Dockside House was the only inn in Derton, save for a bait shop with the word VACANCY written in the dust of one of its shattered windows, Resi wasn't asking for much. In fact, the only confirmation she needed in order to lodge at the Dockside House were the words *WILL TRADE* written boldly on a beaten-down board by the front door.

Cautiously, she entered the front room, a dismal space covered in an inch of dust. The living area was decorated with only a desk, a chair, and a sad floral-print couch. The stuffing oozed out of it onto the uneven floorboards like lava. For several minutes, she waited impatiently, certain she'd picked the wrong inn before realizing a small, bug-eyed creature was staring at her from behind the desk.

Few people stayed in Derton for longer than a few days, but those who considered themselves local knew Ms. Shummacker as the woman who drooled on her way to the fish market. There was no question that she was ancient. Her once-brown eyes were now heavily discolored from years of staring at the sun's reflection off the water.

Gladys Schummacker's nose barely cleared above the worn desk, but what she lacked in size she made up for in throat-clearing. A long, irritated grunt came out of her before Resi got the hint to approach. Without a word, she marched to the desk and plopped the diamond necklace gifted to her by Sequis directly in front of the innkeeper. The woman's eyes bulged as her creaky fingers reached for her glasses. Once on, the spectacles made a show of her, enlarging her eyes to the size of two glassy saucers. Without missing a beat, she groped the pocket of her dress and handed Resi a long, thin key. A coin purse filled with enough change to last a month on the road plopped onto the desk in exchange.

"Stay as long as you like," Gladys cooed, her voice laden with years of pipe-smoking.

The room at the inn held only a bucket and a bed. Resi didn't wish to spend time wondering what the bucket was for, so instead, she crashed into a pile on the mattress, not caring whether the innkeeper had thought to wash the sheets between guests. Exhausted from travel, she slept soundly that night, feeling as far away from the Tristeland and Sequis as she could ever be.

The following morning, she'd snuck out of her room unnoticed. She had reason to believe she was the only person staying at the Dockside House during the offseason; the inn had remained quiet all night. Her suspicion was made correct when she descended the front stairs and caught Gladys in a private moment. Gleefully, the innkeeper eyed herself in a cracked table mirror, pawing at the diamond necklace around her neck as if it were the key to life eternal.

The streets of the town were almost always deserted, except for the occasional sighting of a drunk sailor stumbling his way home after a long night at sea. Resi didn't so much mind the village. It was quiet, desolate, the type of place that made it easy to disappear for a few days.

There were very few women about the town, which did make remaining unnoticed rather difficult. Resi, however, was content to spend the day ducking in and out of pubs, perusing the wacky bait shops and walking the foggy streets.

That night, she returned to the Inn to find Gladys passed out behind the desk. An empty glass rested before her, and further, a letter opener that rested atop an opened envelope. Gently, Resi snagged the small dagger from underneath Gladys's snoring mouth and tucked it into her cloak. It was smart for her to be armed.

An hour later, Resi looked over the cut pieces of her golden-brown hair on the dusty floor. Though a necessity for money and added concealment, she couldn't stop herself from sobbing into her hands. What would Mags have said? Would she have held her while she cried? Told her everything was going to be alright?

She felt much better the following afternoon after exchanging the cut locks for another two coin purses from Gladys. But no amount of coin could bring back the years she'd spent growing out her hair. She sulked all that day, pulling on the short ends, feeling as sorry for herself as the day her parents had disappeared.

For the better part of the next two days, she walked the streets and hid out in pubs. As far as she knew, the people about town probably suspected she was the troubled granddaughter of some wealthy Patrian. She certainly could pass as such, especially now that her brassy locks had been chopped from her head. Autonomy was her only ally. She could blend in, become whatever she wanted to be.

She heard whispers, of course; bar staff exchanging elaborate stories to each other as they wiped the counters and swept the floors at the end of their shifts. The people of Derton were privy to the fact that something bizarre had taken place at the Tristeland, but what, they couldn't be sure. Some were certain a proposal had taken place and that Sequis had finally decided to take a bride from the North. Others had the notion that it was a kitchen fire that had cut the evening short. This second story was the most amusing to Resi. After all, it *had* been a fire that had ruined the night, only, the fire had started in her stomach and not in the belly of the Tristeland kitchens.

Whenever Resi found herself in moments of extreme seclusion, be it down a slimy alley or in the pitch-black of night that swelled her room, she tried to gather the courage to carry out her escape west and to combat the looming heat in her belly. She'd come to think of her monster much like an unwanted child that had been conceived out of some horrible trauma, often patting it as if it were doomed to give her misery for eternity. Since arriving in Derton, she'd been grateful to be rid of the outbursts that had haunted her time at the Tristeland. But still, the heat was always there, reminding her of the burned skin, the blind and bloodied eyes, the lifeless arms and legs, tangled and left alone in the wilted grass. It didn't matter how many glasses of cider she took down in the course of an hour. The faces wouldn't leave her, and some mysterious part of herself told her there would be consequences if they ever did.

Her favorite pub, the Rusty Hook, had become her regular late-night place of dwelling, a destination she sought out to drown herself in ale until her thoughts strayed to days spent in the sun with her mother. Despite the fact that the Rusty Hook smelled of stale fish guts and days-old vomit, Resi had come to enjoy it. She found the rough, raw atmosphere comforting. She liked the way the pillar candles burned so low that the wax dripped on the floor. But what she loved most was the fact that only the loneliest souls came through the doors, souls looking only for a pint and not for conversation.

On her third night in the village, Resi found her way to the darkest booth in the darkest corner, ordered a cider and a small spread of cheese and fish, then watched a group of broad-shouldered men make themselves comfortable at the bar; old friends of the barkeep. They spoke slowly, languidly, as they chugged their frothy drinks. Resi couldn't help but be amused. Long gone were the days of spying on Marion and her porch birds sipping on Rowgar. Based on their unshaven faces and outgrown mops, it was clear that these men were no strangers to the streets and the sea and every place in between. True men of the regions, as Mags liked to call them.

"Strange news from the Tristeland," Resi heard one of them say to the barkeep, a white-bearded man with a rigid nose. "Not sure what to make of it. You know how those spoiled Southerners are, always making up stories."

Resi's spine straightened. Her chew slowed.

"Still," replied another, a younger man wearing a beaten, straw hat. "Can't deny the kind of money he's offering to bring the 'Lick in."

Without warning, the fish lodged in Resi's throat. She sputtered and spewed, drawing the attention of the three men and the barkeep. Busily, she rushed to pull the coins from her cloak before plopping more than enough on the table, all the while coughing and clinging to any breath she could get. Frustrated, she pulled the cloak over her head, wishing it suddenly had the ability to make her disappear from existence. As she headed for the door, she felt the sting of eyes on her back. From the front of the pub, a man whose face was concealed by a dark cloak threw his change down on the table, then quickly finished his ale.

Hastily, Resi raced her way up the winding cobblestone, cursing herself for staying too long in one place, for getting too comfortable with her newfound freedom in a town that didn't quite feel like a town. She rounded the corner and sighed when she saw the warm glow radiating from the windows of the Dockside House. But then, two shadows passed before its light, men dressed in gleaming charcoal armor. Together, they embarked up the rickety front steps of the Dockside House before being greeted by a bejeweled Gladys Schummacker.

Resi hid herself behind a pillar, watching the guards take in the sight of the hideous woman. She drew the cloak tighter around herself, then turned back down the winding road that led straight to the sea.

She'd find shelter for the night; hide herself in a fishing boat, stay safe and dry alongside the bait and decay. She continued walking towards the docks even after hearing approaching footsteps from behind. The Eastern Guard's boots thumped along the street the same as they had at the Tristeland.

Impulsively, she turned down a thin alley, knowing immediately she'd made the wrong choice when she noticed a dark figure, the same man in the black cloak from the Rusty Hook, approaching. Still, the guard's footsteps turned after her.

"Hey!" the dark figure ahead called out. The voice was deep and rough. Resi veered for the other side of the alley, but the cloaked man responded by doing the same.

Confused, she turned over her shoulder, certain the man was speaking to the approaching guards. Only, he wasn't.

"You!" he called out again.

Resi stopped in her tracks, unsure of where to turn. She was stuck in the alley, trapped between the approaching guards and the cloaked figure. Then, light from the streetlamp hit the man's face. She didn't recognize him. Still, he approached her as a friend, someone he knew.

"Roaming the streets after dark again?" he said as he grabbed her, his voice loud enough to wake the entire street from their slumber. "You know, I was really starting to worry. I knew you'd snuck off to the pub. Your father will be *furious* when he finds out you've fallen off the wagon. For a *third* time."

Resi was stunned speechless. She peered into the formless face shielded by the night.

"*Go with it,*" the cloaked man said under his breath. He began to lead her deeper down the dark alley.

"Uh, that's right...*Uncle,*" she started, although, not convincingly. "Can't keep me away from the cider."

The man gave her a strange look, then led her onward. Hesitantly, she peered back at the guards, then sighed a breath of relief as she watched them turn back for the pubs.

"Follow me," said the man as he unhanded her.

Resi waited in the alley, fearful of what might follow. She couldn't go back to The Dockside Inn. She had no other alternative.

The man was short and stocky in an important, but nonthreatening way. Proudly, he waltzed ahead of Resi as if he made a living of walking prominently in front of people. Resi followed after him in silence for what felt like hours, passing the dilapidated docks and rundown ships in the small harbor before turning down a dirt lane leading out of town. The man went for a door belonging to a crooked, two-story cottage tucked into the trees. Resi watched a strong nose extend out of his black cloak as he looked in all directions for anyone that might be following them. Uncertain, he unlatched the door and signaled for Resi to go inside. She stalled, then finally tucked herself inside the warmth of the cottage.

The space was cramped with piles of thick books laid about the floor and chairs. Dust lined all corners. Resi was beginning to think Derton should've been name *Duston*.

"Cozy," she spoke quietly. She watched curiously as the man peered through a sheer curtain at the front of the house. He then pulled a matchbox from his pocket and went for a lantern resting on top of a pile of books.

"Wasn't aiming for charm," he huffed. "Just something abandoned." He lit the lantern, then unveiled himself. His face was strong, but still round at the cheeks. He had the kind of golden-brown eyes that made the angles of his face appear warm, but there was a fierce restlessness behind them, the kind brought on by many years of experience and mishaps on the road. Resi watched as he bent at the waist to throw firewood in the hearth, then lit it with a match.

"Now's as good a time as any for you to tell me who in the Sept-Regions you are," Resi finally spewed. The weight of the question filled the silence of the room like rushing water. The stranger turned, his eyes meeting hers for the first time.

"Just another person looking for the 'Lick that caused such a stir at the Tristeland."

Resi's heart quickened beneath her cloak. "So, you're what—a town patroller?"

The man sighed through his nose. He wasn't amused. "No. I'm Vegari."

Every Aliquian had heard stories about Vegari: Patrians hired to track down runaway Aliquians that could be of use to a wealthy employer. Elusive and cunning, a Vegari's reputation was synonymous with double-crossing. Their tracking almost always ended in disaster. Aliquians lucky enough to escape to the western regions were usually sold into terrible situations at the hands of Vegari. Resi had overheard a story in the fields about an Aliquian man who'd escaped northern Ter with the help of a Vegari. Unfortunately, the man fell into the lap of a Codian farmer who had a certain fascination with torturing runaways. After her little bout at the Tristeland, Resi hadn't thought about being followed by anyone other than Sequis and his Eastern Guard. Terrified, she reached deep into her cloak pocket and retrieved the letter opener from Gladys's desk. She pulled it on the stranger, closing in on his throat.

"And who, exactly, is your employer?!" she demanded.

The man looked down at the dull blade as if it were nothing more than a pesky gnat fluttering in front of his face. He raised the back of his hand to it and simply brushed it away.

"I'm surprised you'd try to interrogate me, considering all the *other* methods of violence someone like you could resort to."

"I asked you a question."

The man lurked with his back to her as he peered again out the window. There was an air of paranoia about him. His hands twisted together nervously. "I'm from Dirig. My employer is Patrian. As am I."

"You came all the way from Dirig?" she asked. She hadn't noticed until now that the small dagger was still outstretched in her hand.

"When rumors start swirling about a gifted Aliquian in the South, you go."

Resi's weight shifted uncomfortably on the tattered tapestry. The heat shimmered from her extended hands, and the man took notice. He pretended not to be threatened, but his eyes widened before he raised his hands cautiously in front of his body.

"Look, I'm not going to hurt you," he spoke. "And neither is my employer."

Resi's hand with the dagger fell to her side. She knew he was telling the truth. If he had reason to harm her, wouldn't he have by now?

"Name?" she asked.

"Rolf."

"Resi," she replied. "But, of course, you already know that."

"Your name has become quite the talk around these parts."

"I'm beginning to see that," she shrugged.

"Stupid move, by the way—selling that necklace."

Annoyed, she huffed. "Girl's got to eat."

The man adjusted his pants beneath his round belly. "You need to be more careful, alright? Diamonds like that don't make appearances in towns like this."

"Ok, ok," she retorted, feeling as if she were a child being chastised by a parent.

"Smart move with the hair, though."

Confused, Resi looked up at him, noticing the lines near his eyes. "How would you know about that?"

"You were described as having long hair. I, however, assumed someone in your position, if you were *smart*, would do everything possible to change your appearance." He took a deep breath. "Everyone in the Sept-Regions is on the hunt for you."

Resi put her head in her hands. "I should be burned alive after what I did." She waited as Rolf crossed the room and placed himself in front of the fire.

"Sure, there were casualties," he shrugged. "And people were burned."

"I don't need a walk-through."

"I was *trying* to tell you that even though many people were hurt, only one was killed."

Resi felt a sense of relief wash over her at this news. At least lives were spared. All but one. "Yeah, and he was second in command of the region," she growled.

"True," Rolf sighed as if examining a wound that would never heal. "Can't really help you out with that one."

Another hot breath left Resi before she looked over to see Rolf warming his hands near the fire. The orange glow highlighted a small patch of gray in his thinning hair.

Resi looked to the floor. "How did you find out about me?"

"Word spreads fast. Abolitionists were alarmed to hear that an Aliquian girl had been selected as Sequis's portrait artist. This made my employer curious. *Very* curious."

"Luther was the only one that knew I was Aliquian," she spat.

"Rule number one about being on the run; assume most people know most things. Aliquians. Guards. Vegari. My employer received an anonymous letter. Said there was reason to believe you were gifted."

"What reason was that? My power didn't fully reveal itself until..." she stopped herself as Rolf suddenly sat forward in his seat. Her eyes searched the corners of the room for an adequate answer. "—the night of the Ball."

Disappointed, Rolf relaxed into his chair. "You don't know much about Aliquian gifting, do you?"

A huff left Resi. "I've always known there was something strange about me," she said as her hand touched her stomach. The fire was there, just quieter, as if it were taking a nap now that she no longer felt threatened. "Stories about people like me were always told to ease depression during harvest season, but I never expected this."

Rolf downed another gulp from the flask. "Most stories, even if they seem far-fetched, have some level of truth to them. Even you know that."

Resi wasn't certain she followed, but even so, she found herself nodding in agreement.

"Your love of painting—when did that start?" Rolf asked her.

Resi thought back to all those weeks ago in Scottis's study. "Only a few weeks ago."

Rolf gave her a strange face. "Not earlier?" He put down his flask on the uneven table before him.

"I sketched, but Sequis's portrait was only the second one I've painted."

Incredulous, Rolf began to pace the room. "Wow, you *really* have no clue about Aliquian gifting, do you?"

Resi didn't need to respond.

"Aliquian gifting is not the same as sorcery, although it's led many great men with power into the practice of dark sorcery if not learned and trained," Rolf told her. "They're two very different things. "

Resi leaned forward in her seat, trying to catch every word. "I'm not a witch?"

Rolf simply laughed. "Have you ever practiced blood rituals? Sacrifices?"

"No," Resi coughed.

"Then you're not a witch. I assume you know the old Aliquian story of the two men traveling up the mountain..."

Resi waited, then shook her head when no such memory of this kind of fable came to her.

"*Why did I even ask?*" Rolf mumbled to himself before he readjusted his position in his seat. "Two Aliquian men embarked up a mountain, one carrying a great stone on his back, and the other a pebble in his pocket. The man with the pebble climbed the mountain swiftly and with a spring in his step. He arrived at the peak with plenty of breath in his lungs, but in his arrogance at having beat the other man to the top, he ran back down the mountainside and slipped to his death on the return journey. The man carrying the great stone, however, took his time ascending the mountain, and gave up his journey many times over, but in his suffering and anguish, he found immense strength and perseverance. His legs grew muscular and tough. His mind became pure and still. By the time he reached the peak, he had transformed into a great warrior of body, mind, and heart. His return to the base of the mountain was filled with beauty and reverence for having overcome the many obstacles he faced."

"So...Aliquian gifting requires time and patience. Sorcery can be accomplished quickly, but without long-term reward."

"Correct. Aliquian power first shows itself in the form of enhanced talents. Those who will eventually show signs of power have tremendous gifts, whether it be towards music, combat, *painting*... you name it. It's what makes Aliquian gifting so different from sorcery, which is born out of restlessness and lack of purpose and passion. Your power is completely unique and individual to you. And as far as I can tell, you have no clue what you're capable of."

Resi leaned back again on the couch, feeling herself fall into its moth-eaten velvet as if it were eating her alive. So that's why the fire had raged during her portrait sessions. She'd sensed this, but hearing it spoken from a stranger was altogether different. "And that's why you traveled to see me? Because there was *reason to believe* I had powers lurking behind my ability to paint?"

"It's also why Luther brought you to the Tristeland. Your artistry was your giveaway."

"Still," she spat, "that's not enough to go off of. I mean, how would Luther be sure that I'd have a display of power?"

"Aliquian power *has* to respond to sorcery," he huffed. "Luther probably thought bringing you to the Tristeland under the guise of '*portrait artist*' would eventually lead to the discovery of your real gifting. After learning of your real identity, your gifting, *and* denying him a marriage proposal, Sequis would've been angry enough to display his descent into sorcery, which in turn, would've pulled out your first show of power."

In shock, Resi huffed. "Great. That's just great."

Rolf snickered knowingly. "This is bigger than just you, Resi. Sorcery and Aliquian-gifting have had a long-standing feud ever since the days of King Aliquis. Once one is drawn out, the other has to respond." He reached for the flask, then, realizing it was empty, stood to search a nearby cabinet for a replacement substance. "What's your trigger?"

Resi glared at him. "Excuse me, my *what*?"

"Your trigger—you know, a strong emotion that activates your power?"

Resi searched her mind. "I wouldn't have the slightest idea."

"Luther had to have known what it was," he said, nodding. "Did he ever size you up? Ask you questions?"

Resi shrugged. "He delivered me to the Tristeland from the Offenheimers. Asked me some things."

"What things?"

"About my parents. But nothing much else."

"What about your parents would be significant?" Rolf asked as he crossed the room to snatch a cobwebcovered bottle filled with a dark liquor off of a nearby cart. He filled his flask, then took a large gulp of it.

Resi's eyes went to her lap. The idea of opening up the baggage of her past to a total stranger felt too exposing, especially in the glow of a warm fire in a home belonging to someone presumed long dead.

"Give me that," she said, extending a hand out for the newly-filled flask. Rolf looked down at the cork container with a strange sort of pride, then handed it to her. Resi took a big gulp, then almost choked it out.

"Not up to your high standards after all the fine wines at the Tristeland?" Rolf jeered.

Resi's face contorted to ease the blow of the taste. "Even a homeless drunk would turn that stuff away."

Amused, Rolf joined her again by the fire, sitting in his chair as if it'd belonged to him for many years. Resi's mind still lingered on Rolf's question from before. She didn't want to, but Resi blurted it out.

"They escaped the farmhold when I was a girl. Left me behind."

A sad wash crossed Rolf's face before he nodded. He was thinking. "Luther knew abandonment was a weak point. Let me guess, he kept you isolated? Alone? And worse, you were sworn to keep a terrible secret. He was winding you up."

"Are you saying my trigger is loneliness?"

"I'm saying," Rolf scooted his chair closer to the fire, "that your real trigger is anger. And, it seems Luther knew how to pull it out of you—by isolating you, reminding you of your past."

Resi's eyes glazed over as she recalled all the times she'd felt the fire roar within her stomach as a girl. "The angriest time in my life came right after my parents left. Why wouldn't my gifting have revealed itself then?"

Rolf's eyebrows raised. "Are you so sure it didn't?"

Resi started pacing the room. Rolf was trying to get it out of her, trying to fuel the fire in some way. "The heat...it started not soon after they left. But I never had an outburst."

"What heat?"

Resi was tempered enough to feel the growing boil from inside. She reached for the back of Rolf's hand and quickly brought it to her belly.

"Ow!" he cried, whipping his hand back and forth from the pain.

"*That* heat." For a fleeting moment, Resi swore she saw fear in his eyes. But just as quickly, he rid himself of it with a shake of his head.

"Just so you're aware," he said through a soft belch, "this street will be flooded with guards come morning. You have a better shot of making it west by my side than you do on your own. I know the regions better than most."

She crossed her arms defiantly. "And what of your employer? What will he do with me?"

Rolf sighed, clearly wishing for some shut-eye. "I can tell you everything you need to know come tomorrow. But what you need right now is rest. All I can ask is that you trust me. As far as I can see, you don't have anyone else in your corner right now."

Resi eased, knowing he was right, but she feared the idea of finding sleep. She hadn't had a full night of rest in so long.

"I'll take the sofa," he offered as he wiped at his tired eyes. "There's a room upstairs. Not much, but it beats the streets."

Hesitantly, Resi peered up the steps. She felt like saying thank you, but she had yet to discover if Rolf's rescue was something to be grateful for or not.

"Sleep," he said. "We'll get a move on before dawn."

And surprisingly, Resi did sleep. She dreamed of blurred faces, of wedding gowns, of tunnels that wound their way deep into the heart of the Sept-Regions, of buckets of piss and dusty-floored pubs. She only wakened once, and with a fright, after having a nightmare of a giant peering out over darkening cliffs. His cape snapped in the breeze and his eyes hungered for one thing and one thing only; her blood.

CHAPTER 15

THE CABIN

For days, it seemed the sky did nothing but cry, cry, and cry some more. The meadows went slushy underfoot as the forest's canopy wept large tears. It was the kind of weather that forced many civilians of northern Ter indoors to sit by a warm fire with a hot cup of folly tea to avoid catching a cold. But for two weary travelers, it was the perfect time to run.

Neither she nor Rolf wished to complain, but Resi suspected she wasn't the only one cursing to herself under her breath. It seemed both of them were content to remain quiet and focused on the task ahead. They were together in their misery, and as long as the rains continued to dampen and soak through their clothes to the bone, they'd remain silent.

They'd been on the road five days, five nights, only stopping for sleep as they headed north for the safety of the small towns lining the border into the region of Sterch. They rotated sleeping, someone always on watch while the other wrestled to find a comfortable spot on the ground. The first night, they'd tried to settle in an old barn belonging to a quiet property. But soon enough, the combination of damp hay and a pair of twitchy rats made the decision to continue the journey through the night far from difficult.

They'd spent the remainder of the dark hours that night plodding through the murky forest, hearing the noises of the wood settle beneath the pitter-patter. At least, Resi had told herself, constant movement kept their bodies alert, on edge. She'd been afraid that if she attempted to rest for longer than an hour at a time, she'd forget how to walk after so many hours of journeying.

To make matters worse, food was running low. Resi had rationed the bread given to her from Ana, nibbling on it every now and again when she needed something to distract herself from the cold. Stealing was also an option; northern Ter was littered with farm after farm after farm, all quiet, sleepy establishments. Swiping an egg or two wouldn't have been so difficult. But, Rolf, it appeared, wasn't the kind to improvise. Anytime Resi even mentioned the idea, Rolf would shake his head in protest. He wouldn't so much as allow Resi to hunt a squirrel or rabbit.

"No fires," he'd said to her through a clenched jaw. "We need to keep moving."

Resi had thought many times along the journey about poking at Rolf with more questions about her gifting. She'd contemplated mentioning their conversation from that first night at the sleepy cottage, bringing it up casually like she'd brought up so many conversations to Mags in the hours after dinner on the stoop. But anytime she'd go to say a word, she'd stop herself, remembering Rolf's blue lips and determined stride.

Try as she might, she couldn't wrap her mind around the concept of her monster inside being labeled as a *gifting*; as if her ability to shatter lives had been delivered to her in a beautifully wrapped package, one with flowers trapped helplessly beneath perfectly tied strings. She was reminded of her paintbrushes delivered from Sequis, each a holy creation, each unique in its design and function. What she wouldn't have given to have had one last canvas to introduce them to. Given the chance, she'd paint the best damn painting in the world.

If only her hands weren't so numb.

Finally, in the afternoon, they came to a wide stream surrounded by large boulders.

"Not much further," Rolf spoke as he aided Resi over a rock.

Stunned, Resi stopped in her tracks. "The Vegari speaks."

Rolf didn't need to respond. The way he proceeded to trudge mercilessly through the trees told Resi enough.

"Where to?" she finally asked.

"A friend's."

For one reason or another, Resi had pictured Rolf and her marching along just the two of them for eternity, making their way through sunshine and snow and every season in between until both of them were so old that their teeth would fall out.

"Can we trust them?" Resi heard herself say.

"They owe me a favor."

Resi looked down at her foot as it stomped on an acorn. "That's not an answer."

Rolf sighed, then turned back. "They have shelter. They have food."

"Do they *know* we're coming?"

Rolf didn't so much as glance at her as he continued walking. "They don't."

Maybe it was the cold. Maybe it was the hunger. Either way, Resi found herself laughing like she had when she was a child all those years ago under a holed blanket. "So, we're just going to stroll up and ask for a place to hide out? *'Oh, by the way, this here is Resi; a Witch-'Lick who killed the Advisor to the Governor! Mind moving over so she can share your bed?'*"

She continued laughing and gripping at her hot and hungry stomach until suddenly, Rolf turned around, his expression serious. "Don't ever call yourself that. Not ever."

"What, *Witch-'Lick*?" Resi asked.

He warned her with a tilt of his head. "You're not one."

Confused, Resi nodded. She watched Rolf make his way forward, his steps wider and longer than before. She trotted to keep up.

"Under no circumstances, should you reveal who you are. Got it?" he threw over his shoulder.

It seemed silly to promise anything else, but still, Resi feared she wouldn't be able to hide the truth from whoever crossed their path.

Too many lies had already been spoken; she hated to tell even just one more.

They walked on, passing a small gathering of stone homes that sat perfectly nestled on a hilltop in the mist of early evening. Further, they came to a narrow path leading back into the trees. Rolf had to brush the wild branches away with his forearm; the path had gone unused for quite some time. Together, they marched up a steep hill, using the trees with their hands to get them to the hidden wooden home. It had been painted the color of the pines long ago, but the paint was chipped and cracked now, longing for love. A stone chimney raised high into the trees, sending smoke into the darkening sky.

"Not a word," Rolf reminded her. Resi rolled her eyes at him, happy the light of day had gone so that her antics went unseen.

Hesitantly, Rolf went to the door. He raised a fist, then knocked. Curious, Resi peered into one of the fogged windows. Candles were lit inside. They waited for a minute or two before Rolf raised his fist again.

"Amos, I know you're home!" he called as he knocked a second time.

Movement came from the back of the house. A shadow passed behind the window, then the door opened only a matter of inches. A blue eye, a nose, and a small tuft of white hair poked out. All Resi could think of was Theodore Offenheimer.

"Who is it?" a small voice asked.

"It's me, Amos. It's Rolf."

The door closed with a creak before a latch was unlocked and the door flew open.

Amos was a petite man with round, concerned eyes. White and thinning hair sat at the front of his head, revealing a copious amount of sunspots at the top. He was dressed in an old, untucked shirt and suspenders that had been unlatched.

"What is it?" he fearfully asked, looking between the two of them. "Is there some kind of trouble?"

"No, no," Rolf assured him, although Resi wasn't convinced.

"May we come in?"

"Who's she?" Amos barked. He scanned Resi head to foot. She felt as if she should've stepped forward to stick out her hand for him to shake. Instead, she curtsied, a habit from too much time spent in Court. Amos was struck dumb by this act, as if he were meeting a princess from overseas dressed in nothing but his underwear.

"This is my niece," Rolf said, this time, convincingly. "We're traveling west. I'm to deliver her to my sister in Rowan."

Amos shuffled in the doorway, taking a moment to look behind him up the stairs and further on to the back of the house. Finally, he stepped aside and motioned for them to come in.

The home was comfortable and filled with all the amenities that Resi had once imagined would exist inside a shabby woodland home; blankets lining the sofa, an ancient, holed chair next to a three-legged side table. She couldn't help but let her eyes linger on the amateur paintings on the walls.

"Must be hungry," Amos snorted, his eyes shifty. "I'll see what Myrtle has on the stove."

He hobbled to the back of the house, leaving Resi and Rolf alone by the fire. Resi closed her eyes and breathed in the smell of broth. When she opened them, she caught Rolf having a similar moment.

Then, a woman's voice rose in the kitchen. A minute later, Amos came into the front room, his face alarmed.

"I'm afraid you must be on your way. Myrtle isn't feeling all too well, and she wouldn't want either of you coming down with it, especially with most of the journey still ahead of you." The poor man couldn't look either of them in the face as he walked himself to the door and opened it for them to leave. "Happy travels."

Resi waited for Rolf to lead them back out into the rain. But he didn't. He stood his ground on the shabby rug. "Amos," he started. "We only ask for one night. We won't be any trouble."

Amos's eyes grew frantic. "Any *trouble*? You barge in here with a complete stranger, and you expect me to believe that?!"

"We've been traveling in the cold for five days. We need a warm place, just for the night." Then, after a breath, "You owe me."

The rain continued to fall as Amos watched it drip from outside the door. It was several seconds before he turned back to them, his eyes serious.

"A spot of food. Then straight to bed with you." He looked at Resi indignantly. "*Both* of you."

The petite man led them back through a swinging door to the kitchen. A long table sat at the center of the room, and huddled over the stove was a woman, Mags's age, stirring and sniffing over a boiling pot. As soon as the visitors entered, she anxiously spun around. She had steely eyes, the kind that could make anyone shrivel to the floor with just one glance. Her wild ginger hair was pulled back under a bandana.

After glaring at the newcomers, Myrtle shot a terrible eyeful at her husband before turning back to her stew. Without a word, she went to grab three wooden bowls from a cupboard before bringing them across the room and slamming them down on the table. She ladled the contents of the boiling pot into each bowl, her eyes drifting over Rolf and Resi as if they were children that had been caught poaching on their property. Then, she all but threw the pot back on the stove before shuffling off through the swinging door and out of sight. A few seconds passed before loud footsteps went up the front stairs.

Amos sighed. "Myrtle's not one for spontaneous visits."

Rolf and Resi wanted to be polite, but there wasn't much stopping them from throwing a leg over the bench and scarfing down the stew.

"Go on, now," Amos ordered, sensing their hunger.

They clamored to the table. Resi groaned as the first taste hit her tongue. The warmth of the broth was a delicacy after days spent dodging the rain. It was better than anything she'd ever been served at the Tristeland.

"Thank you," Rolf said as he blew at the soup.

Amos kept lingering near the stove. He crossed his arms, his gaze on the floor, but every so often he'd glance up to look at Resi, his face studying her like a book.

"Just what is it that you're running from?" he finally asked, his voice rough.

Rolf immediately set down his spoon. "She needs to go west," he said, which, Resi reasoned, wasn't a lie. "I'm taking her there."

"I may be a simple man, but I'm not blind," Amos chortled. "I know a 'Lick girl when I see one."

Slowly, Resi looked up at him, somehow feeling both seen and completely invisible. Rolf simply waited in the silence.

"If she's who I think she is, then you're in some kind of a sticky situation," Amos said, shaking his head.

"If you have something to say, please don't hold back," Rolf said, his mind more on his stew than on Amos's silly accusations.

Again, Amos looked upon Resi with a kind of certainty that made it impossible for her to continue eating. "I can't help but think that this girl is w-worth quite a lot to the Governor."

Resi's stomach sparked. She turned to see Rolf finally turn away from his stew. He stood defiantly.

"And what if she is?"

Amos shifted his weight uncomfortably from the other side of the small kitchen. His eyes fell to his feet. "I don't mean to be a pest. Only wish to know who's sleeping in my home for the night."

Rolf's chest bobbed defiantly in the silence. "I'd be careful to throw out accusations if I were you, Amos. Especially with all the secrets you keep."

Amos's mouth quivered as he wiped his sweaty palms against his slacks. He nodded sheepishly. "Make yourselves comfortable in the front room," he said. "And I don't have to remind you that you best be gone before sunrise." The man shuffled his way to the door, then disappeared.

Rolf gave a few sighs of relief, then sat back down to his stew. Resi waited for some sort of explanation, just one answer to all the strange glances that had taken place between Amos and him. But nothing followed. Instead, she blew at her stew and slurped it down until there was nothing left.

She tossed and turned that night on the old sofa, hearing the shifting noises of strange footsteps upstairs. She couldn't help but wonder how many other civilians were on the lookout for a young traveler on the run. How many eyes were waiting to witness the power she held? Had word spread of Sequis's sorcery? And if so, what did his many supporters have to say about his show of wonders?

The following morning, Rolf wakened Resi with a push of his hand to her shoulder. "Best be going," he whispered.

Without a word, Resi got to her feet and threw her cloak over her shoulder. She breathed in the warmth of the cabin one final time before following Rolf out the front door. But as she went to close the door behind her, she noticed a shadowed figure at the top of the stairs.

A young boy, maybe even younger than her, lingered in his night robes. He looked at her with a strange sort of curiosity. His eyes and hair were dark, too dark to be Codian. All she could think to do was nod to him. She knew what it was like to be confined in a home, and much as she was grateful for her time with Scottis, she would never choose to return to it.

Thankfully, the rains had ceased overnight. The temperature was still cool, but Resi welcomed the slight warmth from the early morning autumn sun on her cloak. She and Rolf continued walking in silence for a few hours before a boldness came over her. Maybe it was the newly dry air. Maybe it was a better night's rest in the warmth of Amos's home. But something in her emboldened her to finally start asking the questions she needed answers to.

"If I'm not allowed to call myself a Witch-'Lick, then what am I?" she called out to Rolf who stomped ahead of her.

Briefly, he paused, looking around the forest as if expecting someone to pop out from behind a tree.

"I don't think the squirrels will tell anyone," Resi whispered playfully.

Rolf turned back to her, his face somewhat amused, but still steeped with stoicism. He continued forward. "Call yourself gifted, but you're not a witch. That's something different."

Resi huffed, picking up a twig and knocking it against the bark of a nearby tree. "I might as well be a witch. Witches kill people, right?"

"A witch or a sorcerer uses the power of *trading* to gain access to their abilities. Your gift is free. It comes to you without you having to sacrifice anything. So yes, it is different."

"What do you mean by *trading*?"

Rolf paused in the sun, looking into the distance. The formidable mountains of Sterch were visible to them now. They'd made progress. "No different than how you traded your necklace for coins," he told her. "Witches trade all sorts of things. They make blood sacrifices. They speak in riddles and different tongues. They do all sorts of wacky things to move forward in their power."

"Wouldn't what happened at the Tristeland be considered a blood sacrifice?"

"Only if you meant to kill Luther, which, I'm guessing you didn't. Your powers were protecting you. You're not trained, and Aliquian gifting takes years to master. Many find that in order to move forward in their gifting, they have to go through many stages of failures and successes. But first, you need to learn how to control your emotions so you can control your abilities. Enter, me."

Resi froze in the trees. "*You're* going to teach me?"

Rolf moved on, laughing under his breath. "No. That's my employer's job."

She waited. "Now might be a good time to tell me who he is."

Finally, Rolf turned to her, his expression light and easy. It was the first time in days that he appeared content to simply be alive. "He's a good man. But I can't tell you his name. If we're caught, his identity needs to be protected."

Resi's eyes fluttered angrily. "How do expect me to believe he's a good man if you won't even tell me who he is? I mean, I've been following you for almost a week, and I still don't know anything about you, anything about him, anything about where you're taking me. For all I know, you could be working for Sequis."

Rolf turned to her angrily. "I wouldn't work for that power-hungry sadist if my life depended on it."

"Ok, then what gives?" she shrugged.

Exhausted, Rolf sighed. "Like I said, my employer is Patrian. He helps people like you; shelters gifted Aliquians. He teaches them until he can bring them into the Hidden Realm."

Shocked, Resi waited in the shadows of the forest, suddenly aching for the sound of her own mother's voice, for the touch of her soft hands against Resi's girlish face. The hidden realm Belaflor, the city of a thousand stories. It existed after all.

"Don't tell me you haven't heard of it," Rolf went on.

Resi assured him with a nod, although still confused. "My mother used to tell me stories of a place where no one saw illness or death. A place beyond comprehension. But, it's myth. Most believe the tales are describing nothing more than a hole in the ground where Aliquian runaways go to rot."

Another small laugh left Rolf. "Try again."

"You're telling me there's an entire *city* of Aliquians hidden away somewhere in the mountains where no one can find them?"

Rolf shrugged simply. "Yep."

All at once, an idea hit Resi like a flash of lightning from the sky. Her parents...if they were alive, it was possible they'd made a run for the city. It was all her mother had spoken about that summer before their disappearance. She watched Rolf cross his arms over his body, his face sullen.

"It's not an easy place to get into," he confided. "Only Aliquians get access. Someone like me can only be brought into the Belaflor if they're accompanied by an Elder of the city. Or, by a Xylo."

The city had a name; Belaflor. But the other words? Resi's face twisted with all the new information. *Xylo? Elder?* "Excuse me, what language are you speaking?"

Rolf huffed. "The Elders are those put in place to protect the city; they're the lawmakers, the court system. If there's ever a problem within the realm, they're the ones responsible for fixing it."

"And the other word?"

Another huff left him, this one long and drawn out. "Xylo is the name of a tree that grows only in Belaflor. They represent a symbol for the city, one deeply connected to the power of the Great King, the same power that exists in the gifting inside of you."

"But," she stopped him, "you said the word as if it belonged to a *person*."

Rolf sighed, choosing his words carefully. "Xylo refers to an Aliquian with unparalleled ability. It's said that once a large enough group of them enters into Belaflor, they will unite their forces to search the regions for the next heir to Aliquis's throne. This heir, this *ruler*, will help guide Aliquians out of bondage forever."

Resi's eyes widened. "You're speaking of some sort of prophecy?" She watched Rolf's face harden.

"Probably a load of mule dung."

"So, these Xylos; they already exist?"

A fleeting look of remembrance crossed Rolf's eyes. "There's only one that I've ever heard of. He was brought to the city years ago."

Resi waited, feeling somewhat stupid. "By...you?"

Memories flooded Rolf's eyes as he chuckled. "Many years ago, a handful of Elders from Belaflor scouted the regions for trackers, men like me, to bring freed or traveling Aliquians into the city."

"And?" Resi asked as her spine straightened. "Did they hire you?"

Rolf smiled, trying to hide his ego. "They would've been idiots not to."

The realization hit Resi hard over the head. "Then, you've seen Belaflor?"

Wistfully, Rolf sighed. "Certain Vegari were granted access to the city. I'd leave on a mission for a few months and then come back until they'd send me out again."

She huffed, then regretted it.

"Spit it out," he demanded.

"Are you still working for the Elders now?" she asked, changing the subject.

"Not anymore, no. Got too old. Too tired." He turned to her with a wink. "Besides, I prefer working alone."

Unsurprised, Resi smiled. "Is the city everything they say it is?" she asked, feeling foolish. It was hard to believe such a fantastical place was real, that a safe haven for people like her could exist in the midst of running and feeling fear around every corner.

Rolf let his eyes settle on the horizon. Memories flashed before them. "And more."

She rolled her eyes. It was possible that he was lying, leading her to believe stories that only led into a hole underground. "But, unless you were traveling with an Elder or a Xylo, how did you get through the portal?"

Rolf turned to her, impressed. "Someone's a quick learner."

A small smirk came to Resi's face. "When you've been in the dark for as long as I have, you better be."

"I never traveled alone," he finally answered her question. Then he added, "They really teach you nothing in Ter, do they?"

"Blame the system," Resi shrugged. "Most of what you just told me has been reworked into myths. It's a miracle that I even know how to read." Her mind drifted back to Amos's cabin, now unseen through the trees. The boy on the stairs... "That boy—he was looking at me as if he knew me."

Rolf stopped in his tracks. "You saw a boy?"

Resi didn't say anything. She didn't have to. Instead, she settled her gaze on the back of Rolf's head, noticing the balding spot she'd grown so used to in the previous days.

"The boy is Amos's son," Rolf eventually said.

Confused, Resi's face shriveled at the center. "But, he was Aliquian?"

Allowing Resi to fill in the blanks, Rolf continued walking. Finally, after the realization hit, Resi caught up to him with a few quick gallops.

"Amos asked you to find him, didn't he?"

Rolf didn't even look at her. "Amos used to be a lobbyist in Dirig. Spent many years building a career. But, unfortunately, he had a weakness for Aliquian women; something he and Sequis share in common."

A chill ran up Resi's back as she watched Rolf shrug disappointedly. The giants' lothario ways were evidently well known.

"Wasn't until a few years ago that Amos learned he was a father," he went on.

"Where did you find him?"

Rolf sighed. "At the worst possible property in Dirig. And he was alone. His mother is deceased. He had no other family that he knew of, besides Amos. I helped him escape, then brought him here. Amos relocated south to protect his name and his fortune. But mostly, to protect his son."

Resi waited, listening to the sounds of the morning birds in the treetops. "Makes sense why Myrtle isn't your biggest fan."

"I don't blame her. Their world of social gatherings, campaigns, and political events was uprooted all because Amos hired me."

Resi didn't know how to answer. She walked stiffly alongside Rolf, settling back into their regular routine of silence. Ahead, the mountains separating Ter from Sterch continued to reveal themselves in the distance: large, purple beasts capped with hats of the purest white snow.

"They're something," she said aloud, although mostly to herself. The mountains, the sky, and the sea were probably of no more value to Rolf than her damp cloak was to her. She wondered if he'd ever spent time as a young man looking upon the Sterch mountainside with eyes of wonder. It was odd imagining him that way—naïve, innocent, unstained by years of travel and danger.

They trotted onwards, allowing the sunshine to warm their cloaks and faces. After a time, the air of the forest began to wear thin. Resi could feel the sting in her lungs as they started up the foothills. Still, she maintained pace with Rolf, trying as hard as her legs would allow to keep in stride beside him.

"You're not one to follow, are you?" he finally asked her.

Resi huffed. "Being out of breath is better than staring at your bald spot for hours on end."

It seemed impossible, but Resi could've sworn she heard a small exhale of laughter come from Rolf. The thought of him letting loose eased her in some sort of way, as if they'd crossed over the same line at the exact same time. Somewhere in the last week, they'd spanned the distance from that of two skeptical travelers to somewhere closer to acquaintants.

Resi could hear the wheels in Rolf's brain turning; he wanted to say something witty in return, but instead, she was alarmed to hear a strange click come from the treetops. Instantly, Rolf stopped in his tracks, putting a hand out cautiously for her to do the same. They waited in silence, listening to the creeks of the wood until, SWOOSH!

A mess of ropes lifted them both into the sky, tangling their arms and legs. A trap. A few seconds passed before she and Rolf realized what had happened.

"Now would be a good time to get out that handy letter opener of yours," he instructed her.

Resi obeyed while Rolf dug for a small dagger at his hip. The letter opener was still dull, but over the course of their travels, Resi had found time to press a forest stone against it to sharpen it.

"What kind of trap is this?" she asked.

"Quiet," he hushed her. "Whoever set it could be nearby."

Frantically, they went at the rope, using as much force as they could to break through. But it wouldn't give. Even more bizarre; the more pressure Resi applied, the tougher the rope became under the blade.

"Something's—er, wrong with this," she said through a grunt. She looked up to see Rolf wipe the sweat from his brow.

"This isn't ordinary rope," he said.

"Yeah, no kidding," she spouted as she reluctantly put the blade back inside her cloak.

Just then, the ground beneath them began to rumble, like the distant echoes of an earthquake.

Rolf's head hung low. "Brace yourself," he instructed.

Over the hill came a tremendous stampede. At first, Resi suspected it was nothing more than a wild group of horses blazing through the forest. But after a few seconds of watching the beasts furiously trample the forest floor, she was certain her eyes were deceiving her. Indeed, they were beasts, with bodies built like stallions. But their faces...

"Centaurs," she heard herself whisper.

CHAPTER 16

THE MAP

The ground beneath the trap continued to shake as the centaurs thundered through the underbrush. The stampede grew in mass until nearly a hundred of them had poured over the hill, all armed with viciously tipped spears. They made their way closer until, finally, they circled the net. In one smooth motion, they all pointed their weapons at their captives, but they did not advance, seeming to wait for a command before striking.

Resi was too transfixed by their beastly forms to even hear the hammer of her heart. The centaurs' coats were rough and patchy, almost like the hair of a matted cat. They were many different colors—chocolate brown, moonlight gray, and deepest black—and their bare chests were broad and well-muscled, like true warriors. What was most startling, however, were their faces; their eyes, piercingly dark like that of a horse, and their noses, long and thin with a bridge that extended deeply into the hairline. Many of them sported long braids down their backs that roped into their fur.

Resi watched as the tribe stepped aside one by one to make way for their leader, a white-coated warrior with giant antlers like that of a regal stag. His size was much more impressive than the others—his chest was massive, his legs built for speed and power. He sported a necklace comprised of many wooden charms around his thick neck.

"Looks like we lucked out, boys," he spoke, his voice rolling like thunder. "*Two.*"

The tribe let out a symphony of sinister laughs before Rolf rearranged himself within the net to face the leader.

"This is some sort of mistake," Rolf said, his voice sure. "For years, this mountainside has been traversable."

The leader looked upon Rolf as if he were nothing more than a small rodent. "I wouldn't be so certain of that. Governor Sequis has had this border protected ever since he came to reside in Ter."

Resi wanted to scream. *Reside* in Ter—like all Sequis ever did was come to live there, like he hadn't seized the land and beheaded its previous leader.

"Have we traveled too far North?" Rolf asked.

The beasts laughed again, their spears wavering inches from the bottom of the net. The leader scoffed. "That would be assumed," he said, his voice deep.

Rolf's eyes peered toward the mountains. "We're headed west. It's possible we made a wrong turn."

"Nice going," Resi grumbled at him.

Rolf didn't answer. Instead, he shot Resi the kind of look indicating that if she said another word, his knife would find its way from his hip to her chest.

"A wrong turn indeed," the leader responded. "Not many travelers would dare to cross into the foothills. At least, not without being questioned."

Resi shuddered in the net. The leader spoke with an air of mystery that led her to believe that the word "questioned" meant something closer to "eaten."

"Surely this can be worked out," Rolf reasoned. "I'm on special orders from a Patrian noble to bring this woman to Dirig."

"And what is *she*, exactly?" the leader asked, his beady eyes shifting to Resi. He glanced her up and down in much the same way that Rolf had eyed his stew the night before.

Resi's stomach lit. The fire had been dormant for the past few days in the chill of the rain, but now, it felt like a match striking against her insides.

"What does it matter?" Rolf asked, his tone sure.

The leader's face stiffened like stone. One of his hooves lifted from the ground and dropped with a thud, sending a cloud of dust drifting up into the net. Rolf and Resi blinked violently as they coughed for air.

"It matters," the leader began, "because the Governor has ordered that every 'Lick from here to the southern shore be kept within the region until further notice."

Rolf was temporarily stunned, his eyes landing on Resi. He seemed to collect himself for a split second, then he turned back to the lead centaur again. "There's no need to be hostile," he said with a newfound confidence. "This woman has been sold to the West. There must be protocols in place for a situation like this."

The leader turned around himself once, then looked up at Rolf amusedly. "Believe it or not, there aren't."

The tribes' spears lifted higher towards the net as the giant centaur took a few steps back and turned to his nearest warrior, apparently asking him a question in a low undertone.

"Any chance you're close to getting angry?" Rolf murmured to Resi, his eyes never breaking from the warrior tribe.

"Working on it," she replied.

The leader faced the net once again, his gaze sure and unwavering. He knew. "The girl," he stated. "If my suspicion is correct, then it's money you seek in exchange for getting her to her next destination. I, however, have a better proposition to offer you."

"We're not interested," Rolf chuckled.

"Don't be so sure of that," the leader spoke as his eyes glanced between the two of them. "Depending on who and what she is, I can make you an impressive trade. Money? Supplies? Free passage through Sterch? You name it. But in the meantime, is there anything you wish to confess to me about your *young traveler*?"

Rolf took a deep breath as the weight of the question landed on him. Then he shot a quick look of improvisational charm at Resi, followed by a wink. "Only this."

Without warning, he raised his elbow sharply and hit her square in the nose. Hard. She reared back in pain, bringing her hands to her face in shock as she felt every part of her go boiling hot. Only a second passed before she and Rolf heard a sizzling sound, like a piece of meat searing on a pan; she realized it was the rope of the net, breaking down under the heat of her body.

Suddenly, it snapped, sending her and Rolf tumbling to the forest floor. They landed together on their backs, still tangled in the now-smoking rope of the trap. Rolf spat as he quickly brought himself to his feet, but Resi was in worse shape, coughing as she rolled over, her lungs begging for the air that had been eaten up by the fire within. For a brief moment, everything was still around them as the centaur leader came to the realization of who he'd captured: Luther's murderer.

"Uh oh," Rolf whispered.

In perfect unison, the tribe reared on their hind legs, shrieking and spitting.

"Come on, come on!" Resi called out loud to the fire that wanted to blaze, gesticulating frantically at her stomach. But it wouldn't rise past her navel. She was too fearful, too consumed by the snorts and the stomps. She gathered herself to her feet and backed into Rolf.

The centaurs stamped and whooped, waiting for their leader to give the command to kill her. But no such call came; instead, his angry face went suddenly slack, and he began to strangely turn about himself in circles.

Resi was reminded of how a dog would chase its tail until it passed out from the endless cycle of failure. She looked over her shoulder at Rolf. "What's happening?" The Vegari only shook his head. Both of them watched in stunned confusion as, one by one, the entire centaur tribe began turning on themselves.

Then, out of the shadows of the forest, a voice began to rise. It was a wordless melody, simple and sweet, and sung by a shaky male voice. The centaurs grew drowsy from the melody, swaying and nodding off as if they'd consumed too much wine. Like shot pigeons, they each passed out on the forest floor, the ground quaking under the weight of their falls. Rolf and Resi watched on in disbelief. The last to succumb to it was the leader; try as he might to resist whatever magic was afoot, his eyes began to flutter and close. In one last effort to regain his composure, he took a few steps forward towards them, swaying and rocking like a drunk. But his knees buckled, and he crumpled to a mighty heap near Resi's feet. If it hadn't been for Rolf lifting her out of the way at the very last moment, she would've been trampled to death.

The mysterious melody continued, taking center stage in the otherwise silent forest. Rolf and Resi listened intently, walking hesitantly forward as they followed the song around the trees. A minute later, the song ended, leaving them on edge in the ensuing quiet. After a few tense moments, a young man in a dark traveling cloak jumped down from a nearby tree, landing perfectly on his strong, steady legs. He faced them and threw back his hood, grinning broadly as he approached.

Resi took in his appearance, eyes widening, knowing it couldn't be true. The copper-brown hair. The deep, soil-brown eyes. She'd seen his face only in golden-lit daydreams since leaving the Farmhold.

"You can thank me now or thank me later," Corey said smugly.

Resi blinked, half-expecting him to disappear. "Corey...what in the Sept-Regions?" She almost reached out to embrace him, then contained herself.

Rolf's hand went to his dagger under his cloak as the young man drew closer. "You two know each other?"

"Sort of," Corey replied, smiling crookedly again.

Suddenly feeling self-conscious, Resi toyed with the uneven ends of her short hair. "He worked for the Offenheimers."

Still eyeing Corey suspiciously, Rolf took two steps forward, placing himself squarely in front of Resi. "Rolf," he said, putting out a hand for the newcomer to shake.

"This is Corey," Resi introduced him.

Rolf nodded, his face stiff. "I believe we owe you a thank you."

Corey shifted his weight. "Don't thank me. Thank my mother for telling me the stories of the Centaur Legion as a boy."

Resi didn't quite understand what he meant, and it was clear as she looked to Rolf that he had no more of a clue than she did.

"Come on, Resi," Corey baited her. "You've read the story."

Though flattered by Corey's confidence in her, she shook her head. "Can't say that I have."

Embarrassed, Corey rolled his eyes. "*Centaur Legion, where's your keep? Centaur Legion, go to sleep. If ever one should come to pass, sing loud and it shall fall on its...*" he stopped, blushing. "Mom used to say '*face.*'"

Resi withheld a laugh. Rolf, however, seemed less pleased.

"Stories say that centaurs fall asleep at the slightest sound of a melody," Corey said. "I didn't expect it to work, but it did."

"I'd almost swear you were following us, judging by your timing," Rolf chided. He clearly didn't trust this new traveler.

"Rolf, he's a friend," Resi protested, her voice soft.

"I'm only asking for him to explain himself," Rolf persisted.

Resi conceded with a sigh, then turned to Corey. "Why are you here?"

Corey looked deflated, as if he'd expected a welcoming committee but had instead been met with a criminal's questioning. His eyes flickered to Rolf briefly before finding safety again with Resi. "After word reached the farmhold that you'd escaped the Tristeland, everything went upside down."

Resi was momentarily taken aback at the sudden realization that Corey might be literate, too. They were around the same age, but then she remembered that Corey had grown up in the western region of Rowan, where he would have been given a free man's education in his youth; Aliquians in that region were still being educated today. Rumors had been circulating about the regions that Rowan was headed in the direction of the abolition of Aliquian bondage, much like the region of Dirig.

"Marion was on a warpath," he went on. "She wanted every 'Lick checked for signs of gifting. She demanded that patrollers search the lean-to's. Those discovered with any sort of illegal materials were sold to different properties within the week."

Resi's heart sank. "Who?"

Corey couldn't meet her eyes. His hands fiddled with the clasp of his cloak.

"Corey?" she raised her voice, moving closer to him. "*Who?*"

All he could do was shake his head with resignation. "I'm sorry, Resi. I know you cared for her."

The forest echoed his words back a thousand times before Resi could take a breath. Mags, left alone and confused by Resi's leave of the Farmhold, then convicted of a crime she'd never committed and sold. Resi had forgotten that she'd left Mags's note under her mattress in her chambers at the Eye, and she'd also left her small piece of sketching parchment in their lean-to. She'd meant to burn the note, but once news had arrived from the Tristeland, she'd been too consumed with fear to remember Mags's simple request. "It's because of me," she finally said. "They sold her because of me."

"Don't say that," Corey protested, taking a step closer to her.

But Resi's world was caving in on itself. All of this, only to see Mags suffer. She couldn't hold back her tears. "Do you know where they sent her?"

Corey had no answer to give to her. He shook his head, then looked to the ground with shame.

Resi reached her hand out to Rolf as if she might faint. He grasped her forearm, then guided her to rest on a nearby boulder as Corey followed behind.

"There was nothing that could've been done," Corey tried to comfort her as he knelt beside her.

"What about you?" Rolf asked him. "Did you escape?"

Corey shook his head. "After that week, Theo called me into his office. He handed me a pile of papers and told me I was free to leave the farmhold."

Rolf raised a skeptical eyebrow at him. "He offered you your freedom?"

Corey smiled. "He didn't explain much, but I have a feeling

I'm not the first person he's helped to leave. He woke me in the middle of the night and led me to a boat in the woods. Told me to head north along the coast until I made it to Derton."

Resi felt a thrill of gratitude, remembering the boat by the berry patch. It had been useful, at least, for someone. Perhaps it had belonged to Theo all along. And that meant maybe, just maybe, he'd been involved in her parents' escape...though that still didn't explain why Resi had been left behind.

Sensing that she was becoming overwhelmed, Corey grabbed her hands in his. His voice softened. "I think he freed me in the hopes that I'd find you."

Surprisingly, Resi didn't find herself recoiling at the warmth of his touch. But she was still a bit confused. "Why would Theo do that?" she asked skeptically.

Awkwardly, Corey cleared his throat as he averted his eyes from hers. "We spoke about you. Well—*I* spoke about you...asked about you."

A strange, warm sensation hit Resi square in the stomach, but it wasn't the fire. There was something disarming about the way that Corey couldn't quite look at her as he explained himself.

"That still doesn't explain *how* you found us," Rolf said as he stood to his feet.

Corey's face lit up in a mischievous sort of way. He bent at the waist and retrieved a long, folded piece of browned paper from a leather satchel slung on his back. Delicately, he unfolded it, and there, in the sunlight, was Theo's map—the same map from the upstairs hall of the Eye, with its faded lines delineating the region of old Caplia swirling about the parchment.

"Theo gave it to me before I left," he said proudly.

Resi outstretched a hand to it, remembering how far away the map had seemed behind the safety of its glass frame. Her fingers almost brushed against it before she pulled them away, worried that one touch of it against her skin would cause it to crumble into ash. The feeling reminded her of how she'd feared that Scottis's fragile foldings would break apart at even the smallest touch of her hand all those weeks ago.

"I know this map," she said with a slight smile.

"But it's not just an ordinary map," Corey said.

Rolf sidled up to him, his eyes scanning the parchment. "Theodore Offenheimer gave it to you?"

"It was one of his prized possessions," Resi interjected. "He kept it framed. Said it was rare."

There was a small breath of silence between the three of them as Corey took Resi's wrist in his hand. "Watch," he said, nodding to her encouragingly. Again, Resi tried to ignore the rough feel of his skin against hers as he cautiously brought her hand to touch the map. As her fingers touched the ink, the black lettering reacted, evaporating from the parchment like fire embers. A rainbow of color ignited across the parchment in its place, raising into mountains at the center, coalescing into lush, green forests to the north, and further south, dribbling into the many tributaries that flowed off the end of the map where the coast met the sea. It was the Sept-Regions in all its glory, just smaller, and simpler.

"Amazing," Resi said in wonderment. The three of them stood marveling over the map for some time before she spotted iridescent sparkles hovering amid the mountains of Dirig. "What's this?" she asked, pointing to it. She turned to Corey, but he didn't have an answer.

Rolf took a step back from the map, his eyes wide. "It can't be."

"What?" Resi asked.

Rolf exhaled forcefully, as if he'd been holding his breath for the last hour. "Son, do you realize what you possess?" he asked, eyeing Cory warily. Corey shook his head. Rolf gestured for the map, and with a slight trepidation, Corey handed it to him.

Something like a thunderclap rang out over the map as Rolf's hands gripped its edges. The colors blurred together before fading back into black ink.

"Huh," Corey said, his mouth frowning. "That's new."

"It's *ancient*, actually," Rolf corrected him. "The map only reveals itself to the same lineage as its maker. This is a genuine Aliquian map, probably made nearly two hundred years ago when King Aliquis was on the throne." Rolf shook his head in bewilderment, still processing his own discovery. "And that small light in the mountains of Dirig marks the portal into the Hidden City. Into Belaflor."

It was all Resi could do to keep breathing. This map proved the stories from her childhood to be true. Belaflor was a real place, a real city, and one that resided in the mountains of Dirig.

"It gets better," Corey nodded, touching the map again so it revealed its secret once more. "See that?" He pointed a finger to a small star of light, gold and pure, that hovered over the foothills of the mountainside leading into Sterch. "It's us."

"It's tracking your location?" Rolf questioned.

"No, no," Corey said, his head shaking.

Annoyed, Rolf pursed his lips together; clearly, he didn't much like the notion of being incorrect.

Corey turned excitedly to Resi, his face pure. "It's you. It *has* to be you."

"*Me?*" Resi asked.

"This is where it gets really weird," Corey admitted. "I discovered the map was special on my first day on the river, but this star didn't appear until a few days later. During the rains, I came to an old broken-down wagon in the forest. It was abandoned, so I crawled inside to get warm. But my cloak was soaked through. I shook the whole night, hoping I'd be dry by morning. But then, in the middle of the night, my bag lit up from the inside. I thought it was a fire, so I started putting it out with my foot—only, it wasn't. It was this map, lit up, and hot as boiling water with this new star floating over the foothills. And just when I needed the warmth. It was like it knew I needed it, or something."

Resi tried to figure out the timing of the star's appearance on the map.

"And you chose to follow the star...why?" Rolf asked.

Corey sighed. "Call it intuition. Or curiosity. But never in my wildest dreams did I..." he turned to Resi, his face not quite concealing a new emotion, one vulnerable and seeking.

Too many questions filled her mind at this, so Resi opted to redirect the conversation slightly. "I don't get it," she said, leaning her back against a nearby tree. "Why would Theo want you to find me?"

Corey looked at her, his face sincere. "He probably didn't want you to be alone."

"That doesn't explain why Resi is connected to that light on the map," Rolf pointed out. "Or how Theo would know that."

Corey shrugged. "I can't begin to know."

Rolf's eyes then narrowed in on Corey with a vengeance. "Where exactly do you plan on going with such an important relic?"

Corey's height shrank a few inches. "I planned on going to northern Rowan. I want to find my sister. We were separated before I was brought to the Offenheimers."

"You're headed west too?" Resi asked, trying to hide the warmth of hope in her tone. Her eyes flickered to Rolf, who was still watching Corey as if he might make a sudden move. Corey smiled and nodded.

"I hate to break up all the excitement, but I must insist upon seizing that map from you," Rolf said gruffly, his stance widening.

"Ex—excuse me?" Corey stammered.

"That one piece of parchment is worth a lifetime of labor," Rolf said, jabbing his finger angrily at the map. "Maybe even two. That, in and of itself, is reason enough to never let it out of your sight. The fact that it has the location of the portal marked on it makes it property of the Elders of Belaflor. It needs to be protected, looked after by someone who can see that it gets inside the safety of the city."

Resi felt the fire rear itself into gear. She stood quickly, meeting Rolf's eyes. "What makes you think that Corey doesn't understand the responsibility of carrying such a relic? Theo entrusted it to him. You can't just demand he hand it over. And—don't think for a second that I've forgotten about what you did back there." She nodded back to the broken net, surrounded by the sleeping centaurs on the other side of the clearing. Her nose felt the ache of his jab.

Rolf looked away from her in a physical denial of her accusation. "I got us out of there, ok?"

But Resi remained firm. "Punch me again, and I can't ensure that what happened at the Tristeland won't happen twice," she said hotly.

Corey looked between the two of them before taking a step back. Then, over Rolf's shoulder, Resi saw one of the centaur's legs twitch.

"No more bickering," she said. "We need to get a move on."

Rolf adjusted his cloak, his eyes still locked on Corey, clearly still full of mistrust for the young man. "If there are more of these creatures along the border, we'll need to take a mountain pass."

"Wait..." Corey said, his voice filled with trepidation. "You wish for me to join you?"

"If we continue north, then we'll most certainly have to stay together," Rolf said.

Resi looked north at the expanse of mountains. It was the only other alternative. She turned to peek at Corey, whose face was stuck somewhere between confusion and absolute terror. "We're going into *Sterch*?" he said, dumbfounded.

"We either take a small pass that will take us into Sterch, or go west and risk the chance of more traps," Rolf answered as he nodded to Resi. He then pointed to the centaur herd. "Let's also remember that Sequis will be notified that you've been spotted near the border once these things wake up. And besides, Sequis will assume we took the foothills west. Only the most skilled travelers could make the trek into Sterch and come out unscathed. He won't suspect you made that choice."

A chill ran down Resi's back. Going into Sterch was almost certainly a death sentence. Too many unknown creatures waited in the shadows; the mountains surrounding Sterch's border were the only thing that kept a plethora of creatures from entering neighboring regions.

"Do you know the way?" she asked Rolf, desperately hoping for him to say no.

Smugly, Rolf turned for the mountains before speaking to them like old friends. "She asks if I know the way..."

Corey and Resi hesitated in the clearing with the map still open in the sunlight. Neither wanted to be the first to agree to Rolf's new plan, but it was Corey who caved first. He shrugged at Resi before trudging after Rolf, and Resi soon followed suit.

"We're going to need to step up our pace," Rolf called out to them. "Sure you'll be able to keep up, kid?" he spat at Corey.

Corey nodded, his face bright and sure. Resi, however, wished she felt as confident. After almost a week on the run from Derton, she was desperate for a slower pace. She tried to muster all of the strength inside of her as she shielded her eyes from the light of the sun with a hand. They needed to find shelter before nightfall.

As she watched Corey stomping ahead, however, she felt her spirit ease. It was possible her luck was changing. Watching Corey's agile frame bound through the woods was better than having to stare at Rolf's bald spot for days on end, and that in and of itself was reason to smile.

"Everything alright back there?" Corey spun back to Resi, jolting her out of her thoughts. Feeling somewhat caught and embarrassed, Resi nodded, her eyes lingering on him as he tucked the map tightly in his bag and took after Rolf.

CHAPTER 17

THE ENCHANTMENT

I f there was one thing that Resi learned about Corey as the three headed for the mountains, it was that he was physically incapable of keeping his mouth shut for longer than a few minutes at a time. He was, as Rolf had so accurately remarked to Resi only an hour into their hike, *unyielding.*

"Is there *no end* to your babbling?" Rolf finally snapped at Corey. Resi snickered to herself. Rolf had taken a stumble on the rocks only a few seconds prior, and was clearly trying to assign blame to Corey for distracting him. All Corey could do was give a look of embarrassment to Resi.

"Nervous talker," he shrugged.

Resi couldn't deny her own amusement at Corey's constant chatter—just watching it drive Rolf crazy was entertaining in and of itself. In her mind, she'd always imagined the boy with the soil-brown eyes as stoic, wise, and mature in a way that kept him quiet. But Corey, in all his innocence, was anything but. At the very least, his talk kept Resi's mind far from Sequis, far from the dread of thinking about the Tristeland.

After some time, Resi sped up her pace and passed Corey to walk in stride with Rolf.

"How's that heat?" he asked her without even so much as a glance in her direction.

"Better," she said with disdain. She sighed. "You almost got us in trouble back there with the centaurs. I could've killed you, and everyone in that forest."

Rolf chuckled under his breath. "Trust me, Resi. I know the limits of Aliquian power. Your fear was too great in that moment to elicit any sort of massive outburst. I suspected a more minimal display, and that's what you gave."

Resi huffed. "You're unbelievable. You know that?"

"So I've been told," he smirked.

Feeling suddenly too tired to keep up with Rolf, Resi slowed her pace once more and let herself fall in line with Corey. She gave him a polite nod, then she noticed the curiosity in his eyes. "He's Patrian?" Corey asked.

Resi nodded, realizing that many of the questions that she'd had about Rolf when they'd first begun their journey together were now weighing on Corey. As they walked, she filled him in on what she knew about the Vegari. As the miles went by, she found herself in perfect stride alongside Corey. Their conversation flowed as if they'd known each other for years. They spoke of many things: Scottis's foldings, Theo's compassionate move to free Corey, Resi's love of painting, and of Mags.

"You and Mags were obviously close," Corey eventually said.

Resi's mood suddenly took a tumble. "After my parents left, she brought me up as her own. Of course, she can be intolerable at times," Resi laughed, "but she has this easy way of making everyone feel immediately comfortable around her."

Corey nodded along with her story as if he knew exactly what she was referring to. "You miss her…"

Resi found herself looking deeply into the kindness behind his eyes for a long beat before she forced herself to look away. She nodded. "Although, I can't say that I miss the way she used to tease me about certain things."

"Teasing?" Corey smirked as he pulled aside a branch that was blocking the path for Resi to pass. "What about?"

Resi shrugged, trying to forget the way her stomach had flipped over on itself when he'd smiled at her on the night of Shina's punishment, and the way that Mags had called her out afterwards. "Oh, just, typical things."

"She was proud of you, you know," Corey said. "After everything that happened."

A pain hit Resi square in the chest. "You spoke with her?"

Corey nodded. "She talked to everyone. It was the only way she could calm herself. When the stories from the Tristeland made their way through the field, she went a little crazy worrying about you."

Resi shook her head, forcing the image of Mags out of her head—abandoned, fearful, and ravenous for answers. She avoided Corey's eyes and walked on.

The lush grass of the southern regions soon receded, changing gradually underfoot into thick, gray rock. The mountains surrounding Sterch had appeared ominous from a distance, but up close, they were downright unwelcoming, as well as difficult to traverse. To make matters worse, the air continued to grow thinner the higher they climbed.

After a time, it became clear that the centaur tribe had finally wakened. All three travelers stiffened as they heard the pack rouse from far below, their hissing and shouting rising to the highest peaks of the mountains.

"There's got to be a better way through," Resi said as she appraised the steep and narrow ravine before them; filled with giant boulders, splintered trees, and other debris, it looked like there had been a landslide only a few days prior. "They'll catch up to us in minutes."

"This pass is too narrow for the centaurs," Rolf told her. Like a skilled mountain goat, he hopped and darted ahead over the rocks with ease. "The only passable route for them is farther west."

Resi relaxed a little. Still, she couldn't quite shake her fear that they might bump into the centaurs a second time.

An hour later, the wind picked up as they approached the summit. Crunchy snow lined the path, and short bursts of snowfall began to spit at them from above. Resi paused in her tracks, transfixed by the sight of the flakes falling from the clouds as if each contained its own small bout of powerful magic.

Corey lifted his face to the snowfall. "Can't say that I'll miss winters on the farmhold. Rowan rarely gets snow."

"Your family; they're still there?" Resi asked, trying to sound nonchalant, like she was just making polite conversation.

"Just one," he said with a heavy sigh. "My sister."

"She'll be happy to see you." Resi smiled, thinking of Mags.

Corey didn't answer. Instead, he quietly moved along, leaving Resi behind with more questions than she'd initially had.

"If you two don't quit your yapping," Rolf called proudly from ahead with his hands placed on his hips, "you're going to miss the sunset."

Resi led Corey to the top, being careful to avoid any loose rocks. She joined Rolf, then looked out over the expansive view. The hazy late-day sun hovered behind them to the east. A chain of mountains tapered into the western horizon like a long, purple spine. She peered over the rocks. The land below was dark in the shadow of the peak.

"Sterch isn't for everyone," Rolf sighed, "but even I have to admit; it sure is something to see from up here." In that moment, Resi could see the child in him, the one she knew had been buried so deeply inside of him but couldn't help but peek its way out from time to time.

Corey pulled the map from his knapsack, removing it cautiously so it wouldn't blow away in the wind. Once he unfolded it, he placed his strong hand atop it. Resi and Rolf watched again as the map exploded with life and color. "Never gets old," Corey smiled up at them. He looked over the map, pointing to the small star over the mountains leading into Sterch.

"I still don't understand," Resi shuddered, pulling her cloak tighter over her chest. "Why is the map tracking me?"

Rolf looked at Corey with a strange sort of suspicion. "That's the question of the hour."

Corey remained silent for a time, then turned to Rolf with new questions in his eyes. "So—you're a Patrian Vegari," he said bravely to Rolf. "But like, a renegade too?"

Rolf looked at him with a peeved expression.

"I mean no offense," Corey retreated, "but, you seem to know a lot about Aliquian gifting for someone who's just paid to deliver Aliquians."

Rolf looked past Corey as if he were speaking to nothing and no one at all. "It's my job to be well-informed on every culture within the Sept- Regions. If we get into any sort of trouble, I'm the one who's *paid* to get us out of it. The more I know, the less likely someone like you gets killed."

Corey had no more to say. His lips pursed together tightly as if he were trying to prevent himself from inserting his foot any further between them.

"We need to make camp," Rolf said sternly. "Let's start the descent."

After the light of day had vanished completely beyond the mountainside, the three found a small unsheltered clearing on the north face of their mountainside, each trying to ignore the far-off sounds of the centaurs on the hunt. As Rolf had predicted, the herd had misjudged the travelers' route; they could be heard to the west, their leader heading the charge into the foothills. Only a few minutes passed before their stampede quieted. Resi let herself take a deep breath. For the moment, the three of them were safe.

Corey settled in to try to sleep by curling up in his cloak on a small patch of grass. Rolf took first watch, but after an hour of staring up at the black sky instead of sleeping, Resi joined him, sitting beside him as he sharpened the blade of his dagger with a small rock.

"Tomorrow isn't going to be any easier than today," he warned her, his face dark and moody. "You should sleep."

Resi shivered, wrapping her cloak tightly around her shoulders.

She grunted sarcastically as she looked at the stiff ground. "Too used to goose-feathered pillows, I guess."

For a few minutes, they listened to the shrill of wind that passed through the mountainside. Rolf continued to sharpen the blade, but Resi could've sworn she saw the corners of his mouth curl. He shot her a meaningful glance.

"Alright...what's on your mind?" he finally asked.

Resi winced. "I just have so many questions."

"Look," he sighed, setting down the knife. "What's happened to you would be a lot for anyone to process. I want to help you, but only at your own pace. Don't forget; your power is young. It's still ignited by raw emotion. And I can't control how you might react to new information."

Resi tried to fight it, but she smiled anyway. "Are you afraid you'll tell me something I might not want to hear?"

Rolf released the held breath from his lungs. "Just trying not to stir up any late-night forest fires."

A small laugh left Resi, reminding her of all those nights spent with Mags on the porch.

"So," he prodded. "What is it?"

She waited for a time, nervous to ask her next question, but finally she went for it. "How does someone know whether they're a Xylo?"

Giving her a knowing smile, Rolf winked. "Why do you ask?"

Resi let the heat from her stomach find her cheeks. "Well...could I be one?"

Rolf clung to the silence for a time, seeming to weigh his next words carefully. Finally, he let out a controlled laugh. "No."

"What do you mean, *no*?"

"I've met a Xylo," he smirked, "and you're not one."

Again, she peered out over the dark void of the valley. "What were they like?"

"He was young," Rolf recalled. "But he had something special. Something *different*."

Resi shook her head, confused. "But, there must be others like me, right? Gifted Aliquians, but ones that aren't Xylos?"

As if the news shouldn't be of any surprise to her, Rolf nodded. "The city's full of people like you. But, of course, they've been trained not to have massive outbursts."

Since the time it had fully revealed itself at the Tristeland, Resi had despised her gifting, wishing she could strip it off like a damp cloak. But learning she was just another gifted Aliquian in a lineup of many who had similar tricks up their sleeve somehow made her newfound gifts seem dull and anything but special. Part of her was relieved, but another part of her, one that felt hungry for the same validation she received at the Tristeland for her artistry, was anxious at the thought of her power being ordinary.

The air grew crisper, the wind blasting their cheeks like prickly pine needles. A yawn pulled at the back of Resi's throat as her eyes drifted back to Rolf, his gaze dreamy and far off over the mountains. She lacked the stamina to ask any more questions. Without a word, she laid back on the cold ground. "That's all for tonight. Don't want to run the risk of lighting what little hair you have left on fire."

Rolf shook his head derisively. "Goodnight to you too."

THE FOLLOWING morning brought with it many aches and pains. The ground was stiff and frozen, and on top of that, the temperatures had plummeted overnight, leaving behind a blanket of snowfall on the mountainside.

Resi woke up shivering, and with a groan, she rubbed at her shoulders. She'd thought she'd known pain; harvest seasons of the past had worn her legs so ragged that at times she'd felt she might keel over in the middle of the day. But this type of pain, especially after days of hiking, was different—stiff, cold, and achy in places she didn't even know existed. As they started their descent, she reminded herself to keep her wits sharp. The downslope wasn't making the journey any easier. Each step brought with it the worry of a potential spill down the snowy mountainside.

Corey, on the other hand, seemed to have slept as soundly on the ground as he would have in a bed made for a king. Resi fought the urge to punch him in the shoulder as he passed her with a spring in his step.

"I meant to tell you," he said, looking back at her. "The hair...I like it."

An agitated scoff came out of Resi in response. She pulled at the dry ends of her hair, missing the smooth, soft greeting that its length had once given her. "It was out of necessity," she replied shortly.

Corey concentrated on his footing as one of his feet landed on a loose rock. "I figured as much. Still, it's nice."

Resi desperately wanted to crawl inside herself to hide. She wanted to muster all her power to grow her hair back, to take the pain from her body, and to deliver her safely to this mysterious employer so she wouldn't have to make any more awkward small talk with the boy she'd once stared at all those weeks ago from the stoop of her lean-to. Even so, she found herself struggling not to watch Corey's strong legs as he courageously took the descent. With all the mountains in the distance, she couldn't quite keep herself from enjoying the view.

"What? You don't like it?" Corey asked her, gesturing again to her hair.

Resi shuddered. "It'll grow back."

A small laugh left him. "Someone hates compliments."

Immediately, Resi was back at the Tristeland, bathed in warm firelight; her first meeting with Sequis. *You take a compliment like a sword to the rib.*

Another shudder, but this one cold as ice down her spine. "So I've been told."

"You better get used to it," Corey said, his face beaming back at her as he paused for a breath. "The way everyone was talking about you at the Farmhold...if the stories are true about you, then you're a hero."

Resi wished that Rolf would object and say something to prevent her from having to address Corey's onslaught of praise. But instead, Rolf kept moving forward into the valley, his bald spot gleaming in the sun as if to mock Resi in its wake.

"You'd be calling me something else if you would've seen the Tris-teland after I left it," Resi said as she passed Corey. But he caught her arm.

"What? A *witch*?"

Agitated, she shifted her weight before ripping herself free from his grip. "Something to that end."

He looked at her sincerely, as if he were addressing a child, stopping her in her tracks with the earnestness of his gaze. "Words have power, and the ones you speak about yourself inform what you believe about yourself," he said gently. "You have something special, something unique only to you." He smiled at her proudly. "Don't you see that what you did has changed the course of history for our people?"

She scowled. Rolf had told her the exact opposite; that she was just an ordinarily gifted Aliquian. She couldn't be sure which of the two of them was more right about her, but something deep within, be it the fire or the kind way Corey looked at her, made her want to believe that there was something much larger at play within her. Perhaps what Rolf had told her was pure fallacy, but if so, why would he choose to hide her own potential from her? All the same, she still didn't trust herself or her powers enough yet to decide. "Pissing off a giant-turned-sorcerer and denying him a marriage proposal is changing the course of history?" she finally replied. "I think not."

Corey paused with his hands on his hips, his face suddenly screwed up into a twist. "*Marriage proposal?*"

In as much detail as she could remember, she told Corey of Luther's plan to set her up as a liar, a Witch-Lick in pursuit of slaying the giant. She explained her many portrait sessions with Sequis, and the dress that had been delivered to her, the one intricately designed with lace and jewels.

"So, wait..." Corey said, his hands brushing the front sections of his hair back from his face. He wiggled his eyebrows suggestively. "I don't mean to be crass, but how would making an heir work, exactly? With him being a giant, and you, well, *not* being a giant?"

Resi shot him a death glare. "If you're referring to what I think you're referring to, then you're disgusting."

"What?!" Corey spouted, his hands in the air. "It's a valid question!"

"*Convenience* in that department certainly doesn't hold Sequis back from bedding every other Aliquian woman that crosses his path," Resi scolded him.

The air between them felt suddenly uncomfortable, and Corey shut his mouth for what felt like the first time in hours. Resi couldn't help herself; at the look on his face, she let out a laugh unlike any she'd had in a long time. She let it build in her chest until she couldn't catch her breath, and soon Corey had doubled over with his own laughter beside her. It wasn't until they saw Rolf positioned stoically ahead of them on a boulder jutting out of the path that Resi's laughter subsided. The older man seemed to be inspecting something to the northeast.

"What is it?" she asked as she approached. But Rolf didn't budge. His attention was focused on the adjoining mountain as if he were a hungry wolf on the hunt. Corey joined them, huffing out large puffs of condensation, and followed Rolf's eyes. After a moment, they both saw it: out of the distant treetops emerged a long tail of white smoke.

Corey snorted derisively. "Those idiots will be hunted down by sunset."

Out of the corner of her eye, Resi saw Rolf shaking his head in protest. "No one is dumb enough to light a fire in these parts," he intoned. "Whoever it is isn't worried about being hunted."

"What do you mean?" Resi asked.

Rolf took a deep breath. "It means that the person responsible for the fire isn't the type to be categorized as *prey*."

Resi's mind flooded with the possibilities. A forest troll? An ogre? A—her stomach dropped. "*Sequis.*"

"Judging by the smoke, he's not alone," Rolf said. "The centaurs must have led him into the region."

Resi's heart was beating so ferociously she swore it was only seconds from leaping out of her mouth. "How many guards with him?"

"Hard to tell," Rolf said, spitting at the ground. "They're on the move. Looks like the fire was put out at dawn." He turned to the two of them, his hands placed sturdily on his hips. "We need to step up the pace. Stay hidden." His eyes drilled into Corey. "Keep *quiet*."

And they did. For the remainder of the afternoon, the three traveled in complete silence, steadying their gaze on their feet and only looking up anytime an unfamiliar sound met their ears. The descent became trickier once off the trail. Rolf continued in the lead, followed by Resi, while Corey skulked behind, keeping focused on the difficult task of keeping his mouth shut.

After a while, Resi could only feel the growing throb in her feet as they trotted on. They kept low as they descended, and Resi, unable to look at anything else, kept her eyes focused on the smoke still rising from the trees.

They were still descending when a dull ache between her temples began to pull at her thoughts. At first, it came on like any ordinary headache—like the ones that sometimes came on after hours in the fields without water. But soon, she began noticing small dots lining her vision. She grew faint, occasionally tripping over her feet. Her mind drifted to Mags—alone, forgotten; to Scottis, locked up in his study, his folded creatures destroyed before him; to her parents, their necks snapped, their legs swaying in the wind as a faceless patroller spit and laughed at their corpses.

Something was very wrong.

"What's happening?" Corey said dreamily behind her. "Are we lost?"

Rolf's bald spot disappeared as he turned back to them, his face dreary and tired. "It's the forest," he said, turning around on himself. "It's been enchanted."

Resi brought her arms around herself. The fire was gone. She was cold, inside and out.

Corey turned back to her before bringing his palms over his ears.

e...teasing me." He spoke like a small boy waking from a bad
am.

Without another thought, Resi stomped back to him. Madly, she
went for his satchel.

"Hey!" Corey objected as he wrestled her grip. "Stop it!"

"The map! We need the map!" she demanded. But Corey
persisted. He did all he could to keep Resi from getting into his
satchel, his face twisted like a wild, rabid animal.

"What's your problem?!" he snarled.

"We need to find a way out of here before we all lose our minds!"

Finally, Rolf snapped, shushing them. "Be quiet!" His eyes were as
hazy as the cloud cover over the forest.

Hesitantly, Resi looked up towards the sky. Softly, voices began to
hiss at her. But where were they coming from?

Go further and die.
She knows nothing of this place.
So far from home and mind.
She will have him soon.

All of a sudden, Corey began pounding his head with his fists in a
fit of rage. His face went ghost white; it was as if he were going mad.
Resi feared she wasn't too far behind him in descending into her own
craziness. Her headache worsened the longer they wandered around in
the trees.

"Corey, don't listen to them. It's not real," she said as she went to
grab him by the shoulders. But the forest voices continued to grow
louder, angrier. "It *can't* be real."

Without warning, Corey fell to his knees before her as he
continued to pound at his head. Resi winced as she watched his fist hit
hard near his eye.

There was no more time to waste. She ripped at his bag, clawing
for the map until she felt the rough edges of it in her hands. Desperately, she opened it, placing her palm on its center until it blazed
again with color. The star, her star, was directly over the dense

forests of the mountains into Sterch. But there appeared to be no way out.

"Come on!" Rolf yelped from ahead of them. "There's a lake at the base of these trees."

Resi looked down to the map. He was right—between the trees was a hidden path, one steep and rough that went off the main trail. Only a small trek downhill separated them from a mass of very dark water.

She'll kill you.
There's no way out.
Run, but you won't escape her.

Resi wanted to crawl inside the warmth of her stomach, to beckon it forward. But it was nowhere to be found. She took a breath, then mustered all her strength before grabbing Corey's arms and lifting him to his feet. Rolf was quickly at her side, aiding her with Corey's lifeless weight.

"Get yourself out of here, Resi," Rolf ordered.

"I'll help you with him, I'll—"

"*Run!*"

Resi didn't object to his last command; it was rare to witness any sort of worry in Rolf's eyes. Wildly, she led them through the trees as fast as she could, cutting her legs on vines and bushes as they descended to the base of the mountain. "I see it!" she called back to them when she noticed the black water sparkling in a patch of sunlight. But Rolf was struggling to balance Corey's weight. She watched in horror as his foot met a patch of slick mud, causing him to slip. Corey fell out in front of him before they both began tumbling down the mountain until WHAM—Corey smacked into Resi, knocking her over. The tree tops circled her vision as she knocked into their trunks, and all the while, the haunting voices continued their hissing.

You'll die in this place.
Running won't save you.
She is waiting for you.

The wind left Resi's lungs as she landed hard on her back in a mangled heap beside Rolf and Corey. A harmonious mix of groans rang out—Rolf's, deep and peppered with coughs; Resi's, choking at the air; and Corey's, high-pitched and childish.

"Everyone alright?" Rolf asked as he pounded at his chest.

Resi could only nod as she fought to get breath back into her lungs. Corey, on the other hand, ceremoniously stretched his arms into the air before lightly springing to his feet, almost as if nothing had happened. He smiled, welcoming the newfound silence of the clearing. "That's one way to descend a mountain," he said as he reached his hand out to help Resi to her feet.

Unamused, Rolf huffed. "A minute longer in the trees and you would've pissed yourself."

Corey scoffed nervously, his hands going again to his copper hair. "I had it under control."

"Tell that to the bruises you're about to have all over your face," Rolf smiled. "You were punching at yourself like a bag of sand."

With a dreadful sigh, Corey lifted his hands to his cheeks. He winced in pain at the touch.

"*Totally* under control," Resi said playfully, smacking him hard on the back.

Corey winced again. "What is this place?" he asked as he defiantly ripped the map from her hands.

Rolf brushed at the new accumulation of dead leaves on his cloak. "Lake Seka—the only source of water in Sterch."

"That can't be," Resi said as she looked over Corey's shoulder. But the map proved his proclamation to be true. The entire region of Sterch appeared as a dark green mass of mountains and valleys, save for the one tiny dot of darkness beneath the floating star.

"I've been traveling the regions for many years now. Not much I don't know," Rolf stated proudly.

"For one that claims to know so much, you neglected to mention the forest voices," Resi said, as her eyes traveled back up the mountain from where they'd fallen.

"Enchantments and charms are centaur tricks," Rolf explained. "Sequis probably put them up to it in an attempt to draw attention to any travelers. Ten minutes spent in that kind of enchantment can cause seizures. Or," he shot a knowing look at Resi, "outbursts of violent emotion."

Resi nearly choked on her own breath. She tried to force out the image of Rolf and Corey's burned bodies strewn across the landscape.

Rolf cleared his throat with an air of command. "We'll keep out of the trees. Stick to the roads."

Try as she might, Resi couldn't deny the looming fear that crept under her skin as she looked out over the dark lake. It was too isolated, too solitary in the middle of such dense greenery. She watched as Rolf turned west. It appeared he was in no mood to slow down.

With a sudden burst of energy, Corey grabbed up a pebble from the shoreline and turned, defiantly skipping it across the water. Much to Resi's astonishment, the stone remained visible for a time under the surface, despite the apparent darkness of the water. Based on color alone, she'd assumed the body of water to be murky and stagnant, but the pebble's long and extended fall under the surface proved otherwise. The pitch black of the lake's silted depths tricked the eye, but the water of Lake Seka proved to be ethereally pure. More than likely formed by a glacier. Resi found herself transfixed by the pebble's dance; it was almost as if it were falling into a clear night sky. She watched Corey glance over his shoulder at her, and together they drank in the wonder of such a moment. When the pebble finally disappeared into the black, they both exhaled in unison before turning to follow after Rolf.

But then, a bubble came to the water's surface. Resi heard it pop, then turned back to find new circles enlarging on the water. She lingered just long enough to watch the water turn still and resume its place as the dark, silent heart of Sterch.

"Am I imagining that?" she turned for either Rolf or Corey. But they were already many paces ahead.

Probably an after-effect of the hallucinations, she comforted herself. Her head certainly throbbed in the aftermath of the enchantment and her tumble down the hillside. She was still on edge. Sensing no immediate danger, she took a breath of relief, then turned back to catch up to the others.

CHAPTER 18

THE DOLUS

T he remainder of the day was littered with plenty of paranoia. Every so often, Resi found herself looking back to the path from where they came, fearing the discovery of Sequis and his army on their heels. Or something else.

Still in the lead, Rolf had set a mean pace. This didn't bode well for Resi; blisters had begun to rise on her heels, making it hard to think of anything but the pain. As she trotted onward, she closed her eyes and tried to remember the smell of the sweet stew from Amos's cabin in the woods. What she wouldn't have given for one good night's sleep spent someplace warm and dry, tucked into some small corner of nowhere.

"Remind me why we decided to take this route?" she heaved to Corey as they slushed through a deep and muddy trench off the side of a dirt road.

"I can't complain," he said, his voice light and breezy. "At least we're no longer in the thin air of the mountains."

Resi shrugged off his optimism with a roll of her eyes. It was beginning to irk her.

The three continued to travel along the exposed dirt road, keeping themselves as hidden as possible in the trench. Surrounding them was a green and lush valley, its edges rising steeply along the horizon to meet the protective Sterch mountainside.

At first, Resi was relieved by the lack of life amongst the beauty of the valley. But the more they traveled, the more she doubted Rolf's decision to take the mountain pass. Not a single village, house, or even a shack was seen along the journey. No birds chirped in the trees. Not even a squirrel skittered across the path. The valley belonged to someone, Resi reasoned, but not to the likes of men. This realization left a miserable feeling in all the cold and terrible places inside of her that refused to be warmed, no matter how many times she pulled at her cloak.

Her hands went to her stomach like they had during her days at the Dockside Inn. The fire had been out for over a day now. She was surprised it hadn't rung out when the enchantment was taking its effects on her. Was it because of fear? Much as she loathed her gifting's existence, she found herself wishing that it was present, possibly because they were in Sterch. So many horror stories had trickled into the Farmhold from other regions; horses being stolen in the night by creatures made of pure darkness, entire platoons of military men from the city of Turbus vanishing in the mountainside. Resi had been so certain back then that those stories had been nothing more than a way to pass the time, but witnessing the magnitude of Sterch up close, as well as its unsettling way of making any unwelcome travelers notice their own isolation, was beginning to make her feel otherwise.

She turned to Corey, desperate for a distraction. "In the forest, when you heard the whispers in the trees..." she hesitated, then sighed and went for it. "What did you hear?"

Corey's eyes went to the mud on his boots. He put another strong hand through his hair. "You really want to know?"

Resi's eyes stayed on his face, noticing for the first time the freckles along his nose. Then she turned forward again, only to see Rolf's newly sunburnt bald spot dip down into a dried gully some ways ahead of them. If this were a race, he'd have lapped them twice by now. "I can't decipher whether we all heard the same thing or if the trees were speaking to us individually," she spoke.

Corey sidled next to her, matching her footing for the first time in hours. "They told me I was weak...that I'd be—" he paused. "Prey."

Resi tried to hide the chill that ran its way down her arms. *Prey*; as if Corey were nothing more than a prairie rabbit. "I heard them say something else," she replied. "Something about a '*she*'."

Corey's silence said everything; he'd heard it too. He nearly tripped over himself as he attempted to keep his pace while walking backwards beside her.

"*She will have them soon*," Resi repeated softly, shivering under her cloak at the memory of the trees' icy taunts.

Corey stopped her, grabbing her by the arm again, but this time, Resi didn't shrug him off. "They didn't mean you, Resi." His eyes were serious.

"Look around," she hushed him. "Do you see another '*she*'?"

Corey sighed, watching Rolf trudge up the other side of the gully. "Why would they be talking about you?" he asked.

Resi tore past him, her arms folding in on herself as she went. The memory of his skin on hers lingered on her forearm. Her words tumbled out as she staggered on. "What if I lose control and hurt Rolf? Hurt you? What if we've traveled this far, only for me to—"

"Resi, you won't," he said, catching up.

"You didn't see what I did to all those people."

The awful, blinding reality of her crime came flooding over her like a tidal wave. She couldn't get Luther's dead eyes out of her mind. And the heat—it was back now, rippling and turning over itself.

Out of the corner of her eye, she saw Corey swing around, attempting to grab her by the shoulders. But he pulled away quickly, feeling the boiling beneath the surface of Resi's skin. Based on the shocked look on his face, it was the first time he'd experienced anything like it. Still, he wasn't frightened.

"You have to forgive yourself, Resi," he said softly, his arms still outstretched towards her. "It's the only way you can guarantee you won't lose control again."

"Forgive myself?!" she spat.

"Your power is controlled by your emotions, right? Well, right now, your guilt is sending you into a tailspin. Neither you—nor us," he said, pausing to spot Rolf watching them suspiciously from the other side of the gully. "*None* of us can afford that."

Without another word, Resi marched off down the dip in the path and up again to meet Rolf. Corey trailed behind, his hands nervously playing with his hair.

"I'm a Vegari," Rolf whispered to her as she brushed past him. "Not a chaperone for two teenagers in some sort of lover's quarrel."

"You know, I think that might be a new record," she scoffed.

"New record?"

Resi snorted as she set her sight firmly on the path ahead. "It's only been two hours since the last time you bragged about your occupation."

They spent the rest of the morning and the afternoon hiking across the valley, then made the small ascent up the next mountain, eventually making camp at its summit around sunset. Corey had managed to find a berry patch as they'd climbed, but Rolf had insisted that what he'd found was poisonous. After much unnecessary squabbling between the three of them over their shared hunger, Rolf removed himself from the conversation by putting a makeshift tent together made out of a few branches and the cloak off of his own back. Barely a minute after it was erected, Corey passed out asleep beneath it, curled up in a puppyish way with the map tucked firmly beneath his armpit. Resi and Rolf sat outside, watching the sun go down beyond the ridge.

"You'd think he was a drunk," Rolf grumbled to Resi. "He sleeps like a drunk."

"One would make the assumption you speak from experience," Resi replied, then remembered something; a memory from that dusty cottage in Derton. "Whatever happened to that trusty flask of yours?"

His face falling in disappointment, Rolf reached into his pant pocket and retrieved it. He unscrewed it and tipped it upside down, but nothing came out.

Resi huffed. "And just when I was beginning to like you."

Rolf settled on the grass with a wry grin, wiping the mud from his worn boots. "What was that all about, anyway? Back at the gully."

"Oh," Resi shrugged. "It was nothing."

Rolf smirked again, stuffing the flask back into his pants. "You and Corey...Corey and you...whispering softly to each other...looking deeply into each other's eyes..."

"Would you keep your voice down?!" she spat, turning back towards the makeshift tent. She spoke again, this time in a whisper. "It was nothing. Really."

"Nothing, huh?" he laughed.

Resi shot him a look of disgust, but she couldn't help but smile a little inside. He was almost as bad as Mags. "He was just reassuring me."

"*Right,*" Rolf nodded knowingly.

"If you must know, he was helping me keep my emotions in check."

Rolf perked up. "You were angry?"

Resi shook her head, frightened of revealing the deep guilt inside of her for what had happened at the Tristeland.

Rolf settled back again, evidently deciding not to push Resi on the issue. The two breathed in the cold night air; somewhere between their earlier tumble down the mountainside and now, the silence of the region had become stifling. They sat in its ominous chill for a few moments before Resi briefly explained about what the trees had been whispering to her and Corey, and her confusion about the mysterious "*she.*"

"All forest enchantments are aimed to provoke whoever passes through them," Rolf told her, waving his hand dismissively. "That enchantment was trying to make you doubt yourself. Make you question your gifting."

Slowly, Resi released the buildup of air in her lungs. She turned back to the tent to ensure Corey was asleep, but it was too dark to know for sure. She could just barely make out the holes in Rolf's cloak. They reminded her of nights spent beneath tattered blankets, and of days filled with far-off stories.

"Forgiveness is the only way forward..." she spoke, remembering the words as if in a dream. "Without it, we all would be stuck somewhere between the present and the past."

Rolf drank in the words like a poem. "Who taught you that?"

Resi raised her eyebrows at him. "My mother...but don't be so impressed. She also said that the sky was made of sapphire candy and that clouds were just balls of cotton swept up by the wind."

Rolf chuckled.

"My father hated that about her," Resi continued. "Her *whimsies*. In fact, I don't think he knew her at all. He used to watch her in the fields like she was a stranger. Like she was no one to him."

Rolf cleared his throat. "And you?"

Resi drew her legs into her chest. Her father's face came to mind; long, gaunt, and disappointed at the end of a long day. "I was just another responsibility he didn't want to take on."

Rolf cleared his throat uncomfortably. "Did you ever try to look for them?"

At once, Resi's heart ached for the freedom of the woods on the farmhold, for her plot to escape its boundaries without anyone having noticed her leave. All her plans, now swept under the rug. Would she ever get the answers she'd so desperately needed after all these years? She sighed. "I guess I was never meant to."

"You know," Rolf started, his tone softening. "Belaflor is a place of belonging for many displaced Aliquians. It's why so many travel great distances and risk their lives to get there."

Resi sighed, fearing her own uncertainty of her parents making it into Belaflor, but realizing Rolf might be right. She'd never pictured her parents making it so far as Sterch, let alone to the mountains of Dirig. For too long, she'd assumed the worst. Unfortunately, her anger at them for leaving her behind had overpowered any hope she'd had of them surviving that kind of journey.

After another few minutes spent in the silence, Rolf finally shifted himself to his feet. "I'll take the first watch," he said. "You get some rest."

"It's okay," Resi said, not moving an inch from her place in the grass. "I'm not one for sleep these days."

Rolf didn't object much; instead, he thanked her with a yawn, swiping his hand at the air as if to give up. He turned back for the tent, and Resi found herself alone.

For a long time, she peered out over the darkness, contemplating what Corey had said to her that afternoon. If forgiveness was the momentary key to keeping her power at bay, then who deserved it most? Herself? Or her parents? And besides, what if her guilt was the only thing holding her back from committing the same crime as she'd perpetrated at the Tristeland twice?

She let the silence of the valley become her ally, allowing it to engulf her. She felt the weight of her exhaustion pull her down until all that was left of her were the slow beginnings of heat in her belly. Annoyed at her fatigue, Resi slapped herself in the cheek a few times, but her many sleepless nights on the road ultimately won out. The darkness forced her hand, and before she could rouse herself once more, she let her eyelids close, and every shrieking voice inside of her slipped into the quiet.

A CORNFIELD, with stalks that stretched high into a darkened sky. Bare, bleeding feet running quickly beneath a white, tattered dress. A cliff, one surrounded by black water on all sides. There was no escape. The only way out was to jump.

Resi jolted awake with a gasping inhale of breath. Only a dream. Even so, the sharp brush of the stalks on her forearms still bit at her skin as if it had been real.

Quickly, she peered through one of the holes in Rolf's cloak, then breathed a heavy sigh of relief as she saw two blackened lumps in the grass beneath it. All three of them were safe. She couldn't risk making the same mistake again—at least, not while Sequis's army was near. She looked out over the valley, now teeming with the promise of early daylight. She'd been out the entire night.

Eventually, she rose and made her way beneath the cloak, nearly stumbling over Rolf. She reached out a hand to wake Corey, but his form before her was stiff and leathery, too easy to move. Her hands rummaged desperately over what she now realized was only Corey's pack. But there was no Corey.

Hurriedly, she bent to shake Rolf awake. Rolf's eyes flew open wide at her touch, his hand reflexively pulling the knife from his pocket and nearly cutting her clean across the throat before he registered who she was. "Resi," he groaned when he took in the sight of her face.

Resi took a step outside the makeshift tent, her eyes nervously on the dagger. "Corey. He's gone."

Rolf rubbed at his eyes in bewilderment before looking around the tent. His eyes widened when they landed on Corey's abandoned pack. He brought his weight over his legs. "Weren't you keeping watch?"

"I—I must've nodded off."

Resi felt a tremble course its way down her spine as she watched Rolf's face suddenly contort in fear.

"The map!" he cried. Sloppily, he seized Corey's pack and rummaged through it frantically, emptying its contents completely; he produced another change of clothes, a worn journal, and a piece of molded bread that Corey had probably forgotten he had. But the map wasn't in sight.

"He had it on him when he fell asleep," Resi recalled. Desperate for answers, she stormed out of the tent and peered out over the valley, the sky reddening at its edges. "Corey!" her voice echoed over the mountains. "Corey!"

In an instant, Rolf came after her. He clasped her hard over the mouth with his hand. "Have you gone mad?!" he spat hoarsely, yanking her close. "Every creature from here to Malig could hear a leaf fall in this valley!"

But Resi didn't care. She bit at Rolf's palm, and he reared back in pain. "Corey!!" she yelled again, this time more frantic. "Corey, where are you?!"

Now angry, Rolf grabbed at her collar before pushing her to the ground, pinning her beneath his weight while keeping ahold of her. Resi froze beneath him, watching as he brought a quelling finger to his mouth. Together, they listened for any commotion, but only the same, eerie silence of the valley surrounded them.

Rolf relaxed slightly, giving her a severe look. "Let me make myself perfectly clear. *No* screaming."

Her tears subsided, and Resi nodded.

"Now, the next order of business," he said. "What was the last thing you remember before drifting off?"

Resi tried to recall, but the tears were streaming so heavily down her face that she could barely breathe. "I was in the darkness. Then I fell asleep. I had the strangest dream."

A mix of emotions paraded across Rolf's face before he shook her in his hands. "A dream? What kind of dream?"

"I was—I was in a cornfield. And there was water all around me. I had to jump, only I couldn't."

Rolf's face twisted; then he suddenly released her, getting quickly to his feet before decisively taking off in the direction from which they had come the day prior.

"Rolf? Rolf, what is it?" she cried after him.

But Rolf had nothing more to say. It wasn't until Resi watched him break into a run that she flew after him. He knew something, something awful, something beyond her own comprehension, but what, Resi couldn't be sure.

They ran along the dimly lit path, clambering their way back over the gully. Terrified, Resi found herself frequently turning over her shoulder, hoping to find Corey trailing behind them; but instead, she was only met with flashes of the strange images from her dream.

Finally, after descending the small mountain and tearing through the mud of the valley, they arrived at a familiar clearing. Resi nearly gasped. She and Rolf had backtracked all the way back to the lake where they'd come to earlier the day prior. Lingering on the shore was Corey, his face pointed out over the water with his broad shoulders hunched forward.

"What is he doing here?" Resi turned to Rolf, her heart fearing the worst. She recalled the widening rings in the lake.

"No," Rolf whispered into the dawn, not registering Resi's question. Paralyzed with fear, he stared forward, his body stiff from head to foot. "It can't be...not here."

"Rolf!" she nudged him. "Rolf, what's going on?!"

Still nothing. All he could do was stare blankly to where Corey waited at the water's edge.

"Forget it," Resi bristled at him. In a rage, she descended the hill to the water, all the while forcing herself to hold back a scream to catch Corey's attention. But as her boots clashed against the rock of the shore and still, Corey did not stir, an icy feeling came over her, one that told her something dreadful was about to take place.

"Corey?" she murmured. She reached out a shaking hand and tapped his shoulder. Slowly, he turned to reveal his face.

His warm brown eyes were gone—they were now completely black and as cold and vacant as the very water before him. He peered through Resi as if she were nothing but mist, then turned himself to look out over the lake once more.

Just then, the center of the lake began to bubble. The water shifted and swirled, vibrating and pulsing with an evil nature, until a long mat of thick, black hair raised from beneath the surface. The curve of a woman's naked form followed after, head bowed and face hidden beneath the tangle of hair that fell down the length of her entire body; Resi couldn't see the ends of it beneath the lake's surface. Motionless, the woman floated above the water, her skin gray and translucent. She hovered there for a moment, her face still hidden— until she tilted her chin up to meet the rising sun to the west. Where her eyes should have been were only two hollow, black voids of empty space that swallowed any and all light.

Resi fell back on herself and hit the shore with a thud. She clamored at the sand and the stone to pull herself closer to the safety of the grass.

"Corey!" she breathed. "Corey, get back!"

She watched in terror as Corey trudged forward, his boots sinking deeper into the lake until the creature locked her eyes onto him. Without another breath, Corey fell head-first into the water.

This terrible creature, the *she* from the forest enchantment's taunts—Corey was hers now. His weight sunk lower into the dark water, nearly submerging him, and in response, the long, tangled webs of black hair spilling out from the creature began to weave their way towards him under the surface. Resi's stomach writhed in horror as she saw them snake towards him like swimming vipers, sending up a violent hissing sound before latching themselves onto Corey and dragging him further under.

Without another thought, Resi launched herself into the lake. Ignoring the chill of the water, she kicked her legs and arms until she reached the long, tangled mess of the black hair. But the hair quickly wrapped itself around her, mercilessly encircling her stomach, her chest, and her throat. She could barely see Corey through the murk; his mouth had opened in a scream under the surface, his empty eyes still managing to call for help. Desperately, Resi cried for Rolf.

"The map, Resi!" she heard him scream from where he stood on the shore. "The map!"

But the water blinded her as the creature's living hair dragged her under, until all she saw beneath the surface were her own two legs dangling above a starless, predawn sky. She fought, ripping at the hair with her hands before she grasped for her dagger tucked inside her boot. She cut at the creature's hair and heard it react with a high-pitched hiss that traveled quickly through the water. The dagger slipped from Resi's hand, and try as she could to find it amongst the chaos, she couldn't. The hair's grip slackened just enough for Resi to kick her way back to the surface again, welcoming the cool shock of the morning air on her face.

"Corey!" she coughed.

But he was with *her* now—she could see his body, floating lifelessly beneath the creature's figure, his limbs lost in the chaos of water and hair.

"No!" Resi screamed. "Corey, no!"

Helplessly, she watched as the creature lowered her body above his, her hair positioned around him like a shadowed halo. The creature's jaw unlatched, creating an opening wide enough to swallow him whole. But she didn't; instead, a sap-like liquid came flowing out of it. The liquid dripped like honey into Corey's open mouth, until it suddenly hardened, creating a kind of cord. Resi's entire being filled with fear as she watched a spark of light ignite from Corey's mouth. The seconds passed slowly as the creature began to lure the light through the cord, drawing it ever closer into the void of her own mouth.

Resi's stomach flipped with dread; the light made up the very essence of Corey's fragile life. "No!" she cried, clawing again at the hair, but the creature was growing stronger as the light traveled up the cord. As she thrashed, Resi looked briefly into Corey's eyes. There was nothing in them.

All at once, the fire roared inside of Resi. No longer could she hear the hissing of the snakelike hair or the screams from Rolf on the shore. All that existed was a shrill noise—a frequency shift in the air. It rang loudly between her temples, and as it built in intensity, the water responded around her.

Two ropes of water raised themselves around the creature, like two strong arms. They hung there, suspended in space; as if in a dream, Resi watched the creature let out a terrible scream before the water laced around her neck and plunged her deep beneath the lake's surface. Resi felt an animalistic, violent pull coming from within herself; she was somehow using the water to strangle the monster, to drown her in her own lake. Try as the creature might to break from Resi's strength, she could not. The creature clawed at the water that had constricted around her neck, using her hands and hair, but to no avail. At the last, the monster let out an earsplitting shriek. The sound ripped like an explosion beneath the surface of the water before it was released in a horrific blast that tore through the clearing in a wave of sound and light. Resi watched, feeling a detached sense of satisfaction as the creature's lifeless body sank deeply into its black hair before it disappeared altogether into the dark depths of the lake, just as she and Corey had watched the pebble fall beneath the water the day before.

Resi's eyes found Corey in the chaos. The cord had snapped, and his body, which was no longer supported by the creature's hair, had begun to sag below the surface. Shaking herself back into her own body, she dove after him, welcoming the crush of the water against her as she came back to herself. She used all of her remaining strength to get to him as the darkness swallowed both of them whole. But when she finally got hold of him, she couldn't kick him to safety; she'd been under too long. Her senses began to dull as her lungs involuntarily took a large breath in and filled her body with water.

She convulsed and twitched, and then something strong latched onto her chest as if it were taking her hostage. She didn't fight it. Instead, she welcomed the eternal black that wanted to creep its way into her. She shut her heavy eyes, surrendering to a terrible vision of a corpse lost in a bottomless lake, lying still next to a boy with dead, open eyes.

A FOUNTAIN of water ejected itself onto the stone of the shore. Resi coughed for her life, feeling the relief of the air filling her lungs as she rolled onto her side. She blinked in the daylight until her eyes adjusted. Rolf hovered over her, his face taut with worry, and a fresh cut lashed across his forehead.

He'd rescued her. But it had almost been too late.

Without a word, Resi slowly raised herself to her feet. Panicked, she searched for Corey along the shore, noticing the destruction along the banks. The clearing had been torn to shreds. Not a single tree stood around the lake; only ash and stone remained.

Finally, she spotted Corey, lying on his side farther up the shoreline. Rolf had wrapped his cloak around him. Corey's face had gone pale and his lips were blue, but his chest still bobbed with labored breath. He was alive.

"He's alright," Rolf sputtered. "You're both alright."

Relieved, Resi lay back on the shore and closed her eyes as she caught her breath. She needed to let the morning sun warm her face, let the panic and fear shake its way out of her before she could even think of dealing with Rolf. In the face of death, he'd been nothing but a coward. And she—she'd become something else entirely.

Out of nowhere, a call from a horn, one brassy and bright, rang out from the mountainside. Resi and Rolf looked to the top of the nearest peak. Positioned proudly upon it was a member of the Eastern Guard on horseback. His horn briefly glinted in the sunlight before he turned around and disappeared beyond the mountain.

"They've found us," Rolf groaned.

Resi wanted to slap him clean across the face. After the creature's shrieks and the explosive blast from her power, what else had he been expecting? She looked at Corey, focusing herself on the task at hand. "We need to get him up."

"There's a cave," Rolf offered. "There."

Resi followed his pointed finger over the calmed surface of the water. A leaning rock formation lay hidden beneath a newly fallen pine only a small hike away. If they hurried, they could make it.

Together, she and Rolf lifted Corey, dragging him along the rocks of the shore. "Resi," Rolf whispered, his voice laboring under Corey's extra weight. "I'm—"

If he was trying to apologize, Resi pretended not to hear it. Whatever Rolf's excuse was for abandoning them would have to wait; it wasn't the time or place for explanations. They needed to get to safety. They'd have to wait it out until Sequis and his army passed through the valley.

As they came to the cave, Resi lifted the pine branches, and she and Rolf hauled Corey's weight into the shelter. Corey began to sputter as he coughed up some of the lake water. Resi pretended not to notice the strange black liquid that came up with it. As Rolf rested the young man with his back against the rock, he rushed to open Corey's shirt, then gasped. Corey's chest was black and veined.

"The dolus—its venom is killing him," Rolf whispered.

Dolus, the name for a lake demon. It had never occurred to Resi that one would exist so close to the border of Ter, so close to home.

Her heart sank deep into her stomach as she watched Corey struggle for his life. Not him. Not here.

"There has to be a way to stop it," she said, her voice quaking. But Rolf didn't have an immediate answer. "Rolf, there's a way to stop it, right?!"

"There are medicinal remedies, but only in Dirig and Rowan," Rolf answered. His breath quickened. "I've never known a dolus to come this far east."

"What is it doing here?"

Rolf covered up the sight of Corey's darkened chest with his own cloak. He winced as he turned away. "No idea."

"Well—w-well, we have to do something! We can't just let him die!" Resi stuttered. She couldn't make sense of the horror of losing Corey, not in the cold of an abandoned cave; but it appeared to her that Rolf's energy had run dry. He had nothing more to offer her; no wisdom or council, not even after such a horrifying attack. His chest bobbed as he caught his breath. "Would you do something!" she finally yelled at him.

"I don't know what to do!" Rolf snapped. "I don't have all the answers here!"

"You promised!" she scolded him. "You said that you would be the one that would get us out of trouble if it ever came our way. Well, here's your chance, 'all-knowing' Vegari! Prove you're more than just your title!"

"I'm not a sorcerer, alright?!"

They both went silent, fear growing in the space between them. Resi's thoughts raced back to the Tristeland, to the moments before she'd exploded with power. Sequis had been healing Luther. It was possible that he could do the same for Corey. She could see in Rolf's eyes that he had reached the exact same conclusion. But her mind clamped down on that hope; it was foolish to even think it.

"Don't say it," Resi said, beating Rolf to the punch. "We can't."

"It's the only way," Rolf whispered.

"And *how*, exactly, do you think we'll convince Sequis to keep him alive, huh?" she spewed. "He wants my head on a spike. Why wouldn't he want both of yours, too?"

Rolf started to pace, his arms crossed over his chest. The angles of his face twitched. "I don't know. But it's the only hope we have of keeping him alive."

They both turned to Corey. His gray face blended into the stone. He didn't have much time. Resi didn't have to think. She ran to him, putting the warmth of her own body against his.

From beyond the cave, they heard the clatter of horse hooves on the ground, and another cry from a horn pierced the silence. Rolf peeked out beyond the branches of the pine tree. His jaw clenched. "They're here."

"What do we do?"

Determined, Rolf crouched on his feet. He brought his eyes closer to hers. "Resi," he said. "Do you realize what happened back there?"

A flash of black hair streaked across Resi's vision. "It—it must have drowned itself," she shuddered, willfully ignoring the reality of what her power had done. "It—"

"You vanquished it," Rolf insisted, his eyes fierce. "You accessed your gifting, and just in time. I was only there to pull you to shore."

"Don't even get me started on that—"

"Listen to me!" Rolf's command echoed through the endless space of the cave, reverberating into a chorus of deep tones. "You're right," he heaved. "I have no excuse for what happened back there. But you have no excuse for what happens next. You're capable of calling your power on command. You just have to believe that you can."

"Believing in a power that's killed and injured too many isn't going to get us out of this mess," Resi sputtered stubbornly. "It'll only make it worse!"

Rolf carefully released the air in his lungs. Resi knew he wanted to scream at her, to knock her around until she agreed to his horrendous plan. "No, it won't. It may feel out of your control, but it isn't." Something shifted in his face, and he fixed her with a serious gaze.

"Think of how you feel right before you paint. You're not worried it will turn out alright. You just have a desire to engage with it."

Resi let the words sink in as she watched Rolf swoop Corey into his arms and head for the opening of the cave. How did he know all of this?

"What are you doing?" she asked as she scrambled to her feet after them. Rolf turned back to her with only a nod and a knowing glint in his eye.

"You'll know when the time is right."

And with that, he and Corey disappeared beyond the pine branches.

For a time, Resi waited in the dark. She finally maneuvered her way to the edge of the cave, concealing herself beneath one of the pine trees to view the scene.

The sun had disappeared beyond the ash and smoke from the dolus attack. Rolf was squinting as he attempted to see anything beyond the lake, but the smoke was too thick. He moved forward, heaving Corey's weight above him, occasionally losing his balance on the wet sand of the banks.

His feet were at the shoreline when he looked out over the water again. Fog had descended over the smoke, and both consumed the decimated clearing like a disease. But sure enough, as the sun came alive once more from beyond the cloud cover, Resi saw the shadows of a dozen armed soldiers appear on the other side of the lake. And at their forefront stood a soldier several feet higher than the rest; a green-eyed sorcerer, not quite man, not quite giant.

CHAPTER 19

THE WEST

The cohort of soldiers followed after the Governor on horseback, with muskets, long and heavy, hung over their shoulders. At the tip of each firearm was a long, sharpened blade. Sequis was dressed in a suit of dark armor. He walked purposefully as his steps fractured the earth beneath his feet, crushing the sand in splintered patterns across the shore. Resi fought every urge within herself to exit the cave as she watched Sequis approach her bedraggled companions.

"Your Lordship," Rolf started as he fell under Sequis's shadow. "I don't believe we've had the pleasure of ever meeting." He winced as he moved Corey from his shoulder to the sand. "Rolf," he said, extending his hand.

But Sequis didn't reciprocate the gesture; his massive paw remained at his side. "There's a rumor floating about that a certain tracker has been escorting someone who very much belongs to me," he spoke, his voice ringing out.

"That so?" Rolf mused.

"Let's not hop about the issue," Sequis said. His mass bent over at the waist, the golden tendrils of his hair nearly brushing Rolf in the face. "I know she's here."

Rolf couldn't help it. His eyes flitted to the sand to look upon

Corey.

"Whatever your employer is paying, I'll triple it," Sequis said calmly.

The water lapped at the shore as Resi watched Rolf peer around Sequis to his soldiers. He shifted on the sand uncomfortably. "I don't want your money. But I'm willing to offer something else in exchange for healing the kid."

"I'll be the first to inform you," Sequis said bemusedly as he examined Corey's grey face, "Giants aren't ones to barter."

Rolf's eyes worriedly flinched to Corey. "Please. I'm begging you. He's badly injured."

"And?" Sequis said coolly.

Again, Rolf didn't have an immediate answer. Still, he stalled. "He's a free 'Lick, sir. If you provide him with healing," he gulped, "I'll tell you where she is."

But Sequis was done playing games. "Search the area," he said to his guards, and they scattered. He then reached out a hand and grasped Rolf by the collar, lifting him slowly from the ground. Rolf's legs flailed about like two limp noodles. "Spit it out, tracker," Sequis seethed. "*Where is she?*"

But Rolf wouldn't concede. He stared quizzically into the emerald of Sequis's eyes. "Huh..." he struggled to say as he noticed the jagged stitches along Sequis's face. "New scar?"

In a flash, Rolf was spread wide on the sand. He watched helplessly as Sequis stomped his way to where Corey rested. Angered, the giant lifted his large boot and gently pushed it down on Corey's venom-filled chest. A loud, desperate cry left the young man.

Less than a moment later, Resi revealed herself from behind the pine's trunk and stepped into the sunlight along the rocks of the other side of the small lake. As if an invisible string connected her to Sequis, he looked up to watch her walk up to the shore in the sun.

"What do you say, Resi? Shall I even the score?" he yelled madly over the water. "Your dolus-poisoned friend for my Advisor?"

Resi surveyed the horrific scene: Rolf, lying twisted and pained on the rocks, and Corey, poor Corey, trapped beneath Sequis's boot. The dozen soldiers, their teeth bared and muskets pointed right at her. The world slowed once more like it had at the Tristeland, and she felt the nausea hit her hard in the gut.

Immediately, she felt the fire descend from her feet to connect with the earth. But it stopped there; she wouldn't let it find its way into the world, not like it had with the dolus or at the Tristeland. She was too fearful, too worried to move, to breathe, to think of anything but Corey's screams.

A crack of blue light suddenly came flying at her, hitting hard at the ground beneath her feet. The dirt gave way, throwing her, and she landed hard on her back, groaning. An icy feeling, like sinking into a frozen pond, came over her legs; she'd been hit. She tried to raise herself to her feet, but couldn't. She was paralyzed from the waist down, her legs lost somewhere in a cloud of dust and dirt.

One by one, the guards crowded her and dragged her across the shore to their leader. They dumped her on the ground beside Rolf before tying her hands to her feet behind her back with a rough piece of twine.

"You really thought you had a chance of outwitting me?" Sequis asked, lifting his boot from Corey and languidly taking a knee on the shore beside her.

Resi turned to her right and left, seeing the bright light in Corey's eyes beginning to give out to one side of her, and Rolf clutching at a broken leg to the other. "You only pick fights you know you'll win," she spat at Sequis. "But the trick's on you. You even said it yourself. You're *weak*." She pulled at the heat, trying to flame it around her. But her legs couldn't find it. They were nothing to her now; just two stumps of dead flesh and bone.

Becoming enraged, Sequis wiped a small bead of sweat from his cheek before it could drip over his new scar from the night of the first attack at the Tristeland. "If I recall correctly, it was *you* who ran away from the wreckage you caused that night. Too afraid to face the consequences of what your violence caused."

"You were trying to kill me," she pointed out.

His eyes widened and his nostrils flared. "You *dare* speak about murder as if it were beneath you?"

Resi coughed, feeling the guilt well in her abdomen. Combined with the heat of her power, it was a nasty sort of sick, the kind that wanted to bring itself up to the surface. She wanted to tell Sequis that killing Luther had been an accident, but who was she to think he would believe her? "Hadn't you almost killed Luther yourself?" she struggled to ask.

Dissatisfied, Sequis huffed out a snort.

"Kill me," Resi begged him. "Just don't hurt Rolf or Corey. Please."

A peculiar laugh bubbled over Sequis's lips. "Playing the martyr won't save any of you," he said. "And besides, we have traditions within the Eastern Guard, especially when we catch runaways."

The soldiers snickered behind their muskets, their heads bobbing in agreement.

"My crest," he continued, pointing to a simple golden circle on the breast of his armor. "A circle; infinite; a shape with no beginning, or end. Much like the establishment of Aliquian servitude. It's as old a tradition as any, and as long as I'm in power, it always will be. It's rare that I come across a 'Lick that steps out of bounds, and for your courage, I commend you," he snickered. "But I'm not above reminding you of what you are."

Sequis turned to Corey; black venom dripped from the corner of his mouth. He reached his gloved hand to swipe some of it with his fingertip. "And to think...I nearly offered you the world," he told Resi. "Still, it seems you and I have more in common than I'd once suspected."

"You're a monster!" she cried vehemently, rejecting his statement with every ounce of defiance that she held within.

"Ah," Sequis cooed. "One might say the same about someone like you, Miss Flood. In time, you will come to see that. Your so-called 'gifts' will be your demise. You've killed once..." He lowered his mouth to her ear, then whispered, "What makes you think you won't do it again?"

Desperately, Resi wriggled beneath the twine, scratching her wrists raw against it. Sequis watched her intently, almost delighted by her will to fight, and seemingly drawing power from it.

"I've imagined you this way..." he said, his voice softening. His head tilted sinisterly to the side. "Tied up in my bed chambers, waiting for me. *Begging* me to have you."

Hungrily, he bent at the knees, drawing his massive face closer to hers. She could smell the alcohol on him, the aftermath of many rough nights of travel and the grief of losing his longest friend. He studied her face before bringing his large mouth to hers. The kiss was rough and violent. Horrified, she reared back before spitting at him square in the eye.

Sequis took a deep breath with his eyes closed before wiping the saliva from his face. "I'll enjoy this."

All at once, he pressed the black venom against her forearm, and drew a circle; he was marking her, just as Horris had marked Shina. Resi shrieked at the top of her lungs as the venom and power of Sequis's sorcery burned at her flesh. All the while, Sequis's eyes drilled into her, taking in the pleasure of her pain.

The smell of cooked flesh floated through the clearing as Resi's shrieks quieted. Exhausted, Resi lay still on the sand, feeling cold and hot at the same time. The flame in her stomach was dying out, giving way to another feeling, one desperate and searching for anything powerful to draw life from.

"Dolus venom," he spoke, taking a victorious sniff of the smell of burning flesh in the air. "It should kill you within minutes."

Resi gasped for breath, feeling the heat of the venom work its way from her arm down to her fingers.

"I want to be the last thing you see," Sequis glowered as he brought his face closer to hers once more. "The last voice you hear... take this to the grave with you, 'Lick: until the flesh rots from your bones, you will be marked with the brand of a criminal 'Lick. Forever shackled. Forever a prisoner. Forever bound under my rule."

The venom was spreading quickly, consuming Resi, threatening to eat her alive. She wriggled in the dirt, her mind picturing Rolf and Corey somewhere beyond her sight, bound and gagged, the two of them crying out for the heat she couldn't muster. She could feel her breath slowing and her heart reaching for more. The sky was brightening, coming over the clearing like a new day.

But then, a soldier cried out. Surprised, Sequis looked up from Resi's face. It was barely another moment before a drum echoed somewhere in the distance; a sound much like a heartbeat. Then came the beat of wings, followed by a descending shadow over the clearing.

But all light was fading. The heaviness of the venom engulfed Resi as she fought to keep her eyes open. She let the cool brush of the wind whip against her face before the clearing vanished altogether. She resigned herself to the venom, hearing shrieks from the soldiers as her consciousness began to dwindle. The last thing she heard was the clash of metal on metal and the explosion of gunfire, as a burst of blue light danced across her fading vision.

———

MORE LIGHT CAME, but this time, it was bright, radiant, almost holy.

Resi awoke covered by white sheets. Her eyes darted about a cavernous room. Hesitantly, she peeled the sheets off of her, noticing the dampness of her hair on her cheeks. She was dressed in nothing but a nightshirt, and at some point, she'd been bathed.

The bed was small, as if it had been made for a child. Above, a skylight brightly revealed a crisp blue sky. Deep cherry wood beams rose high into the ceiling, and the sound of the sea played outside like a soothing melody.

Resi's mind began to race; everything was too lavish, too much like a nightmare from the past. Not the Tristeland. Not again.

Just then, the door squeaked open, and waiting in the door frame stood Rolf. He was dressed in clean trousers and a new cloak, and a fresh splint ran up his right leg. Resi didn't have to think; she ran to him, hugging him as if she hadn't seen him in years. He was alive, and he smelled fresh and soapy.

"I see you're feeling better," he quipped.

Resi let go of him and turned about herself, taking in the grandeur of the room. "Are we dead?"

Rolf laughed. "Not sure the afterlife could beat a place like this," he said as he motioned to the open window. "But it might come close."

Resi walked out on the balcony, smelling the foam of the sea for the first time since leaving the Tristeland. They were raised high above a rolling vineyard in a giant fortified compound made of wood and steel. The surrounding valley, green and yellow, teemed with birds and livestock.

"What happened?" she asked him. She raised her arm, noticing the new bandage on her forearm. The clearing, the dolus venom, the Mark—it had been too violent to be a dream after all.

Rolf's eyes crinkled slightly as he reached into a pocket to retrieve Corey's map, and once Resi placed her hand on the parchment, she watched it respond. The star, *her* star, hung delicately above the western side of the Sept-Regions near the Peri Sea, a sea that often brought travelers from near and far by ship to the western coast of the regions.

"No," she said, looking up at Rolf in disbelief.

"Welcome to the wine country of Rowan," he nodded.

Resi tried to remember the moments before she'd passed out from the venom. "We were rescued?"

Gently, Rolf ushered her back inside. "By an old friend."

"How did we get here?" she asked. Then, remembering the lifeless eyes beside her in the clearing. "Corey?!" she blurted as she rushed for the outer door, but she stopped short when the worst possible thought entered her head. Had he survived?

Rolf sighed, sitting back on the bed. "He's...alright, Resi."

Resi let the good news wash over her like a cool current. "Can I see him?"

A hand went to Rolf's thinning hair. He fluffed the front of it, as if that one small action might unleash a wellspring of follicle growth. "It's best—" he paused, finally meeting her eyes. "It's best we let him rest. After everything he survived, he needs to recover."

Resi found herself nodding emphatically, but she wasn't sure why. All she wanted was to wrap her arms around Corey and hold on, to tell him that he would one day find his sister. "Your leg," she suddenly remembered. "It was broken."

Defeated, Rolf peered down at the splint wrapped around his thigh. "Thankfully, this place is known for its healing remedies. It was reset." He smiled, but for some reason, Resi took it as a warning. "I'm sure you're familiar with stories of fairies."

She almost doubled over with laughter. "As in, '*little people with sharp teeth that fly about like mosquitos*' fairies?"

"Well," Rolf said, reasoning. "That's one kind of fairy. The Pix clan lives in southern Rowan. Terrible things. They've had it out for Queen Tasmin ever since she was crowned."

"I'm sorry..." Resi said slowly. "*Who?*"

Rolf sighed, placing his hands in his lap. "Tasmin—Queen of the Meade-Valley fairy clan."

"Oh..." Resi said. She'd never heard stories or myths about such a thing.

"We owe her our lives, Resi," he continued. "Tasmin was hunting down the dolus we came across. She'd been tracking it for months, trying to kill it after it'd escaped the western bogs. But she and a few of her best warriors came across us instead. Luckily, she was able to extract the dolus venom with a medicinal remedy that she'd brought along; she had enough to heal an entire army."

"How did we make it out?"

"Fairies may look fragile, but they're anything but. Tasmin is trained in almost every form of combat. Feisty thing, she is," Rolf smiled slightly. "Lovely, but, not one to be tested. It wasn't a minute after she and her stallions arrived that they'd fished us out of that mess."

Resi suddenly recalled the wind on her face, along with the beat of wings. "And Sequis?" she asked.

Another sigh escaped Rolf, this one tense. "We managed to get out in time to escape, but Sequis is alive. He'll recruit more men, especially if he plans on attacking us here."

"He's coming?! Here?!"

"He knows we're with Tasmin," Rolf shrugged. "And Sequis isn't one to quit, but Corey's not strong enough to journey on foot."

"But, but—if this *Queen* is so great at healing, why can't we leave? The three of us could head north tonight!"

Rolf finally stood to his feet, his face downtrodden. "The dolus did more than just sap Corey's strength, Resi. Doluses lure men from their beds and prey on them in their dreams, but they do much worse damage to their minds. The effect leaves many with serious trauma."

"What are you saying?" Resi breathed. "That Corey has gone crazy?"

Rolf's arms wrapped in front of his torso. "The creature got into his head—messed with him. He hasn't eaten. Doesn't want to sleep. He's not prepared for the journey."

Determined, Resi charged for the door. She had to see Corey, had to hold him in her arms like she had in the cave. But Rolf forced himself into the space of the door before she could leave. "Resi, no. It's not a good idea."

"Don't be ridiculous," she huffed, trying to slip past him.

"Stop!" he yelled, pushing her back into the room with a nudge at her shoulders. "He's asked not to see you. *Specifically.*"

She shuddered, imagining a pale-faced Corey making the request to deny her visitation. "You've seen him?"

Rolf sighed. "He's not well, Resi. He needs time."

She didn't want to admit it, but she knew that Rolf was telling the truth. Still, she persisted. "You're lying."

Rolf sighed, then briefly glanced over his shoulder into the darkened hall. "I know you have a lot of questions. And they'll be answered."

Indignant, she placed her hands on her hips. "Just not by you, apparently."

Rolf gave up the fight. He turned away, heading for the hall, then paused to point a finger towards a smaller set of doors at the other end of the room; a closet. "Get dressed," he ordered. "The Queen would like a word."

CHAPTER 20

THE FORTRESS

As soon as she'd dressed, Resi joined Rolf in the hall. She'd picked an olive green, lightweight linen shift from the closet for her first meeting with the Fairy Queen. The color brought out the color of her eyes and suited her well. Even so, she lacked any confidence. She tugged nervously at the dress as she followed after Rolf.

Still tense from their earlier conversation, the two kept quiet as they walked along the hall, passing by door after closed door. Each was made of wood and had been marked with swirling symbols that Resi had never seen. The ceilings were incredibly low; so much so that she and Rolf had to duck down whenever they turned a corner. Every so often, they'd pass an open window and Resi would pause to breathe in the fresh ocean air. The chill weather of the east had yet to arrive here in the west.

Together, they wound their way through the long halls, weaving their way closer to the heart of the fortress and passing no one along the way. After a time, Rolf paused before a particular closed door, one that was even more intricately carved. Fragrant herbs hung from the top of the door frame.

"He's here," Resi said, sensing Corey's presence beyond it.

But Rolf didn't say anything. Instead, he continued on, keeping his head down.

Finally, they entered a cavernous space, one damp and cold. They found themselves at the top of a stairwell carved out of the trunk of a massive, ancient tree. Surrounding them was a room in the shape of a dome. Light poured down from large openings in the ceiling. Stunned, Resi let her eyes follow the rays of light down to where they pierced a white onyx floor far below.

"What is this place?" she asked.

"The Western Fortress," Rolf told her. "The residence of the Fairy Queen and the Meade Valley warriors. They've lived here for centuries, long before even the Codian migration."

Resi looked out past the stairwell to where the domed room gave way to a massive terrace, hanging out over the turquoise water of the Peri Sea like the bow of a magnificent ship.

"Food awaits," Rolf chimed as he accompanied her down the stairs and through the magnificent ballroom. Resi brushed her hands against the smooth bark of an array of small trees that grew their way through the space. Their branches reached high into the room above them, deep green leaves canopying the sunlight from the large openings far overhead, leaving only pockets of sunshine for Resi to feel on her shoulders as she passed through.

Further out on the terrace, a floor table awaited them loaded with colorful fruits, cheeses, breads, and vats of Fet and milk. Men and women, some fair and red-haired like Codians, others with dark hair and dark eyes like Aliquians, lay about the pillows lazily, their cheeks reddened by the fresh sea wind.

Resi's eyes were drawn to a child, a young girl facing the sea, leaning happily over the balcony with a smile that could light up the night. Her skin sparkled in the sun, and she wore a cream chiffon dress that perfectly complemented the black of her hair, which was braided and knotted at the back of her head. Resi was captivated by the sight of her.

Only, she wasn't a child. The girl turned around to reveal that she was actually a woman—petite, athletic, and built like a warrior. The smile stayed on her face as she noticed the new guests approaching.

"Resi," Rolf breathed. "This is Tasmin, Queen of the Meade Valley fairies."

Happily, the Queen skipped to them, her dress dancing behind her in the breeze. Resi stuck out her hand, but was instead greeted with a forceful hug. "Let me guess," Tasmin said, her voice soft like rain. "You were expecting wings?"

She released her, and Resi took a deep breath. "Not entirely, no."

"Don't worry," Tasmin chimed. The smile spread wider on her face. "You wouldn't be the first."

Suddenly aware of the eyes on her, Resi turned to view the group congregated around the table. Their chewing slowed as they took in the sight of her for the first time.

"You both must be hungry," Tasmin said, extending her arm towards the table. "Please, sit."

Resi and Rolf perched awkwardly on the pillows, hesitantly reaching for whatever food was closest. The fairies, Resi noticed, were all built the same as Tasmin: no taller than four feet, their eyes bright, earnest, kind, and warm. Still, their gaze stayed on Resi, watching her every move.

Tasmin suddenly snapped at them, her tone embarrassed. "You act like you've never seen a human woman before in your life!"

Surprised, the group jumped in reaction. They all stood and filed out, one even snatching a bottle of Fet off the table before snickering his way after the others and back into the safety of the dome.

"Please excuse them," Tasmin apologized to Resi. Gracefully, she reached for a glass and poured herself a helping of Fet. "We haven't hosted a visitor in quite some time. Especially one like you."

Resi choked slightly as she swallowed a too-large bite of bread. "Like me?"

"Oh, don't be modest," Tasmin said. "First, a display of power at the Tristeland. Then, a dolus vanquisher? In my seventy-six years, I've never known another Aliquian to cause such commotion."

It was almost too much to take in. Resi turned to Rolf as she processed it. *Seventy-six years?* Tasmin looked no older than fourteen.

At her reaction, Tasmin shot a look to Rolf, then muttered something under her breath; something along the lines of, *did you tell her nothing?*

Feeling uncomfortable, Resi changed the subject. "Rolf said you were friends," she started. "How long have you known each other?"

The smile didn't leave Tasmin's face. Instead, it softened and warmed as she recalled. "Close to twenty years now."

Rolf huffed. "Makes me feel old."

"Well, aren't you? I've come to understand that a certain someone celebrated a fiftieth birthday this past year," Tasmin chuckled.

"This, coming from the seventy-six-year-old fairy."

"Hey," Tasmin warned him with a raised brow. "Don't push it."

"I knew I liked you," Resi smiled at Tasmin.

Tasmin smirked at Rolf. "I met this Patrian brute all those years ago when he'd just been recruited by the Elders of Belaflor. The Fortress used to be a hub for many Vegari."

Resi couldn't help but give a smile to Rolf. It was a joy to imagine him then, so young and full of optimism. "You came here with your traveling partner?" Resi asked him, reaching for her glass. She watched a strange look pass between him and Tasmin.

"Yes," he spoke softly before taking a large gulp. "We often stopped here on our way north."

"Oh, he was so charming," Tasmin cooed. "Good-looking too. All of my Sairons were crazy for him."

Another word Resi had never heard. "Sairons?"

Tasmin swallowed her Fet, then motioned to where the other fairies had gone off to. "Female fairy warriors; said to be the most beautiful of all women in the Sept-Regions," she said before looking back at Rolf. "And out of all the men that visited here, they thought this one was the most handsome of them all."

"That's enough," Rolf batted away her praise.

"And if I recall correctly, you liked your Fet back then too,"

Tasmin said, raising her glass to him. Rolf wavered before finally clinking his glass against it.

"As you can tell, not much has changed," he smiled.

"So, who was it that accompanied Rolf?" Resi asked Tasmin, feeling the warmth of the Fet beginning to heat her cheeks. "Whoever it was must've been a saint to spend all their time on the road with a man that walks at the same pace as most people run."

Rolf shot a fleeting look at Tasmin. "Trixa," he said. "Trixa was her name."

The name hung ominously over the table for a few seconds.

Finally, Tasmin spoke. "They traveled together for three years, scouring the regions for gifted Aliquians, like you."

Resi watched as Rolf's gaze drifted to his lap.

"Enough about us," Tasmin continued. "I was surprised when my warriors and I finally tracked you down. We'd just crossed over the ridge when we heard screams."

"She saw everything," Rolf told Resi. "What you did to the dolus."

"When we reached the clearing, we couldn't believe what we were seeing," Tasmin confessed.

Perplexed, Resi turned to the fairy queen. Her beautiful, tiny face was aglow with excitement.

"You're something special, Resi," Tasmin exhaled.

A small wave of pride swelled over Resi. But then, it just as quickly crashed and dissipated.

Tasmin then gripped her hands with purpose. "I want to help you defeat Sequis."

"Help *me*?" Resi stuttered.

Tasmin nodded. "With my warriors and the strength of your gifting, we could easily overwhelm him."

Resi looked at Rolf, but his face was devoid of any opinion on the matter. He simply shrugged.

"If you think I'm up for any sort of fight against him, you're wrong," Resi tried to explain to Tasmin. "You saw what happened. My powers aren't strong enough to compete against his."

Tasmin shot her a look of disbelief. "Let me get this straight...you slip through his fingers not once, but *twice*, and you still don't think you have what it takes to stand against him?"

"Correction," Resi said, with a mouth full of cheese. "I *ran* from him, then I was almost *killed* by him. If you hadn't shown up at the clearing, we wouldn't be having this conversation."

"You're welcome, by the way," Tasmin said, her eyebrow arching.

"Thank you," Resi responded. "I don't know what I—what *we*—would've done without you."

Briefly, Resi's mind floated to Corey. How was he doing, all alone and cooped up in his room? Desperately, she wanted him here to defuse the tension. He always knew how to make even the worst situations humorous.

"Let's see it," Tasmin said, reaching for Resi's arm and gently flipping it over in her hands to view the bandage. Gingerly, Resi unveiled the circular mark from where the brand had burned her. It was raised and still visibly pink, but far more healed than it would have been if it hadn't been treated by the finest of Rowan's medicinal remedies.

"The Mark..." Tasmin said gently. "He won't stop until he sees you dead."

"But if I make it North, then I have a chance of being protected," Resi said, looking to Rolf for reinforcement. "We could outrun him. Even make it into Dirig by the end of the week."

"And go where?" Tasmin asked. "This is the safest place west of Sterch."

"Not entirely," Rolf interjected.

Resi withheld a laugh. She could only imagine he was talking about Belaflor. "Rolf's taking me to his employer," she told Tasmin. "Some unnamed abolitionist who shelters and trains gifted Licks like me."

Tasmin shot Rolf a surprised expression. "Unnamed abolitionist?"

Rolf shifted uncomfortably on the pillow beneath his backside. "He prefers to remain anonymous. He's protected that way."

Briefly, Tasmin's gaze lingered on him. Then, she quickly stood from the table, her expression tense. "I need to show you something," she said. She extended a hand out for Resi, aiding her to her feet. When Rolf didn't budge from his pillow, Tasmin glared at him. "Both of you."

Tasmin trotted off into the darkness of the dome, her dress dancing behind her like the tail of a kite. Quickly, Resi and Rolf followed her across the expansive onyx floor, their footsteps echoing about the space like distant claps of thunder.

Soon enough, Tasmin led them through a long, covered walk that brought them back outside to a large field. "We keep the stables near the vineyards," she threw over a bare shoulder.

Confused, Resi turned to Rolf, who shrugged at her yet again. Resi shot him a look of disbelief. What was with him, anyway? First, he'd panicked during the middle of a dolus attack. Now, detachment? Apathy? She needed to talk to him, but didn't want to broach the subject with him until they were alone.

Determination in her stride, Tasmin crossed the grass in her bare feet, hopping over a tall fence nearly twice her size as if it were nothing more than a small stone in the way. Resi turned about the field, noticing how the fence circled to become some sort of pen; a paddock for horses and cattle.

Finally, Tasmin came to the first stable, one broad and long atop the hillside. She brought her small hand to an old door, then turned back to them.

"It would behoove you to thank them for what they did for you the other day," she said with a wink.

Immediately, she opened the door, letting the light of day explode through the darkness within the stable. And there, in large individual stalls, awaited nearly three dozen white horses. Each stood exceptionally tall and broad; some were even larger than the centaurs of the Sterch mountainside. But their uniqueness lay in the fact that each possessed a large set of breathtakingly beautiful wings. One in a nearby stall gave a stretch and a flourish of its wingspan for Resi as she slowly marched past. Surprised, she gasped at the sight. The horse let out a satisfied neigh in response.

"You were expecting wings?" Tasmin chimed. "Well, here they are. The *Wings* of the Meade Valley fairies."

Resi froze. "They're...they're—"

"Astonishing?" Tasmin finished for her.

Resi could only nod as she followed after her. From somewhere out of sight, she heard a shuffling noise, which turned out to be a male fairy bending to check the hooves of a stallion who had been tethered in the aisle at the other end of the barn.

"Normally, they'd be free to roam the hillside," Tasmin said. "But after we came upon the likes of you three, they needed to be checked for injuries."

"Where did they all come from?" Resi asked, looking to Tasmin for reassurance as she dared to reach a hand through an opening door of a nearby stall. "May I?"

Tasmin nodded proudly. "They're called Puras, and they're native to this valley. When my ancestors settled here after the War, it was as if they were here, just waiting for us, gifted by the regions. They're friendly," she smiled. "Immensely loyal."

Gently, Resi touched the beautiful creature above its nose, trying her best to recall what war it was when the fairies were displaced—when *everyone* was displaced—and Caplia, a once united peninsula, had become seven separate regions, each with their own political structure. At her touch, the stallion cooed like a pigeon against the warmth of her hand.

"Oh...and sometimes they decide to act like birds," Tasmin scoffed.

Resi giggled. "So, it was them that I heard?"

Tasmin tilted her head, confused.

"Before I passed out in the clearing, I heard the beat of wings," Resi told her. "I thought I was dreaming."

Tasmin turned provocatively, continuing on down the aisle. "They tend to have that effect on people," she said breezily over her shoulder.

The two made their way through the barn, pausing every so often to meet another stallion that poked its nose out from a stall. All the while, Rolf trailed silently behind them, his face tense.

"He's not one for animals," Tasmin whispered to Resi. "Thinks anything that doesn't talk can't be trusted."

Resi held back another laugh. Rolf was almost too predictable.

The three nodded at the shy farm hand before exiting out the other end of the barn. They were greeted by a spectacular sunset that donned colors of tangerine, magenta, and lavender. Resi couldn't help but be reminded of her last night at the Tristeland, and how she'd ached to paint it.

"One more stop," Tasmin said, her expression suddenly grim. "This way."

Hesitantly, she turned towards the darkening sea, leading them down a narrow path that winded its way through the tall grass. And there, snuggled close to shore, rested a tiny shack. Its boards were weathered and peeling with white paint.

"I must warn you," Tasmin said, suddenly turning about to face them. Her lungs filled with air before she released it in a long sigh. "What you're about to see is not for the faint of heart."

"Something everyone likes to hear," Rolf murmured.

Tasmin approached the shack slowly, her face filled with a complex emotion that Resi couldn't quite place. The door to the shack had been bolted shut. The only opening into it was a small slot by the floor, presumably used for food.

"Take a look," Tasmin gestured as she took a few steps away, her eyes pained.

Cautiously, Resi peeked between two of the boards, but saw only darkness inside the shack. But then, a dim red light began to slowly appear. It spread like a mist in the black before it revealed its source; two nostrils, and then, a pair of fiery red eyes. The black mare suddenly reared inside the small hut, snorting and kicking as it sensed them, its' midnight wings flaring and twitching.

Resi quickly pulled herself away, nearly knocking Rolf over to the ground. Swiftly, he caught her, then took a look for himself.

"What happened to it?" he asked Tasmin. But she was nowhere in sight. Resi scanned the shore and found her along the beach, her arms crossed in front of her as her dress whirled around her like a tornado, her eyes locked on the building waves. Resi was the first to get to her.

"She was mine, you know," Tasmin confided as she wiped a lingering tear from her cheek. She didn't tear her gaze from the sea. "She was given to me by my father when I was just a girl. We've seen the regions together. But when that monster got ahold of her—"

"What monster?" Resi interjected.

"A dolus," Tasmin breathed, finally meeting Resi's gaze. "They attack men in their sleep, luring them through vivid dreams to mate with them, and then drown them. But if one of my Puras takes a single glance at one, they're instantly possessed by some terrible evil. I keep trying to find some sort of cure, some medicinal remedy." She glanced about the fields. "You'd think out of all places..."

Confused, Resi waited. Is that what the dolus was attempting to do to Corey? *Mating* with him? She waited for an answer until Rolf finally joined them, his face worried.

"Many years ago," Tasmin told them, "King Romilius, The Patrian King in Turbus, appointed my Meade Valley Warriors to watch the borders into the bogs in exchange for our support. The bogs are the perfect nesting ground for the doluses. Wet, humid..."

"Miserable?" Rolf finished for her.

"Anyone from here to Malig knows that if you want to run into a demon, head west," she went on. "But for years, everything was quiet. The dolus breed was content in the bogs. We patrolled the region for any of them that might have slipped through the cracks, but none ever reached as far as the border into Rowan."

The breeze whipped around Tasmin fiercely, pulling her dark hair behind her like a flag.

"But a few months ago," she continued, "we noticed something odd. More and more doluses were venturing out of the bogs. It was as if they were being called, beckoned by something. They were curious, reckless even. Some of the Puras ran off during the night."

Rolf turned to Resi. "You must know, Resi...a dolus likes its privacy. It's not like one to travel outside of its habitat. For one to be found in Sterch isn't just strange, it's—" he stopped.

Tasmin scowled. "Purposeful."

Resi waited, trying to understand.

"It was around that same time that Governor Sequis began making his way about the regions this past spring," Tasmin went on. "Many spoke of his desire to rekindle his dying relationship with King Romilius. He was the closest thing Sequis had to a father, but they had some sort of falling out a few years back. Romilius is rumored to be leaning towards Aliquian abolition. But Sequis, it seems, has some sort of plan to take over the regions with his sorcery. Maybe he'd never intended it to become public knowledge, but because of you, it is now."

Resi remembered back to her first meeting with Sequis; he'd been drunk, vulnerable. Hadn't he just visited King Romilius? It would make sense that his anger on that day stemmed from his desire to change Romilius's mind on abolition, and based on their first portrait session, it hadn't been successful.

Interested, Rolf looked to Tasmin. "You suspect there's a deeper reason for Sequis's travels?"

Tasmin stared deeply into the water. "The doluses began making their way out of the bogs when Sequis was rumored to be in Dirig. He was close. The timing is too coincidental."

"So, what you're saying," Resi said calmly, "is that Sequis is recruiting some kind of dolus army?"

"We're not sure," Tasmin answered. "But if he is, then something must be done."

"How would he be able to form an army of those awful things?" Resi asked, remembering the encounter with the dolus in Sterch. "From what I saw, they don't seem to listen too well."

Tasmin and Rolf exchanged another strange look at each other.

"Ok, you both have to stop doing that!" Resi ordered. "It's driving me crazy."

Rolf sighed, then ran his fingers through his thin hair. "We forget how little you know, Resi. The lack of education given to Ter's Aliquians about their own beginnings is stifling."

"Knowledge is power," Tasmin huffed. "Sequis knew that when he decreed the Ban of Aliquian Education."

Angered by her own lack of understanding, Resi took a step forward towards the sea. "Where did the doluses come from?"

"They were born out of sorcery," Rolf stated. "Dark magic is their life force."

"The morning Corey was attacked in Sterch..." Resi suddenly turned back to him. "How did you know that Corey had been lured away by one?"

Rolf tensed. "Doluses only attack men, Resi. When a dolus leads a man to be killed, any others around him will experience intense dreams that keep them asleep until the victim is lured away from the group." He took a deep breath. "I had a dream that night, too."

The smell of autumn hung in the chilly air. Graciously, Rolf turned to give a shivering Tasmin his cloak. She wrapped its length tightly around her shoulders before her eyes warmly went to Resi.

"Tell me what you know about King Aliquis," she demanded Resi.

Resi released the air in her lungs; it was the same question that Mags had asked her every Fourth-Year Festival. "Only that the legend of him proceeds him," she remembered. Although she knew more, she didn't allude to it.

"A better question;" Tasmin diverted her. "What do you know about his successor, a man named Anton?"

Anton...Resi hadn't heard the name in years. Her mind flashed to a simpler time, to a summer spent under the glow of green leaves picking berries. "*King* Anton?"

"That would be the one," Rolf growled.

Resi closed her eyes. "I know that not a single 'Lick on the Farmhold named their child Anton without knowing their kid would be bullied by other children."

"And there's reason for that!" Rolf snarled. "Anton was like a son to Aliquis; his second in command, not unlike Sequis's relationship with Romilius. But selfishly, Anton strayed from his real gifting and delved into sorcery, the same dark practice that Sequis is tapping into. After forcing Aliquis from the throne, Anton used sorcery to terrorize the regions for many years."

"And what so few people know is that King Aliquis stepped down and willingly gave him the throne," Tasmin said with disdain.

Shocked, Resi shook her head, trying to understand. "Aliquis *willingly* gave a sorcerer the throne?"

"It still remains a mystery," Tasmin chimed in. "Had Aliquis remained in power, perhaps your people would've been spared from hundreds of years of servitude. The Codians and Patrians weren't going to stand by and watch another Aliquian King, like Anton, resort to sorcery. He destroyed everything that Aliquis had built during his reign...too many lives were lost. Too many lands were destroyed. So, the Codian and Patrian lawmakers finally sided together after years of unrest to put every Aliquian in chains."

Resi's mind suddenly went to a long-forgotten memory: her mother in the fields, telling Resi the story of the Great King's Fall—his fight for power ending in a massive battle, his escape from the regions and that he was never seen or heard from again. He would be known forever as the almighty ruler who ran from his people, her mother had spoken, one who had left them to fend for themselves when the Decree of Aliquian Servitude fell upon them for his cowardice. But Anton? No one dared to mention the name. Resi had always assumed that Anton had rightfully claimed the throne, not that Aliquis had willingly given it to him after Anton had fallen into sorcery. The notion seemed ridiculous, something straight out of the handbook of "*What Not To Do as King.*"

"This is why Aliquians despise the story of Aliquis and Anton," Rolf said, his hands on his hips. "No one can understand Aliquis's reasoning behind passing the throne to a psychopath, one who ruined the reputation of Aliquian power for generations to come."

Resi shook her head. "Why would King Anton give up his gifting for sorcery?"

"Aliquian gifting requires training, patience, time," Tasmin explained. "But anyone—be it Codian, Patrian, or Aliquian—can move quickly in sorcery, so long as they're tapping into the right kind of trading; rituals, blood sacrifices...you know—the *creepy* stuff. It seemed Anton wasn't willing to wait for his time. He wanted power, and he wanted it fast."

"Why would Luther want Sequis to come out as a sorcerer to the public if the Codian population has always despised sorcery? If they put Aliquians in bondage because of Anton's choice to practice it?"

The three went silent for a time, listening to the waves crash along the shore as the sun dipped beyond the horizon.

"Sequis is the most beloved politician the South has ever seen," Rolf replied. "If there's anyone who could get the Codian population to warm to the idea of sorcery, it's him. Now that sorcery is on the rise in the criminal city of Letz, and is rumored to be spreading in Turbus as well, Luther wasn't about to miss an opportunity to be a part of the next wave of sorcery."

It was all beginning to take shape in Resi's mind. While at the Tristeland, she had pieced together that Luther had desired a land that would once again bow to dark sorcery, bow to Sequis.

Then, suddenly, she had a deeper realization. "Luther must've been practicing it too—maybe even introduced Sequis to it."

Curious, Rolf and Tasmin perked up.

"The entire plan to reveal Sequis's sorcery was Luther's," Resi explained frantically. "In fact, Sequis was furious that Luther went against his desires to reveal his sorcery to the public. If anything, Sequis is new to it. He may have even been attempting to step away from it."

Resi calmed as she briefly allowed herself to believe that there was a part of Sequis that didn't want to be known as the giant who took over the regions with the aid of a dark Advisor. The memory of his parting words, however, sent a haunting chill down Resi's spine. *Forever shackled. Forever bound under my rule.* Something had snapped in him, something vile and frightening. Romilius had denied him. His Advisor had betrayed him and had been murdered in a terrible attack. The girl he'd meant to take as his wife proved to be nothing more than a Lick girl disguised as a portrait artist. He was truly alone, and Resi knew the kind of recklessness that came with isolation better than anyone.

"Then maybe we have a fighting chance of defeating him," Tasmin said, trying to hide her optimism.

Terrified, Resi met her eyes. "Sequis may be new to sorcery, but he's not to be underestimated. If anything, he feels even *more* dangerous."

Tears then began to fall down the fairy's face as she turned back to the dilapidated barn with the dark Pura inside. "It's one thing to release the doluses from their bogs to start an army," Tasmin said haltingly. "But taking over the souls of my Puras to turn them into vengeful beasts that he can manipulate with his dark magic and use for his tyrannical plans?" She turned away, hiding her face. "It didn't use to be personal. But now it is."

Resi shivered in the chill coming over the water. The once beautiful vineyards of Meade Valley suddenly appeared lonely and dark in the minutes after sunset, clouded by visions of black Puras along the hillside and gray-skinned demons crawling out of the ocean.

Tasmin's hands went to Resi's shoulders. "I'm asking you to help me. Begging, in fact."

Resi didn't want to allow the weight of Tasmin's request to fully land on her; it was almost too much responsibility. She didn't have an immediate response.

"Don't worry—I will give you time to think," Tasmin reassured her. "You have two days to give me your answer. But in the meantime, rest. Enjoy everything the fortress has to offer. At the earliest, Sequis and his men will be here in a week's time. If your answer is yes, then we fight. But if not, I will have some of my best warriors escort you and your fellow travelers into Dirig while I evacuate the valley."

"Evacuate?"

Tasmin nodded grimly. "Without someone like you to stand against Sequis's sorcery, my people and I are as good as dead."

CHAPTER 21

THE TRUTH

The sun had withdrawn and brought about a breezy, and romantic night. Barefoot and dressed in nothing but a slip, Resi crept back through the low-ceilinged halls of the fortress, tracing her fingertips along the cold stone walls. Finally, she came to a familiar door and placed a gentle hand against it.

The door opened forward, revealing the dark room behind it. It was very similar to Resi's room: a healing space, but one obviously dedicated to tending more difficult maladies. Herbs hung from every inch of the ceiling, and odd-looking medical objects lined the furthest wall. At the center of the room, moonlight shone starkly along the drawn-back sheets of an empty bed.

"Corey?" she whispered into the nothingness. She wanted to remain calm, to go back to her room and forget why she had ever left it in the first place. But Corey didn't have a positive history when it came to wandering off in the middle of the night, and even in this fortress of safety, she couldn't fight down the panic rising in her throat.

Frantic, she made her way back through the halls. It wasn't long before she found the massive tree at the center of the fortress, and further in, to the domed onyx haven that had sparkled in the sun at last light. The air from the terrace hit Resi's face a moment before she saw Corey looking over the water, bathed in moonlight. His hands roughly clasped the rail before him. He was dressed in a thin shirt and linen pants, and his wavy hair blew about as if it had been possessed by the wind.

Resi faltered. She didn't dare sneak up on him, but she couldn't wait a minute longer before speaking to him. Hesitantly, she shifted across the white onyx, taking each step as if it might lead to a sudden calamity.

"You shouldn't be here," Corey spoke, without tearing his gaze from the rumbling sea.

Feeling caught and ashamed, Resi froze mid-step. "Neither should you."

The silence went stone-thick between them as she gradually approached the rail. She took a moment to really look at him up close; the skin beneath his eyes was dark with lack of sleep. All she desired was to comfort him, but Corey's stiff body language told her to keep a distance. Instead, she settled beside him, pretending to be equally transfixed by the churning of the water.

Finally, she mustered the courage to look at him. "You can't ignore me forever," she reasoned. "At some point, you're going to have to tell me what happened."

Corey's brow softened slightly, and he nodded reluctantly, his lips biting into each other. "You could be right."

"You know I'm right," she quipped. An optimistic voice inside of her hoped that her playful banter would lead to an alternate universe where they could fall back into who they had been before the dolus attack. Maybe Corey would tease her back. But after a few more moments of silence, Resi was certain that the old Corey that she'd come to know on the road had not survived the attack.

He'd been left to die in the clearing that day.

"Resi," he said firmly, his eyes now fixed on the ground near her feet. "Go back to bed. Now."

"And what if I say no?" she demanded. "What if I stay here until you finally tell me what happened to make you hate me so much!"

"I don't—" he started, then simmered. "I don't hate you."

"Then what?!" Resi said, throwing her arms in the air. "You demand not to see me. You're not sleeping, which we both know is a serious sign that something is wrong."

Corey went rigid, as if he were fighting to keep from scratching an itch. "Just leave me. Please."

Resi's legs shifted awkwardly beneath her. "Two days ago, Rolf and I couldn't get you to shut up. And now I can't get you to say a single word? "

All of a sudden, a rage lit in his eyes. He looked at her, his eyes wide and panicked before he lunged on her. Only, he grabbed her fiercely, scooping her into his strong arms before bringing his face to hers and kissing her roughly.

The thought of sharing a moment like this with Corey had come to Resi sporadically along the trails into Sterch. Within the walls of her imagination, her first kiss with Corey had often unfolded somewhat awkwardly; him fumbling over his words in the moments before and failing to meet her eyes. But her imagination had never conjured anything quite like this, a quick moment that was forced and unnatural.

Panicked, she bit Corey's lip firmly, and he reared back with a groan.

"What in the Sept-Regions are you doing?!" he roared.

"Uh, what am *I* doing?" Resi retorted, her heart pounding and her head spinning.

Embarrassed, Corey slunk off to a bench near the railing. "I'm so messed up," he said to himself. "I knew I'd mess this up."

Resi watched as his head fell into his hands. What was happening to him? Without another thought, she went to sit beside him.

"Corey..." she exhaled. "Tell me what happened. Please."

He couldn't look at her. "Anything I'd say would just sound...stupid."

She heard the weight of his embarrassment in his voice, and felt her indignation for his cool behavior temporarily leave her. "Try me," she said, her tone lighter.

"It's just...I'm not sure how to explain it, what that *thing* did."

Corey packed so much hatred in just one simple word; when he spat it out, it was as if the dolus had stripped him of all of his goodness. Then he seemed to crumple. His face fell into his hands again, and he stayed there for longer than was comfortable for Resi. Just when she was about to say something, Corey finally spoke.

"It started like any dream," he began. "But—not." He looked up over the rail to take in the sight of the churning sea. "Since I was little, I've always known when I was dreaming. Colors are too bright. People I know and love suddenly appear as if they're not dead, or—"

Awkwardly, Resi cleared her throat. The dream she'd had the night of the dolus attack had been real for her, too, like a memory that she'd stuffed away somewhere deep inside that had resurfaced against her will.

"But this dream was *real*," Corey said, before a smile came to his mouth. "No different than the day we first noticed each other on the lane. The day Shina was marked. Do you remember that day?"

Resi nodded. The only comfort she'd felt in the moments before Shina's cries had pierced through the dark forest was in the warmth of his eyes. Had it meant something to him, too?

"This dream was like walking into a memory. Every thought was my own. Every sense was tangible. And you..." he turned back. "You were so beautiful."

Resi's heart skipped a beat. "I was in this dream?"

Corey's face warmed, but the quake in his voice remained. "It started off in a meadow. There were flowers in your hair, and the sun was lighting it golden in a way I'd never seen before." He paused, uncertain. "You kept calling out to me."

Nervously, Resi's hands twisted in her lap. She didn't like seeing Corey this way; apprehensive, undone, and seconds from flying off the handle.

"But then, you ran off," he said as his face went pink. "You called for me to follow. I ran until my heart felt like it was going to burst out of my chest, chasing you deeper and deeper into the trees until I found you." He swallowed hard as his eyes averted to the ground. "When I did, your dress was wadded up along the shores of a secret cove. You were leading me into blue waters so clear you could see rocks the size of carriages along the bottom."

Resi made herself take a breath for the first time in what felt like minutes. She choked on the air, nearly coughing.

"I tried to leave, but you kissed me," Corey said, his face softening. "You kissed me so purely, I felt as if I could do anything. Be anything."

Resi couldn't help but feel uncomfortable, but still found herself hanging on every word.

"Next thing I knew," he went on, "the cove turned upside down on itself, and the light around you darkened into crimson, then black. Your eyes went inward, and you were sucking the very life out of me."

"The dolus," Resi breathed.

"That thing nearly drowned me," Corey growled, his tone hard. "But worst of all—it concealed itself inside the thought of you."

Resi felt the air in her lungs release in one long sigh. Corey finally looked up at her, his eyes searching hers, until he seemed to come to some conclusion in his mind. "I'm in love with you, Resi," he confessed. "I think I have been for awhile."

Nervously, she laughed. Wasn't this what every girl wanted to hear? Mags had told her to want such a thing...but still, something wasn't right. "Before a few days ago," she said with another clear of her throat, "we'd never spoken to each other."

Corey's brows furrowed in protest. "Does love require certain conversations?"

For a moment, Resi was dumbfounded. "No—no, I'm just saying—"

"I was alone when I first came to the Offenheimers," Corey interrupted. "My family and I had been separated. I had no one. Nothing. All I wanted was a place to call home, a place to belong. But no matter where I looked, I couldn't find it in any other face I met in the fields."

Resi knew that feeling of dejection and isolation. But then, at least she'd had Mags. Still, she'd always assumed Corey was popular amongst the others their age. She'd noticed more than one Lick girl eyeing him in the fields. But never had she thought of what was going on behind those eyes. Corey had been just as lonely as she was.

"I saw you for the first time one afternoon working beside Mags," he recalled, his smile widening. "You were laughing. And suddenly, I saw it. My home."

He said the word as if suddenly he felt a deep peace in his heart—as if the word now had new meaning. Resi still couldn't find any words to speak.

"I spent every morning watching you walk alone to the fields, and every night forcing myself to look away from your lean-to," he laughed. "I was so worried you'd notice me. But when you finally did, you didn't look away."

Resi's mind flashed back to that night, that pleasant evening she and Mags had spent angrily fighting over their stew. Hadn't Mags been the one to encourage her to find that place of belonging, that special person who could make life just a little easier to bear?

"Corey, I—" But there was nothing to say. Resi's mind had run dry, like an ancient waterfall that had eroded into a mountain.

In a flash, Corey was beside her once again on the bench, his eyes locked into hers like he meant to keep her there forever. He bent slowly, and this time, he kissed her softly, almost hesitantly, as if fearful of the words she was holding back. His lips were warm and soft, just as Resi had imagined them during all those days on the foothills. But just as she felt the beginnings of bliss beginning to ignite inside her, he pulled away to rest his forehead on hers.

"I want you to come with me," he whispered. "To find my sister. To find Mags."

Resi felt the bliss begin to slip. "You and I both know Rolf won't have that."

"Screw the tracker," Corey said, playfully nudging her shoulder with his.

She laughed, all the while breathing in the smell of his freshly washed skin. "It can't happen, Corey. There's a price on my head. Rolf needs to get me into Dirig."

"Then what happens to us? We just...forget this? Forget us?" he said, pointing between the two of them.

Resi liked the sound of that—us. She sighed, her eyes shutting hard, forcing that thought away. "If you don't want to come with us to Dirig, then for a time, we'll have to. And besides, there's the fact that I've only ever brought danger to you since you met up with Rolf and me."

"What if that's a risk I'm willing to take?" Corey insisted.

"Doesn't matter," she shrugged, finally meeting the warmth of his gaze. "I won't allow you to take it."

His face suddenly hardened. "Does that mean you're not going to stand with Tasmin and fight?"

Resi pulled away, surprised. "How do you know about that?"

"I may have been incapacitated for a few days, but I'm not deaf," Corey shrugged. "Fairies talk. And loudly, might I add."

Resi tried to push away her frustration with a sigh. "I'm no match for Sequis, and Tasmin knows it. Standing with her would ensure the destruction of this entire valley. The best thing for everyone is to get me as far away from Meade Valley as possible and out of sight. Then Tasmin can evacuate the city."

"And what about you?" Corey demanded.

"What about me?"

"You plan on hiding yourself away with some mysterious abolitionist until you can finally enter the city, while the rest of the regions fight Sequis on their own?"

Stunned, Resi stood to her feet. "Since when am I expected to protect the regions?"

Corey stood as well. "Resi—Sequis is threatened by you. Why else would he chase you into Sterch? He knows you're a suitable opponent, and he won't stop until he sees you defeated."

Hysterical, Resi began to cackle madly. "Are you hearing yourself? Seriously, Corey...even Rolf told me that I'm not anything special when it comes to my gifting."

"You honestly believe that?"

"Yes, I do."

Corey shook his head. "He's lying to you."

"And why would he have reason to do that?"

"Because he's hiding something," Corey said with a new hush in his voice. "I can feel it. Has he given you any indication of where he's taking you?"

Resi had nothing to offer in response. She couldn't deny Corey's argument; Rolf had been acting strange ever since the dolus attack, and when Tasmin had asked him directly about his employer, he hadn't answered. A crippling fear came over her. If he'd lied to her about the nature of her power, then what else had he lied about? And why?

Corey, who had been studying her face, now sighed before he clasped his hands together tightly. "The way his face looked when he saw the map...there's something about it that he's withholding from us."

Resi stilled as she remembered the night of the dolus attack: Rolf, freezing up on the shores of Lake Seka as he cried for the map. "I've been planning on talking to him."

"I'm surprised you haven't already."

Resi started to speak, but nothing came out. "I don't want to seem suspicious of him," she finally said.

"Why?"

"Because he's brought us this far! And, as far as I'm concerned, he has every right to sell me to Sequis and claim an even larger price for me."

"He wouldn't do that. Even if Sequis offered it."

Resi started pacing the terrace, listening to her footsteps along the concrete. "I'll talk to him. Tomorrow."

"Good. 'Cause if you don't, I will."

For a time, they both listened to the waves crash against the rock, until one sprayed over the terrace like the wave of a hand.

"Promise me that you'll think about what I asked," Corey said. "I'll stay here with you to fight Sequis. Then, we can leave. Together. Rolf doesn't have to know." He came close to her until his chest almost pressed against hers. The smell of his soapy skin wrapped around her like a protective shield. "Ditch the shady Patrian. Come with me."

Resi closed her eyes and allowed the warmth and nearness of his body to comfort her. "I'll think about it. But I can't promise to give you the answer you want."

Corey's lips twitched, as if he were fighting back a smile. "Two days."

Resi sighed, then chuckled. "You and Tasmin sure know how to put on the pressure."

He shook his head. "We just both know what you're capable of—something Rolf doesn't seem to understand."

Corey reached out for her hand, then leaned in again for her lips. He kissed her with more warmth and intention this time, and Resi couldn't help but rise to her tiptoes and kiss him back as her hands roped their way through his hair. But Corey withdrew from her as if to keep her wanting more—and she did. Then he smiled and gave her a wink before slinking back towards the onyx hall.

Resi spent what felt like hours peering out over the water, thinking of Mags and the farmhold, though it felt as if they belonged to someone else's memory. For much of her life, she'd dreamt of running; running through the trees to find safety in the west, running from the pitying glances in the fields—from Marion, from Horris, from everything. But something deep inside, beneath the heat and the butterflies from Corey's kiss, told Resi that running away from this nightmare would not free her from the reality of what she carried.

RESI WOKE the next morning and toured the grounds of the Western Fortress on her own. The grounds proved to be mesmerizing. To the south, rolling hills of wheat extended as far as the eye could see, backing up to the castle and wrapping it in a golden embrace. The vineyards were expansive, rolling out to a charming town many miles to the east. Surrounding it all was the view of the sea, shadowed by clouds in the early hours as the sun hovered over the Sterch mountains.

It was still well before noon when Resi came across a stairwell hidden along the perimeter of the onyx ballroom. Curious, she descended them, and at the foot of the stairs she discovered a long, stone room that stretched the entire length of the fortress, filled with countless rows of barrels.

Resi thought back to evenings spent at court drinking Fet that had come from this very cellar. Amused, she laughed to herself in the darkness. If only Marion Offenheimer could see her now.

She knew she was stalling; she needed to speak with Rolf, and soon. What she couldn't make sense of was her nerves. If there was one talent in Resi's arsenal, it was calling people out. But Rolf, in the oddest sense, had become something of a constant these past few weeks, and the only person she'd depended on getting her this far. And by some miracle, he had.

Still, she couldn't deny Rolf's secrecy—his so-called "abolitionist" employer in Dirig; the odd looks Tamsin had thrown at him over her goblet of Fet; and the shady way he'd kept to himself these past few days. He'd avoided Resi like an illness. All this time, he'd asked her to trust him, to rely on him as a companion and as the only person to get her to safety. But since Corey had come upon them, so much had changed. Perhaps he'd been right to doubt Rolf, right to be so angry for being kept in the dark.

Hoping to catch one last peek of the vineyards before they became crowded with workers, Resi decisively exited the cellars and turned for the sunlit fields. As she came to the outdoor corridor where Tasmin had brought them the preceding evening, Resi made out the faint ring of voices, followed by the shuffle of feet on gravel, growing closer.

"Don't you dare run away from me!"

Keeping herself hidden behind a stone pillar, Resi peered out into the sunshine. Her hunch was right; it was Tasmin. And she was running after Rolf.

"Get back here!" the fairy queen hissed.

"Why?" Rolf asked, his black cloak flaring behind him as he turned to her. His face was twisted and heated red with anger. "So you can accuse me more?"

"No! Rolf, please. I only want to understand."

"What more is there to understand? I told you everything."

"You told me something, but not the truth."

Resi watched Rolf's eyes anxiously search the fields for any bystanders. "You can't begin to know what I've been through these past few years."

"Lay it on me," Tasmin said, her arms folded across her chest.

Resi wanted to rush up to Tasmin and cheer her on for demanding answers, but she kept herself hidden in the shadow. Reveal herself, and Rolf would surely not confess to what was truly on his heart. She watched him cross the distance between himself and Tasmin, getting as close to her face as her height would allow. But Tasmin didn't budge.

"And tell you what?" he huffed. "That my reputation has been shattered? That I've been dodging in and out of cities, trying to find work wherever I can, but striking out each time?"

"Oh, Rolf..." Tamsin sighed with pity.

"You asked for the truth!"

"Why didn't you come to me sooner?" she asked.

"Not exactly the way you wish to greet a friend after all these years." He sighed. "Too many memories here..."

Tasmin's shoulders hunched forward. "You were embarrassed?"

"Yeah, well, you would be too. It's what happens to you when you've been convicted of a crime."

There it was. *Convicted of a crime.* Resi gulped, fearful of what either might say next.

"And you're hoping to clear your name by coming all this way?" Tasmin said, her eyes shifting to the walls of the Fortress.

Rolf stopped himself, and Resi could've sworn she watched an unsure glance cross his face, one that spoke of an attempt to brush away the hope that had temporarily bubbled in his heart. "Getting her there is the only way."

Incredulous, Tasmin stepped forward, shushing him with her hands to keep his voice low. "And you're just not going to tell her?!"

Rolf brought a hand to his temple, then rubbed it as if he were trying to summon a better answer. "If I tell her, she's as good as gone."

Resi felt her anger rising, and her gifting rose to meet it, trying to burst its way to the surface, to breathe in the light of day before Resi's instincts to tame it kicked in. Today, however, there was no holding it back, because this time she didn't want to.

In a flourish, she strode through the shadows of the corridor and burst into the sunlight, furiously marching the remaining steps to the gravel path. "I knew it!" she said when Rolf noticed her. "Corey was right! You're a liar! A criminal!"

Rolf stayed frozen in place, though Resi could see the questions in his head running chaotically behind his eyes. Tasmin shuddered.

It could all be done so easily, Resi thought. One snap of a finger, one tempestuous thought, and Tasmin and Rolf would be no better off than the dozens of burned victims in the gardens of the Tristeland. Though she had no reason to hurt Tasmin, it seemed she didn't have the wherewithal to protect anyone from what she carried—so if Rolf went down, so would Tasmin. Resi's anger had won, and anyone in her path was at risk.

"I knew you'd sell me out!" she yelped. "And for what? To clear your name? Put you back in the good graces of your stupid Patrian king?!"

Resi heard a rustling, and turned to see a small crowd of Sairons and male fairies that had gathered near the entrance to the onyx ballroom. Voices hollered out from somewhere inside the Fortress.

"Sell you out?!" Rolf said, his eyes searching her face.

"You heard me," Resi spat.

Tasmin looked to Resi and then back to Rolf, then cautiously backed out from between them.

"Resi, you don't know anything," Rolf scoffed rudely, turning to stomp off.

"I know enough!" Resi insisted, following him. "You're a liar; nothing but a criminal looking for a buck! And had you told me that when I met you, I never would have agreed to travel with you!"

Rolf kept stalking towards the Fortress. "You wouldn't have made it another day had it not been for me!" he shot over his shoulder.

"Better to have been killed in Derton than to have been led on a wild goose chase by a con artist like you."

"I lied in order to protect you," he said, finally turning back to face her. "And you're right—had you known everything about me, you never would have come with me. But I was true to my word when I said I would do everything in my power to keep you safe." He turned to start walking again.

Indignant, Resi's stance widened as her hands landed hard on her hips. "So, chickening out during the dolus attack was just a fluke then?"

Rolf staggered on his mending leg. The pain of the break came and went with a wince on his face. "Resi, I said I was sorry."

"You abandoned me. Abandoned us!"

In anger, Rolf turned back to her, shouting, "An Aliquian boy died on my watch, Resi!"

A small gasp came from somewhere in the crowd of fairies gathered on the stairs. Rolf turned a glance over his shoulder, then rolled his eyes, annoyed by their sheer existence.

"What?" Resi asked him.

Rolf hesitated, his face long with the weight of his shame. "While on the road all those years ago, I failed to protect him from a dolus attack. He was a child." He paused for a time, clearly tortured by the memories of the experience. "I freeze up even at the mention of a dolus."

"Why didn't you tell me?" Resi asked, noticing the pain in her palm from her fingernails digging into her skin.

"Nobody wants to hear a sob story," Rolf sighed. "Especially from someone like me."

Resi paced on the gravel. "Corey was right. You're a coward."

Rolf's anger flared. "The kid would've died had it not been for you and me! All he ever did was slow our pace and get us into more trouble!"

"And save our life, you idiot! Had it not been for Corey, you would've been eaten alive by centaurs!"

"We didn't ask for his help, Resi. He was never part of the deal!" As soon as the words came out of his mouth, Rolf looked as if he regretted them.

The surrounding vineyard turned red in Resi's vision. "Excuse me?!"

Rolf's eyes closed regretfully. "That—that came out wrong."

"What deal?!"

He huffed. "I just needed you. Just you."

The heat was raging inside of Resi, but she refused to allow another Tristeland situation again; she didn't want the blood on her hands. She looked down just in time to see a wave of shimmering heat leave her fingertips.

"Just...let's just settle down here," Rolf said, raising his hands protectively in front of him.

Rolf was right to try to calm her down; Resi didn't like where her anger was leading her. She took a deep breath, and the heat temporarily subsided. Her grasp of her power was improving, but she couldn't stop herself from pressing him further.

"Had it not been for Corey," she scowled, "Tasmin never would've found us!"

"And Sequis would not be riding here with his army!" Rolf shot back. "Corey's a leech! A parasitic 'Lick that latched onto us the second he could!"

Resi flinched in disbelief at his use of the slur. "You hypocrite!" she growled.

"I'm just a low-life tracker. We reserve the word for when it's necessary."

The heat fired off again inside of Resi like she'd been shot in the stomach. "I didn't see you telling him to leave the second he opened that map!"

"Excuse me, did she just say *map*?" Tasmin asked with interest.

Two large drops of perspiration slowly fell down either side of Rolf's head. "The kid has a relic belonging to the city," he sighed, turning to Tasmin with a look of absolute dread.

"I finally get it," Tasmin said, shaking her head. "A missing relic from Belaflor grants the carrier immediate access into the city. If you couldn't bet on Resi getting you back in, you were betting on that map."

He avoided Resi's eyes as he answered. "It wasn't the plan I had in mind initially, but two opportunities are better than one."

Resi took a step back. She finally understood. The first thing that Rolf had called out for during the dolus attack was the map. At that moment, he'd doubted she would make it out of the lake alive. His faith in her had been fleeting, so instead, he'd placed his bet on the map.

"You were using me...using Corey," she finally mumbled, dumbfounded.

"We were all using each other!" he defended. "You needed someone to get you west. I needed a way back into Belaflor. I was your guide, someone who could protect you. You were my ticket, the one option that I bet my entire life on. I knew what you were after the dolus attack—" he sighed resignedly, like he was giving up, then he brought his voice down. "You carry something different."

The realization of the full extent of Rolf's lies, and the doubt they'd planted in Resi's heart about the true nature of her gifting, hit Resi like a slap across the face. "Are you saying what I think you're saying?" she asked, ignoring the word that wanted to escape her lips.

"I'm shocked it's taken you this long to figure it out," he scoffed.

Resi tried to calm herself—tried to think of something, anything that might calm the nausea growing in her stomach. Nothing good ever came of the nausea. "You led me to believe that I was nothing..." she breathed. "That I was just another run-of-the-mill girl with a gifting."

"Had you known what you were, your ego would've overpowered you," Rolf declared. "Knowledge of that level has caused too many people to stumble. I didn't want you to kill more people, to regret what and who you are." He looked up to the sky, searching for more words. "Like I said, I promised to protect you—even at the cost of losing your trust."

Evidently nervous that Resi might lose her grip on her powers, Tasmin motioned to the group of fairy onlookers, pushing them back. But Resi managed to withhold her anger, stuffing it deep inside where even she couldn't find it.

Rolf threw his hands up in the air, fixing Resi with an earnest gaze. "I was going to tell you. But everything changed when Corey found us. He was a friend to you, someone you trusted. You didn't need me anymore, but I still needed you."

"I never needed Corey," Resi seethed, finding the words bitter to taste. "He was just a familiar face. And he had a map."

"That's right," Rolf said. "But not just any map—one of the most important maps that's ever been created! I wasn't about to let it out of my sight for a second."

Resi ran through everything Rolf had said, her mind reeling. Then, something clicked, and she panicked. "Wait a minute. If there was no employer, no anonymous letter from the Tristeland, then how did you find out about me?" she demanded.

Rolf looked to his feet. "I heard about you at the same place where most people hear gossip. The pub."

Tasmin shot him a *you've got it coming to you* sort of glare.

Resi swallowed. "So you led us into the most dangerous region in the Sept-Regions with nothing but a half-assed plan and a whole bunch of baggage, and on top of that, you never thought to tell me that I was a..." but Resi couldn't say it. The thought in and of itself was too extraordinary, too ridiculous to comprehend.

"I told you I was good at getting people from point A to point B," Rolf pointed out. "I never said I did it honestly."

Resi cursed at him in her head. "You must've done something pretty bad to get kicked out of the city," she said ruthlessly. "So what was it, then? Murder? Theft? Or did they finally see you for the liar that you are and demand you leave?"

Resi watched a pang of guilt come over Rolf, and for a moment she felt the beginnings of sympathy starting to well inside of her. But she fought it. *He's a liar, Resi. A rotten, manipulative prick that preyed on your powers.*

Corey's words from the night before came back to her. *Screw the tracker.*

"I could tell you everything," Rolf started, "but all of that would be pointless. The only thing that matters now is that I get back," he pleaded, his head wilting. "I have to get back."

Whispers could be heard from the crowd of fairies that were gathered on the stairs. Having had enough of their chatter, Rolf turned over his shoulder to yell at the crowd. "Don't you all have something better to do?!"

Resi watched Tasmin snicker under her breath as the fairies scattered like field mice and departed for the interior of the Fortress. In their absence, the air seemed to have settled between the three of them. Resi let her eyes wander up the height of the Fortress; she feared what kind of danger awaited its walls. As her eye came to an open window right above the stairs, she made out a shadow and immediately recognized its outline; broad shoulders, and a lean build. Copper brown waves. She replayed her own words in her mind, realizing too late how they might sound out of context.

I never needed Corey.

"Corey?" she yelled out. But he'd already disappeared into the Fortress.

She bolted from the gravel, leaving Rolf and Tasmin behind in a cloud of kicked-up dust. She ran as fast as her legs would allow, pushing through the crowd of fairies and through the onyx hall, up the ancient steps. She barreled through the narrow passageways of the Fortress until she came to a marked door. But she didn't even bother to knock. Her intuition knew Corey was already gone.

After all, he was nothing more than a familiar face to her. And he had a map.

CHAPTER 22

THE ELDER

Tensely, Resi paced her room, tangled in a web of her own making.

The third person in the gardens of the Tristeland...come on, Resi! Who was the third person?

The map...why had Theo given Corey the map?

In the privacy of her chambers, Resi let out a rage-filled screech, the kind she only ever reserved for the inside of her arm. She leaned against the open window, letting her groans soar through it until her cries roared together with the sea as one. Fearful of herself, she looked down apprehensively at her stomach; the air around her was shimmering with new heat.

It was all too overwhelming. Sequis's wrath. Rolf's dishonesty. And now, Corey's sudden disappearance. It'd been six hours since she'd spotted him standing in the shadowed window. She had to hand it to him; he had a talent for sneaking off.

Resi had frantically searched the Fortress for any sign of Corey, but had found no trace of him. Frustrated, she'd then barricaded herself in her room by placing a chair in front of the door. She'd refused any and all visitors, only taking in a tray of food that was left for her by one of Tasmin's Sairons when it was time for dinner.

She'd let the time pass slowly as she kept herself warm under the blankets of her bed, remembering the nights when she'd lapped up her mother's stories like warm milk. How she wished she could go back to that time and place, if only to tell the younger version of herself to not believe in fairy tales. Or in people; all they ever seemed to do was lie.

But Corey...Corey was not amongst that kind. He didn't deserve to hear the words that Resi had spoken in haste. They'd been cruel and untrue.

On top of everything else, she'd yet to come to a decision on whether to stand with Tasmin to fight Sequis. Her mind was dizzy with the decision: leave, and force Tasmin to evacuate her people. Stay to fight, and anyone who stood with her would surely be slaughtered by Sequis. Or worse, by her untrained and violent power.

Resi was shaken from her thoughts when she heard shouts coming from somewhere within the Fortress.

Had Corey been found?

She eagerly rushed to the door and pulled the chair from under the handle, then sped as quickly as her legs would allow her down the cramped halls. When she came to the steps carved into the ancient tree at the center of the Fortress, she was met with a wall of sound. A league of civilian fairies had assembled in the hall below. They were buzzing with anticipation.

"Please...please!" Tasmin's voice called out. Tensely, she stood on a raised platform at the other end nearest the terrace.

Resi scolded herself. All this time, she'd been so caught up in her own struggles that she'd forgotten to contemplate Tasmin's. The Fortress was Tasmin's home, a protective place for warriors and for travelers. The fairy queen had so many to look after; her warriors, her Puras, and the people in the surrounding villages. Tasmin had never asked for this fight; she was only defending her homestead and her people. She'd protected Resi, Corey, and Rolf when she'd found them in the clearing after the dolus attack. She'd risked her life to get them out of that mess. So, then, why was Resi so fearful to help her in return?

Resi made her way urgently down the steps and joined the crowd. She turned to the nearest fairy, a small man with bright eyes. She realized that she recognized him from the table on the terrace on her first night at the Fortress. Surprised by her arrival, he did a double take at her.

"What's going on?" she asked him.

"Tasmin is addressing the concerns of the clan," he said shakily. "Many assembled this morning in the village. They stormed the Fortress and demanded access to the Queen."

"What concerns?"

The fairy turned to his right and his left before answering her, evidently hoping to find someone to help him out of this situation. Finding no one, he gulped and stammered out, "Well...concerns about...you."

"Oh..." Resi said with a sigh. "*Great.*"

The crowd hushed as a fairy woman with fair hair approached the stand.

"What is your concern?" Tasmin addressed her.

The woman cleared her throat nervously before raising her voice over the crowd. "As previously stated by other members of the clan, I wish to support the case against protecting the Aliquian girl."

Resi wanted to crawl out of her skin. Maybe, with any hope, she could take a flying leap over the terrace rail and land on the most jagged rock at the bottom of the sea.

"What do you wish to say?" Tasmin asked shortly, her patience evidently wearing thin.

The woman steadied herself, then spoke. "The 'Lick is a severe threat, not only to this Fortress, but to the many civilians in town. People are scared. Some are saying we might be evacuated. Displaced! And all for one 'Lick girl?!"

The crowd erupted in agreement. Even the fairy beside Resi cheered in support. When he noticed her glaring at him, he cowered in shame and fear, then slunk off further into the crowd.

"Quiet!" Tasmin's voice echoed. The crowd took notice, then mellowed. "Fairies of the valley, I hear your concerns, but this fight would have been brought to us one way or another. Sequis has poisoned our land by releasing the doluses from their territory. Should we not side with those who also wish to fight against him?"

This was a bold move, Resi thought. Tasmin had no way to know whether Resi planned to step up to the challenge and trust in her newfound gifting.

"Who's to say she even has powers to begin with?" a male fairy called from the crowd. "We haven't seen any part of her gifting revealed. If she's the so-called 'Giant-Slayer' we've come to hear about, why doesn't she fight Sequis herself and keep us out of it?"

Resi rolled her new title around in her head. *Giant-Slayer.*

The crowd erupted once more, this time louder, angrier. Resi tried to duck out to find a cement column to hide herself behind, but the fairies nearest her were beginning to spread the word of her appearance, their whispers hitting her ears like the hiss of a serpent.

"To say she isn't powerful is to call your Queen a liar," Tasmin threw back at the crowd. "I've seen what she can do with my own eyes. But she's still young in her gifting. Strong—yes. But trained—no. She needs reinforcements, people to come to her aid."

Resi continued to move through the crowd as she listened to Tasmin's words. Something about her delivery seemed forced, as if the queen were only seconds away from breaking down and siding with all the others. Still, the one small drop of hope inside of Tasmin was evident in a glimmer behind her eyes. It was just the kind of reminder that Resi had needed—one strong enough to overcome the anger, the lies, and the doubt.

Without another thought, she went straight for the platform. "Excuse me," she said softly as she attempted to push her way through the angry faces. "Let me through, please."

But the crowd pushed back against her requests. Many of the civilians were forceful towards her, pushing her to and fro. A select few, however, were very hesitant to be near her, as if the Giant-Slayer might lash out at any moment. Resi felt her stomach simmer in protest when a push sent her barreling into another fairy. She was beginning to lose her patience.

"EXCUSE ME!" she bellowed.

Just then, Tasmin locked eyes with her. "Let her through!" the queen called out.

One last push through the crowd brought Resi to the platform, and Tasmin helped her up, her smile wide and sure.

"For a minute, I thought you'd disappeared, too," Tasmin said, her voice childlike and kind.

"He still hasn't been found?" Resi asked. Her mind shifted to the silhouette in the window, to the copper-brown hair that had sparkled beautifully in the sun before darkness overshadowed it.

All Tasmin could do was shake her head. "I'm sure he's just out for a walk in the vineyards. Blowing off some steam."

Resi, however, was sure otherwise. Corey had taken along his map and his satchel. If he was planning on heading north, the patrol of fairies on the route out of Meade Valley would be sure to catch him. At least, she hoped so.

"Do you mind?" she asked Tasmin as she nodded to the crowd.

Tasmin's face showed no sign of concern at the idea of Resi addressing the fairies, and in that moment, Resi felt as bonded to her as a sister. Tasmin trusted her, though Resi couldn't quite understand why.

Resi faced the crowd, and the same nerves that had coursed through her on the day of the Tristeland Ball returned to her. With so many eyes on her, it didn't seem possible to stay calm.

"I know you're all worried. I am too," she spoke with authority. At the sound of her voice, the crowd's anger subdued.

Resi thought of Mags, who had always teased her that she was the type to bury her head in the sand when a problem arose; how right she'd been. The pain of missing her suddenly hit Resi square in the gut like a fist to the stomach. It was a powerful feeling that nearly threatened to knock her right off her feet.

"I didn't ask for this," she said, touching her stomach, reaching out to the heat that had been with her for so long. Some members of the crowd reared back, afraid that her gesture might conjure an outburst of her power. Others looked at her as if she were nothing but a fraud. "But it's in me. It's part of me. I suppose that's something I'll have to live with for the rest of my life. I can't run from what I am.

"I don't question your anger—I'm a strange person seeking shelter in your home. I've led the worst tyrant in the region straight to your doorstep. Hate me, if you wish. But, please, don't aim that anger at your leader," she said, facing Tasmin with a genuine smile. "Your queen is brave. It was she who asked me to fight, she who asked me to stand with her against the most powerful sorcerer since the age of the Great King. And believe me when I say that Sequis will do everything in his power to rid the Sept-Regions of anyone that gets in his way." Resi turned to Tasmin, then grabbed her hand proudly.

"What Sequis did to the Puras...it's..." Resi paused. "He turns beautiful things into monsters. I need you. But you need me, too." She looked down again; her fingertips sparked with heat, just once. "We need to crush him."

The words rang true, but sounded exactly like what Rolf had confessed to her only hours earlier. *I needed you. You needed me.* She couldn't help but wonder if that was the way all things worked outside of the Offenheimer Farmhold gates; that it was just a simple fact of life to borrow and take as much as was necessary from those who could help you.

Finally, a deep voice called out from the back of the group. "Show us!"

Resi couldn't make out who it was, but the entire collection of fairies started to chant the words with him.

"Show them what?" she turned to Tasmin.

"I think they're referring to what it was that I saw at Lake Seka. What you did to the dolus."

Resi took a hesitant step back from the edge of the platform. "It's too dangerous. I could hurt someone."

"Have you ever called your gifting forward on command?" Tasmin asked gently.

Of course, Resi thought. But then, it suddenly dawned on her— her gifting had only ever shown itself out of necessity, out of a pure instinct to survive: the Tristeland at the gallows, the dolus. Never had she been asked to pull her powers out of nowhere, and for nothing.

"I'm not sure," she said hesitantly.

Tasmin's face expanded in shock before she contained herself. "Now's as good a time as any," she said, her hands pointing to the crowd. "Give 'em a little show."

More nerves piled on top of Resi's shoulders as she looked over the crowd. What would happen if she couldn't give them what they wanted? Or worse—what would happen if she did?

She stilled herself, thinking about the fire within, that rage-filled anger she'd tried to keep at bay ever since her parents had disappeared. She could feel its dormant state; low and rhythmic, like a drum. But how could she stir it? In previous outbursts, something dangerous had always awaited her. But her strongest show of power had been the night of the Ball, the moment she'd seen Sequis throw the blue light at Luther's chest.

She couldn't go that far again. She wouldn't.

Resi looked down at her hands. They were shaking with the fear of a very critical realization. In that moment, that nauseous, sickening moment on the gallows floor, Sequis had withdrawn the blue sphere from her and had launched it at Luther. That feeling in the moments after...

Relief. Pure and unadulterated.

But anger? Anger seemed to bring out defensive power. Her power had responded favorably towards Corey during the dolus attack because she cared for him. And she knew she'd do the same for Rolf, even with all his lies. They'd become some dysfunctional version of a family through all of this mess, hadn't they?

Her eyes lingered on the crowd, watching their lips part slowly to chant in unison. She didn't know these people—not like she did Corey, not even like she did Rolf. But maybe, one day, she would.

"I can't," she turned earnestly to Tasmin.

"What do you mean, *you can't*?" she snapped back.

"My gifting doesn't work that way. At least, not yet. I can't just turn it on and off. The situation has to be right."

Tasmin raised an exasperated eyebrow. "You've got an angry mob in front of you that could pounce at any second, and you're telling me it's not the right time?"

"I'm sorry," Resi said. "I need to go. I need to find Rolf."

"You're just going to leave me here? With them?" she nodded to the masses.

Resi gave her a knowing smile. "Something tells me you've dealt with worse."

Tasmin attempted to hide the grin growing on her face by rolling her eyes.

"You know where you'll find him, right?" she asked.

An idea quickly came to Resi, and she nodded.

"I hope you're a fast runner," Tasmin laughed.

Resi winked back at her. If only Tasmin knew about her early morning jaunts through the trees of the Offenheimer Farmhold.

In a flash, Resi escaped to the back of the platform. She zigzagged through the ethereal trees and went for the opposite side of the ballroom, closest to the entrance to the vineyards. The crowd erupted with incoherent yelling, and they soon stormed after her as she departed the ballroom.

She came to the cellar steps, nearly throwing herself down them. She opened the door, then locked herself in behind them. The silence pooled around her until, BOOM! The mob hit at the door, yelling and ranting at her to reveal herself.

Resi turned to face the relative darkness and felt a cool chill come over her. The cellars were dimly lit by torches along the wall; she grabbed the first one she could find and used it to guide her through the darkness. It was the perfect place to find Rolf after their argument —a dark, secluded haven, filled with Fet. If he was still anything like how Tasmin remembered him from his younger years, he'd be here.

She pushed onward, passing the many rows of barrels until she spotted a shadow. Rolf lingered with his back to her. He was pacing down a row, holding an opened bottle of Fet in his right hand.

"You sure know how to piss people off, don't you?" he said upon her approach.

"Something we have in common, I suppose," she responded.

She got close enough to see the lines of his face, but didn't dare get any closer. There was a new heat in her stomach.

"Still mad at me?" he asked.

Resi shot him a look of disbelief. "Still a liar?"

Rolf drew a long breath, then slowly nodded. "Yeah...think so."

"Then, yes."

For a time, they just walked together, slowly taking in the cool of the cellars, breathing it in as if it would be their last opportunity of respite for a while.

"I went looking for him, you know," Rolf said before taking another gulp from the bottle. "He's not in the vineyards. Not in the stables either."

"He's gone," Resi sighed. "Took the map and his satchel." I imagine he's trying to find his sister. She's somewhere within the region."

"Don't worry. He won't make it past the northern patrol."

The harsh undercurrent of his words bothered her. It was so easy for both Rolf and Tasmin to write Corey off, to think less of him for not being a well-traveled tracker and for not being gifted. But maybe, Resi suddenly realized, it was Corey's ordinariness that made him so unique. His pureness of heart was his greatest strength, and his weapon of choice.

"He'd asked me to go with him," she admitted.

"Just now?"

"No," she shook her head. "Last night. If we all don't wind up dead in the next few days, he wanted me to leave with him."

Rolf sighed dreamily, albeit, in an effort to tease her. "Young love."

This poke from him made her even angrier, mostly because she hadn't truly addressed how she felt about Corey. He'd harbored feelings for her for so long, but she still couldn't be quite sure she felt the same. "If I'd had any common sense, I would've said yes," she scowled.

They crossed to another row of Fet barrels before Rolf offered her the bottle for a sip. Reluctantly, she obliged. "I certainly wouldn't have blamed you," he shrugged.

"What would've happened to you? If I'd left with him?"

"I would've gone back to Turbus. Found odd jobs here and there until news of the next Xylo came my way."

She scoffed in the silence, then winced at the mention of the word that she wished she could will from her mind. "You're shameless."

Rolf snickered and stuck out his hand for her to pass the bottle. "That's just it, Resi—love makes people do shameless things."

Resi waited for him to clear the air; there was more he wished to say.

"Well, I *was* in love," he finally told her. "A long time ago."

Again, Resi found herself picturing Rolf as a young man: his hair thicker, his face fuller, his posture taller. She remembered all the strange looks exchanged between Rolf and Tasmin around the table from the other night, and his silence. Then, a realization struck her.

"The woman you traveled with...it was her."

"Trixa," Rolf whispered. He placed a hand on a nearby barrel, as if asking it for reassurance. A sad laugh left his chest. "Funny—we actually shared our first kiss in this cellar."

Resi was just about to tease him before she realized that she, too, had shared her first kiss within the Fortress walls. It was just the kind of place for such romantic matters; for lover's trysts, quarrels, and grand gestures.

"She was something," Rolf laughed. "Drove me nuts, initially. She was stubborn. Entitled."

"You wouldn't know anything about that," Resi jabbed.

"Me? No," Rolf answered sarcastically. He kept walking, his head slung low. "This place was her favorite. I mean, apart from Belaflor, but that was home. She loved Tasmin. They were like sisters."

"She was Aliquian?"

Rolf nodded. "She was an Elder. At least, at that time. She didn't carry any power, which is a requirement for the Elders of the city."

An interesting notion, Resi had to admit. "Why?"

"When King Aliquis recruited the Elders' help to maintain the realm of Belaflor, it was his promise to his people that even those without power could reach great heights," Rolf relayed to her as he rubbed one of his temples with his hand. "And, with such a responsibility over the city, King Aliquis presumably didn't want the Elders to be able to use their power against the people. Keeps the playing field equal, if you ask me."

Resi cleared her throat. "And where is Trixa now?"

The weight of passing time landed hard on Rolf as he brought a hand to his bald spot, and patted the sweat from it. "I don't know."

Even after everything they'd been through, Resi found it difficult to poke Rolf about this. She took another swig, hoping he'd bite. "Care to tell me what happened?"

He smirked. "I know you'll keep nagging me if I don't."

Resi watched him take a deep sigh, the kind that he must have kept pent up tightly in his chest over the years. "We traveled the regions together," he started. "Trixa was the youngest Elder of her time, which garnered her a lot of attention. The Elders chose to send her off on the road with me. We loathed each other those first few months. She was a know-it-all type. Couldn't get her to shut up. After a few weeks, I wanted out. Even requested a new companion."

"And?"

Rolf huffed. "I was denied. No matter how much I couldn't stand her, it was obvious how exceptional she was at locating gifted Aliquians. She had a knack for planning escapes out of cities and had strong connections with what few abolitionists existed in the West at that time. She taught me almost everything I know when it comes to your people. And, she was a good storyteller. Savvy. Smart. Before I knew it, I found myself wanting to see everything about the world through her eyes. Suddenly every quality I'd once hated about her became endearing." He smirked. "I was hooked."

Try as he might, Resi could tell that Rolf couldn't hide the delight of reminiscing about Trixa and of telling their story. It was refreshing to see this side of him, Resi noted; he spoke to her as if he were talking about his past with an old friend—or at least, someone he really trusted. *Had* trusted.

"But her talents were needed back in the city," he went on. "I was given another Elder to travel with, but it was agonizing to be apart. I spent another year on the road without her." He laughed ruefully. "And boy, was I miserable. Every few months, I'd return to the city. I'd do everything I could just to be near her, just to see her. But there was just one problem."

Resi's face twisted in confusion. "What?"

"She's an Elder." A quick shot of pain crossed over Rolf's face, as if just the sound of that word hurt him to hear.

"...And that's off limits?"

Rolf nodded. "The Elders are strictly instructed to keep their bodies clean, which means they live a chaste life."

"She's not even allowed to get married? Have children?"

All Rolf could do was shake his head. He took a large gulp of the Fet, killing the bottle.

"So, what did you do?" Resi inquired.

Rolf raised a hand to scratch the back of his neck. He was avoiding the next bit. "On one of my trips back to Belaflor, Trixa sent me a letter instructing me to meet her in secret. She wanted to keep seeing me, but I knew we'd never have the kind of love that could be seen and remarked upon. I couldn't fathom hiding what I felt for her. We were always sneaking around and finding secluded places to meet whenever I was back in the city."

His head fell, and Resi spoke the words he couldn't. "You denied her."

Rolf couldn't look Resi in the eyes as she watched a wash of regret overtake him. "We would've lived our lives out in secret, fantasizing about the next moment that we could steal away to see each other. But Trixa was willing to risk it all. She got angry at me, told me to leave the city if I wouldn't agree to be with her. But I knew that quitting my position on a whim would've looked suspicious. Trixa and I could've been taken to trial if anyone had ever found out about us. The Elders could've ordered her death. So, I did the only thing I could to take me away from her."

It dawned on Resi. "You committed a crime."

Rolf brushed a hand through the air as if his crime was nothing.

"It was small, really." He paused, and a laugh escaped him. "I stole a goblet from the Elder's Palace."

"Wait..." Resi said with a look of disbelief. "That's it?!"

Rolf nodded, then nearly choked on his wine. "The Elders kicked me out of the city the next day after searching my quarters. Told me the only way I would ever be granted access again was if I found another stolen relic belonging to the city."

"And Trixa?" Resi prodded, trying to keep up.

"I never saw her after that. Of course, I immediately regretted my decision once I was on the other side of the portal. A person can exit the city at any time, but someone like me, someone who isn't Aliquian, *cannot* enter without an Elder or a Xylo present. I've been searching for a way back ever since." He smiled a broken sort of grin. "All that Trixa probably remembers about me is that I'm a thief."

Playfully, Resi nudged him in the shoulder. "I had no idea you were such a romantic."

Rolf grumbled. "*Yeah, yeah, yeah.*"

She sighed, finding relief in the slowness of her breath. Then, a question came to mind. "Why would Theodore Offenheimer have such an important map in his house?"

"Beats me," Rolf said. "But, I'm betting it's a story for the ages."

Another realization. Or hunch. "He couldn't have...stolen it, could he?"

Rolf could only shrug. Still, it was obvious he knew that there was a great possibility that Theo had not come across that map entirely by accident.

"You shouldn't bet on me, Rolf," Resi groaned, hearing her voice echo in the cellars. "I'm not a sure solution to getting you inside that city."

"You could be right," Rolf said quietly. "And even if you're able to get me in, the Elders might choose to throw me out again. Or hang me. But, a map like that doesn't lie. I choose to trust it. If you are what it says you are..."

"Is that why it's connected to me? Because I'm—" she stopped herself.

"Say it," Rolf ordered.

Resi gulped. "A Xylo?" Just then, the fire leapt in her belly, as if just saying the word was enough to give her power for a lifetime.

Rolf leaned back on a barrel. When it budged slightly, he pulled away from it. "In my years on the road, I've never seen a Belaflorian map have a connection to a person. Not like that."

Her mind spun at the news of this discovery. Why her? Why now? "That night in Sterch—you told me there was only one way to truly know if someone is a Xylo or not."

Rolf snickered. "And you're curious about what that might be?"

Her eyes widened at him. "Obviously."

Gently, Rolf placed the empty bottle down on the cold floor. "The only way anyone can be identified as a Xylo is if they show a specific sign of power. In Belaflor, it's called the Bellow."

"The what?"

Rolf rolled his eyes. "*I know*—sounds ridiculous. But if you'd ever heard it, you wouldn't question it."

Resi waited, unsure of what to do next. Rolf got the hint, then continued.

"When a Xylo comes to an understanding of their authority, they are said to show a very large display of power that manifests itself as a roar, or a shriek. Years ago, I watched a young boy exhibit such a power after coming into the city for the very first time."

Resi nearly tripped over herself. "Just when I thought things couldn't possibly get any weirder."

"Nothing's off the table when it comes to Aliquian gifting," Rolf said.

Resi waited. "And this whole prophecy thing?" she snorted. "Where did that idea start?"

Rolf gave her a look of complete honesty. "With Aliquis. *The Great Eight will emerge, but the last of them found is the greatest of all. All peoples of the land will rejoice his name, free and powerful, bound and small.*"

Resi retreated into a giant pit of her own embarrassment. She'd never heard this prophecy spoken aloud until today. "The Great Eight?"

Annoyed, Rolf rolled his eyes at her lack of knowledge. "Seven Xylos that will unite to find the final Xylo, the next ruler of the regions."

"The second I get into the city, I'm getting my hands on a book."

"It's going to take a lot more than that, kid."

"So...let me get this straight," she leveled with him. "Aliquis foretold that one day in the future, a great and fearsome enemy would arise in these lands, and that a group of powerful Aliquians would go on a hunt for the ruler that might defeat him?"

"Apparently."

"Did he ever say when?"

A chasm of silence grew between them as Rolf thought over her question. "One Xylo was named a few years ago, and I suspect the second has as well. This can only mean, Resi, that we are not far behind this prophecy being fulfilled. You should prepare yourself...the coming time will be one of great fear and unrest."

Resi huffed, surprised at her own ignorance. "You don't think this enemy is Sequis, do you?"

Rolf faced her square on, his gaze steady and unwavering. "I guess we'll soon find out."

Just then, the door to the cellars flew open amid much chaos. Tasmin and a handful of Sairons and fairy men dressed in armor came rushing toward them.

"Centaurs," Tasmin said breathlessly.

"Where?" Rolf asked.

"At the border. Our patrol saw them fleeing East into Sterch." She looked around the cellars, avoiding Resi's eyes. "And they found this."

One of the guards stepped forward, his face hitched with fear. He held out something in his hand, and Resi stepped forward to see it. A second later, she fell on her knees to the cellar floor.

The fairy held out a small leather satchel, well-worn and familiar.

"Where they've taken him, we can't be sure. But we must act fast," Tasmin ordered.

Resi mustered her courage and threw away her worry. She wasn't fearful of what might happen to Corey, at least, not quite yet. She came to a simple conclusion. Sequis; he'd made an improvised move in order to get their attention. "They're using him as bait. The centaurs will leave some sort of trail."

"If that's the case," Tasmin said, her eyes searching Resi's face, "then Sequis must be ahead of schedule. He'll have the upper hand on where we fight."

"At least you won't have to evacuate the valley," Resi said. "It's what Sequis wants. He has a plan."

"Wait," Rolf turned to Resi. "Are you planning on fighting?"

Resi looked to Tasmin, remembering her words to the crowd. "He has Corey," she said. "Isn't that reason enough?"

Then, Rolf's face went suddenly white. He turned to one of the guards with fear in his eyes. "Empty the bag."

The guard stood there limply, confused. He shivered, not knowing whether to take the command.

"You heard him!" Tasmin yelped. "Empty it!"

The guard did as he was told. A few loose items trickled out, but the map was not one of them. Resi watched in horror as Rolf's face hardened into a scowl.

"We leave at dawn," he ordered, before hobbling back towards the cellar door. Tasmin and Resi didn't need to ask any more questions. Instead, they just nodded to each other, then followed after him in silence.

CHAPTER 23

THE REGIMENT

B y nightfall, a group of five hundred fairies—some villagers, and some Tasmin's warriors—had been called upon for war and were beginning to set up camp in the vineyards. Because Rolf's splinted leg prevented him from fighting alongside the others, Tasmin recruited him to be the leading strategist for the battle. He appreciated the honor. For many hours, he hobbled up and down the vineyards, introducing himself to everyone in sight before he eventually peeled back to the commanding tent to meet with Resi and Tasmin.

It was all rather poetic, Resi thought. According to Rolf, one of the final battles of the Great War, the war that had settled the score between Anton and Aliquis before Aliquis had handed over the throne, had taken place at a site located at the border of Sterch and Rowan—only a mere matter of miles from where Corey's bag had been found.

"That's where Sequis will be," Resi assured Tasmin and Rolf. The three of them were bent over an old war table loaded with similar markings to those found inside the halls of the Western Fortress. "It's serendipitous for him."

Tasmin began to pace nervously. "We can't be sure."

"It makes complete sense!" Resi said, throwing her hands up. "Sequis is intentional. It'll mean something to him to fight there."

Rolf brought a hand to his chin. "We need to throw him off somehow."

Much as she loathed the idea, Resi put herself out there. It was the only choice they had. "He wants me. Just me. Send me in first...*alone.*"

Both Tasmin and Rolf sized her up, their eyes loaded with warning.

"Putting you within arms length of Sequis is not an option, Resi," Rolf told her. "If we lose you right off the bat, then we're all screwed. You're too important in this fight."

That was the way it always was with Rolf; Resi never had a say. She didn't like the image of a stranded army certain of its own demise, but she didn't like the other option of watching her friends be killed while she helplessly stood by.

"You're not going in alone, Resi. Remember—I have a bone to pick with him too," Tasmin chimed in. "Nice try, though."

Rolf nodded in agreement. "Our one advantage is the Puras."

Anxious to see her reaction, Resi turned to Tasmin. Much as the queen tried to hide it, a terrified expression crossed her beautiful face before it just as quickly disappeared. "We'll put our best archers in the air," she finally said.

"Now," Rolf continued. "There's the issue of the map. We need to get that map."

"I know you're chomping at the bit to get back into Belaflor with it, Rolf. But it might be too late to get it back."

Resi took a deep breath. "But we *have* to get it back. It's one of the few maps ever created that has the portal into Belaflor marked on it. Chances are that Sequis has seen it by now—probably forced Corey's hand, *literally*, to reveal itself. If that's the case, then we have a whole other set of problems on our hands."

"Still," Tasmin reasoned. "Sequis won't be able to get into the city on his own."

Rolf nodded. "Yes, but him discovering the location of the portal is a big enough issue. It puts the security of the whole city at risk," he said before hesitating and then looking at Resi. "If he gets ahold of you..."

Resi suddenly realized that if she were truly a Xylo, the sanctity of her power would then make her that much less safe within the regions. How many other people were looking for someone like her to aid them into the city? She then realized that this was the exact reason why Rolf didn't want her to meet with Sequis alone. If captured, Sequis could use her power to access the portal, and the entire city would feel the wrath of Sequis's sorcery. The consequences of something so disastrous would be massive.

"Bet Corey wasn't thinking about that when he left with the map," Rolf said under his breath.

"He was hurt," Resi glared at him. "No thanks to you."

"And you!" Rolf snapped.

"Really mature, guys," Tasmin said, her hands raising to bring down the volume. "Playing the blame game. That's really going to help us win this battle."

"Use me as leverage," Resi said. "Hand me over, and Sequis might hand over the map."

Tasmin crossed her arms. "That is, unless he's already seen where the portal is marked. If he has, then none of this even matters."

The dust settled on their bickering. All of them sighed in unison in a trio of different tones.

"If I don't talk to Sequis first, then you should," Resi said, turning to Tasmin. "You're our best bet as negotiator."

Tasmin took a cautious step back. "Have you fallen down a flight of stairs and bumped your head?" She folded her arms across her body, then jutted her hip out. "I became Sequis's enemy the moment I rescued you from that clearing. And from what I've heard, Sequis doesn't negotiate."

The three looked down over the dismal map on the war table, each secretly longing for the relic that Corey had brought out of the valley with him.

"I hate to admit it, Rolf. But Resi's right," Tasmin finally sighed. "We have a chance at getting that map if she goes to him first."

Rolf shut his eyes, clearly angry with the queen for siding with a plan he hadn't concocted himself. Typical, Resi thought.

"I'm just one person," Resi said to him. "But if Sequis studies that map long enough, his next plan of action will be finding a way into Belaflor. We can't give him that option. We need that map."

Rolf's jaw clenched. "I don't like it. Not even a little bit."

The three of them spent the next hour planning. The final decision was made by Rolf to keep Resi safe and away from battle unless it was absolutely necessary. When Sequis was at his weakest and the numbers of the Eastern guard were slashed, she would take a stand against him.

After their plotting session, Rolf had demanded Resi wear full armor for the duration of their ride north to the border, which she pitched a fit about. Still, Rolf wouldn't take no for an answer. He'd already received the armor from a fairy attendant and was aiding her into it.

"Is this absolutely necessary?" she asked him scornfully.

"You never know when danger will meet you, Resi," he spoke roughly as he adjusted the armor on her shoulders. "And I'll be damned if I have to recruit any more fairies to bring you back from almost dying by the hands of a sorcerer, giant, psychopath, womanizing-turned-nut-job, monkey brain—"

"Ok, quit your babbling," Resi interrupted him with a laugh. Leave it to Rolf to go off on a tangent at absolutely the wrong time. Once Resi was fully dressed, she attempted to adjust to the stiff hardware near her ribs, then found herself thinking that maybe the corsets she'd worn for weeks within the Tristeland weren't so terrible after all.

Tasmin led Resi to the stables, where she was kind enough to offer her a young Pura for the ride. The Pura was smaller than many of the others, but Resi was just grateful to be given one at all.

"Are you sure?" she asked Tasmin when she was presented with the bridled mare.

The fairy queen smiled, and Resi was suddenly reminded of Scottis's sweet face after she'd made him laugh for the very first time. "I figured she would be safest with you. After all, you're really the only one who could protect her from a dolus possession. You've fought one before."

Tasmin's trust was an honor to receive, but still, Resi felt uneasy. "So," she said, changing the subject. "We fly?"

"No. Their wings will need all of their energy in the coming days. Tomorrow, they're just good old-fashioned ground transportation. Nothing more."

Resi nodded as nobly as she could. There was a part of her that felt a wave of disappointment at the thought of not getting to experience the Puras in flight.

"Her name's Lambweed," Tasmin said as she stroked the Pura's long white mane. "If she had her way, she'd eat every last bit of it from the fields."

Resi couldn't help but hear the deep affection in Tasmin's voice. "I'll take care of her," she promised.

Once Tasmin had decided upon two dozen of her best Puras, she assigned the same amount of Rowan's finest archers to ride them out of town the following morning. As night fell upon the valley and Resi made her way back to her chambers for one last good night's rest, she couldn't help but feel a sense of pride in her decision to help Tasmin's cause. Even so, fear bristled beneath her skin.

Was this what true bravery felt like?

Anticipating the dawn, and whatever horrifying destiny awaited her, she slept lousily that night. Finally, when a morning bugle rang out before first light, she rose from her bed and threw her cloak over herself.

The vineyards were already bustling with activity. After families kissed their loved ones goodbye and every last warhorse and Pura was brushed and bridled, the muskets were loaded. Resi threw on her armor and mounted her Pura clumsily. Rolf easily lifted himself onto a stallion by her side, and threw her a reassuring wink. There was nothing left to do but start the journey.

The entire regiment left just as the sun rose over the hillside, leaving the Western Fortress and the vineyards behind. Rolf was determined to make it to the northern edge of the valley by nightfall. They'd camp there, then enter Sterch the following morning.

As Resi settled on her saddle, she looked down and grimaced at the dirt beneath her fingernails. She gripped the bridle tighter. She had never ridden a horse, let alone one of such sacred majesty; pure as snow. Calloused hands shouldn't be allowed to control such a perfect creature. Her eyes raised to the surrounding hillside, and for a brief time, she relished in the raw beauty of the west. No wonder Rowan was so popular amongst the wealthy for long holidays. The many colors belonging to Meade Valley, which was enormous in size, were striking; greens to golds, lit brightly by the sun.

The allure of this place, Resi noted, was bold. A place so remarkable needed no introduction and no explanation. Its power was ancient. In that quiet moment, she wished more than anything that she could see herself in the same light.

As expected, the soldiers kept away from Resi as they trudged through the mud of the valley. Their reticence concerned her, though she understood why they kept their distance: after all, the only other person besides Rolf who had witnessed her power was Tasmin. She didn't blame the soldiers for doubting her, or for doubting Tasmin. Still, she wished it were possible to warn each of them of what Sequis was capable of, what they could expect from a giant-turned-sorcerer. The more she thought of it, however, she was convinced that no amount of storytelling could convince a person of what sorcery—or Aliquian gifting, for that matter—looked like up close; the violence, the heat. Both were phenomena that were hair-raising to witness firsthand, and unbelievably difficult to explain.

As they rode, Resi attempted to stoke the fire within her along the journey. Cautiously, she worked with her anger, trying to recall memories of her parents: the sad way that her mother had looked at her on the night before her parents' disappearance; her father's disappointment anytime he had dared to turn his face to her in the fields.

But that was just it—the only feeling that Resi could identify within herself was disappointment; empty, bitter, disappointment.

That, and fear—gut-wrenching, piss-your-pants fear. If anything, these feelings dampened the fire, even threatened to put it out completely.

After an hour or so of no success, she gave up, convinced that her attempts were all in vain. It was possible that calling her power on command was just a shot in the dark, a flash in the pan. Feeling frustrated, she pulled Lambweed to the rear of the riding group; she didn't want Tasmin or Rolf to see the disappointment on her face.

As midday fell upon the mountainside, a light emerged at the base of the hills: a city, and it glowed with promise. Resi would've nearly missed it had she not turned back to see the expansive view of the valley from the foothills. Beyond, the sea churned large waves onto the shore. It was a charming haven of quaint shops and wineries. Carriage after carriage paraded down the long avenue leading out of town, appearing as a shimmering necklace along the widening shoreline. Resi pulled on Lambweed's reigns, slowing her trot until she came to a stop. It was the first time Resi had ever laid eyes on a free city. The region of Rowan was one of the few places where all peoples and creatures worked and lived together as one, and all because of the ruling of the Meade Valley queen, Tasmin. Her ancestors, as Resi had come to understand, had always stood in a position of neutrality when it came to the rights of all people.

A spark flamed within her as she processed a new feeling that emerged: conviction to fight. All she desired was the chance to experience freedom for herself. A vision of her and Mags walking arm in arm down the streets of a thriving city came to her, and her spirits lightened.

The fire inside Resi responded in turn with a sharp kick to her gut. It was her right, this power. Her sword. And it was time she learned how to properly wield it.

Lambweed neighed, shaking Resi from her thoughts. She pulled onward with a heavy heart. Yet again, she found herself in the perfect place at the wrong time, and with no resources to paint.

Like clockwork, Rolf nobly circled back to her on his stallion only a few minutes later. "You alright?" he asked shrewdly.

Resi knew she didn't need to answer Rolf, at least not in a moment such as this. Too many emotions moved in opposition within her. And besides, she wanted to enjoy her first ride. She stayed quiet, but she smiled at the notion of having him by her side.

"The town's called Ashant—named after a Patrian socialite who used to travel all the way from Turbus to summer here," Rolf informed her. "You should see it at night."

Resi chuckled to herself. "Better cover up, Rolf. Your Patrian is showing again."

Rolf tried to hide his pride, Resi knew, but he couldn't. Instead, he just trotted along beside her, his eyebrows rising and falling as he seemed to replay their conversation in his head. Perhaps, Resi hoped, Rolf was finally beginning to understand his own need for validation.

The hours passed before the wind picked up, bringing with it the first cool burst of air that Resi had felt on her skin since the trek through the Sterch foothills almost a week earlier. Too many accompanying thoughts came to mind at that memory. She turned to see Rolf leaning back to view the early show of stars in the sky.

"You know, Trixa would've spent her whole life fighting to live here if it weren't for her responsibilities in Belaflor," he said.

Resi pulled her cloak tight around herself. "You speak about her as if she's a ghost, " she remarked, watching the last fleeting look of joy leave Rolf's face before it hardened back to its normal state.

A puff of condensation left his mouth. "In some ways, she is."

Resi's throat tightened as her mind drifted to Corey. That night on the terrace, she almost felt he'd become a ghost too. He'd stood as still as a statue as he'd looked over the water. "If anything happens to Corey," she whispered, "I'll always blame myself."

"It was his choice to leave," Rolf said. "It was his decision."

"Only because he—"

"No matter what he heard, Resi, it doesn't matter. It can't change the fact that he left. But you're doing something about it. Now."

"It could be too late." Resi felt goosebumps run along her arms. Sometime while they spoke, it had turned into a true fall evening, the kind that Resi had always looked forward to after harvest season.

Autumn always came on that way—unexpectedly, and often, too soon. And now, just like that, so much of her familiar life was over, she realized; gone were her days of toiling in the fields, along with everything else in Ter. Gilda, the old wretch. Marion, in all her ridiculous dresses. There were so many aspects of her old life that she was happy to leave behind.

But others? Resi thought of Scottis, alone and shut away in the mansion. And Mags—Resi couldn't think of her for too long; at least, not without crying. But she couldn't shake an image from her mind—one of Mags alone, forgotten, and getting frailer by the second in an unfamiliar place. Resi surrendered to her fears and allowed the tears to fall freely until she felt one land on the exposed skin of her neck.

"Uh," Rolf wavered. "I'm not really equipped to deal with, uh, female *emotions*."

Resi couldn't help but laugh at Rolf's reaction. "If that's your attempt at cheering me up, then you're an idiot."

It was another shared moment between them, like the one they'd had in the foothills after staying at Amos's cabin. Rolf's care for her showed in his eyes for a brief time before he turned away from her. As her tears subsided, Resi felt the pull of forgiveness yanking on her heart like a child yanks at their mother's sleeve.

"I'm just a lying, idiotic tracker, so don't take my advice," he reflected. "But in times like this, belief, whether in yourself or in others—" He looked around to the many men and women armed to fight. "In whatever form it takes—is your fiercest weapon on the battlefield."

Resi let the words linger on her like dew. "Is that some sage, Patrian wisdom passed down through the generations?"

"No," Rolf said. "I told you not to take my advice. So, it's not."

It only took one long look at him for Resi to figure out where he'd heard it. "How in the Sept-Regions did you manage to land such a woman?" she wondered.

Rolf's hand landed hard on his thigh. "Beats the hell out of me."

"So—belief, huh?"

"In whatever form it takes." Then, a further word of wisdom

came to his eyes before it left his lips. "Stop thinking you need to show up for your power. Instead, let it show up for you."

Resi had heard this before from him, but it suddenly occurred to her that she hadn't really been listening the first time around. "You told me the same thing in the cave after the dolus attack, but it didn't work. I couldn't defend you and Corey against Sequis."

Rolf gave her a weak smile, but a genuine one all the same. "Where there is shame, belief will flee. But where there is love? Joy? Purpose? Belief will follow."

With nothing more to add, he rode off to join Tasmin once more. Resi, happy to take in the silence, stayed a few paces behind.

It was a long day's journey before the entire regiment made it to the northern end of the valley at nightfall. The meadow where they would camp for the evening was nothing more than a green pasture marked only by its few inhabitants; a handful of lost sheep that had wandered over from a nearby farm.

Tents were pitched and fires were lit within the hour of their arrival. Rolf, eager as ever, met with the archers to solidify plans for the air raid while Tasmin and Resi made haste to their tent.

"It'll be hard, but you need to sleep," Tasmin urged as she tucked herself in for the night. "We keep moving at first light." Resi took a long breath and tried to imagine what kind of rest she would be getting if they were still at the Western Fortress.

"Here," Tasmin said, reaching under her pillow. She passed Resi a wet and leafy sort of plant. "Sleep Seaweed, we call it. Might taste like raw fish, but it does the trick."

Resi took it, but her stomach heaved in protest when her fingers stuck together from a filmy residue that the plant left behind. "I think I'll pass."

"Suit yourself," Tasmin said. She snatched it from Resi, then swallowed the entirety of it in one yucky gulp.

The hours of night ticked by slowly, and the camp grew quieter and quieter as more and more soldiers settled in for the night. Resi stared up at the underside of the tent until it began to spin in her vision, then decided to look over at Tasmin. The queen was a mess of blankets and snores; the seaweed had certainly worked. Relieved, Resi tilted her head closer to the opening of the tent. No voices rang out from the center of camp, and it had been close to an hour since she'd heard anyone passing by.

It was the time to run.

Quickly and quietly, she threw on her cloak and exited the tent. All the fires had been put out for the night, save for one near the commanding tent; Rolf and the archers were still solidifying their plan for the morning.

Resi didn't quite know what she was doing, but she knew that keeping out of sight and slipping through the cracks was what she was best at. She narrowly dodged a group of drunken fairies making their way back to their tents by throwing herself down on her stomach in a patch of tall grass near the makeshift paddock holding the Puras. After they'd passed, Resi paused to watch Lambweed pull at the grass with her teeth alongside the other Puras before she slipped through the fence at the eastern edge of camp. It had briefly crossed her mind to bridle the mare and take her along, but she didn't dare run the risk of Lambweed becoming prey to a midnight creature on the loose in Sterch.

Resi breathed in the dry mountain air. She was alone, really alone, for the first time in what felt like months, and the sudden rush of freedom, like the kind she'd found in the woods surrounding the farmhold, pushed her legs into a strong run. She'd missed the open space of night and the concealment that darkness gave to a wandering traveler. So much had happened since those dreamy mornings spent placing the markings in the trees. And somehow, Resi's goal had remained the same; to run without being seen.

This trip, however, would be different—a last stand, of sorts. There would be no coming back to a lean-to, and no rescue from a fairy queen if things went sideways. She was unprotected, and completely on her own, but it was exactly how she'd wanted it. The dagger she'd stolen from the Dockside House was now lost at the bottom of Lake Seka, and she'd defiantly chosen to leave her heavy armor behind. Rolf had instructed her to let her power show up for her, and so she would. She'd confront Sequis alone, and hopefully, no other life would be taken. The thought of even just one more soul dying because of her power had solidified her choice in leaving, and there was no turning back.

Focusing her attention on the present, she brought her eyes to the mountain pass ahead. The muddy trail was freshly marked with large hoof tracks. There was only one thing on her mind; it was time that she lived up to the name of Giant-Slayer.

CHAPTER 24

THE CAMP

s Rolf had described it to Resi over the war table, the site of the Great Battle between Anton and Aliquis was just inside the western border of Sterch. The large meadow was surrounded on both sides by steep hills that gave way to a thick forest. As it lay, it was a perfect bowl carved right out of the land: a scar in the middle of the wood.

Resi settled behind a tree, then peered around it to look for any movement in the meadow. The woods lay still as far as the eye could see. Resi let her eyes linger over the trees surrounding the bowl; they appeared to have been blown back by some unknowable force, and their roots lay exposed even now, their still-barren branches fanned away from the site as if there had been a horrible explosion. What had taken place here during the Great Battle? And further, where was Sequis and his army? Resi raised a watchful eye to the sky; not a single smoke signal from an errant campfire caught her attention. She huffed quietly to herself and could just barely make out the condensation from her breath in the darkness. Sequis should've been here by now.

Determined, she moved on, keeping her stance low to the ground as she followed the centaur tracks beneath her feet. The frosty air of the northern regions had certainly made itself known during the night hours; the wind carried with it a dry, evil sort of cold, one that kept the mind distracted from everything but its bite.

Resi decided to rest her aching legs when she came to a fallen tree across the path. She'd packed a small piece of bread in her cloak pocket, and she bit into it nervously. It would be her last meal for a while. Or, ever.

It was possible that Sequis and his army had never planned on visiting the site of the Great Battle in the first place, Resi reasoned. For all she knew, he and his army were a hundred miles away, parked some-place deep at the center of the region, where anything could be waiting along the path.

She took down the last of her bread, then picked up the tracks again. They were fresh; startlingly so. Desperate for any clues, she looked up through the trees—only blackness as far as the eye could see, save for a small patch of clouds lingering above the tree line a few miles away. She kept walking, keeping her eyes on them as she did. They were bizarre clouds, tinged blue by her faulty eyesight in the darkness.

Blue. Blue, like water. Blue, like the hottest flame.

Quickly, Resi brought herself off the path and dodged through the trees. She ran until she was out of breath, until her lungs wanted to collapse with exhaustion, until finally, she came to a dip in the wood. The footpath was still visible to her through the trees, and her eye followed it as it sunk lower and lower into the earth.

Another hole in the woods, similar to the site of the Great Battle. This one, however, was massive, and protected by trees of all kinds. And there, safely nestled in the center of it all, was a camp.

Resi gasped. It would've taken her a month to count the number of tents. A new chill ran up her back as she pulled the hood of her cloak over her head. There was an eerie stillness over the entire camp; no lit fires, no soldiers floating about making small talk. The gargan-tuan campsite was still in a snoozy state in the hours before sunrise. Dormant. Vulnerable.

A sleeping giant.

Resi looked up to see more of the blue clouds ascending into the darkened sky. It appeared Sequis had been preparing for her arrival.

Even if she had an eternity to look, there was absolutely no way she would find Corey. She needed to get the lay of the land, to see the formation of the camp in its entirety. If she could figure out where Sequis was in all of the mess, then with any hope, she'd find Corey; if she wasn't already too late.

Resi stalked tactically back toward the path, being careful of where she placed her feet; centaur traps were likely positioned throughout the entire surrounding wood. She hid herself behind a tree, one that put her within feet of the dip in the path. She waited, letting her breath slow, feeling the pulse of the trees. Then, she made a dash for it, feeling the sludge of the mud beneath her boots. She set her sights on the camp, only to freeze mid-step. A familiar face, one sullen, but gentle, was coming up the path towards her.

Commander Lee.

He was guarding what appeared to be a checkpoint into camp. Frightened, he grabbed at the musket around his shoulder and aimed it at Resi, like a hunter spotting a deer through the trees. It was only a few seconds before a look of realization crossed his face. Slowly, he lowered the barrel, his eyes never leaving her. They both stayed that way for what felt like hours, suspended in disbelief, each examining the other and wondering what to do next.

Then, a chorus of voices sounded from the path behind him. Resi didn't hesitate, scampering off and hiding herself well inside the trees along the other side of the path.

She couldn't see the other guards through the dense wood; just the firelight of torches, silhouettes, blurred cloaks, and hushed words. After a time, the group began stalking closer until their footsteps strayed into the woods. Their movements were precise, practiced. She would be found within minutes.

Without another thought, she bravely revealed herself from her position, raising her hands high above her head to show she was unarmed. Within seconds she was seized by two members of the

Eastern Guard, their charcoal armor reflecting the orange light of the glowing torches.

"What did you find, Lee?" a deep voice finally asked from somewhere out of sight. Footsteps crushed through the leaves of the forest floor, until finally, the man revealed himself from behind the others. Resi nearly fell back in disbelief; it was a figure from her nightmares, one she'd hoped never to lay eyes on again.

Horris, the Foreman of the Offenheimer Farmhold. Memories of the horrible night of Shina's punishment raged through Resi's mind, and she felt her heat bloom beneath her ribs. She was utterly dumbfounded; what in the Sept-Regions was he doing with Sequis's guards? In Sterch? Resi watched his curly mustache twitch beneath his hooked nose. He took in the sight of her, eyes shaded beneath the covering of a tricorne hat, his nostrils flaring wide with victory. He was dressed finely in an ornate blue waistcoat and breeches—a bold fashion choice, even by his standards.

"Fascinating," he seethed, spitting over the consonants. "So much has transpired since we last spoke, Miss Flood."

Resi watched as a sly smile formed beneath Horris's mustache. She tried to recall when she had last laid eyes on him—it had been the morning after the Fourth-Year Festival. He'd just slipped out from Marion's chambers. She'd met Luther only a few moments later.

Horris's eyes didn't leave Resi as he brought a lit pipe to his lips, and a long trail of white smoke released from him in a long sigh. "Bring her to him," he spoke triumphantly.

The two guards forcefully grabbed Resi by the arms and began marching her down the path. Every so often, Resi stole a glance at Lee, who followed close behind. He couldn't meet her eyes.

Early daylight cast a murky blanket over the entire regiment, which made it easier for Resi to make out the boundaries of the encampment. Further north, an open pasture revealed the silhouettes of the sleeping centaurs, each one curled up on the forest floor. Resi sneered; they must've been recruited by Sequis after the dolus attack.

She kept her eyes moving as the guards led her into camp. Her gaze settled upon a massive tent in the distance, one taller and wider than all the others, with the gold governor's crest proudly displayed on its curtains. Surrounding it was a spacious square that marked the center of camp.

The guards led her in silence through the rows of tents, which seemed endless, until the group finally came upon the center square. Resi watched with questions in her eyes as Horris parted the curtains of the large tent to go inside.

Resi tried to make sense of it. Horris? Here? What would've brought him to Sequis? How did they know one another?

Desperate, she turned to find Lee. He paced along the perimeter of the square, keeping his eyes low. She wanted to thank him for leading Ana and Alby to the tunnels that awful night at the Tristeland, but he evidently had no desire to look for her in return. He kept his eyes firmly planted on his boots.

The minutes passed slowly, the mud growing wetter underfoot as the sky began to spit out a cool mist. Men arose from their tents, yawning and stretching, taking in the first light of day. Before too long, a small crowd had gathered in the square.

Voices mumbled from beyond the tent, before finally, the governor's crest on the curtains parted. A sheath of blonde hair emerged first, and Sequis's green eyes found Resi's not soon after. Resi turned away when she noticed him buttoning his pants. It wasn't long before a young Aliquian woman with long, dark curls fumbled her way out of the tent after him, dressed only in a slip. Frantic and embarrassed, she fled from the square with her dress crumpled in her hands

Resi felt her stomach curl and ignite at the same time. It was Horris who emerged next, his eyes set on Resi, his gaze proud and firm.

"Well," Sequis said, his grin softening. "I wondered just how long it would be before you showed up. Tell me, was it difficult to escape your regiment?"

Resi kept her eyes on him, never wavering. You're here for Corey. Remember Corey. "Where is he?" she asked as she wriggled in the guard's grip.

Sequis smoothed back his long hair and slicked it behind his ears.

"Who, exactly?" he asked, his grin spreading wide again. He was testing her.

"Hmmm..." Resi mused. "I didn't think your arrogance could make you any less bright. Apparently, I was wrong."

Sequis shot her an irritated look. "Oh, you mean the weak 'Lick boy we came across at the border?" He sauntered his way closer, boots sinking deeply into the mud under his mighty weight. "At first, I was just going to order his death by hanging. But then, I recognized his face. Thought he would be of good use." He snickered. "Little did I realize just how important he would become."

Resi's chest bobbed frantically. "You got what you wanted," she spat. "I'm here."

"Yes. You are," he said as his eyes flitted across the square. "Lee!" he called. Commander Lee made his way closer, his eyes still stuck on the ground. "Commander, it was you who came across the witch-'Lick in the woods, yes?"

Lee nodded, his arms crossing in front of him. "Yes, sir."

"And you're certain she was alone?" Sequis asked, his voice light and airy.

Lee nodded again, then finally managed to look up at Sequis. The square tensed, then relaxed under his strained breathing.

"A man of very few words this morning, Lee," Sequis said.

Lee said nothing once more.

Sequis took a look over his shoulder at Horris, then faced Lee once again. "Are you absolutely sure?"

Lee's eyes quickly darted to Resi. "To my knowledge, yes, she was the only one in the wood."

Sequis's head shook slowly, his eyes locking onto Lee with a new sort of determination. His smile fell. "My new advisor has informed me of your dishonesty."

Resi refused to believe the words. Out of all the men in Ter— Horris? As Sequis's new Advisor? The notion was too far-fetched, too ridiculous. Then again, he and Luther were not too different from one another; each had a peculiar sort of sliminess about them.

But Horris had authority to be able to practice small levels of sorcery, hadn't he? Perhaps, he was looking to climb just one more step up the ladder as Sequis's new Advisor.

In an instant, Sequis's massive hand roughly closed around Lee's throat. He lifted him from his feet, bringing him level with his face. "For weeks, I've wondered which one of my guards had betrayed me the night of the ball. I questioned you. Even believed you. But your guilt has given you up, Commander. You never planned to inform me of Taresia's arrival today, did you? Just like you never intended for me to discover that it was you that sent those two 'Licks into the tunnels all those weeks ago!"

Lee's feet kicked violently as he struggled for breath. His face darkened with blood. Still, Sequis looked at him without sign or show of any mercy.

"Pity you couldn't save the two 'Lick maids," Sequis seethed. "And pity you can't save the witch-'Lick. Or yourself."

Lee's neck snapped like a twig breaking under someone's weight. His lifeless head fell in Sequis's hand before his corpse was violently thrown. It landed feet away in a clearing like chucked garbage.

Resi let out a pained gasp that rang through the square. She went limp in the guard's arms as her legs turned into mush in the mud. Ana and Alby were dead. And now Lee—and it was all because of her. Horror enveloped her and rendered her hopeless.

All was quiet in the square for some time before Sequis flexed a strain in his right hand. He signaled to Horris. "The boy."

Horris nodded, then turned quickly on his heels for the south of camp before finally disappearing beyond a faraway tent.

Resi couldn't fight the doubt and fear that was holding her power at bay within her. She was stupid for coming here, even stupider for thinking she could've made the journey alone. Whatever had possessed her to believe that she had the power to save anyone, let alone herself?

Mud sloshed beneath a multitude of approaching boots. Resi looked up as Corey was brought forward by a group of guards, Horris following close behind. Part of her was relieved to see him; at least he was still alive. But she felt her stomach flip when she noticed a new limp in Corey's walk.

"Our guest of honor!" Sequis called.

As Corey came closer, Resi's breath left her lungs. His face was extremely swollen and bruised near his eyes. He could barely open them.

"What have you done to him?!" she cried.

"Oh—you'll see," Sequis said as he reached into his pants pocket. He removed half a dozen rings, then slid them onto his large fingers. "In the meantime, why don't we discuss one little detail, shall we?" he said, motioning to Resi. The guards brought her forward and closer to where Corey sat slumped in the mud in the guards' grip. "There's something important the three of us should discuss," Sequis said rationally. "I'm sure you can gather what I'm referring to."

A chill ran down Resi's spine, but she kept her wits. "Let's pretend for a moment that I'm the stupid one," she spat.

A murderous look flashed across Sequis's face before his eyes lingered over her mouth. He took a long, rigid exhale. "Believe it or not, you have information that is very, very important. And not just to me." Sequis signaled a guard to step forward with his hand. The guard opened his coat to retrieve a piece of rolled-up parchment. It was just as Resi had feared; the map.

Sequis smiled at her terrified expression before he unfurled it. "To your average idiot, this map is ordinary. But, for a man of my position, it represents much, much more." He motioned to Resi's right, and the guard forcefully pulled her hand to the parchment.

"No!" she cried. She fought to pull herself away. Kicked. Screamed.

"I like you this way," Sequis said, his face amused. "Scared."

The guard forced Resi's hand onto the face of the map, and within moments, the map reacted with color. "So beautiful," Sequis crooned. "Almost like...a painting." Impressed with his own wit, he peered pompously into Resi's eyes. "I've seen dozens of these maps in my lifetime. Maybe even more. But never in my wildest dreams did I dare to believe that one would mark the exact location of the 'Lick

City." He took a long breath as he turned back to the map, inhaling the aging scent of the parchment. "Hidden in plain sight, in the northern mountainside of Dirig, of all places. Naturally, your people will have gone to extreme lengths to make sure that someone like me could never enter the city. But in due time, I will make my way inside its gates. And when I do," he said with great satisfaction, "I will burn every last inch of it to the ground."

Resi looked up at him menacingly through her damp hair. She wriggled in the guard's grip as she watched Sequis take a long and calculated breath. "But there's one other concern I have about this map. Care to take a guess what?" Sequis asked. Resi stood her ground, remaining quiet. "No?" he questioned. "I can't blame you for being in the dark. Very few 'Licks get the chance to view a map like this up close."

"Bite me," Resi seethed.

"Don't tempt me," Sequis replied, his voice falling into a whisper. "It appears this map has some sort of special connection to you, of all people." His brow furrowed into a line between his eyes. "Why?"

Resi shuddered. "Even if I knew the answer to that question, I wouldn't bother telling you."

A small laugh left Sequis's chest, one heckling and cruel. "I thought you might say that." He looked over at Corey before drawing back his massive arm and plunging his fist into Corey's chest. The blow landed hard. Corey groaned loudly, and the sound of it echoed through the square.

"Stop it!" Resi shouted.

Sequis leered. "Only if you answer me."

"I told you! I don't know!"

Sequis began to roll up the sleeves of his shirt. "No?"

"I don't know why! Just stop, please!"

Sequis looked down on her, his nostrils flaring wide. "I'm afraid that's just not good enough." Another fist came down on Corey, this time on his side. A crack emanated from his ribs as another bright groan filled the square.

"Enough!" Resi screamed.

"It's really very simple," Sequis instructed. "You tell me what you know about this map, and I'll stop."

Resi winced at the desperation in Corey's swollen face. She knew that if it were up to him, he would never tell Sequis the truth about what Resi carried. But Resi didn't have the strength to watch Corey suffer anymore at her side.

"There is a reason the map is connected to me!" Resi cried with a heavy heart. "It's because..."

The words had no sooner left her lips than she noticed Horris stepping forward to Sequis's side. The movement was sudden, almost as if he were intrigued by the news and was desperate to hear more.

"Ah...yes. It makes sense now." A twisted smile formed on Sequis's lips. "It has some sort of allegiance to you because you're *special*. At least, that's what I'm assuming the tracker has told you—that you're valuable. Worth the world. A chosen one of the king."

Horris's chest bobbed with breath as his eyes furrowed on Resi.

"Do you believe the tracker?" Sequis asked her. "Do you believe you are what he says you are?"

Resi faltered in the guards' arms, and her feet slipped in the mud. Her eyes searched Corey's face for more answers, but all she could see were his two swollen black eyes. She didn't need to answer Sequis, she realized. He wasn't looking for any more explanations. "You're stalling," she spoke.

A low and threatening chuckle came from Sequis. "Then why don't you prove it?" He nodded to the guards before they released Resi with a thud to the earth. "A friendly duel never hurt anyone. And besides, I could use the practice before I pillage your people's precious city."

Slowly, Resi brought herself to her feet and brushed the dust from her knees. She looked to Horris. And that hat; that gaudy, ugly—

The first hit came at Resi's feet, knocking her to the ground. Sequis had missed, but not by much.

"Get up, 'Lick," he taunted her. "Show me your newly discovered gifting!"

Resi searched deep inside herself to try and find the heat. But it wasn't there. It was replaced by an icy-cold numbness, a prickling in her gut. She tried to ignore the laughter coming from the surrounding guards.

The second blast clipped her shoulder and threw her back a few feet into the earth before the wind was knocked out of her. She waited in the dirt as the dust settled. Her shoulder rang out in pain as if she'd been stung by multiple bees. The cloud of earth finally cleared around her, revealing Horris's silhouette: his strong, thin build; the odd tricorne hat.

It now made perfect sense; the third person in the gardens of the Tristeland...the darkened shadow in the night. It had been Horris. After Resi's painting of Scottis had been discovered by Marion, Horris had recognized Resi's gifting and had contacted Luther. It had all been one massive setup—one big plot to force Sequis's rise to power and for him to reveal his sorcery to the rest of the regions.

Resi clamored to her feet once more. The heat was beginning to flicker on inside of her like the spark of light at the moment of a new day. She thought of Shina's Mark. Of Mags. Of Scottis. Of Theo. She remembered Rolf's words about belief, and the smile that lit Tasmin's face anytime she talked about her Puras.

The fire flamed inside her, warmed by the memories, bubbling quickly to the surface. Resi felt ignited. The fever sent her head into a spin, and before she could register what was happening, she unleashed the heat from herself as if it were an arrow being released from a tightly strung bow.

A small shockwave rippled through the square, knocking the guards off their feet. Sequis stumbled as he felt the blow in his temples. Resi watched Horris's hat land on the ground beside him before the muscles in his jaw tightened.

The camp went silent. The release of power hadn't been like the blast at the Tristeland, one uncontrolled and violent. Resi's power had rippled out like a warning before the final showdown.

"You're learning," Sequis said, his smile forced. "More controlled. Still, this isn't the work of a Xylo. Just a poorly trained witch-'Lick."

Resi boiled within, patiently waiting. "We both know you've never met anyone like me."

"You may be right," he said, the blue sphere of flames swirling over his palm. "But that doesn't mean you're special. You're nothing more than a maggot that just so happens to be in my way, a stupid 'Lick girl abandoned by her mommy and daddy..."

The sphere from his palm cracked, then sent forward a lasso of light that cast the square in hues of cool azure. It wrapped around Resi, burning into her clothes before it met her flesh. She cried out, but not for anyone. She was alone. No one stood behind her to back her up.

The lasso tightened around her, tearing through her shirt and burning into the muscles on her arms. Resi shrieked fiercely against the pain. She was violent with anger, enraged with the Sept-Regions and all its corruption, with Sterch and its many evils. But mostly, she was angry with herself for all the time she'd spent wondering about her parents and fighting with the ghosts of them in her head. Her family had abandoned her long ago, but her new family—Corey and Rolf, and even Tasmin—they needed her now.

They needed *all* of her.

She let out a ragged scream, one that came from deep within. It was a full release, a guttural, strained sensation that occupied the space around her and engulfed her like a wide dolus mouth. She fell to the ground as Sequis's blue light fled from her in all directions. It soared over the camp like the wings of a bird and pierced through the early morning until nothing remained. Only a ringing that drowned out muffled voices.

Resi looked about the square, but could only see dust clouds in the air. She wasn't greeted by burned faces or by blood-stained hands. The blast had torn through the camp like a storm but had left no one hurt. It was defensive, not aggressive. Powerful, but not deadly.

Resi didn't have to think. She pulled her cloak over her head before scrambling to her feet. She panned the square to find Corey, but the dust was too thick. Finally, she spotted him lying alone in the middle of the square. His body was curled in on itself as if he had no more energy to give. Resi nearly tripped over herself as she clamored through the dirt to get to him. When she got to him, she bent at the knees to view him up close; he was in even worse shape than she'd thought. He couldn't even raise his arms. Quickly, she picked him up, and he let out another loud groan before she took on the load of his weight. He cried out in pain.

"Corey, you dumbass," she whispered to him. "I'd yell at you now, but we need to keep moving."

"I'm sorry," he managed to say through a cough. His voice was breathy and ragged. "I'm so sorry."

"Find them!" a voice called. Resi turned around, barely making out the form of Horris through the haze, pointing aimlessly towards the camp. She searched further, but couldn't locate Sequis through the smoke.

Resi began to lead Corey on, but try as she might, she couldn't ignore the disturbing sights of the disarrayed camp. Soldiers stumbled hysterically out of their tents, their faces marked with ash. Spooked horses scattered across the encampment as men tried to wrangle them. But Resi didn't stop for anything. Even with every part of her body screaming in protest, she kept a steady pace with Corey draped against her, doing his best to help keep them moving forward.

They trudged quickly through the muddy high street, then hid between two tents when a group of guards ran in the opposite direction. Resi took the opportunity to look up the path that led west out of camp; the way was flooded with guards, each armed and prepared with muskets the length of centaur spears. Where were the centaurs anyhow? She looked north over her shoulder to try to view their pasture, but it was still lost in dust.

They needed to keep moving and find higher ground. Resi drew her cloak tighter. They'd have to traverse the steep and muddy terrain to get out of the bowl. She heaved Corey through the cramped tents, sliding past guard after guard until the ground began to slope towards the sky. The air was thick with the smell of damp earth, of grubs and moss.

"You're going to have to help me," Resi said, grabbing Corey by his chin and waiting until his eyes met hers. "We need to climb."

Corey nodded weakly. He put one hand in front of the other, grabbing at the muddy hill with all the strength he could muster. Resi put a hand on his back and lifted him by the shirt every so often as she managed to pull herself higher. With each attempt, Corey would let out a painful groan, one that ripped through Resi's chest every time she heard it.

Three musket shots, sharp and bright, suddenly rang out towards the western checkpoint; guards guiding the way for the others in the square. They were trying to rally together.

Resi gave it her all. It took her five tries, but she managed to pull herself and Corey up the steep hill, finally making it to level ground. She brought him to his feet, and as the first signs of golden light warmed the forest floor, the two hobbled west into the comforting arms of the woods.

"Time to lead our giant to slaughter," Resi said to Corey. She could've sworn she saw a smile cross his mouth, small and fleeting. "Don't worry. We're almost there," she told him.

It didn't matter much to her that she was lying. She had no idea how long it would take to get Corey to safety, but she knew that she would say anything to keep the smile on his face. She wanted to hold it there until she and Corey were back with his people—her people. Their new family.

Chapter 25

The Battle

The leaves sparkled with frost in the early daylight, and finally it was light enough for Resi to find a direct path to the Great Battle site, the same one that she had come to earlier in the day. Carefully, she placed Corey in the dirt along its perimeter. He rested his back against the same fallen tree she'd come to. Resi watched on in fear as Corey's chest bobbed frantically. He clutched at his side as if he were bleeding out. Cautiously, Resi lifted his shirt to take stock of his injuries. She tried not to react when she saw the spreading bruise, deep purple beneath the skin near his ribs.

Paranoid, she looked back over both shoulders. "We haven't got much time here."

Corey huffed. "You need to keep moving."

Resi shot him a crazed look. "Don't be an idiot. They'll find you here."

"That's right. They will. But you—"

"Don't say stupid things," she interrupted as tears began to well in her eyes.

"But I *am* stupid," Corey joked before he began sputtering, coughing up blood into his hand. "I should never have left you. I was—"

"Shh," she ordered. She pulled his bloodied hand away from his mouth. "You're not to blame for anything. What I said...Corey, I didn't mean it."

"But you did," he corrected her. "You were right. You never needed me. You've never needed anyone. I mean, look at me." He coughed again. "If anyone needs rescuing, it's me."

She wiped the sweat from his forehead. "Let's not forget that it was you who found Rolf and me strung up in a centaur trap. I'm just repaying the favor."

"Do you know how repayment works?" he asked sarcastically. "I've been in your debt since the dolus attack." His eyes softened on her mouth. "You saved my life."

Resi couldn't help but laugh. It was what Corey always provided; laughter, even in the midst of the horrific messes she made, even when it came at his own expense.

"...Get to Tasmin...and Rolf," he murmured.

Resi turned west, hoping to find Tasmin proudly atop one of her Puras standing at the other side of the bowl. But the woods only responded with echoes, ghosts belonging to the many soldiers killed in a battle that had long been over.

"Besides," Corey continued. "You need to give them this." He scrabbled at the inside of his cloak, but his hands were shaking too violently. He was too weak. Resi stopped him and placed her hand inside his cloak. When she felt the familiar touch of the rough parchment, she gasped.

"You didn't..." she said in disbelief as she opened the map. At her touch, it ignited with color and hope.

Corey smiled dashingly before his swollen eyes closed. "You should thank yourself. It was lying right beside me after the first blast."

Without a thought, she slapped him victoriously in the chest, then immediately regretted it when Corey howled out in pain. "Sorry!" she retracted.

"You're a lousy flirt," he told her through a groan. "Always were."

She looked at him and saw the boyish face beneath the bruises. Tenderly, she bent to kiss him and tried to ignore the cool temperature of his lips against hers. When she pulled away, she saw and felt Corey's eyes dreamily linger over her face. "How's that for lousy flirting?" she asked with a grin.

Corey took a moment to respond. He was still lost in the kiss. "It's a definite improvement."

She couldn't help herself. She kissed him again, this one urgent, as if it could be their very last. She'd held back the tears, but couldn't any longer. Without a care, she let them fall down her cheeks, watching as they landed on Corey's face, taking away the stains of ash that had darkened his cheeks. But then a horrible dread came over her as his eyes began to roll back in his head.

"No, no, no, come on!" she insisted. She tried to lift him to his feet again, but he gave them none of his weight. "You can keep going! We can keep going!"

Just then, the woods rang out in pain. A burst of blue light hit a nearby pine like rogue lightning before the tree split in two. Resi sheltered Corey beneath her and splayed her cloak over him like a shield. "I can't leave you!" she cried as more light shot through the air. "I won't leave you like this!"

"You don't have a choice!" Corey spoke with a sudden hoarse authority, as if he were using the last of his energy to tell her this one final thing. Resolutely, he placed the map in her hands. "You have more than just me to protect now."

She couldn't believe herself for nodding back to him, for agreeing. But he was right. Somehow, Corey was always right, even in his stupidity. She kissed his forehead swiftly and tried to mark this time and place in her mind. She wanted to always remember the soapy scent of his hair and the salty taste of his forehead.

"I'll come back for you," she said, the words sounding like the fading squeak of a broken toy. She squeezed his hand tightly before covering him with a mess of fallen leaves until he was hidden. Then, she broke out in a run, using the thick trees against her arms to push her forward as she let her tears freely fall down her face.

More blue light sparked at the trees and flew through the air before the forest began to fill with the stench of burning wood and leaves. Resi paused at the rim of the bowl, then turned back to the forest.

A giant came barreling at her through the trees. Sequis was headed straight for her, his teeth bared, his scar shining brightly beneath his eyes. He was followed by a massive fleet of centaurs, more than Resi and Rolf had met at the border into Sterch. Their spears were at the ready, and their beastly bodies coiled with tension as their eyes focused on their new target. Their leader, the warrior with antlers of a stag, was at Sequis's side, keeping in perfect stride; another beautiful monster in a different form.

Resi threw herself down into the bowl, feeling her boots fill with sand and mud as she slid down the steep hill. She rolled sloppily, brushing her arms against wild thorns and bushes until she came to a stop on the ground. Quickly, she brought herself forward to the middle of the circular site.

She only had to look out for herself now. There was no one else to be concerned for, no one to fear hurting by accident.

She waited in the heart of the bowl as the pregnant prologue of Sequis's impending arrival overwhelmed her like the smell of rain before a storm. Every word that had ever been spoken to her of Aliquian gifting darted through her mind. She let out a frustrated screech at her own lack of understanding of her own power. It was all too overwhelming. She wished she'd had more time to get to know it better, to have become friends with it.

The stampeding hooves grew louder along the forest floor, shaking the trees around the bowl. Any moment now...

Rolf had said it simplest: *"Belief unlocks Aliquian gifting like nothing else."* Resi closed her eyes, repeating the words in her mind like a chant. Strangely, the memory of the strike of inspiration she'd felt before painting Sequis's portrait came to mind, and the rush of emotion that had overcome her prior to painting Scottis's precious face hovering over his book. It had all come from one small space inside of her.

A spark of creativity had flowed through her veins ever since she was a child. It was a restful, peaceful place, and in her talent, she carried an understanding of her own ability, a trust that she had in herself to carry out the task before her. And it had all come from the simplest love of doing it. It stemmed from joy.

It was true that she loved to paint, more than anything in the world. But to kill? To end someone's life? She took no pleasure in doing that, and she knew she never would. Her mind went to the horrific night at the Tristeland. The attack in the gardens, her most powerful display to date, had come out of purest relief, a fleeting release of the fear she'd been holding within her when Sequis had tossed the blue flame at Luther, and not at her. But how was she expected to call forth the same feeling here, now, on the brink of getting blasted into a million pieces by a homicidal giant-turned-sorcerer? The heat within was nowhere to be found, not even an ember. Resi was too filled with terror.

Sequis and the centaur leader finally appeared at the rim of the bowl. The governor was dressed in his armor with his hair slicked back. His face was hardened with dust. Beside him, the centaur leader stood proudly, his antlers rising high into the forest sky like two thick branches.

Without a word, Sequis smiled down at Resi in the bowl, and the blue sphere lit once more in his hand. Then, surprisingly, he threw the first blast at a tree along the perimeter of the bowl. It ignited in an instant, sparking indigo before the forest floor caught fire. Rapidly, the flames began to spread from tree to tree.

Resi turned about herself with panic. Sequis was trapping her in the bowl. And all she could think of was Corey, alone, burning in the flames of the forest.

The centaur herd came next, their spears reared back and their chests painted red for battle. They snorted and stamped along the bowl.

"Your move," Sequis called down to her.

But Resi had nothing, not even a retort. She had nowhere to run. Delirious with fear, she staggered back on herself before she fell on her behind.

Sequis laughed deeply at her clumsiness. New sweat from the heat of the fire gleamed on his forehead. The flames were spreading on all sides now, cutting Resi off from the western border into Rowan, from everything.

In one valiant jump, Sequis leapt the distance between the rim and the bowl, hitting the damp grass with a massive thud. The wet ground collapsed beneath him as he straightened his back vertebrae by vertebrae, followed by the glorious reveal of his angular face, his scar, and his vengeful, emerald eyes. The sphere spit and hissed over his hand, enlarging and shrinking.

"I want to see you try, just once, before I kill you," he marveled.

Promptly, Resi got to her feet, but she felt her defeat come over her like a wave of newfound freedom. She didn't have the ability to fight him; not anymore. "Kill me," she sighed. "You've won."

"I'm afraid I can't let you give in that easily," he answered her. "I'm a lion, and you, witch-'Lick, are my mouse," he smiled darkly. "I want to play."

The blue sphere slowly enlarged to the size of a carriage wheel over his hand—the biggest she'd seen. It reverberated like a drum, singing a terrifying melody of light and color. "Go ahead," he cooed. "Show me." His face was alight with curiosity, a horrific intersection where pleasure met power.

Resi plunged deeply into herself, searching her emotions. She didn't feel anger. In fact, she felt pity, and not for herself. Sequis had every means necessary to destroy her in an instant, and yet, all this time, he hadn't been able to do it.

Because he doesn't want to.

It suddenly dawned on Resi. If Sequis had one terminal weakness, it was her. She was his one fatal flaw. He was never going to be the one to kill her—not at the Tristeland, not in the clearing, not now.

She knew her next move. She didn't stir. She didn't blink.

"Show me!" his tone darkened unnaturally.

She flinched at the sound; not human. But somehow, she continued to hold down her fear like she would a nauseous stomach. She wanted him to beg, to plead. Curious, she glanced up at the centaur herd; confusion hung in the air between them.

"Don't look at them!" Sequis roared at her. He shot blue light high into the air above them, above the clearing in the trees, above the forest fire that threatened to trap Resi forever. "Look at me!"

Another blast, and another. And another. They filled the sky like gunfire, each exploding like a cannon. "Damn it, 'Lick!" Sequis finally bellowed. He spat at the ground, then stomped across the space to her before forcefully grabbing her by the waist. He lifted her from her feet so easily, like an angry child would their doll. "Fight me! FIGHT ME!"

Resi went limp and held her breath in her chest. Sequis threw her about, and she grew dizzy in his arms, her eyes occasionally lifting to the centaur fleet. Someone stood beside their leader; it was Horris, with his burnt tricorne hat resting unevenly atop his head. His face was stiffened like that of stone. Resi watched as he dismounted from his horse, his eyes narrowing on Sequis.

"Why won't you fight me?" Sequis cried to her, his voice cracking. His arms gave out before he gently placed Resi down in the grass, and he fell to his knees beside her. And there, once again, was the man from the parlor, the one Resi had met all those weeks ago in the Tristeland; the handsome-faced ruler that wanted desperately to be freed of his responsibilities...the broken boy, alone and burdened with pain.

In one last attempt, Sequis raised his eyes to hers before he grabbed her face in his hand. His grip was so tight that her teeth cut against the inside of her cheeks like blades. His hands could snap her neck almost too easily.

"Why you?" he asked, his voice broken and bent. "Why did it have to be you?"

Resi whimpered in pain as her eyes flitted back to Horris. He watched on in disbelief from the rim. Resi swore she saw his mouth cursing underneath his breath.

All of a sudden, a war cry, vibrato and quick, rang out. Sequis turned to the centaur herd, searching the group. But the sound had come from the other side of the bowl.

Like a mirage, a child-faced warrior stood at the other side of the rim. The fire lit her dark features ablaze. She was a woman of no mercy, a queen at the peak of her power.

Tasmin.

One hundred horses with one hundred warriors of the fairy clan lined the rim, their muskets raised, their armor gleaming with the reflected fire. Like water spilling over the top of a glass, the fleet charged into the bowl, Tasmin at the fore. The centaur herd responded in turn. Men, horses, and centaurs poured into every space and filled every patch of available grass.

The crash of metal on metal hit Resi's ears like the piercing cry of a bird. The fairy clan sprang into action, Tasmin leading the charge. Resi watched in awe as Tasmin dismounted from her Pura stallion with a valiant somersault, then plunged the sharp end of her spear deep into the torso of the nearest centaur. The other fairies were just as quick. Rolf had been right; the Meade Valley fairy clan was gifted at combat, moving so fast it was as if every other soldier was moving in slow motion.

Sequis reacted savagely, caving to the pressure of the battle. He threw a blast, narrowly missing Resi. Desperate, she moved herself, landing hard on her back. The air was knocked out of her. For a brief moment, she lay there, listening to the sounds of battle. Men crying out in agony. Muskets blaring out like exploding trumpets. Centaur and horse hooves scratching and marking up the once-unbothered grass.

Chaos. Pure and unfiltered.

But then, she was suddenly swooped up onto a passing soldier's horse with a long and powerful stride. Resi looked up from the soldier's arms. It was Rolf, his eyes forward and focused, carrying her out of the battle and into safety.

"I thought you weren't supposed to fight!" she called to him as she noticed his splinted leg.

"You're not the only one allowed to improvise!" he said, not looking at her. She didn't have to ask. She knew how betrayed he felt by her disappearance. He circled back, fighting off the centaurs with a small pistol. Resi did as best as she could, using her legs to kick off members of the Eastern Guard.

"—Corey," she suddenly remembered. Then louder, "Corey!"

Rolf finally looked at her. His eyes went wide.

"He's badly hurt," Resi told him quickly. "I left him at the top of the rim beneath a fallen tree. He's hidden."

Without missing a beat, Rolf brought a hand to his mouth and whistled between his thumb and first finger. A nearby fairy soldier, one with rugged good looks and a longer haircut, turned to him from his horse.

"There's a boy on the rim!" Rolf called. "—Badly injured beneath a fallen tree. Rally two men and fish him out!"

The soldier nodded, then ran east.

"He saw it," Resi finally told Rolf. "Sequis saw the map."

Rolf couldn't look at her this time. Disappointed, Resi reached into the top of her shift and retrieved the map, placing it trustingly in his hand.

"You can thank Corey for bringing it back to you," she finally said. Rolf didn't say a word, his guilt running loose in his eyes.

They trotted west until the horse came to the steep ascent up the rim. Rolf kicked its sides as it slowed. It nearly slipped going up the ascent, but with one final 'hyaw!' the horse scampered over the rim.

"Where are you taking me?!" she demanded. "I can't abandon Tasmin! Or Corey!"

Rolf showed no reaction to Resi's protests as he kicked his leg over the saddle, then lowered Resi to the ground.

"Rolf!" she screamed.

A fire burned bright in Rolf's eyes, a flare she'd yet to see in him. "You almost got yourself killed!" he railed. "You—" His arms raised above his head, his breath ragged and spent as he paced back and forth before her.

"I'm okay, Rolf," she tried to placate him. "I'm—"

"You almost forfeited the entire battle!" he called out. "Without you, we have nothing, you hear me?! Nothing!"

Resi's breath slowed in her chest. "You mean, *you* have nothing?"

she accused, before glancing down at the map in his hands. "Bet you're relieved that both of your tickets into the city have returned."

Rolf looked up to her, his eyes bloodshot and disbelieving. "No, Resi—"

"Forget it," she said, throwing her arms up. "I did what had to be done to get Corey and the map out of there. And besides," her speech slowed. "Sequis won't kill me."

Rolf's arms went to his hips. "What?"

Resi nearly laughed over the words. "Something is holding him back. I gave him a clear shot, and he wouldn't take it."

"But...that doesn't make any sense."

Resi's head shook quickly, a reaction to her own disbelief. "You can't force me out of this fight, Rolf. I caused all of this. I have to go back."

Rolf's arms landed on her shoulders before he took in a quick breath. "Resi, this isn't just about this battle. It's Tasmin's fight, too. But you—you need to be brought to the city, brought to safety. Your people are counting on you to join the other Xylos."

"Oh, would you quit it with all the Xylo talk?" Resi said, fed up at last.

"You may not understand it now—"

Resi moved quickly. She mounted the stallion, feeling Rolf's hands try to rip at her ankles.

"No!" he cried out after her.

But she'd been too quick. She sped off into the woods, leaving Rolf and the dust in her wake.

CHAPTER 26

THE BELLOW

When Resi returned to overlook the bowl of the Great Battle site, she cowered in fear at the sight before dismounting the horse and releasing it to run away from the spreading fire. The bowl was lit up like a lantern and the flames of the forest fire sent smoke high into the sky above the trees. The horrible sounds of battle—metal on metal, shrieks of pain and battle rage, and the explosion of gunfire—filled every available pocket of sound between the crackles and groans of the destruction of the forest.

Resi staggered forward as her lungs filled with smoke. She coughed and shielded her eyes from the sting of the heat as she moved towards the bowl. She had to keep her wits about herself to avoid being clipped by small trees that were falling left and right in the mayhem. A wave of nausea hit her in the gut. Initially, she thought her power had returned to her, but she realized soon enough that she'd been wrong. Her insides were sick with the smell of burning flesh that had begun to fill the air.

Finally, the rim came into view. The trees around it were gone, revealing nothing but mass hysteria down below. The centaur army had been weakened; only twenty or so stood. The rest lay dead on the forest floor, their bodies limp and bloodied. Their leader was amongst them, his magnificent antlers coated in the same mixture of blood, ash, and mud that now covered almost the entire meadow.

Desperate to find Tasmin, Resi's eyes scanned the carnage. She was horrified by their decrease in numbers. The fairies had held their own, but their earlier enthusiasm for battle was beginning to wear thin. Many could barely wield their weapons in the heat of the fire.

Stiffly, Tasmin stood in the middle of it all, watching, waiting. Her skin gleamed with sweat. In the sweltering heat, she'd ripped off her armor. She was looking for something. For *someone.*

Resi followed her line of sight, and found Sequis. He stood perfectly in the center of the bowl, his eyes fierce, focused, and filled with rage. His golden hair hung in limp strings against his face, streaks of ash turning it prematurely gray in places. He, too, had removed his armor, and as a show of power, he'd removed his under-shirt, as if to brazenly encourage anyone that might dare spear him in the chest to try to do so without hesitation or fear.

Resi drew a quick breath as she watched him march towards Tasmin. Steadily, he brought his hand up to face her, the sphere glowing brilliantly above his palm. He threw a large blast at Tasmin, but the fairy queen leapt a dozen or so feet in the air, neatly avoiding the blast before somersaulting her way back to the ground. But Resi noticed she'd injured her leg somehow in the process; still, she limped forward determinedly, never wavering for a second in Sequis's path. Resi had to do something, but what?

Then, she watched Tasmin bring her fingers to her lips. The queen let out a screeching whistle that rang out over the fire and the battle. Alarmed, Sequis aimed to shoot another blast in her direction, but before he could fire, a formation appeared in the sky.

It was the Puras and the archers with their bows at the ready. Their arrows shot into the bowl like a rainfall of terror, wiping out a group of centaurs and a handful of guards. The fairy warriors protected themselves with shields before Tasmin called them forward to fight off the remaining guards.

Still, Sequis's focus never wavered. Fascinated by his stillness, Resi watched him. Moments passed before the blue sphere vanished, reabsorbing into his hand.

It appeared he desired a more fair fight with the queen.

The warrior inside of him emerged as he lunged forward at Tasmin. Tasmin fought back, using her agility and flexibility to maneuver around him like a cat. In one swift move, her tiny body crawled up the space of his back. She wrapped her strong legs around his thick neck, squeezing until his face turned a beet red. But Sequis was stronger. Almost too easily, he gripped Tasmin's legs and threw her down on the ground beside him. Resi winced as she watched Tasmin stagger to her feet once more. She was hurt, but not gravely.

Without another thought, Resi clamored her way into the heat of the bowl, tripping over herself, wincing at the pain from the cuts along her back and arms. Her strength was dimming, and the chaos around her was winning. She watched in horror as the sphere's light appeared again on Sequis's hand before he threw it at a nearby fairy in passing. It was as easy to him as swatting a fly. The fairy's body flew back and hit hard against the dirt wall of the bowl.

Finally, Sequis spotted Resi. The same look as when he'd nearly kissed her in the Tristeland gardens quickly crossed his face—as if he were nervous, vulnerable, totally seen and totally naked. It was a fleeting moment, but Resi watched on as Sequis closed his eyes and tilted his head to the sky. He took a knee almost submissively, as if he were collecting himself. All the while, the battle and the fire raged on around him. He appeared as a beautiful sculpture stationed in the middle of it all. Then suddenly, his eyes opened.

Resi trembled. They were black as a dolus's.

A screech called out over the day like a dagger in Resi's back. A cloud of darkness appeared on the opposite rim of the bowl. Resi turned towards it, her stomach sinking with fear. Long, inky black hair spilled into the bowl first, followed by a translucent gray body; then another, and another. Resi shrieked. There wasn't just one dolus; at least two dozen others floated about the rim like horrific shadows suspended in the wind.

Resi reared back and landed on a young fairy soldier beside her.

"Run!" she called to him as she watched his eyes take in the horrific sight of the lake demons.

She let her eyes go to Sequis; he stood still amongst the chaos, his eyes darting back and forth, evidently directing the doluses. He was controlling them with his mind, pointing them to their targets.

The doluses slipped into battle, their translucent gray bodies hovering in the air over their male victims. Men ran for their lives with terror-stricken faces; they'd not yet seen this kind of horror.

The doluses snatched their prey one by one before the syrup-like liquid fell into the mouths of the caught soldiers. Next followed the snap of the stiff cord and the pull of life, until the body beneath went stiff. Then, each of the doluses seemed to split down the middle, each half becoming a new whole; a splitting of one into two.

Resi's breath was ragged in her chest as she tried to blink away the terrifying scene. The demons were mating and multiplying about the meadow like a plague.

She ran and yelled to other fairy soldiers to clear from the bowl. She searched the face of each person she came across as she ran for her life. Where was Tasmin? Where was Rolf?

She looked up and immediately regretted it. A dolus attacked a fleeing Pura and its horseman. Resi couldn't look away as she watched the pure white coat slowly dim into a dark night sky. The archer's eyes followed suit, turning black and becoming the creature's next victim.

The sounds of war engulfed Resi until they overwhelmed her and tore at her insides like claws. She clamped her hands over her ears before clamoring up the dirt wall to get to the rim. But then, WHAM! A blast hit right above her.

She turned back towards the bowl: Sequis. His eyes were still black as night. She let her eyes search his face, but found no tenderness in it.

Then, out of nowhere, she was suddenly struck by a quiet memory: Scottis, his face hovering over his book in his study. Resi had first discovered her love of painting only moments later. She could see the colors of Scottis's concentrated face as the sunlight peeked in through the window. It was a moment of innocence. Rest. Joy.

Then, a ringing hit her ears. Everything went quiet and slow around her, as if she had just entered a dream. There was no fear inside of her, but there was also no peace. Just numbness. The heat inside of her was gone, leaving just an empty void that pulled at her from inside.

And somehow, it was greater, this memory; greater than the battle, stronger somehow. Strong in its simplicity. Even at their weakest, her friends like Corey used joy as their sword. And Mags—sweet, kind Mags. They'd always been stronger than Resi; braver, too. Not because of their will to fight, but because of their pursuit of purity and wonder.

Resi opened her eyes, and the vibrancy of the fire within found its way into her senses. The sounds of battle were crisp and exact. The scene of battle flooded her sight like a slow-moving painting, depicting the fear of man and beast suspended in a moment in time. Resi was momentarily transfixed. The colors of the forest were brighter and crisper than they'd appeared to her before. She felt as if she were seeing for the very first time.

She didn't have to do anything. *Be* anything.

Her eyes returned to Sequis. In all the mess, she saw one thing clearly for the very first time. Sequis had been right. He was no different than she; both of them had been rejected, abandoned, and betrayed.

They were one and the same.

And finally, the heat flickered inside of her, but then instantly cooled. The power inside of her became as chilled as the purest mountain water. It eased the sting of the forest fire on her skin and silenced the shrieks from the fairies. The usual nausea and the fever that followed her power's awakening were nowhere to be found. Instead, there was only stillness inside of her. Resi felt as if she were falling into a cool pool after too many miles of running.

A certain sense of destiny and impending greatness came over her. The cool rose from her stomach and suffused her face, as gentle as sea breeze, before she felt her mouth stretch wide. Her voice rose only to a whisper.

"Enough."

From where she sat in the dirt and mud, a roar sounded out over the forest; deep, authoritative, and commanding above all others. Her power released from her like a river maneuvering its way over rocks and logs and everything in between. It was quick, unwavering, and it touched everything in its path. It was a force as ancient and as powerful as the deepest currents of the sea.

And then, it seemed as if the forest reached for the silence and clung to it. The woods became still once more, as if they'd just awoken from a nightmare. There was only peace.

Resi's vision went dizzy as she took in the sight. The forest fire had simmered down to ash. The doluses were nowhere to be found, almost as if they'd been wiped out of existence entirely. Along the opposite side of the bowl, the few remaining members of the Eastern Guard scrambled to the dirt walls and clamored to find safety.

Resi felt herself ease. Their troops were pulling back.

"Resi!" came a call from above her. Rolf waited for her with his hand extended from the rim. She crawled up the wall and grabbed it, then fell into a heap beside him.

For a brief moment, the two sat in stillness as they looked into the ashen meadow far below. Resi took in the quiet morning air like sleep. Neither could say or speak about what had just happened, what had been confirmed. They didn't need to.

But then, movement stirred from amidst the ash. Sounds of coughing followed before a massive form rose from the ground. Sequis sputtered and wheezed as he stumbled to and fro in the middle of the bowl. He gained his bearings before looking to the rim. But he did nothing. Instead, he stumbled back as if he were drunk, then stared at Resi in shock.

Then suddenly, his eyes widened in confusion as his body was lifted from the forest floor. Slowly, he rose into the air, higher and higher still. He was clearly in a state of shock and bewilderment from the last attack, rendered helpless by his complete disorientation.

"Resi?" Rolf questioned her.

But Resi ignored him, transfixed. She watched Sequis's body rotate and wriggle like a worm on the line until his massive form was raised high above the clearing. He stayed suspended in the air for a time like a gorgeous archangel—a giant in the sky. Then, CRACK! His body twisted in midair. He let out a pained scream unlike any Resi had ever heard; worse than Shina's, worse than Corey's.

His head turned to where Resi waited along the bowl and his lips quivered as he tried to utter words.

"Forgive me," he coughed as his eyes strained for her.

His body hung there for a few moments, his mangled and twisted legs pointing unnaturally in opposite directions, until his form wilted again to the ground. Down he fell until his body plunged into the meadow floor and threw ash in all directions. A cloud of dirt rose slowly into the air.

Resi let out a dreadful scream and she fell to her knees along the rim. A part of her celebrated this moment and the relief it brought, but another part of her grieved the smallness at the very core of Sequis; the great man that so desperately wished he could be a child.

"Resi!" Rolf cried, lifting her face to his. "Resi!"

But she couldn't tear her eyes away from the face that she'd once captured in color, now twisted and white on the meadow floor. Sequis's eyes were wide, and darkness consumed them.

A figure appeared at the other side of the rim, and Resi's eyes drifted towards it. One soldier remained; Horris, with his face covered in ash and his eyes locked directly on Resi. Resi watched numbly as he took one breath of silent submission before he kicked his horse in the side and disappeared beyond the smoke and deeper into the forest.

"Resi!" Rolf continued to cry out. He shook her at the shoulders and tried to get her attention, but his attempts were strangely muted under the ringing of Resi's newfound power.

She couldn't believe it had felt so easy. No emotion. No rush of cool or hot. She'd felt nothing in the moments before she'd killed Sequis. Just, nothing.

CHAPTER 27

THE CELEBRATION

T he sun set purple and pink over the mountainside as Rolf and Resi came to the camp at the border. They'd spoken nothing to each other on the quick journey; Rolf only checked in with her by occasionally patting her leg in a proud, fatherly way. Still, there was something about his manner that was withdrawn. Resi was no longer the small girl with an untried Aliquian gifting. She was a Xylo, and one who had just reached a new height of power. It seemed even Rolf wasn't immune to that.

His jaw clenched tightly as he helped her dismount the Pura, then pointed her to the medical tent. "I'll catch up with you," he nodded. He then passed the Pura onto a fairy before peeling off for the commanding tent. There were preparations being made to depart for the Fortress the following morning.

Resi made her way inside before a flurry of Sairon nurses swarmed her, their dresses stained with blood from tending to so many wounded. The tent was filled with warriors—men and women, all battered and many wailing in pain. Soon, Resi was quickly laid out on a table, then examined. After a minute, the nurses went quiet.

"You're—" one of them started, a young woman with long black hair. "You're fine, Miss."

"That can't be right," Resi corrected them. She probed the painful places where Sequis's blue light had pierced her skin, but her fingers found no traces of blood or injury.

The women around her smiled in victory, their faces as bright as morning light. One bravely stepped forward to Resi. "We never thought we'd see the day; a Xylo, in the flesh."

Resi exited the tent a minute later in stunned silence. Her breakthrough of power had revealed a new strength; she had the ability to heal, but only herself, it appeared. Or had others been spared?

She walked through the camp in a daze. She couldn't get the image of Sequis out of her mind; his mouth dripping with blood, his golden hair sooted black. She'd forever be known as the Giant-Slayer —the girl that took down Governor Sequis. She once thought that she'd feel relief upon the news of Sequis's death. But her guilt in that moment was overwhelming. Had she meant to do it? Was it truly what she'd wanted?

She pushed on, noticing that camp was quiet; too quiet. Resi could only imagine how devastated Tasmin was to lose so many warriors. She looked east to the pasture. Only fifteen white Puras; nine had been attacked, and now, she supposed, they were no different than all the other monsters of Sterch.

Resi came upon a few uninjured fairies. As she approached them, they looked at her with wide-eyed curiosity. "Where is Tasmin?" she asked one. Timidly, he pointed to a small grouping of fairies to the west. They stood huddled together before a tent. Resi felt a flurry of mixed emotions at the sight of their faces; some were celebratory, others were clearly burdened with the loss of family and friends. Resi couldn't help but smile, however, when she saw Tasmin had made it out of battle mostly unscathed. Out of her battle armor, Tasmin appeared even tinier than usual. She stood proudly amongst the group in a beautiful blue cloak with a fur-lined hood. A slight smile played across her childlike face.

Resi raced up to the group before Tasmin saw her approach. Immediately, the other fairies turned to leave before Tasmin burst into tears. She leapt at Resi and gave her a tight hug. "You," she said. "You saved my people. Saved me."

Unsure and confused, Resi pulled away from her. It wasn't the reaction she had been expecting.

Sensing her confusion, Tasmin stroked Resi's face. "This way," she said. She ushered Resi further into camp, passing more groups of celebrating faces, and other faces in mourning. They came to a shaded patch of frosted grass beyond the Pura pasture.

Resi waited in the chill. She was still suspended in a dream world. Where were they? What had just happened? Why was Tasmin standing so calmly before her, as if a war had not just taken place a few miles east?

"I've never seen anything like it!" Tasmin said as she began pacing. "You were—I mean, you were *amazing*, Resi! You were sitting there in the dirt, looking, well—" her expression turned apologetic for her next words, "kind of pathetic, actually. But then! You just..."

Resi exhaled vacantly as she recalled the roar that had erupted from her chest. Her eyes glazed over. "I screamed. And then it was over."

Tasmin cautiously approached her. "Resi, it's over. You won the battle."

"*We* won this battle," Resi corrected her.

The fairy queen took a reluctant step back. "But, it was you that ended it. Accept that. Be proud of that."

Resi couldn't feel anything. No fire. No water or wind in her gut.

"You're not injured?" Resi asked Tasmin. "I saw Sequis—"

"A few bruises, but barely. We fairies are stronger than we look," Tasmin winked.

"And the doluses...?"

Tasmin smiled. "They were vaporized instantly once your power revealed itself."

Resi supposed the same thing had nearly taken place at Lake Seka, then realized that her new ability to scale back her heat had provided her with even greater destructive capabilities. She wasn't quite sure how to feel about where the nature of her power was headed. Like shooting an arrow into the night sky, she feared it would only ever prove to strike her down.

Then, her heart sank. "Corey?" she asked.

Tasmin's face wilted. "He's injured—has a few burns. He's being treated in his own tent now."

"Can I see him?"

Tasmin nodded, her eyes pitying and sad. "When he's awake."

"I couldn't save your Puras," Resi spoke softly as her head dropped in disappointment.

"Stop that," Tasmin ordered her before she lifted a quick hand to wipe a tear that wanted to trail down her cheek. "You can't save what was already gone."

A breeze came through the pasture, crisp and biting. Resi released a heavy sigh as her mind drifted to the final moments of battle, to Sequis. "It just doesn't feel right...I don't think I wanted to kill him."

With concern in her eyes, Tasmin placed two soft hands on Resi's cloaked shoulders. "No sane person ever wants to harm another, but some people need to be defeated, Resi. Think of Belaflor. Think of your people."

Resi supposed it was the way all great rulers spoke to each other. *Think of your people. Even if it means compromising your own integrity.*

Tasmin smiled. "You Aliquians are all too nice." Then, her attention was suddenly pulled beyond Resi's shoulder. "And speaking of nice, here comes its opposite."

"I heard that," Rolf chimed as he approached.

Tasmin patted Resi on the shoulder as her eyes searched Resi's face. "I'll see you. Soon." She then gave Rolf a raised eyebrow before she headed back to camp.

"So..." Rolf started. He shifted awkwardly, warming his hands by rubbing them together. They drank in the silence together, both letting it soothe the trauma of the day's events. It was how they interacted best; standing in quiet solidarity in the aftermath of terrible situations. Perhaps that was why they'd stuck together for so long.

"You must be confused," he finally said. "I mean, I would be."

Resi's head lifted to the sky. "I didn't feel what I normally feel."

"The power changed?"

She nodded. "It was easy—too easy. And with Sequis...it was like I wasn't in control. It just...happened."

Rolf faced her, his eyes serious. "I don't know everything, Resi; certainly not the power of a Xylo. I've heard things. Seen things." His tone softened. "But I know one thing for certain; you need to be trained. Taught. And by people who actually know what you're going through."

There was an uncomfortable beat as Resi thought of the topic that neither of them wanted to address. She feared Rolf was thinking the same thought.

He scratched his head. "Look, Resi—"

"You don't have to apologize, Rolf. I've been reckless," she chuckled. "We both have."

He sighed. "Go with Corey. Find Mags and your parents, if it's what you really want. I'll even go with you. When the time is right, I'll lead you to the city."

It all sounded too good to be true to Resi. But even so, she found herself disagreeing. "I'm not so sure that's the course I can choose anymore."

His gaze narrowed on her. "What do you mean?"

Resi felt the cold of the northern regions wrap around her, and she welcomed it. "I've wanted to go after my parents for so long now that I don't know what it's like to just be in one place. My mind's always been moving forward; to next week, next month, next year. When will I escape? When will I find them? When will I finally get answers? But, now that Ter is so far gone, all I want is to be still." She took a deep breath of the cool air. "I'm tired."

She watched as Rolf nodded in agreement.

"And," she continued, "I'm guessing more than just Sequis had a peek at that map. The Elders need to be warned."

Rolf's eyebrows raised with surprise at Resi's newfound sense of purpose. "Spoken like a true Belaflorian."

She grinned at him. "I like the sound of that."

He suddenly tensed. "If you still need someone to take you there, I can. But please know that I don't expect anything else."

Hearing the sincerity in his voice, Resi laughed. "If you think I'm going in there alone, you Patrian brute, you're crazy."

Rolf smiled broadly. It was the first real grin Resi had ever seen spread wide on his face, and she was left breathless by it. There he was; the Rolf that Trixa had fallen in love with. The man who knew the regions so well, the husky tracker that had somehow become a trusted friend to her along their journey.

"Tomorrow," he said softly to her. "Tomorrow."

BY SUNDOWN, the Rowgar and Fet were flowing in spades, and Tasmin declared she had no plans to stop drinking until the sun was to come up. Expertly, she maneuvered her way around camp with two bottles in hand, laughing and drinking as she reveled in the victory of her people.

Resi stayed out for a few hours around the colossal fire that was built at the center of camp. She tried to enjoy the festivities as best she could; some brave, drunken fairy men tried to flirt with her by regaling her with stories of war and travel. Still, Resi couldn't stop thinking of Corey. Of saying goodbye. Of Mags. Of her parents.

Finally, as the stars peeked out through the cloud cover and the moon settled over the mountains of Sterch, Resi snuck off to find Corey. Rolf noticed her flitting between the tents as he chatted up a young-buck fairy surrounded by beautiful Sairons, and waved her on. "He's up," he mouthed to her.

Resi moved quickly to the west side of camp, breathing in the cold and feeling as far away from Ter as she might ever be. Finally, she found Corey's tent, noticing before she entered the first signs of snowfall. She put out a hand, only to discover that it wasn't snowfall at all; the ash from the forest fire had finally descended over the camp.

At the sight of Corey, Resi covered her mouth and tried to keep her fear at bay. But she couldn't. He lay stiffly on a bed made of hay, his face warmed by the light of the lantern at his side. Bandages cinched tightly around the core of his body. "You came," she heard him mumble in the darkness. His voice was weak; just one more thing the fire had claimed.

"Of course I did," she spoke. All she wanted was to touch the warmth of his skin, to feel the softness of his hair, but she remained controlled.

"Resi..." Corey breathed. "Tasmin told me everything. I'm so—" He couldn't finish through his coughs. But he didn't have to. Resi knew how proud of her he was. She let her tears fall down her cheeks.

"You and everyone else, it seems."

"You sound disappointed."

She smiled through her pain. "I guess it only feels right hearing it from you."

They breathed together in the cold as they both listened to the music of fiddles and drums from the center of camp.

"Fairies certainly know how to throw a party," Corey finally said in an attempt to ease the tension. "I should be good as new in a month or so. Tasmin's taking me back to Meade Valley before escorting me south to help me locate my sister."

Resi sighed. His optimism, as usual, shined through even in the darkest of moments.

"Corey, I have to go," she said in a whisper. "Tomorrow."

He sighed disappointedly. "I know."

"You do?"

He stifled another cough. "Rolf came to me earlier. Offered me back the map. But I refused it. Besides, it's always belonged to you."

Touched, Resi wiped the tears from her face and tried to calm herself. He was too good with words, too great at pulling together the pieces of her that wanted to fall apart. "I hope that's not all he did," she said, rolling her eyes.

"He apologized," Corey rasped. "In his own way."

She sighed, hating the cold tent and the wounds that kept her from holding him. Worst of all, she hated the decision that was keeping them apart.

"It's the only way," she sighed. "I wish I could—"

"You don't have to explain yourself, Resi. Not to me."

Giving up the fight, she reached for his nearest hand, which was wrapped in bandages. "I'll carry you with me," she pointed at her chest. "Show Belaflor to you."

"I'd like that," he said half-heartedly. "I'd like that."

She laid her head down beside him on the hay. "What am I going to do without your loud mouth always getting in the way?"

He didn't answer, but she could feel the terror in his heart over losing her, over possibly never seeing her again.

"I'll find her, Resi," he whispered. "I'll find Mags, and when I can, I'll bring her to you."

He spoke it as a promise, and without asking him any further questions, Resi believed him. She began sobbing quietly at the thought of years without his laugh or his funny way of easing every moment. She felt a growing ache beginning to take root inside of herself. Still, she spoke softly to him. "Tell her I love her—that I miss her so much sometimes that I can't sleep."

"I will," he said, his voice quaking. "I will."

"Thank you."

"Just one thing, Resi," he asked, his voice sure.

"Anything."

"Promise to remember me," he said, his words soft and as pure as a child's. "But not like this; like before."

Deep inside, Resi knew that he wanted to tell her the words that he'd often held back in fear of her reaction. But there was no more room for heavy exchanges in an already cramped tent. Even he knew that.

She lifted her head before kissing him gently on the forehead. "I promise." She lay back next to him and settled in to listen to his quiet breathing under the sounds of celebration. She tried to draw forward the healing waters of her new Xylo power, tried to understand it enough to give it away to him. But nothing came. She suspected she was too heartbroken, too fearful of this being their last day together. As her tears flowed down her face, she pledged to herself to keep Corey locked away in her heart forever. She'd always remember the boy with the soil-brown eyes, the one who looked at her and saw his home.

CHAPTER 28

THE PORTAL

asmin woke Resi in the hour before the sunrise, then led her to the pasture. Unsurprisingly, Rolf was already waiting with his cloak tightly fastened at the neck. Resi couldn't help but smile; she'd never seen Rolf so excited.

"It's three days' walk to the portal into Belaflor," Tasmin said. "But, I thought I'd cut your journey short."

Gracefully, she swept her arm towards Lambweed in the pasture, the small and beautiful mare that Resi had met from the regiment's initial journey to the border of Sterch.

"Tasmin, I could never accept..." Resi protested.

"Slow down," the fairy said, her face tensing. "I'm not giving her to you. Just letting you borrow her."

Rolf released a guffaw of laughter, doubling over on himself in mirth. He was still high on the energy of battle and on the prospect of their journey, and Resi supposed she was too. Soon, the three were laughing together until any tension that had grown between the three of them in the previous two days had been completely destroyed. Somehow, Resi believed that this one small moment now bonded them even more than the battle.

"But how will she get back?" Resi asked as she turned again to watch Lambweed bend to eat from the pasture.

"The valley is her home," Tasmin said as she led Resi to Lambweed. When Tasmin touched the Pura's nose, the horse cooed like a pigeon. Tasmin gave Lambweed a playful snort of disapproval for acting like a bird, much like she had at the stables of the Fortress. She then smiled at the Pura with delight. "She'll find her way."

Resi turned back to see Rolf standing behind them. He shielded his eyes from her, but Resi swore she saw the faint glint of tears in them. The past few days had brought up new emotions in him, and like her, he was sad to be saying farewell to Tasmin. Resi laughed to herself. The tracker was human, after all.

"Off you go," Tasmin said before she gave Lambweed a kiss on the nose. "Come see me, alright?" she then said playfully to Rolf. "Let's not make it another ten years before I can make fun of you again." They embraced before Tasmin turned back to hug Resi.

Resi nodded back toward Corey's tent. "Take care of him?" she asked.

Tasmin winked at her before giving her a hug, the kind Resi imagined a sister might give. "I'll protect him."

Lambweed gave a neigh before Tasmin turned back for camp; too emotional to watch them all leave. Resi gave one last look at the meadow on the border, making a wish to never relive the events of the Tristeland or this place ever again. Then, she and Rolf mounted the Pura mare, and with a burst of Lambweed's wings, they were off.

The sensation of flying was somehow a perfect combination of freedom and fear, of buoyancy and gravity. Resi held on tightly to Rolf, but enjoyed the cool breeze that tickled her face. They flew over bright meadows, and mountains with waterfalls that fell over the green, rocky cliffs like thin, crystal tears. Rolf proudly pointed out when they crossed the border into Dirig, and Resi, feeling more alive than ever, shouted at the top of her lungs with a great whoop. Feeling equally inspired, Rolf threw his head back and joined in on the fun. Together, they both released their arms wide. With Lambweed, they were a trio of wings high in the sky, as untouchable as the sun and the wind.

It was late afternoon when Rolf nudged Lambweed gently in the side to begin their descent. They'd entered a deep valley, one with snow on the peaks of the mountains surrounding it. The grass was a breathtaking green in the meadow far below. Purple flowers dotted the foothills, and to the east, the monstrous mountain chain leading south graced the border into Sterch.

Lambweed slowed and descended toward a pine-covered peak. All the while, Resi found herself questioning the thick surrounding forest. Wasn't the tree line far below?

They landed in a small clearing that gave way to a breathtaking view of the valley. With a tremble of her hand, Resi laced a small purple wildflower in the saddle before they bid Lambweed farewell. Together, she and Rolf watched her soar over the sunset-soaked valley in silence until she was out of sight. It was the most peaceful scene Resi had ever viewed. She swore to paint it one day, maybe even soon.

"What is this place?" she finally asked Rolf.

Rolf handed her the map. "Take a look for yourself."

With tremendous excitement, she opened it and watched the small golden light appear right over the bright mark of the portal. Their lights shone as one, and she couldn't help but feel the significance of such a moment. But fear followed next; their only way forward was through a steep and narrow mountain pass, one that appeared impossible to navigate.

"We better get moving. Want to get there before sundown," Rolf said as he predictably fell back to what was most natural to him—leading valiantly, with his bald spot proudly on display.

The two started the hike and Resi quickly realized just how strenuous the terrain would be to navigate. They started through a narrow, untamed pass that overlooked the valley, then found themselves in a sticky situation. The trees cut away completely to reveal a secondary jagged, but open pass that turned a hairpin around the face of the mountain. Some areas of the pass were so narrow that had either of them taken one clumsy step, they would've found themselves falling hundreds of feet into a ravine of boulders. In some places, they were forced to shimmy along the path with their bellies skimming the stone. Even so, the spectacular views of the quaint villages nestled into the valley far below made it worth the effort.

After an hour of silence along the route, Resi couldn't help but notice a change in the trees. Their color, once a deep forest green, had lightened to a summer lime; odd for mountain pines, she thought. In the golden light of early sunset, they almost seemed to sparkle.

A mile further, Resi began to feel a strong pull in her chest. It came on like the feeling of saying goodbye, or like hugging an old friend for the first time in years. She was captivated by it, but then felt a familiar feeling of dread trying to threaten it. Had she come under a similar enchantment like the one they'd encountered leading into Sterch?

Seeming to read her thoughts, Rolf turned back to her. "It's the air," he informed her. "I don't notice anything. But for an Aliquian... the city is close. That feeling lures you to keep searching."

Suddenly, he stopped and pulled out the map. Resi placed her hand on it and the white light appeared. The blue light marking the way into Belaflor was gone; her star had replaced it. "The city wants me to find it?" she asked herself in wonder.

"Quick!" Rolf turned about the forest. "Look for patterns! Similarities in the trees!" he barked. "Reflections in the light! Something that's repetitive!" Resi could hear the excitement boiling inside of him. Were they really here? Was it really time?

The two of them fumbled in the dirt for quite some time, each standing on their tiptoes, bending at the waist. "Should I be looking for some type of door?" she eventually asked, her eyes squinting in the fading sunlight.

Rolf stopped in his tracks before his face went hard. "It's a portal into a new *realm*, Resi. Not a quaint passageway into some woodland home. Think bigger."

Embarrassed, Resi smacked her lips together, then nodded. "Right."

Finally, after what seemed like an hour of searching, Resi heaved a huge sigh and extended her arms high above her head. Her body was beginning to ache miserably after the battle. She pulled her hands from left to right to get a side stretch, then noticed a peculiar sight amid the tops of the trees.

Two large birds, identical in size and shape, flew overhead. They soared together in tandem, as if attached by some invisible force. Their wings parted and flapped in complete unison, sending them further up the mountain until they flew out of sight over the treetops.

Curious, Resi began to walk in the direction they'd flown. What kind of birds were they, anyway? And where were they headed all the way up here on the mountainside?

Then, as if calling to her, she noticed an oddly-shaped tree. Its branches spread long and spindly towards the tops of the pines, but its base was fat. A breeze then made its way through the clearing, sending the branches of the strange tree into a whirl. Resi watched it dance before she froze mid-step. An identical tree on the other side of a large mountain boulder moved and whirled in harmony with the one before her.

"Rolf?" she called significantly. Without question or a word, Rolf clipped the distance between them, then placed a heavy hand on her shoulder. "Look...there—" she said as she extended a finger to the identical trees.

She turned just in time to see Rolf's face light up. "Excellent! Excellent, Resi!" He bounced his way forward between the two trees, and the air went still as he took a large breath. Then, as if expecting to touch something invisible, he reached a shaking palm out to the forest. Like a hand to water, the air before him rippled and sent a multitude of rings spiraling in all directions. The ripples made their way to the top of the trees, and a sound followed like the thud of a distance ship hitting waves.

"Well, what do you know," Rolf said warmly. "The Aliquian found the portal, after all." Resi could hardly contain herself; she smiled excitedly back at him. "What do you see?" Rolf probed her out of sheer delight. Resi looked into what she believed was the furthest depths of the forest. But then, taking a turn around, she began to see the patterns. It appeared as if they were staring into a mirror. The only noticeable difference was that she and Rolf were missing in the reflection.

Then, it dawned on her. Earlier, she had only seen one bird in the sky; the other was merely its mirrored twin reflected in the surface of the portal. "Wild," she said with a giggle.

She turned to watch Rolf's eyes search high into the treetops. They were filled with gratitude. But then, his face fell quickly with shame. Resi noticed a few tears fall from his eyes to the ground.

"Rolf, what's wrong?"

"I've been nothing but a coward these past few weeks, Resi," he breathed. "A selfish, thoughtless coward."

Resi recognized guilt better than anyone. She'd carried it with her from the Tristeland. She still carried it with her now, especially after what fate had come to Sequis. She knew Rolf felt remorse for his actions, but she didn't desire for the burden to stay with him any longer than was absolutely necessary.

"I don't doubt that you wish to see what lies beyond this portal," he continued. "But I must tell you; it is purely your decision upon whether I enter with you."

Resi gave him a look of reassurance. "I meant what I said at camp, Rolf. From now on, you're with me."

Overwhelmed with joy, Rolf swept Resi tightly into his arms and lifted her from the ground. The hug took Resi's breath away, but soon enough, she found herself melting into it, all the while feeling a wave of gratitude that he'd miraculously entered her life when he did.

Still, she couldn't resist a joke. "I'm not one to handle, uh, *men's emotions.*"

Rolf chuckled as he let his emotions settle. "Well, then," he said after Resi's feet made contact with the ground. He tried to hide his excitement by readjusting his cloak at the shoulders. "I suppose it's time."

The forest went unsettlingly still as Resi waited for what would follow. Since she'd left the farmhold, all she'd wanted was to find a safe harbor to land after weeks of travel. Now that she and Rolf had arrived at the entrance to the city, she found herself wondering if such a place of divinity could even exist within the Sept-Regions. After all the horrific things she'd seen along the journey, she was beginning to fear that such a place could only be imagined in the mind.

Her thoughts drifted to memories of her parents, of their disappearance. She dared to hope that they might wait for her on the other side, then thought better of it. What would it matter, anyhow? Her once desperate questions that needed answering had gone mute within her many weeks before. She felt peace steal over her as her mind turned to Mags instead. The woman had always tried to get Resi to see it her way—that Resi's place of belonging existed inside a person, or a place. But as wise as Mags was, Resi had learned otherwise since she'd left the farmhold. For Resi, she'd found her belonging, but not in anyone else. Her home was in the knowledge of her destiny, and she knew that hers was waiting inside the city gates.

Sensing her panic, Rolf grabbed her hands in his. His eyes flitted to the falling sun before they returned to her. "Are you ready?"

"Is anybody ever ready to enter a new realm?" Resi asked as her voice quaked in her throat.

Rolf suppressed a laugh, but his eyes continued to dance to the edge of the mountain. "There remains one thing," he said. "You must invite me in."

"Invite you?"

"The portal must be made aware that a Patrian has been granted access."

"How do I do that?"

"It's simple. You state my name, and then ask me inside. But you mustn't place your hand on the portal until after you've done this. Otherwise, the portal could kill me when it is opened."

"Oh," Resi added casually with a shrug. "So...no pressure then?"

A nervous smile crossed Rolf's mouth before Resi squeezed his hands and looked to the shimmering mirror before them.

"Rolf," she stated, "I, Taresia Flood, would happily wish you access to the city of Belaflor." The words came out so easily that it seemed ridiculous to imagine Rolf's life depending on them. Then, they moved together to place Resi's shaking hand on the glimmering portal.

The mirrored reflection felt much like water on her palm, but it was neither hot nor cold to the touch. Only a few seconds passed before the liquid-like surface began to vibrate slightly along her fingers. Then, a bright, golden light appeared within the mirror beneath her palm, as if her touch had awakened it. The light began to trace its way up the surface of the portal, spreading in a dozen directions like veins on a leaf. The glow from the golden veins became so bright that both she and Rolf had to shield their eyes. It climbed higher and higher; then finally, when the lines reached what appeared to be the tops of the tallest trees, the portal began to crumble into flaming embers that drifted into the air like burning parchment.

As the portal crumbled away, the tops of the trees were drenched in light from beyond the veil, spreading through the surrounding forest like wildfire. A fierce wind from beyond the portal suddenly rose and ripped violently through the forest, throwing Resi and Rolf down to the forest floor. What's more, Resi felt the presence of a frighteningly powerful force emanating from beyond the light. It was ancient, connected to the earth and sky, and no different than the fire and water that waged war inside of her.

The wind continued to howl, swaying the trees of the forest and sending a cloud of dust barreling in all directions. Resi and Rolf came together, holding onto each other as they watched the portal fall away. Fear coursed through Resi as the light grew even brighter, and the power behind it swallowed them whole, making it impossible to see, to breathe, to think.

Seconds later, the ground began to quake underfoot. Splits in the forest floor separated Resi and Rolf in an instant. "Now, Resi! We go now!" Rolf called to her through the chaos. He had fallen into a small crevice and was desperately clawing his way towards the light. The whole world was falling away around them. The ground rumbled miserably, causing a large pine tree to split down the center of its trunk.

Resi leapt from her position, landing with a thud on a still-intact portion of the shuddering earth. She shielded her eyes as she recklessly ran toward the wall of pure fire and light. Her lungs let out a scream before the world around her seemed to vanish completely in the wide mouth of the portal's light, as if they were willingly running into the sun. A heat like what had emanated from the heart of Sequis's forest fire sprang forth from the portal, stealing the oxygen from the air and clouding every thought in Resi's mind. She could only concentrate on putting one foot in front of the other.

Then, as suddenly as it had arisen, the heat dissipated and the air became brisk. Resi's legs had stopped running, but when, exactly, she couldn't be sure. She opened her eyes. The bright light had faded, and she found herself standing behind a waterfall with water the color of the purest tanzanite. Its mist fell upon her, delicate and welcoming. For a brief moment, she just stood there, her hands suspended before her to test if she was dreaming, or if she was dead.

She'd nearly forgotten Rolf was beside her. He was clearly in a similar state of shock, his eyes still blinking away the aftermath of the light. The ground at their feet, which had seemingly crumbled into nothingness not seconds prior, was now made of some type of crystal-clear green stone.

Rolf chuckled as they playfully touched at the water together. It was cool on their skin, but their clothes remained as warm and dry as if they'd been left out in the sun. Rolf reached out his hand to Resi, and she clasped it; then they passed through the waterfall to the other side.

They'd entered into a brightly lit grotto and were standing atop a small stone ledge that protruded from beneath the waterfall, which came in from the top of the cave and fell into a wide, deep pool, which lay just a short drop below them. Resi looked about; their only apparent route forward was to dive into the water and swim out of the cave, which presumably had an exit point somewhere below the surface.

Resi took a moment to breathe in the clean scent of the grotto. The air was tropical, temperate, as if they'd just crossed into the mist of a hot spring. The water that fell thunderously from the waterfall swirled about in changing colors in the pool below—amethyst purple, turquoise blue, emerald green. Resi shielded her eyes as she looked upward at the sun, which was poking through a hole at the top of the opposite side of the cave. The light reflected off the water below, splaying small rainbows across Rolf's cloak.

"I'm not so sure this isn't a dream," Resi said in disbelief. She wanted to absorb every molecule of her surroundings. Even the smallest details were noteworthy.

Her eyes continued to dart around in amazement, trying to take everything in as their feet moved along the thin stone ledge. She watched Rolf dive into the color-changing water, and trusting him, she followed after. She swam deep under the surface, following his shape in the water before her, and together, they exited the grotto through a small opening in the bottom of the rock. They broke the surface and caught their breath as they swam to the shore of what seemed to be an inland lake that was surrounded by tall and thin trees. Resi looked about the surrounding land, which sloped along the horizon in perfect green hills.

After Rolf helped her out of the water, he led her to a stone path that curved its way between two hills. As the sunlight hit her skin, she looked down in amazement as she realized that neither of their clothes were wet. She and Rolf could only smile at one another as they reveled in the miracle of it all.

"Welcome, Resi, to the Great King's realm of Belaflor," Rolf sighed, his face alight with joy.

Resi raised her eyes to the horizon cautiously, afraid it would all vanish. A light along the emerald hills caught her attention; a faint shimmering of water. There it was, a city of many colors, surrounded by a horseshoe of misty falls and domineering emerald mountains. It was just as Rolf had promised her without ever having to describe it. No words could or ever would capture this kind of mystical beauty.

They stood there for a time, catching their breath as they took in the sight of the city. But then, a flurry of wind suddenly came barreling through the surrounding trees. Resi thought she might enjoy the breeze, but its force was noticeably violent and carrying power that demanded attention. She looked down at her feet and thought she was seeing things; her untied laces were somehow lacing themselves. Scottis, she thought, would've loved it. Surprised, she turned to Rolf, then took a cautious step away from him as she noticed the gray in his hair fading to a deep brown.

What was happening?

Soon enough, the wind had circled the entirety of Resi's body, completely enveloping her. For a moment, she panicked as her legs lifted from the ground, and she floated in suspension as the wind danced around her. Panicking, she looked to her forearm, only to find nothing but smooth, tanned skin. The Circle of Infinity, the mark once branded and forever burned into her arm by Sequis, had vanished. She gasped as her hair, spiky and short, suddenly fell long and weighted to her waist. In an instant, it appeared that she and Rolf had been healed of every wound they'd ever carried. Once the wind had settled around them, they laughed and jumped in amazement at the miracle like two children. The notion of a power so formidable and so pure brought tears to both of their eyes.

As Resi realized this place was not a figment of dreams, but *real*, as ordinary as the dirt that still lingered beneath her fingernails from the farmhold, she felt a deep rest come upon her soul. She was no longer in bondage. She was no longer a 'Lick, but she was certainly proud to be an Aliquian. The chains that had kept her self-belief shackled and bound had broken. She was freed.

Awestruck, the two stood facing the path to the city in silence. Another grand journey awaited them. With pride, Resi allowed the stories of this remarkable place, once thought to be a myth, fill her heart. Just as Resi's mother had taught Resi all those years ago, the realm of Belaflor had opened its gates wide to her, and for the first time in her life, Resi felt certain that she was home.

ACKNOWLEDGMENTS

There are entirely too many people to thank for aiding me on the journey that brought *The Aliquian* to life. Putting a novel together takes a village, and the village of people that God has brought into my life during the process of creating my debut novel has been full of heart, generosity, and creative passion.

I'd like to first thank my support group of family and friends who have encouraged me to drop everything to write this book. The seeds of joy that have been planted through your encouragement have helped this series grow into a widespread tree, one that has transformed my life for the better. From the bottom of my heart, thank you.

A big shout out to my soft-but-spicy Slytherin friend, Lauren Corbett. I owe a tremendous amount of gratitude to you for your initial support for my writing journey, and for introducing me to the fierce and mighty Rebecca Job. To Rebecca: no words could express how exciting it was to introduce you to the first draft of my manuscript. Your patience, kindness, insight, and sense of humor made the experience of developmental editing such a joy. Thank you for your belief in me. Thank you for keeping it honest and real.

To the one and only Christopher Blackeby: I can't imagine this book ever forming shape without having heard your messages of fullness. Try not to let it get to your head, though, buddy (insert wink emoji here). To my wonderful spiritual parents, Kirby and Fiona, and our WowLife family, THANK YOU! Thank you for the friendship, guidance, counsel, wisdom, and laughter that you have brought into my life. We are an intelligent church! Much love.

I am so grateful to the inspiring Grace Melrose for introducing me to Streamline Books. Thank you, friend! And to my team at Streamline; Will, Trevor, Annika, and Hannah...the experience of publishing by your side has been a dream. Thank you for trusting my vision and for being such a legendary hype-team. To the epically talented Taylor Mahurin: your dedication to bringing Resi's artistry to life through your illustrations has completely blown my socks off. I have no other words besides '*AHHHH!*'

To Reid Coe, my husband and best friend... Seven years ago, we were living in a shoebox apartment in New York City, and I first expressed my heart to you about creating a purpose-driven book series. You listened with intention and excitement, and you've been listening with the same level of care every day since. Your belief in me, in so many ways, has been the ethanol fuel behind my writing journey. Thank you for your generous investment in me and into our marriage. I honor you. I love you so much.

And lastly, and most significantly, to my heavenly Father, my *God*, who has given me boundless joy through writing this book. Tender words were spoken to me beneath a starry sky many years ago: "*In you I will do great things.*" You spoke it to me as a promise, and as a beautiful show of your love for me. I asked you for a story, one that could be used to pour a sense of greatness and purpose into the next generation. What you gifted me was far more than I could've ever imagined. You gave me the gift of my own transformation, my own self-belief, and my own perfectly crafted story. I am endlessly grateful. Let's ride this ride, Papa!

ABOUT THE AUTHOR

The Aliquian is author Mary Coe's debut novel. Her love of purpose-driven stories began on the stage. She graduated with a BFA in Musical Theatre in 2013 from the prestigious program at the University of Michigan before performing in regional and professional productions all over the country. Mary now resides in Michigan with her husband and two co-authors: her cats, Amelia and Abraham. She is currently working to complete the four-part series of *The Aliquian*.

Made in the USA
Columbia, SC
10 November 2023

25913456R00236